Pr…

MICHELE HAUF

"Dark, delicious and sexy."
—*New York Times* bestselling author Susan Sizemore on *Her Vampire Husband*

"Cleverly engrossing dialogue, overwhelming desire and intriguing paranormal situations are skillfully combined to make this an irresistible read."
—*Cataromance.com* on *Moon Kissed*

"A novel twist on a vampire tale…Hauf mixes well-developed characters and sparkling dialogue with a paranormal tale and comes out with a winner."
—*RT Book Reviews* on *Kiss Me Deadly*

"With dangerous encounters, a myriad of paranormal beings and even some subtle humor, *The Highwayman* is an enchanting love story packed with riveting adventures."
—*Cataromance.com*

"In this action-packed delight, Hauf's humorous writing and well-developed characters combine for a realistic story—in spite of its supernatural basis."
—*RT Book Reviews* on *The Devil To Pay*

Also available from

MICHELE HAUF

HQN Books

Her Vampire Husband

Harlequin Nocturne

From the Dark
Familiar Stranger
Kiss Me Deadly
His Forgotten Forever
The Devil to Pay
The Highwayman
Moon Kissed

Silhouette Bombshell

Once a Thief
Flawless
Getaway Girl

LUNA Books

Seraphim
Gossamyr
Rhiana

MICHELE HAUF

SEDUCING THE VAMPIRE

ISBN-13: 978-0-373-77538-5

SEDUCING THE VAMPIRE

This edition published by arrangement with Harlequin Books S.A.

For questions and comments about the quality of this book please contact us at Customer_eCare@Harlequin.ca.

www.HQNBooks.com

Printed in U.S.A.

To Michelle Grajkowski, for believing in me.

SEDUCING THE VAMPIRE

Let me not to the marriage of true minds
Admit impediments. Love is not love
Which alters when it alteration finds,
Or bends with the remover to remove:
O no! it is an ever-fixed mark
That looks on tempests and is never shaken;
It is the star to every wandering bark,
Whose worth's unknown, although his height be taken.
Love's not Time's fool, though rosy lips and cheeks
Within his bending sickle's compass come;
Love alters not with his brief hours and weeks,
But bears it out even to the edge of doom:
If this be error and upon me proved,
I never writ, nor no man ever loved.

—William Shakespeare [Sonnet 116]

PROLOGUE

Paris, 1785

NEVER HAD TERROR LOOKED lovelier.

Blood oozed from the punctures in her neck. The choker's honed iron points penetrated pale, powdered flesh, piercing muscle and even bone.

Thick crimson blood purled down the curve of clavicle, detoured across alabaster shoulder, and then plunged toward the voluptuous breasts imprisoned behind silk damask and lace.

Kohl drawn around blue eyes emphasized her horror. Yet the plump lips—carmine rouge caressing the pouting lowest lip—did not gape in pain.

The witch's spell had frozen her for time unending.

He stepped away from her and unhooked the bone crown from around his wrist. Tapping the circlet of rat skulls against his palm, he took it all in.

Imposed in stillness, she yet possessed the incredible and annihilating ability to seduce. Always she had bewitched, ever aware that her carefully crafted appearance, her practiced movements, her well-thought words could render all men gibbering fools.

He lifted a hand to stroke the enticing curve of her bosom, but cautioned that connection.

It had come to this. Even as her blood scent filled the air and curled beneath his nostrils, he could not force himself to lean forward. To smell her wine-lush skin. To breathe in her life. To overdose on her terror.

He needn't, for the heady mixture of her essence surrounded him in an exquisite caress. For the first time, he suspected, she feared. And he had been the master of that rare condition.

If only he could have mastered her in body and blood.

Holding the crown before him, high enough so that her fixed stare could sight the object, he rattled it. Dozens of rat skulls strung about a leather cord. New white bone, stripped of flesh, fur and muscle, still reeked of rodent blood and the sewers beneath the city.

The sewers? Ah yes, a most clever notion.

Placing the crown upon her black hair, always scented with summer wine, he pressed until it sat firmly and would not slip off.

"I crown you—" the wicked edge in his voice cut his tongue—or maybe it was his fangs "—Queen of the Rats."

She did not scream. Rather, she likely *could* and was at this moment. Silently. Ragingly. The spell had immobilized her entire body.

Cursed to become a living Pandora doll, frozen on the outside, alive and stunningly aware on the inside, she could now but accept punishment for her wicked, devious ways.

"You had your chance," he whispered, allowing admiration to soften his tone. "And now I condemn you to eternity."

CHAPTER ONE

North of Paris, 1785

SLAMMED AGAINST THE CARRIAGE wall, Viviane La-Mourette braced her forearms against the padded interior. The impact forced her to bite her lower lip. She swore sharply as the carriage tilted. Her body was wedged against the wall, one hand slapping the glass window. The fragile glass cracked and sharp edges lacerated her palm. The scent of blood imbued with wine and dust tainted the small compartment.

She could tell from the coachman's agitated yelp that he had fallen from his box. It was the middle of March, yet the weather had been unseasonable. Snow as high as a man's knee blanketed the countryside. The country roads were barely traversable, save for a few major routes directly to Paris.

The brass foot warmer beneath her seat had slid against the wall and now spilled out white coals. The wool blanket draped over her lap had become tangled in her arms and the lace *engageantes* at her elbows.

"Insufferable."

Struggling against the meddlesome twist of fabric, Viviane tried with futile effort to keep blood from smearing onto her damask gown. The fabric was the color of deep forest moss, and she had only brought along one additional gown for this visit.

She licked the blood from her palm. The cut had healed.

A gut-clenching scream paused Viviane from her preening.

Accompanying the coachman's hideous cry rose snarling, growling, and—Viviane's bile rose with recognition—the sound of *tearing* at human flesh.

The horses stirred, tugging at their restraints and jostling the carriage. The commotion stopped. The snow muddled the clod of retreating hooves. The coachman must have cut loose the team of two.

Why release their only means of transportation? She would never make Paris now, and most importantly, not before dawn.

Instinct prompted her to assess her clothing. She wore a satin underskirt that could be used as a hood to protect her head, if she needed to start walking. Gloves covered her hands and wrists, and she did have a leather mask that covered all but her eyes.

The letter Henri Chevalier had sent her weeks earlier crinkled against her breast where she'd tucked it between her chemise and corset. He'd written in expectation of her visit this spring. The mention of Constantine de Salignac had almost kept Viviane from making this trip. Henri had intimated Lord de Salignac, leader of the esteemed tribe Nava, desired her hand in marriage as a means to strengthen tribal bloodlines.

The abominable suggestion now distracted her. Viviane would marry no man, even if he were a tribe leader. Salignac could only have his eye on her because she was bloodborn. She did not care to be any man's chattel.

The fact Henri had patroned her for two centuries following her parents' cruel deaths and yet had granted her great freedom had probably spoiled her.

Better spoiled than enslaved.

"I will never arrive in Paris to even face the presumptuous Salignac if I do not extract myself from this detestable situation."

A low growling snarl set her heart racing.

With her shoulders crushed against the tilted carriage wall, Viviane now listened attentively. Tearing flesh sounded as if a dull blade was cutting through leather. It wasn't an awful sound, save for the context.

More growls trickled dread up her chest and thudded at the base of her throat. "Wolves."

But fear did not follow. Fear was for the weak, those lacking in discretion regarding their personal boundaries.

Shoving the blanket away, Viviane flinched at the sound of a pistol and then gripped the broken windowpane.

The wolf barked. It must have been hit. She concentrated and listened. Heartbeats. Two of them. Neither was human—which left herself and the wolf.

If it were not badly injured the animal would next come for her.

"I am not prepared for death tonight. I suppose I must see to this matter myself. Curse the bloody animal for my shoes!" Her shoes were new, and the velvet matched the color of a rich chocolate. A former lover had carved the porcelain roses that dotted the toes.

Stepping up and pushing open the door set the carriage to a wobble. The warning creak of wood and snow indicated she had made a wrong move.

Viviane pressed herself against the seat and groped for a hold on the padded fabric walls as the carriage fell completely to its side. The landing snapped her head against the windowpane.

Outside, the mournful whines did not cease. Wolves in

France were abundant, but someone had once told Viviane there were as many lone wolves as there were those who traveled in packs. Pray this one was a lone wolf.

The struggle out through the door facing toward the sky was difficult with the hindrance of skirts and corset. Her long dark hair, which she had unrolled from the curling papers an hour earlier, impeded her movements as heavy curls slapped her face and got caught under her elbows.

Perched upon the carriage side—which was now in position to face skyward—Viviane's breaths clouded before her. Snow crystals falling from overhead branches sparkled in the darkness.

Divining the warm scent of human blood, she could not see carnage from this angle.

Jumping into the loose snow beside the overturned carriage, she landed with a curse. Snow sifted over her face and under her skirt. Her night vision proving quite fine, she sighted the coachman. His neck had been torn. Blood soaked his dark wool greatcoat, jabot and face. One hand extended above his head, loose fingers still held the pistol atop a bloom of bloody snow.

The wolf limped and wobbled, stepping on three legs, and collapsing in the snow. It had taken a bullet in the shoulder for the bloodied brown fur.

"Be gone with you!"

The creature dodged the fist of snow Viviane tossed at it. It snarled, baring fangs.

Viviane bared her fangs.

Mourning yips echoed across the countryside. She couldn't risk a pack discovering her alone with little means of protection.

Stalking through the deep snow, and losing one shoe in the process, she gained the wolf. It was large, perhaps as long as she from head to knees, and strong of muscle.

Thick black fur streaked the brown. It would certainly make an excellent trim to a woman's gown or hat.

"A fine replacement for my ruined shoes."

Blood spurted from the bullet wound near the animal's neck. It would bleed to death.

Not quick enough for her peace of mind.

Grappling the beast's head securely, Viviane twisted it under her arm and along her side, making sure to pull up so the skull moved sharply away from the neck. An alchemist who studied dead bodies had once told her that severing the spinal cord caused instant death.

The wolf dropped lifeless to the ground.

Viviane wiped her bloodied hands in the snow. Glancing south, she sighted whiffs of smoke curling from dozens of chimneys. Paris. The comfort of a warm home and Henri Chevalier, her loving patron, called.

"So close," she muttered. "And now I shall have to walk. Without shoes." She heeled off the remaining shoe. It would hamper. "Insufferable wolf. You got your just."

Picking up the coachman's pistol, she then rummaged through his coat pockets, finding two balls, powder and a short iron ramrod. Making quick order of reloading, she tossed aside the ramrod. She may need to fend off another wolf. The pistol would give Viviane the advantage of distance but once.

Bending over the coachman, she pressed his eyelids closed. "Rest in peace." She thought to make the sign of the cross over his body, but the detail seemed bothersome.

Pistol in hand, Viviane tromped through the snow. The wolf—she paused, struck by what lay on the snow where once the four-legged creature had been.

"*Sacre bleu.*" It was—a werewolf.

A man, bare and bleeding at the neck, lay sprawled where she had snapped the wolf's neck. In human form he was called *were*. Dark glassy eyes sought hers. Alive yet, despite what she'd thought a spine-severing move.

"I did not know," she offered, nervous suddenly, whipping her head about to scan the periphery. No wolves lurked nearby.

The were's eyelids shuttered. His head sank into the snow and his muscles relaxed with death. Blood spilled from his mouth to stain the scrap of white fabric he'd torn from the coachman's neck.

Minneapolis, modern day

RHYS HAWKES MOVED THROUGH the Irish-themed pub with a swaying stride. It was past midnight, but O'Leary's stayed open until two. The owner, not an Irishman but rather a German who'd married into the family, granted him carte blanche. The high-tech, temperature-controlled cellar was always open for Rhys to select a bottle of wine, whiskey, or to relax in the cool darkness after a long day at Hawkes Associates.

More than just a bank, Hawkes Associates stored treasures, housed certain volatile objects of a magical nature and offered the various paranormal nations, Light, Dark, Faery and otherwise, a safe and lasting place to keep—and exchange for new currency—their money and valuables as they passed through the centuries.

His firm was the only of its kind and had offices in New York, Minnesota and Florida, four more in Europe and one in China. The Paris office served as his home base.

He didn't own this pub, but he was considering buying it.

Rhys didn't get involved in the daily management details of the clubs he collected as if they were baseball cards.

They were investments. And rarely did he mingle with the crowds. He was a lone wolf—make that vampire.

Still clinging to the same excuses.

Not an excuse, just an easier summation.

Tonight he was in business mode, eyeing the place for potential.

At the blue neon bar, two college guys exchanged what Rhys had decided were urban legends. The one about the man with the hook instead of a hand was common. But he'd never heard the one about the mermaid swimming the Gowanus Canal in Brooklyn. He kept the men's conversation in peripheral range for the humor.

A waitress clad in a shimmy of green satin and beads snuck past him and slipped behind the bar. The scent of alcohol made Rhys nostalgic for the real whisky he'd once drunk in Scotland. Not his homeland, but a safe hiding place when the vampires had sought to extinguish the werewolves from France during the Revolution. He hadn't been hiding; he'd been in mourning.

The world had evolved over the centuries, but the disease between the wolves and vampires could never be healed. Most days Rhys was fine with that. Other days he wished he could have done more.

Of course, his situation was the stickiest. There was no definite "side" for him. He had once been persecuted for his differences—by those of his own blood. He and his nemesis had battled for decades. Neither had claimed victory.

Until *she* had become involved. She had changed everything. And since then, nothing had been the same.

It was rare Rhys thought of her, and always those azure eyes.

But for a man who had walked the earth two and a

half centuries it was easy to pine for a long-departed lover who whispered ghostly sonnets in his thoughts.

Rhys smirked at his wistful memories.

"Heartbreak," he muttered. It clung like a bitch with fangs.

With one ear taking in the legends, Rhys's ears perked up when he heard the men start talking about a Vampire Snow White.

"Yeah, you know. The chick buried in a glass coffin by some prince."

"That was a cartoon, dude."

"I know, but listen. They say a vampire chick fell in love with a man who was a vampire or maybe he was a werewolf. I'm not clear on that detail," one of them said.

Rhys slid onto a bar stool. He smiled at the men and pushed the crystal peanut bowl between his hands. They regarded him with nods.

"Vampires and werewolves are fiction," one man said.

"Whatever. So are urban legends, but you wanted one you'd never heard for tomorrow's blog."

"All right, give it to me. So she fell in love with a guy who might have been a vamp—"

"Or maybe a werewolf. But she was being courted by a vampire, too. An evil vampire."

Rhys's fingers curled into a fist. He felt the muscles at the back of his neck tighten. He wanted to grip the man and shake the rest of the tale out of him, but he checked his growing urgency.

"Anyway, so this vampire chick falls in love with the man who wasn't what he seemed and they get married or something. I don't know. I'm foggy on that detail. Only the evil vampire is pissed, see. So something happens to separate the two—the chick and her lover—and the evil vampire locks her away in a glass coffin and buries her like some kind of Goth Snow White."

"That's a dorky legend. Couldn't she have broken the glass?"

"No, dude, get this. The vampire had a warlock put her under a spell. She couldn't move, but would live forever. So she can see out the glass coffin, but can't move or scream. So the legend says she went mad, and she's probably still buried somewhere beneath the streets of Paris. You know they have all those tunnels under Paris."

"Huh. So what if she escaped?"

"Don't know, man. That'd be one freaky bloodsucking chick."

The men tilted back swigs from their beer bottles.

"Sweet. But, dude, so not true."

"Tell me about it. Vampirella gone mad."

"I'd offer my neck to Vampirella any day. She is so sexy."

"She's a cartoon, too." The storyteller swiped an arm across his lips. "You going to put it on the blog?"

"Yeah, we'll see. Buy me another beer, dude, this one's tapped. So what's with the man who was a vampire or maybe a werewolf?"

"I don't know. That's how I heard it told."

"So you mean he's different, like, where his hand should be—" the guy assumed a melodramatic tone "—was a stainless-steel hook!"

Rhys winced.

"No, dude, he was…not right."

The crystal bowl in Rhys's grip cracked in half. The men turned and delivered him wonky looks.

"Delicate," Rhys offered sheepishly.

Not right. The words stabbed Rhys's heart with bittersweet memory. He could hear them spoken in *her* voice. He pushed the mess aside. "Interesting story."

"Yeah, dude, it's an urban legend. You can read all about it tomorrow at my blog."

One guy handed Rhys a business card that simply read: UrbanTrash.com.

"Wouldn't it rock if werewolves and vampires existed? We could all like, live forever."

"Forever is not always appealing." Rhys strode away.

The Vampire Snow White. Once loved by an evil vampire and another who was maybe a vampire or maybe a werewolf. An urban legend?

It was rumor.

But the details were too familiar to disregard.

"*Mon Dieu,* I thought she was dead."

CHAPTER TWO

Paris, 1785

THE PERILOUS JOURNEY THROUGH knee-high snow ended when a rider galloped alongside Viviane. He literally swept her into his arms to sit before him on the horse's withers.

The warmth emanating from his thighs and chest told her that he was mortal. The desire to bite him did not rise. All that mattered was getting warm and shaking the feeling into her left foot. A hasty *"merci"* spilled from her lips.

"The sun will beat us if we do not hurry," he said.

How could he know the sun would prove her bane? "Who are you?"

"They call me the Highwayman. I know you are not human."

"But you are."

"Not like most humans, though."

They made Paris as the sun traced the horizon, and he left her at her patron's home.

As she entered the warmth of the marble-tiled foyer, Viviane tumbled into Henri Chevalier's arms. Shivering and sniffing tears, she took a moment to glance outside. The Highwayman had heeled his mount down the cobblestones toward the pink sunrise, his leather greatcoat flapping out like wings.

She dropped the pistol in her pocket and listened to it clatter to the floor.

"Viviane, what has happened? Where is the carriage?"

"Uh..." Pulled into Henri's welcoming hug, she melded against her patron's body. Henri was all muscle and hard lines and smelled like cedar and lavender. "The Highwayman found me."

"I've heard the legend. He is a good man."

"Like us?"

"No, but immortal. He's no grouse against vampires—but rather demons—fortunately for you. We didn't expect you until tomorrow evening."

"Henri? Oh, dear." Henri's wife, Blanche, touched Viviane's shoulder where wolf blood stained the fabric.

Two years earlier while in Paris on an annual visit to her patron, Viviane had met Blanche and decided to like her. The petite blonde stood like a bird next to Henri's towering build. She gave to Henri the one thing he had never asked of Viviane—intimacy.

"Have the maid boil water and fill the bath," Henri directed his wife. "And draw the curtains in the guest room. Quickly!"

It felt decadently blissful to nuzzle against Henri's chest and cling to the heavy brocade robe that hung upon his broad shoulders. He must have been preparing for sleep. He always did greet the dawn in his dark bedchambers. Vampires required a quarter as much sleep as a mortal did.

"The carriage tending me here...broke a wheel three leagues out," Viviane whispered. Exhausted and starving, she could but speak in gasps. "A wolf...killed the coachman."

"And you managed to escape?"

"I...broke the animal's neck."

Henri's chuckle rumbled against her cheek. "I should not doubt it."

"It was a werewolf."

"Ah?"

She knew well he held no resentment toward werewolves, unlike most vampires. Henri did not take sides, nor did he hate—unless given reason.

He toed the pistol. "Not yours."

"Belonged to the driver, who is dead. *Sacre bleu,* Henri, I did not wish to harm the beast, but I prefer life over mauling."

"Pity the man—or beast—who forces Viviane LaMourette to do anything. You are fortunate the Highwayman happened along."

He kissed her cheek and carried her up the curving marble stairs to the guest room. Half a dozen candles glowed upon a writing desk. Two mortal maids—enthralled by their master—bustled about, pouring boiling water into the copper tub. White linen lined the tub; a frill of lace dancing along the hem dusted the floor.

Before Henri could set her on the bed, Viviane clutched his robe. "I'm unsure if I can wait until you rise later."

He nodded and instead of setting her down, carried her into his bedchamber. Blanche, with but a nod from her husband, whispered, *"Bonjour"* and took her leave, closing the door behind her.

"I shouldn't wish to impose upon her," Viviane said, as Henri set her on the bed. Leaning back onto her elbows, she spread out her hands, crushing the decadent silk bed linens between her fingers.

"It is not an imposition. Blanche will sleep in her private chambers this morning."

Shrugging off the robe, Henri then tugged the gauzy

night rail over his head and dropped it onto the bed to stand in but chamois underbreeches. Built like a Roman gladiator, the man's broad shoulders never did align straight across. He'd broken his collarbone decades earlier after falling from a cliff in Greece and it had never healed properly. It gave him little worry, but he did wince when raising his left arm over his head.

He stretched out on the black-and-gold-striped chaise longue positioned before the hearth fire.

Viviane found her place and nestled beside him, chest to chest, kissing his cheek.

"I've missed you," she admitted. It had been five or six months. "Have you gained another line near your eyes? You are such a handsome man, Henri. So kind to me. I can never thank you for the freedom you have given me."

"Then do not speak," he said. "Take what you need."

Candle glow licked teasingly upon Henri's neck. Viviane tongued his flesh, then pierced skin and the thick, pulsing vein to slake the thirst she could only satisfy with Henri, her patron, a friend and mentor, but never her lover.

He was, quite literally, her lifeline. Without him she would be lost.

Two weeks later...

VIVIANE LANGUISHED IN THE SPA. Henri called the room a tepidarium after the Roman baths he'd once enjoyed in Greece. The stone floor was always warm due to an underground pipe system. Istrian tiles lined the walls and glossy crimson squares glinted amongst the pearly white squares. A constellation of crystals set in a white iron candelabrum reigned over the round pool, which was as wide as Viviane's length should she float across it.

She visited Henri twice yearly, and did like to spoil herself amidst the luxuries of his home.

A map room appealed to her desire for knowledge, though she could not read the words, only trace the snaking rivers and marvel over the shapes of so many countries. The spa and music room strummed her sensual ribbons. Viviane devoured all things sensory and erotic. She was a woman, after all, and would not be kept wanting. Men overwhelmingly agreed, and when she desired pleasure, she took it.

Seven bedchambers, a ballroom and a twelve-stall stable told the world Henri Chevalier could afford anything he desired. Yet he would never be so conceited as to state it himself. Flaunting one's riches was considered lewd.

Blanche generously shared her wardrobe, and kept an entire room devoted to shoes. By delicious coincidence, Viviane wore the same gown and shoe size as her patron's wife.

Viviane's home in Venice was as richly decorated, but it was old. Most furnishings had been acquired in the sixteenth century, and were in desperate need of reconditioning. The plaster walls were cracked and water seeped in the north entry hugging the canal.

Alas, those repairs would never be made. Viviane kept her current financial condition close to heart. It was not dire, but could become so if she did not invest properly, and soon. Pity, the last *notaire* who had invested well for her had died of sudden blood loss.

Sometimes she simply could not control her hunger, especially when sated by a handsome young man.

Ah, but she had survived alone two centuries; she would beg no man for help now.

And no Casanova vampire lord would entice her to

change those principles of independence with the suggestion of marriage. It mattered little that Henri had last evening suggested his approval for the union, if and when Lord de Salignac put forth the offer.

Viviane had attended the Salon Noir twice since arriving in Paris. The Salon Noir mirrored Marie Antoinette's court with lavish clothing, jewels, courtly titles and decadence, save the attendees were vampires, werewolves, demons and other Dark Ones. Faeries from the Sidhe nation, and a familiar or two, attended in fewer numbers. The Light—the witches—kept away due mainly to their differences with the vampires. The vampires did not mind at all since witch's blood was poisonous to them.

If you were dressed well, and not human, it was a given you'd been invited to the Salon Noir.

During her second visit to the salon, Constantine had been preoccupied with his patroned kin until she had sashayed past him. She had heard the thud of a woman's backside hit the marble floor as Constantine pushed her from his lap and sauntered after Viviane.

When Constantine de Salignac walked through a room, all eyes followed his regal lift of chin, those steely gray eyes that saw things before everyone else, that compressed mouth, which could utter a biting jest, or indeed, bite.

Being a tribe leader, Lord de Salignac was expected to populate his tribe with bloodborn vampires. That was possible when a child was born to two vampires. So he blooded mortal women recently transformed to vampire in hopes they would be able to carry his child. It was a long process that could take years before the new kin could even conceive.

Viviane did not care to be another woman feathering his elaborate damask-and-gold nest.

As well, vampire lovers were risky. Most insisted on

sharing the bite, which was a means of bonding to one another through the blood. Taking another vampire's blood was something she had reserved, as most did, for one exquisite relationship that would bond them both in body and blood. It was not to be considered lightly.

Dragging her fingertips over the opalescent bathwater, Viviane sighed and dismissed the dread thoughts. The bath was two parts water, one part milk. Wine and mulled spices had been stirred into the exotic witch's brew.

Portia, Blanche's maid, popped her head inside the circular tepidarium. "What is your opinion, mademoiselle? Is the scent not divine?"

"Devastatingly indulgent," Viviane drawled. "You were quite right regarding my pleasures, Portia. How is it you know so much about what will please a woman when you've led a subservient life?"

"Fantasies, my lady." Portia winked, and dismissed herself.

Viviane wondered if Blanche would allow her to abscond with Portia when finally she returned to Venice. The attentive maid was a prize to hoard.

Viviane had skipped the Versailles soiree Blanche had pleaded she attend. Seeking the king's eye, and Queen Marie Antoinette's favor, interested her little. The gossip Blanche would report upon their return would suffice.

Stretching her arms about the curved marble pool, she closed her eyes. Tilting her hips, she let her legs float to the surface. Her toes popped up in the milky sheen, a string of pebble islands.

An acrid taste suddenly stung her throat. She pressed a hand to her chest and coughed.

That was odd. She wasn't ill. Vampires rarely contracted a human malady. Must be the intense scent of the spices.

A convulsion in her gut forced up a hacking cough. A bead of crimson expanded on the white surface before her.

"What…?"

She touched her lip. Blood painted her fingers. Now she tasted it in her mouth, metallic and hot.

A spike of feverous heat clenched her heart. Sucking in a breath, she slapped her palms on the water. More blood eddied up her throat. She tried to call for Portia but, wrenched forward by the sudden sharp pain in her chest, her head plunged under the milky surface.

Viviane swallowed the odious blend. Surfacing, she choked up another throat-burning spasm. Blood swirled into the white.

She felt a stabbing pain at her breast.

"Portia!"

Thrusting her naked body aside, she landed on the ceramic-tiled floor. Heaving blood, she cried out as the pain ceased.

Three leagues west of Paris, en route to Versailles

THE STAKE BURST HIS HEART. Henri stumbled, groping at the thick wooden dowel. His attacker growled and slashed talons across his throat. Blood choked into his mouth and blurred his vision as he collapsed before the carriage. In eyesight lay Blanche, her head severed from her neck. Crimson spattered her blond ringlets.

The werewolf who had charged the carriage, leaping to grab the coachman from his post, stomped his paw on Henri's head, crushing it into the soft mud.

NO FUNERAL WAS HELD FOR EITHER Henri Chevalier or Blanche. A team of four vampires had been dispatched to clean the scene of assault before dawn and collect the vampire ash. The carriage was burned. The ash was thrown into the Seine.

According to rumor, a werewolf had murdered the couple.

Viviane did not attend the Salon Noir for weeks. But though her heart ached for her patron she was not a woman to dwell in sadness.

Now, more than ever, she must be vigilant for her own future.

CHAPTER THREE

THE HÔTEL DE SALIGNAC SAT at the west end of the Tuileries on the rue Saint-Honoré. Tonight the four-story town palace's cobbled fore-courtyard boasted carriages parked tail to head. A blazing *touchier,* brandished by an iron Aphrodite, held reign center courtyard to welcome the Dark Ones.

It was rumored Lord de Salignac privately entertained the queen and her ladies on occasion. Marie Antoinette was said to be particularly fond of Salignac's aviary, ill contained as it was. The birds had the run—or rather flight—of the palace.

Moving through the ballroom, Rhys Hawkes took in the faces. Among the crowd, the vampires were easy to spot. Pale flesh was not the most obvious giveaway—for mortals used cosmetic powder to achieve the same effect—but rather the imperious lift of nose as they practiced their ill-gotten aristocratic airs.

Rhys was thankful he'd not developed the snobbish mannerism innate to Parisian vampires, though at times like this he realized it best he at least adopt an air so he did not draw the sort of attention he abhorred—disdain.

He did not sense any wolves in attendance, besides his companion Orlando, and that put Rhys ill at ease. The Salon Noir was a sort of safe ground for all breeds of Dark Ones to gather, but Rhys knew well vampires had an irritating manner of labeling werewolves animals and claiming themselves the civilized breed of Dark Ones. As well, find a werewolf eager to embrace a vampire and you'd find an omega wolf ostracized from the pack.

He would stay so long as required to sniff out any suspicious sorts.

Two vampires had been murdered a fortnight earlier east of Versailles.

Rhys had been recruited by the Council, which had representatives from all the paranormal nations, to discover the culprit and the reason behind the heinous act. He would be accepted as a seated Council member after he'd solved the mystery. Field investigation was a lowly assignment, but he didn't mind. A man should have to prove his worth if he wished to claim merit.

The black-and-white harlequin ballroom floor buzzed with an assorted enclave, ranging from the dourly macabre to the flighty giddiness of the Sidhe. A few pairings of four danced an intricate quadrille flowing from three violins and a boxy harpsichord.

Low, black wrought-iron candelabras flickered a circus ring of amber flames. Rococo frieze lined the upper walls with what appeared to be cupids vomiting roses and birds. Rhys noted bird guano smeared the black-and-silver-striped English paper on the wall to his left.

The ballroom was a bustle of animated expressions, studied smiles and practiced gestures. Men dodged powdered and beribboned wigs. Women tapped damask shoulders and the occasional cheek with a communicative flip of their lace fans.

Rhys understood the women could send messages with a flick of their fans. The intricate code bemused him, though he had never bothered to learn it.

The thought to make a connection with a sumptuous

lovely hung in his mind. When in Paris, indulgence could not be ignored.

A minuet twinkled from the harpsichord and the dancers rearranged and re-paired. Rhys noticed Orlando paired with a blushing mortal who wore her blue satin bodice low enough to reveal the rosy aureoles staining her breasts. The young wolf was hungry for a ripe female. The boy's pleasures were not wicked or dark, so he was safe.

Rhys on the other hand, possessed a dark secret, which made him cautious as to whom he chose to engage in a lusty liaison.

An interesting scatter of red roses nestled against fathomless black hair caught his attention. Red, so red. *Like that first drop of blood.* The vampire within him stirred. Tucked within the center buds of those roses were tiny… skulls? Curious.

Rhys followed the woman's gliding procession across the ballroom. Her hair was unfettered by powder or wig. Dressed in bold red, she was attired to captivate.

"Regarde moi," he whispered. Look at me.

She turned. Rhys straightened, lifting his chin. His persuasion never worked on paranormals. She couldn't have heard him. Blue eyes sought his. Unnaturally blue, but not Sidhe, for faery eyes held a violet tint.

The corner of her mouth turned up, a morsel of tease. What sensual delights did that tiny curve of flesh promise? Did her mouth curl so preciously when she cried out in ecstasy?

Sweet mercy, Rhys had not felt his body react so instinctively to a woman in years. His heart pounded and blood rushed to his groin. His werewolf growled lowly, pining for an illicit coupling.

Fortunately, he was vampire now. It was easier to contain the werewolf's lusty desires when in this form. And much safer.

The rose-embellished beauty swept behind a couple who nuzzled nose against neck. The man's gray powdered wig tilted askew as his fangs grazed alabaster skin. The bite. A wicked tease between two vampires that could be construed as a promise to one another, but only if mutually consented.

When had he last taken blood for sustenance? Rhys couldn't recall. Weeks surely. And that was the aggravation of it. When in vampire form, he had to *remember* to take blood; it was not instinctual. Though he assumed vampire form most often, his werewolf mind ruled when in this shape—and the werewolf did not desire blood.

He'd ask about the murders, and find a pretty thing to bring home tonight. Or at the least, find one to wander through the Tuileries with him, the taste of her trickling down his throat after he abandoned her in a swoon beside a lush crop of roses.

Perhaps the rosy beauty with the bright eyes?

Following the pull of desire, Rhys shuffled through the crush of powder-dusted shoulders and silk-stockinged legs. Passing a faery, he accidentally brushed her forearm with his fingers, and whispered an apology. The result of contact sparkled on his flesh. He rubbed his fingers on his coat to wipe it off.

Again she appeared in view. Closer. She received a kiss on both cheeks from another woman Rhys knew was vampire for the fangs her smile revealed. But the blue-eyed beauty, while pale, was vibrant, too much life sparkled in her eyes to be vampire.

He favored mortals. Much less drama. And easier to abandon after the bite with a touch of persuasion. Perhaps that was why she'd turned to him—she was mortal.

Again her gaze fixed to his. Her eyes widened with promise, a touch without tactile sensation, yet it sped Rhys's pulse and warmed his neck.

He nodded and offered a smile, remembering Orlando's coaching: When at court one must never smile to show their teeth, but the smile mustn't be so weak as to be construed false. So many rules and ridiculous pandering. It was enough to make a man's head spin.

It took a lot to spin Rhys's head. And this exquisite beauty did so.

The woman touched her bottom lip with a fingertip, her flirtatious eyes holding his. Just below her left eye a black heart patch beckoned.

Rhys offered her his most charming smile.

She let out a peal of laughter and spun away, an elusive wraith becrowned in skulls and roses.

"What the hell?" Rhys muttered to himself. Had his sensual prowess fallen amiss? He could not let her slip away without a few words.

The investigation could wait.

VIVIANE STRODE THE MARBLE floor in one of many galleries of paintings. She'd needed a moment away from the stuffy ballroom and leering gazes. It seemed all the male vampires were hungry for her. Not because she was attractive or interesting, but because she was bloodborn.

"Bother."

Drawing in the air, she thought of Henri. He had never made her feel like an object.

The clatter of approaching shoes tugged her from the wistful moment.

A man strolled toward her. His swaggering stride made him move like a prowling feline, yet his broad shoulders and stocky build put into Viviane's mind that of a provincial worker, one who lived off the land.

Certainly not an aristocrat, and most definitely not vampire. That put her to ease.

His eyes fell upon her high breasts, tethered behind the cinched bodice. Very well, so he was like the other men.

Licking his lips, he smiled, revealing the whitest teeth and an easy charm that Viviane could not disregard. Hair dark as her own had been tamed into a queue at the back of his neck and tied with a plain black ribbon. But there, on the left side of his head, a gray streak amidst the black gleamed under the candlelight.

Desire stirred. Momentarily, Viviane imagined his hair sweeping across her breasts, gasps huffing from his lips, and she clinging to those wide shoulders. No other at the Salon Noir had been capable of summoning such a visceral reaction, and this man had not yet spoken a word.

She angled so her path would pass him on the left.

He adjusted his trajectory to a direct line before her.

Presumptuous of him. She shuffled sideways. The man matched her feint.

"Pardon me," she said, and her skirts swished across his buckled shoes.

At the last moment, he stepped aside to grant her berth, but not too far, and her skirts crushed against his thighs.

"You are hardly deserving of a pardon, mademoiselle. Such beauty should never be forgiven, but rather indulged."

Viviane stopped walking and swung a look over her shoulder. Romantic blather never impressed her, even when issued in a deep, sure tone. His delving eyes were brown, as was his frockcoat. So common.

Strangely, though, her heart beat faster, anticipating

more than she expected he could give her. Men always disappointed.

One of her dark brows curved sharply. "Who are you?"

"Rhys Hawkes." He strolled around behind her. "An admirer."

Viviane drew a careful study from his hands, along the snug cut of his sleeves and down the front of his frockcoat. Minimal decorative embroidery on his coat, and only a bit on his blue waistcoat. A sorry lack of lace, which further alluded to his provincial origins. Yet she could not know what he was without touching him, or tasting his blood. Mortal or other?

"Are you like me?" she asked abruptly.

"A vampire?"

"You cannot be." He could not be vampire for his ill fashion sense and less than discreet approach. At the very least, he was not a Nava tribe member.

"I am," he confirmed.

"Hmph. You are—" nostrils flaring, she winced "—not right."

The man pressed a palm to his chest and bowed his head. Offended? What had she said? And then she did not care; not if he was here on pretense.

"How did you get in?" she asked tersely. "The Salon Noir is invitation only, and I know Salignac would not dream of admitting an unfamiliar."

He stepped closer. Yet as annoyed as he made her, Viviane's feelings vacillated from cool dislike to lunatic desire.

Could she press her tongue through his smirking lips? Might the man answer her longings, fulfill her desires and entertain her passions?

Possibly, but there was no reward in succumbing too easily.

"I suppose those glances across the ballroom meant nothing?" he said.

"You must be mistaken, monsieur, if you believe I was looking at you. I dare not waste a moment on one so—"

"Not right?"

"Who *are* you?"

"I've told you, I am an admirer." He performed a curt half bow, and came up, gliding his face close to hers. He smelled earthy, like a forest. So different. "There lives a daring challenge in the curve of your smile, mademoiselle."

A flicker of her lashes could not be stopped. Yet until she learned exactly what he was, she daren't appear interested. If he really were vampire avoidance was key.

Viviane took a step to the side.

He matched her with a quick side step.

"Remove yourself from my path, monsieur, or I will scream."

"You won't do that. It's hardly fitting of your character. And I'll press my mouth to yours to capture that scream before you can vocalize it."

The tip of her tongue dashed out to trace her lower lip. Yes, please?

"You are correct," she offered calmly. "A scream is vulgar."

In a sinuous move, she snapped her fan out from where it had been tucked up her sleeve, and slashed it before him. Blood purled from cut skin and sweetened the air.

The man touched his cheek and turned his forefinger toward her. "Does not my blood attract you?"

Her nostrils flared as she scented him. *Wrong move, Viviane. You are always hungry of late.*

"It repulses me," she forced out. "You are not vampire."

"I…am." Why the reluctance in his tone? "But I do not intend to wear out my voice convincing you of what should be obvious."

He brushed his fingers across her cheek. Before she could close her eyes and dip her head into the delicious connection, Viviane flinched away. "The shimmer," she said on a gasp.

She did not speak of faery dust, but the innate sensation two vampires felt when touching. So he was vampire. Yet why did she still wonder at what made him so different?

Rhys stepped aside, offering her ease of escape. "Forgive me, mademoiselle. My passion knows little in the way of boundaries."

"Passion? We've only just met, Monsieur Hawkes. You do not even know my name."

She wanted to tell it, but again, that would be too forward. If he discovered it on his own that would prove his interest.

"Indeed. And I also sense my desire offends you."

"Desire never offends me. Speaking with a man who is not what he claims to be does."

Rhys nodded. "I release you from this uncomfortable tête-à-tête with hopes you will spend fitful moments anguishing over the loss of my presence."

He bowed, spun sharply, and marched away, shoes clacking loudly.

A roll of her eyes could not be prevented. Anguishing over the loss of his presence? Why did they always attempt to win through words and platitudes?

Viviane desired action, a bold approach and a forceful insinuation of passion. Or rather, it was a fantasy she thought of often, but had never the pleasure of experiencing. Rare did she meet a man to match her bold mien.

Pausing at the doorway, the man touched the cut on his cheek. She had marked him.

"But have you the daring to mark me?"

"THIS WAS A DELICIOUS IDEA," Orlando muttered as he joined Rhys.

Orlando tugged at the frockcoat the tailor had insisted be taken in at the arms. The green velvet transformed the pup into one of those Greek forest deities with powerful muscles and the face of an angel, or so the effeminate tailor had commented, much to Orlando's discomfort.

"My ideas are never delicious," Rhys grumbled. "Reckless perhaps, but never bordering delicious."

"Most certainly not wearing such plain attire."

Orlando had taken on airs since stepping inside the Hôtel de Salignac. Rhys would allow the boy his vanity.

He had brought along Orlando, who was much like a son to him, because the two of them named a common friend in William Montfalcon, a werewolf who lived tucked on the left bank's boulevard Saint Germain. It was where they were currently staying, despite Montfalcon's strange absence.

Rhys smoothed a palm down his new coat, brushing at the clinging faery dust. Plain? The brown embroidered silk suited him. The tailor had insisted he call the color by its proper name *la chocolat*, after the queen's favorite drink. Though the ivory buttons were extravagant and over the top, the enthusiastic tailor had insisted they would draw attention in the wake of Rhys's regrettable decision to forego lace *engageantes* on his sleeves. The sky-blue waistcoat lent to what little vanity Rhys could muster.

And while he was a boot man always, the hose and

buckled shoes did not feel uncomfortable, only not quite masculine. Heaven forbid, he engage in swordplay on rain-slippery cobblestones.

At least he'd the principle to forego a powdered bag-wig.

Rhys decided he would make no advances worrying about his attire. It was his carriage and attitude that would win him entrance into the secrets hoarded within the salon.

He leaned close to Orlando and said, "The rumor is that a werewolf murdered the vampires. Have you heard any interesting discussion?"

"Not yet, but I did spy Salignac. Over there."

Following Orlando's nod, Rhys scanned the crowd of wigs dribbled with candle wax and bird droppings and saw, splayed across a red velvet chaise longue, the vampire lord and leader of tribe Nava, Constantine de Salignac.

Blood heated Rhys's neck and he clenched his fists.

Over the years, he and Salignac had traded the role of tormentor against the other. Whenever Salignac found opportunity, he went for Rhys's jugular. They got into rousing duels and malicious dupes. Constantine had even gone so far as causing the death of Rhys's only loved one.

Rhys did not believe in an eye for an eye. Senseless violence proved nothing. Yet the seeds of such violence were always cracked open whenever in Salignac's presence.

He took morbid delight in the idea of walking up to Salignac tonight. It had been a decade since they'd last spoken.

"Here's something you'll find of interest," Orlando said. "Salignac is smitten."

"Smitten? As in…?"

"In love. Or so the whispers tell." Always so comically

dramatic, the young werewolf fit into this false society with an ease Rhys would never possess. "Seems there is a beautiful vampiress who was left without a patron after Henri Chevalier's murder. You know the females need to feed from a familiar blood source to maintain their life essence.

"The thought curdles my blood," Orlando muttered.

Werewolves would never dream of drinking blood from humans, or consuming their flesh. It was abominable. Yet a werewolf bitten by a vampire would develop the gruesome need to take mortal blood.

"Salignac stumbles moon-eyed in the wake of her silken skirts," Orlando reported. "The entire salon is abuzz with rumors he will patron her, perhaps even marry her. It is why no other vampire dares pursue her."

"That is not love, Orlando."

"Yes, but if ever an alpha existed in the vampire ranks, it is Salignac. If he strikes first, the other males cower. I hear the woman is indifferent."

Rhys smirked. "A female not interested in Constantine? The illustrious leader of the failing tribe must be confounded."

"Seems her former patron gave her unbounded freedom."

Interesting. Rhys had never heard such a thing. Female kin were literal slaves to their patron.

"She attends the salon and boldly defies convention," Orlando added. "She is wicked."

"Wicked women are better left to other men to suffer their claws." And yet, he'd never refuse a scratch or two, most especially one from an azure-eyed beauty.

"Perhaps so, but Salignac is relentless."

Rhys had once been in love. With family. With the idea of serenity and an untroubled life. He still considered it on occasion, despite Constantine's best efforts to excise that desire from his heart. The man had taken it all from him, and with a smirk and a nod.

"To each his own," Rhys said.

Yet his tattered heart heaved to know Constantine was in love. And Rhys would ever be challenged to find a woman who could see beyond his darkness and into his heart. *You are not right.* The oath female vampires tended to pin on him with an indelicate stab. Not usually so quickly, though.

Hearing such words from the vampiress, issued with a biting cut, had been akin to pushing him facedown in the muck littering the streets of Paris.

The deuce! He did not require love. Lust suited him fine. And the sensual vampiress would serve that craving well.

Both men observed as a tall woman bowed before Lord de Salignac. Rhys noted it wasn't a complete bow, rather forced actually. She did not deem Salignac worthy of her submission.

Though he could not completely see her face, long curls of raven hair paralleled a slender neck. And the hair was teased, coiled and pinned up with—

"Red roses," Rhys said under his breath. It was the blue-eyed woman who had caught his eye.

"What's that?"

"Can you see if there are skulls at the center of the roses?"

"In her hair? Can't see from here. But don't you adore how the women cinch their corsets so tightly their bosoms have nowhere to go but—"

"Orlando, watch yourself. Is that how you behave around women you do not know?"

"Yes."

The boy's innocence would get him in trouble some day. "You are yet a pup. To win a woman's regard you must not be so vulgar."

"And you are the master of wooing a woman? The last time I saw you with a woman—"

"I do not share all my liaisons with you, boy." Nor did he discuss his affairs.

Rare was it Rhys left the country to seek amorous pleasures. The country women would not think to powder their hair or wrap themselves in ells of expensive fabrics. They appreciated the more rustic male, one whose appetites were fierce and less refined than the city fops.

"I've my eye on someone," Rhys said. "And she will be in my bed soon enough."

"Oh, yes? Which one?"

"The one with the roses in her hair."

"Oh, but Rhys..." The werewolf swallowed audibly.

When Lord de Salignac lifted the woman's hand to kiss, Rhys sucked in a breath. The vampire lord's eyes closed. He lingered over her hand, inhaling her scent, consuming her in a breath.

Rhys knew that look.

"She is the one," Orlando said. "Mademoiselle Viviane LaMourette. The one whom Salignac loves."

Indeed. Rhys closed his eyes. He had chosen incorrectly.

And yet. Was it not his chance for love? Surely Constantine pursued her for one purpose, and that purpose did not require love.

A tendril of spite clutched Rhys's spine. It was always there, forced up by Salignac. What satisfying vengeance to take away from Salignac the one woman he loved?

Decided, Rhys nodded once and drew up his shoulders. "I want her. I will have her."

CHAPTER FOUR

Paris, modern day

"WAS IT LOVE AT FIRST SIGHT?" Simon Markson asked Rhys as they walked through Charles de Gaulle Airport.

"Yes," Rhys said, smirking wistfully as he recalled the foolishness of his youth. And yet at that time every cut to his person had felt like a blade directly to his heart. He had *needed* revenge. And the opportunity had been too perfect.

"She was beautiful. She was like…a hummingbird," he muttered absently.

"What's that?"

"She was a hummingbird—a woman who can never be caged. And should her wings have ceased to flutter she would have died."

"She had wings?"

Rhys shook his head. Simon's head was a veritable database of all paranormal creatures; he'd taken it upon himself to research his employer's world after being hired a decade earlier.

"Why did you never tell me the legend?" Rhys asked his assistant.

"Never thought much of it."

"But you've heard it before?"

"The Vampire Snow White? Once or twice. While on dates, you know." Simon tapped away on his cell phone with his free hand. "It's an urban legend for a reason, Rhys. It's fiction, a story created to titillate and you know how much the women like vampires nowadays."

"I've told you my history. It could be true."

"Yeah, I remember the day you told me everything." Simon whistled. He tucked the phone in his breast pocket. The two walked through the sliding doors to the pickup lane outside. "Who would have thought werewolves and vampires were real?"

Rhys had hired the man as an assistant when he'd needed help adjusting to the technology that moved faster than a hyperactive hare. He'd surrendered to the learning curve with the introduction of the laptop and BlackBerry and the iPod. Now he gladly let Simon handle all the technical stuff.

While Rhys could function in this human-dominated realm without having to divulge his true nature, he was not a man to treat friendship lightly, and always revealed himself to his closest friends, even if they were mortal, which were few. Trust came with truth. Never again would he doubt himself or attempt to hide a part of his nature.

Didn't mean he flashed his fangs to anyone. The rule of discretion applied always.

Simon flagged down his driver three cars back in the queue. He'd contacted the Paris office of Hawkes Associates and made arrangements the moment Rhys had called him about the legend early this morning.

"I still think it'll be like looking for a needle in a haystack," Simon said. "There are over five hundred kilometers of tunnels beneath Paris proper. And some of those tunnels go down five, six, even seven layers deep."

"You made contact with the man who claims to have mapped all those treacherous tunnels?"

"Right," Simon said. "Guy named Dane Weft claims to

have made the ultimate tunnels map. But on his website, he admits the tunnels constantly change. And there are some inaccessible levels. I offered him cash. Didn't even have to break the bank."

"Money does not concern me, Simon, but I do appreciate your frugality."

Raindrops splattered their shoulders. A woman in heels with an immaculate coif stepped back from the curb toward the overhang and bumped into Rhys. *"Pardonnez-moi."*

Bright blue eyes held his for a moment and her cherry-red mouth slipped into a smile.

Not the same. He'd never hold *her* again.

He stepped beside Simon as the car pulled up.

"I don't know what you expect to find, Rhys. Even if this glass coffin does exist, she could have escaped decades ago, centuries, and may have died—for real—when the glass broke."

"If someone had a witch bespell her and the coffin, I can assure you it will be fail-safe against natural disaster."

"I thought the legend said it was a warlock?"

"Witch. Warlock. Same thing, only one is a wanted criminal."

Rhys sighed. Truly, he was jumping to conclusions. And yet, he couldn't *not* investigate. He'd never forgive himself if he ignored what felt so real in his bones.

Could it really be her? Shame on him if it were true.

It hurt him deeply to imagine her locked away, alive and aware, in a confining little box. It had been two and a half centuries!

Simon slid into the Mercedes's backseat and waited for Rhys to follow. "You okay?"

Rhys slid in and confirmed the driver knew his home address. Pushing fingers through his hair, he massaged his pounding temples. "I won't be okay until I see her again, and know she is not damaged for my foolishness. Or...find irrefutable proof she died in the eighteenth century."

If the legend was true, the enormity of the repercussions practically took Rhys's breath away. He was no man for abandoning her.

Don't get ahead of yourself. It is merely a legend.

"Is it possible you are reaching for chimeras?" Simon asked. "She's gone. I thought you saw—"

"I don't know what I saw now. Was it her? How can I be certain? Just think, Simon, if I have walked away and left her to suffer. Could she still be out there somewhere?"

"It's longer than a long shot. It's an infinity shot."

"I have to pursue this."

"You didn't know, man." Simon slapped a palm on his knee in comradely reassurance. "Don't be so hard on yourself. But what if we do find her? I mean, you know what the legend says."

Yes, that she would be mad. Locked away for centuries, aware of the dark, the insects and whatever horrors surrounded, yet unable to utter a scream? Rhys recalled her fear of rats. Her mind must be a macabre store of dread and terror.

Did he want to find the remnants of what had once been the most beautiful woman to ever touch his heart, to know him and accept him, even his dark side? And if he did find her, would he be far more kind if he killed her quickly to put an end to her suffering?

The chance he was merely chasing a phantom legend, a story conjured by firelight to entice and frighten, was great.

"No," Rhys muttered. "I will find her. If I must die trying."

CHAPTER FIVE

Paris, 1785

CONSTANTINE DE SALIGNAC'S voice possessed a soft murmur and felt like warm syrup seeping into her skin. His very presence, taller than she by a head, with broad shoulders and long fingers moving expressively as he spoke, intrigued her.

When he stood near, Viviane could not look away from him.

And yet, she did not feel the necessary spark of passion. His closeness did not provoke desire, twinkle across her flesh, or vibrate throughout her body. Intimacy should be like that. A man's presence should put a woman out of sorts in the best of ways.

Twice now, Lord de Salignac had kissed Viviane. Once in the garden behind the ballroom during a midnight salon. Last time had been four days ago in the planetarium amongst the squawking blue-and-emerald parrots. The kiss had invited their tongues to dance, and yet too quickly it had turned rough. Possessive. But hardly interesting.

Viviane knew what Constantine wanted. Eventually she must succumb. But if a man wished to keep her interest, she required passion. The man must convince her of his conviction.

Now Constantine coiled one long ringlet of her hair about his forefinger. "I am pleased you've attended this evening, Viviane. It is good you've not despaired in the wake of Henri's death."

She tensed. The man gained no regard with his callous prod at her most intimate memory.

A bird squawked nearby. "You've many birds. The peacock in the back courtyard is magnificent."

"A gift from Marie Antoinette."

"Does she know you are vampire?"

"The queen does not believe in the occult."

Viviane recalled Madame du Barry had been ousted from court for her belief in the occult. It was never a good thing when those in power believed, be their beliefs real or superstitious. Always scandal followed. The mortal could be silenced, and usually such reprimand was ordered by the Council.

She strode the hall where earlier she'd met Rhys Hawkes. "Have you hummingbirds?"

"No."

"I should think not." She stroked the gathering of roses above her right ear. The pointed beaks on the skulls pricked nicely.

"What are these?" Constantine inspected the flower buds tucked along the side of her coif. "Rat skulls?"

"I abhor rodents. These are replicas of hummingbird skulls carved by a Venetian artisan."

"Yes, the long beak..."

"I regard hummingbirds as my totem." Always she felt as if she must stay one step ahead, her wings ever beating, to maintain life. "Pretty, yes?"

"They suit you. But one mustn't overlook the value of a plump rat."

"Do not tell me if you drink from them."

The masterful tribe leader lifted a brow, but instead of proclaiming he did so, and completely horrifying her, he said, "I wonder if you would enjoy a stroll in the north hall where I've had the Tiepolo hung? It is a marvelously dark piece."

"Perhaps a few moments," she reluctantly agreed, while her eyes scanned the ballroom for the man with the gray-streaked hair. "It is oppressive in here."

A glance to Portia assured her she would return. Portia liked to wander the salon and figure who was mortal and who was not. The maid was safe from hungry vampires for she wore Henri's mark. To them Portia appeared used, not worth a taste.

The north hall served as a retreat for a few couples walking arm in arm, admiring the massive fresco paintings, which would normally fill an entire boudoir wall. But on the two-story-high walls they appeared merely portraits, one lined after the other. An ostentatious display of wealth. Three candelabras marked the walls at distances, providing low, hazy light.

Viviane realized Constantine could tend all her needs. Save the most vital—freedom.

Constantine offered his arm, which she accepted. The lace blooming from the end of his sleeve spilled across her wrist. He smelled of lavender, wine and the slightest trace of blood. He must have fed before attending tonight, most likely from one of his kin.

Viviane had never bitten another vampire who was not Henri. The bite was very sexual, which had made her relationship with Henri unique. They'd never had sex. That he had respected her enough to allow her freedom, while both succumbed to the orgasmic swoon of her bite, was tremendous.

She would be bound to no man, vampire or otherwise. Yet she was not stupid. A patron was necessary to survival.

"You stand alone amongst the frippery tonight," Constantine said. He placed a hand upon hers, which she curled about his forearm.

"I shouldn't wish to be an oddity," she said. "You don't think I blend well?"

"You do, but your beauty blinds one and all to your true nature." He paused before a velvet settee and Viviane tucked her skirts to sit. "Because I know what wickedness lives in your heart." He leaned in and whispered aside her ear, "Wolf slayer."

Spine stiffening, Viviane tightened her jaw. "It is not a title I admire."

"But you should. The entire salon uses it with respect when you pass."

"Only because you told them the tale of my encounter." That it had already become a *tale* whispered amongst the throngs disturbed her.

"It puts you above all others. A strong, dangerous woman no man shall reckon with. Which reminds me, I have something for you."

He slipped a ribbon from his sleeve. A curved white talon dangled from the length of blue velvet. Viviane touched it tentatively.

The sudden intrusion of warm metal brushing flesh startled her. Constantine stroked her cheek. One of his rings had sharp edges and she flinched, but it wasn't from fear of being cut. All vampires felt the *shimmer* with contact, a glittery vibration coursing through their veins. It was the only way they could recognize their own breed unless they saw fangs or witnessed the other drink blood.

Was Hawkes really vampire? His otherness baffled her.

"From a werewolf," Constantine said, confirming her

suspicions. "One I slayed decades ago. This is the trophy I took. I want you to have it."

"Oh, Constantine, I could not—"

"You must. It is a symbol of our similar spirits. We are both wolf slayers."

Viviane sighed and clasped the dead relic. At least she'd the decency to wear facsimiles of hummingbird skulls. Yet she could not deny her macabre curiosity. Inspection found the talon to be like ivory, and the tip pin-sharp.

Yet what troubled her was his talk of werewolves.

"Henri was never cruel to a wolf," she whispered. "He claimed no enemies."

She wanted to learn more. Because something did not feel right to her. Who had been the wolf who murdered Henri? Was it a retaliatory move because she had slain the wolf in the country?

"Of course, Henri was kind to all," Constantine offered quickly. "Too kind."

"Do you think… Because of what I did?"

"Slaying the wolf? No, mademoiselle, a thousand times no. These things simply happen."

The banal statement struck at her core. Constantine stroked her cheek again. The touch irritated more than comforted.

"For your reassurance, you must know I have already set my men to track the murderous wolf. Though Henri was not a member of tribe Nava, he was an honorary member. And we protect our own."

If Nava were so protective of their own, Henri should not be dead, honorary member or not.

"His head will sit upon a spike in the Bois de Boulogne in no time."

The city park was a sort of haven for Dark Ones after the prostitutes had left with their marks for the night. It was also the place where an example could be made of any who had thought to act against another tribe. Midnight executions were rare but not unheard of.

"Shall I tie it around your neck for you?"

"No." She nestled the talon beside her breast, tucked behind the corset. "The ribbon doesn't match my gown. But I promise I will wear it to the next salon."

"That would please me immensely."

She stifled a shiver to imagine pleasing this man. At this horrible moment she realized her future was tenuous.

"I wonder after your intentions?" she found herself blurting. Very well, so curiosity would kill this cat, or at the least, maim her. "Regarding your pursuit of me."

"As I'm sure Henri told you—"

She put up her palm. "It is not something I can consider at the moment."

Constantine audibly swallowed. "I understand. You and Henri were close. But marriage aside, you must choose a patron quickly. Henri's blood is established in you," he continued. "To take a new patron will require some…restructuring. Time to adjust. You must be blooded anew."

An emptiness eddied at the back of her throat. How much time *did* she have? She had only needed to drink from Henri twice a year. Yet she had felt his death as if he'd been ripped from her very soul.

"I will consider your proposition if you will show me how willing you are to have me in your life."

"You've to ask me anything."

"Understand, just because I am considering your proposal does not ensure that I will accept. But I find it would be extremely challenging, if not socially humiliating, to step under your patronage when you've already so large a harem. I feel I would become lost amongst the throngs."

"They mean nothing to me, Viviane. I do not love any of them. My kin are there to serve a purpose."

"Would I not serve that same purpose?"

"No, it would be different. Viviane, I love you."

The hairs at the back of her neck prickled. What beasties snuck upon her heart?

She maintained decorum. "Then prove it. Send them away."

"All of them?"

"Yes. Cease patronage to your entire harem."

Taken aback, he thumbed the Van Dyke beard on his chin. "They would die without me."

Viviane shuddered inwardly. She was only promising to *consider* his proposition.

"It shall be done," he said.

ONCE RHYS TOOK A PERSON'S scent into his nose, he had it forever. A vampire, on the other hand, must be much closer, within hearing range to track the heartbeat of his victim. Thanks to his mixed blood, Rhys could track Viviane LaMourette anywhere in the city, if he desired.

That was the question. *Did* he desire to track her?

What was he doing? Seeking to revenge the vampire lord. What had become of his initial, and real, attraction to the vampiress?

Those whimsical blue eyes had captivated him. Too bright, too bold. And that mouth. So red, so soft. And that imperious command of independence he had found refreshing. The woman might well be a libertine.

And that teasing curve at the side of her mouth. Like a delicate petal, it begged plucking.

"And what is wrong if I wish to pursue fine things?" To take them, hold them in his hands and crush them against his skin.

What was wrong was he had veered off course. He'd come to Paris on a mission for the Council. And still, no word from William Montfalcon, which was beginning to disturb him.

Rhys had been suspicious of Montfalcon's unlocked door upon arrival. It was as if the man had left for the day and intended to return—yet had not. So he and Orlando were staying in the man's home with hopes he was merely away on holiday. Rhys knew Montfalcon would not mind, and if foul play had occurred, he felt sure Montfalcon would appreciate someone looking over his home.

He had not taken time to question any in the salon after the distraction named LaMourette had turned his head.

"Don't allow her to change your course," he muttered.

Yet his course had altered to include revenge against Salignac. That bit of side play he would enjoy.

Later that evening, Rhys tracked the vampiress's carriage through the tight, dark streets until it pulled up at a stable behind a town house hung with red shutters. An oil lamp flickered above the front doorway, leaving the stables shrouded in shadow.

The maid stepped from the carriage and wandered into the stable, her heels clicking abruptly.

A cloaked figure emerged from the stables behind the maid, a man, perhaps a stable hand. He stepped into the carriage. Closing the door behind him, the maid tugged up her hood and loitered outside.

"The vampiress is out on the prowl."

Vacillating whether or not to approach, Rhys decided he must attend his own neglected hungers, or meet the full moon with a raging madness he could not abide.

"Time to find a donor," he muttered, hating the act as much as he needed it.

CHAPTER SIX

CONSTANTINE DE SALIGNAC settled onto the tattered velvet divan, hastily untying the jabot at his neck. He was eager to slip into oblivion. But it was difficult to concentrate after what his man Richard had reported.

"That bastard is in town," he muttered.

He swiped his palms over his face, and scratched the small patch of dark stubble on his chin.

Richard had reported seeing Hawkes lurking about, sneaking through the salon as if to spy.

"Rhys Hawkes, will I never be free from you? Do you walk this earth only to torment me? To show me what others must never know?"

Richard popped his head into the study. "She's on her way, Salignac."

"Properly spiced, I hope," he snapped.

"Drank the whole bowl of opium," Richard offered with his usual lascivious glee. "She can barely walk."

Constantine's fangs descended in anticipation. Normally Richard waited until he'd been directed to prepare the evening's repast, but for some reason Sabine had gotten into the opium early. She'd cast him a stabbing glance when he had greeted Mademoiselle LaMourette.

Sabine had no right to jealousy, and yet rarely did his glossy-eyed kin ever show signs of fight over him. Pity.

Sabine was his oldest and favorite. He had a few dozen female kin that he blooded regularly in hopes of eventually getting them with child. A mortal woman-made vampire required five to ten years of blooding from her patron before she could accept his seed and grow fruitful. Sabine had been carrying his child for five months now.

Finally, some success.

If she could give him a male heir, a bloodborn vampire to carry on his name, the tribe would be most pleased. His position as leader was tenuous. The ailing tribe needed new blood to grow stronger. Constantine had been named leader two decades earlier, and he'd expressed the dire need for the male members to gather as many female kin as they could in hopes of producing viable male bloodborn vampires. Yet nothing had come of it.

His greatest hope rested upon securing Viviane La-Mourette as kin. She was the diamond amongst the rubies. The only bloodborn vampiress in Paris, she was the key to his remaining leader of tribe Nava. Finally!

Yet she asked him to give up his kin? A bold request.

A petite blonde, wearing a gossamer night rail that revealed her tumescent belly, stumbled against the door frame. She grinned drunkenly at Constantine and brushed the loose hair from her face.

He gestured for her to come to him. Candle glow exposed the road map of blue veins beneath her pale skin. She was growing more delicate as her stomach expanded. He made a note to find her a proper maid who would tend only her. He must not risk his child's life.

She collapsed on him more than sat. Though she was his favorite, he'd gone beyond desire for sex now that she was expanding. Still, her blood was the finest vintage.

"You could not wait for me?" he wondered as he stroked the hair from her neck.

"I thought I was your favorite," she pouted. "I saw you leaning so close to that wolf slayer."

So she was jealous. "You are my favorite, Sabine." For now.

He kissed her neck, grazing a fang along the vein. No passion required, only hunger for solace. Ever polite, only a small cry from her. She clutched his jabot and cooed as he extracted the hot blood from her vein. Laced with opium, it relaxed him and dizzied his world. Made him forget things.

He sucked the sweet wine of oblivion, yet she began to struggle. Normally she slipped into a weak reverie.

Constantine caught Sabine's wrist. "Settle. I am not finished."

"Oh!" Such a shriek could not be because of his ministrations. Sabine squirmed on his lap and slid off, landing on the floor, her head tucked. "It is like knives!"

Licking the blood from his fingers, Constantine stopped and noted what he was doing. He was never so messy. Where had it come from…?

A smear of blood across his lap trailed over the chaise longue. He startled. On the parquet floor, writhing in pain, Sabine bled from her loins.

"Richard!"

Jumping off the chaise and over his kin, Constantine wobbled to catch his balance. The opium hazed his perception. He wanted to recline and drift away, to annihilate the nasty foreboding Rhys Hawkes's presence had embedded.

"Hell, she's losing it," Richard hissed. He plunged to the floor and lifted Sabine by the shoulders. "What should I do?"

"Get her out of here!"

Unwilling to look upon the wailing female, Constantine turned and smashed his fist across the candelabra. Half a dozen tapers clattered against the wall. Flame ignited the English paper but quickly burned out. "Damn it. Will I never have what I desire?"

RHYS HAD TO ADMIT THE HAWKER down the street offered excellent pheasant legs. Roasting for hours over applewood chips gave the meat a soft, sweet flavor. He set aside two cleaned bones on the paper they'd come wrapped in and started on his third.

He preferred meat to blood. Or rather, his werewolf did. And though he was vampire right now—and vampires could not abide meat—the werewolf ruled his thoughts. He would regret this when the vampire retaliated during the full moon.

But until then—his werewolf mind urged Rhys to tear another strip of savory meat from the bone.

Setting aside the cleaned pheasant bone, Rhys scanned the copy of *Journal de Paris* he'd unfolded on the table, yet found he wasn't in the mood to read about the queen's curious involvement with a priceless diamond necklace.

They'd been in Paris a week and William had not returned home. Montfalcon was young, strong and bold, yet he was also gentle and discerning.

Rhys could not figure what would have led a wolf to take Monsieur Chevalier's life, and that of his wife.

Indeed, could it have been William? Certainly would give a man good reason not to be found.

No, he was forming conclusions with little basis in truth.

Nefarious deeds had occurred within the vampire and werewolf communities. Suspicion should point to the Order of the Stake, a covert organization of mortals intent on slaying all vampires.

Mortals or a werewolf? Rhys would rule out neither.

If she had been patroned by Chevalier, perhaps Mademoiselle LaMourette could provide some insight.

"Oh, did I tell you?" Orlando said, interrupting Rhys's thoughts as he grabbed another pheasant leg from the diminishing stack. "I learned something about the slain vampires last evening after you went off to stalk the vampiress."

He would hardly call it stalking. Mild interest, perhaps. "Yes?"

"Seems they were a husband and wife, and…the vampire…"

"Henri Chevalier."

"Yes, he patroned only his wife and one other vampiress. Viviane LaMourette."

"Yes, I know."

"But did you know —" the boy leaned in dramatically "— she is bloodborn?"

Rhys sat back in his chair, stretching out his legs. Bloodborn female vampires were rare, a prize to snatch and hoard. If two bloodborn vampires were to procreate, the offspring would be very powerful.

Lord de Salignac was bloodborn. Rhys was also aware tribe Nava was desperate for new blood. The tribe was in danger of extinction for a mere dozen or so males remained.

"You are sure?"

"A faery told me. And then I stole a kiss from her."

"You should be cautious of the Sidhe, Orlando."

"But you—"

"Have a distinct relationship with their kind." And not one he wished to cultivate. "A man unaccustomed to dealing with those who wield glamour had best stay as far from them as possible."

"I kissed her once. Besides, I've my eye on the mortal

pretties who prance about the Palais Royal and lift their skirts to show their unmentionables."

Rhys shook his head. "Be careful there, too, boy."

So Viviane LaMourette was a bloodborn vampiress. He'd thought only the created vampires required a patron. But then, this was the first existing bloodborn female vampire he had heard about in a long time.

"Bloodborn," he whispered.

Constantine would be a fool to let so valuable a female slip from his clutches. Which would make Rhys's successful seduction as a means to revenge all the more satisfying.

And aren't you doing a spectacular job of that, man?

"I think the murders are in retaliation for the wolf slayer," Orlando said.

"You do?"

A pack wolf had been murdered as spring had arrived. He had been found beside a toppled carriage, neck broken. Yet the killer had not been a mortal, for rumors whispered through the Salon Noir it was vampire.

The packs were careful to keep away from humans, yet the werewolf's humanlike soul required a connection with the mortal world when the full moon insisted they mate.

Rhys, on the other hand, suffered moon madness. Normal werewolves sought to mate during the full moon; his werewolf—urged on by the vampire mind—hungered for murder.

"So how did it go with the vampiress? I thought you intended to seduce her?"

"We got on well enough."

"Isn't what I sensed."

Cheeky boy. Rhys splayed out a hand. "Did you expect she would fall into my arms at first glance? I intend to call on her today. She must have information regarding her patron's death."

"I wager you are the only vampire who dares approach her."

"Makes things more interesting, I suppose."

"How will you take from Constantine the one thing he wants more than life? Will you kidnap and ravage her?"

"No." Rhys chuckled. "It will be far sweeter to win her admiration, then see Constantine and know the woman he loves has been tainted by me."

CHAPTER SEVEN

THE RAIN HAD STOPPED. Clouds blurred the moon.

Viviane navigated the slick cobblestones with airy steps. The women at Versailles had nothing on her balletic rush-walk.

A cat meowed. The creak of carriage wheels a street away slapped the hard stone.

The Dark Ones occupied these spare hours between the theatre and the dawn arrivals. Viviane mused the blood was fresher, healthier even, than from the languorous aristocrats.

A breath pulsed the night.

Viviane paused, but did not look over her shoulder. A survival trait, she never made herself obvious, be it walking through a crowd or alone.

Again a breath teased the air and tickled the base of her neck. Goose bumps tightened her skin. Normally she was the one to produce such a sensation in a victim.

She picked up her pace, clutching her skirt to keep it from the wet cobbles.

Tonight she craved…something. A bite from a stranger. The wanting brush of skin against skin. Sometimes, if the man were clean and reasonably handsome, she would allow his hand under her skirt, but that was rare. She kept her lovers separate from sustenance.

It is not blood; I want to be touched tonight. To feel passion. To surrender to climax.

A carriage rolled by, forcing her shoulder against the limestone wall of a three-story home. A nail jutting from a windowsill snagged her sleeve.

Viviane tugged and cursed as the lace at her elbow tore. She touched her abraded skin and sucked at the bleeding wound. The skin knitted together under her lips, and within a few breaths it had healed.

Moving briskly through an alleyway so tight her shoulders brushed the walls with alternating steps, the darkness overwhelmed. A whisper of wind brushed her ear so tangibly she felt sure someone had touched her.

She would not tolerate an untoward mortal man thinking he could seduce a lone woman this evening—that was an engagement she always controlled. However, if it be a cutthroat, then do follow; she would lure him to an unfortunate result.

Viviane stepped on a moving ropelike bit. Her ankle twisted and upset her footing. The kitten heels were not made for sure balance. Something squeaked. Dread scratched her senses.

"Sacre bleu."

She could feel them teem about her skirt hem and across her toes. Slithering. Sharp, pin-quick claws. A silent swarm. So suddenly they'd come upon her. Had she wandered into a nest?

Odor of rot assaulted the soft tissues in her throat. Terror lifted in her belly. The intensity of her racing pulse hurt her ribs. Her shoulders dropped against the wall. Eyelids fluttered.

"No," pealed from her mouth. "Please, I, cannot..."

Disgust and fear consumed her bravado. An agonizing moan keened from her lungs. Yet Viviane could not cry out for the scream lodged in her throat, clinging as if for safety from the horrible creatures.

Too many of them. The horde rattled.

Which way had she come?

Tiny fangs pierced her ankle. Viviane shook her leg violently. Her skirts hampered movement. The satin corset constricted. She lost balance and slapped a palm to something hard. Should she faint—

"I have you." A man's voice.

Lifted from the ground, her senses blurred. The something hard she'd grasped to steady herself was a man's chest. She gripped him about the neck, trapping a ponytail tied with ribbon under her fingers. Earthy scent. Subtle vampiric vibrations shimmered under her palm.

Strong and focused, he carried her through the darkness.

Aware. So aware of his breath playing across her décolletage.

The heartbeat against her breast pounded steadily. He held her as if a child, secure in his arms. Viviane recognized his scent. Not a stranger.

Nor a friend.

Sacre bleu, she had fallen into *his* arms?

"You're safe," he whispered. "It's over."

He set her down. Clinging but a moment longer to his coat shoulders, Viviane ducked her forehead against his neck. *Safe here. Nothing to fear.*

Still she could feel rats teeming about her ankles. A prick of fang— She lifted a foot and slid it along her leg.

"No more of them," he comforted. "I promise. They swarmed over a dog carcass at the end of the alley. I could smell it. You couldn't have known."

"I…hate them." Humiliating, she could not find her breath or stand and face him calmly. But the memory…

The bodies of her parents' victims, left behind after

the Order had slain her parents. The dead mortals had not been buried, for she was too young to manage digging a grave. Swarming with rats.

"I don't like rats much myself. They are filthy creatures."

He stroked the hair from her cheek. The touch was rough, his flesh not smooth, unlike Constantine's soft, thin fingers. Viviane clasped his hand. She closed her eyes and held him there at her cheek. Chase away the memories. Concentrate on his warmth until she recovered her breath and tendered her confidence.

He was too close, too intimate with her. *So wrong.*

She did not care. Could not think beyond the safe feeling. It wasn't wrong to take comfort, was it? She didn't know. Rarely had she received the like. He must think her weak.

"Are you well, my lady? Tell me you were not harmed? Bitten?"

"Yes, a few bites." Healed now, surely. "So awful. There were too many. I did not hear them until it was too late."

Still gasping for breath, Viviane followed the stroke of her fingers down the front of his frockcoat. Simple pearl buttons wobbled on threads in need of tightening. The coat was old, a comfortable piece. He was not a Nava tribe member then, for they deemed a man worthy by not only his unbaptized state, but as well by his dress and aristocratic bearing.

The observation distracted her, and she needed that. Breaths settled. And her heartbeat resumed a normal pace.

His scent, earthy and rich, like a wide-open meadow or a vast, enclosed forest, appealed. Complex. Not dusty or perfumed as so many of her kind preferred.

Realizing her fangs had lowered she willed them up. Tucking her head, Viviane chastised her body's irrational reaction. Anxiety always put her to defensive mode.

Yet so did desire.

"I thought you were Constantine."

"Sorry to disappoint."

"I am not disappointed."

"Pleased?" he asked hopefully.

"No." She wobbled, grasping for the wall.

Rhys Hawkes pressed his body against her, hugging her from breast to hip. It was a lover's easy pose. His eyes held hers and he bowed to her. Would he kiss her? Dare he?

"We stand outside your home."

For the first time she realized the wall behind her shoulder was the Chevalier stable. Truly her mind was out of sorts.

"I would escort you inside," Rhys said, "but fear the invitation will not be offered."

He slid a hand down her thigh—she'd forgone underskirts for the hunt; much quieter that way—and bent to squat before her. His hand moved over her shoe, tied with red moire ribbon, and up her ankle. Though she wore silk stockings, it felt as if his skin touched hers. Warmth burnished her flesh. He could wrap his whole palm about her ankle, contain her, control her—

Viviane realized he was feeling for the bites, not trying to accost her.

"I am sure any bites have already healed." She pulled her ankle from his touch, yet regretted the lost connection. "Were you following me?"

He shrugged.

"When have I ever given you the suggestion I appreciate

your company? You've spoken to me but once, and that was most unpleasant."

"It wounds me your memory of our meeting was so foul. I found it most enjoyable. I think it was something I saw in your eyes. They are the color of a bright summer sky."

Viviane looked away. The last time she had seen the bright sky…

Deprived of daylight for two centuries, she often wondered what it would be like to touch sunlight streaming through paned windows, and could still recall watching dust motes dance in a sunbeam before she'd been blooded at puberty.

She possessed a vague recollection of summer fields dotted with fresh cornflower and clover. Now all she had opportunity to see was the occasional moth on a suicidal mission toward a flame. Still, pretty in a macabre manner.

"Go away," she whispered.

Monsieur Hawkes leaned in and delivered a wicked grin. "Make me."

He stroked a curl of hair along her neck, so she swatted his hand none too lightly.

"Ouch. Do it again?" He snickered.

Viviane's blood rose at the challenge. A gentleman would walk away. A rogue would have kissed her by now.

"You may like the vintage of my blood, Viviane."

She bristled at his use of her name. It was too personal. He invaded her comfort. "I wager it is a less desirable vintage than I am accustomed to, Monsieur Hawkes."

"Yes, I am to understand you city types sneer at the country appellations."

"Only because they are so uncivilized and ill-mannered."

"Are we still talking about blood, or have you turned to my person?"

"It is all the same."

"Of course. You are the aristocracy."

"You do not claim the same?"

"I am a humble provincial at your beckoning, Mademoiselle LaMourette. Ask me to slay all the rats in the city and I shall."

She could not prevent a chuckle. "If but you could."

Moonlight filtered between the nearby rooftops, gleaming on the harsh planes of his square jaw. Dark eyes glittered with the stars she could not see for the clouds. His thick, long hair was dashed with a gray streak as wide as two fingers. So wild.

He could have her if he but swept her into his arms and carried her inside. And then she would receive the satisfaction she craved this night.

He placed a hand above her shoulder on the wall. "Rumor tells you require a new patron?"

"My patron was Henri Chevalier," she said tightly. Anger spilled over the tender wanting. "Constantine believes a wolf killed Henri and his wife in cold blood."

Rhys shifted against her, leaning in closer. "Not all wolves are vicious."

"What do you care for the wolves?"

"I mark no man my enemy, no matter his breed. As Rousseau says, 'All men are created equally.'"

Henri had once quoted the same. She'd thought him a revolutionary. And she had admired him for his bold, independent thinking.

Her anger subsided as she looked over her rescuer's face. Square jaw and bold nose. Not outwardly handsome, yet indicative of a warrior, and strong, powerful men always attracted her. Desire again scurried to the surface, reducing her need to put up the offensive. Rhys was attractive, more so for his teasing gentleness.

"Thank you for the rescue." And then she leaned in to kiss him.

A connection, two mouths meeting in the night. Testing. Taking measure. Wondering. She kept it chaste; his lips were soft and yet firm, willing to give her her way. This kiss was hers to direct, and while she fought with the insanity of it, she was proud of her independent heart. It never led her too far astray.

Tonight her heart took what she craved. Flesh to flesh. Sharing of body heat. A sample of pleasure she could either pursue or flee.

How she wanted to pull him to her, crush her breasts against his chest, and dive into the deepest of intimacies. But no, this simple moment must be savored. This first kiss, not at all awkward for their mouths met as if destined, she would remember always.

Breaking the kiss, she leaned back, but Rhys followed her, forehead to forehead.

"You surprise me, LaMourette. I thought my presence offended you."

Indeed, she surprised herself.

"Regarde moi," he said.

No, she would not look at him. Could not. Her bold heart grew trepid.

"It was nothing more than a thank-you kiss, Monsieur Hawkes. Lost in a moment of relief." She exhaled resolutely. "I assure you, now I've gained my senses, I will ask you to leave."

"I am honored to have earned your kiss, even if in a moment of nonsensical folly. Good eve, LaMourette. Until we next meet." He glanced upward. "Full moon in less than a week. What is it Shakespeare wrote? *Well met by moonlight?*"

"I believe it was *ill met by moonlight.*"

"Ah? Well then, forget I said that. Meeting you has been beyond a pleasure. *Au revoir.*"

She lifted her chin and did not look until he'd broached the cross street and his silhouette filled the alley. Broad-shouldered and solid. He was built like a peasant who worked the fields. Not refined. Brusque. And such a swaggering walk. Nowhere near the aristocratic elegance she was accustomed to.

Viviane swiped her tongue across her bottom lip. The taste of him did not offend. And the smell of him, so much a part of this mortal realm, crept into her pores and fixed itself there. Complex, yet simple. Dark. Sure of himself.

Yet she could not abandon the ill ease something about the man was very wrong.

CHAPTER EIGHT

"YOU SAY SHE WAS WAITING for William Montfalcon to return to her?"

Orlando nodded fervently. "He'd told her he was bringing money, so they could be together."

Having returned from his nightly visit to the brothel, Orlando's ginger hair was mussed and his shirt untucked from his breeches. But he wore a smile like a badge of triumph.

"Her name is Annabelle," Orlando said.

"Just Annabelle?"

"Yes, just." A wider, more pleased grin had never graced the boy's face.

Ah, the afterglow of a night well spent.

Settling in for the morning, Rhys sat on a stool at the end of the bed, stripping his stockings off before the porcelain ewer filled with boiling water. "How did this topic come up while you two were…?"

"I asked her if she ever thought to stop and leave the world behind."

"Interesting conversation."

"We did more than shake the bed." The boy plopped onto a chair, one arm draping the back, a leg dangling over an arm.

Rhys recalled the drunken high of after sex, and felt a nudge of jealousy. Kissing—or rather, receiving—La-

Mourette's kiss tonight had only increased his frustration.

"I am a gentleman, Rhys. You taught me to treat a woman with dignity."

"Is that so? I don't recall directing you to comment on their assets as if they were confections on display at the market."

"Oh come, man! I am young. I am enjoying myself."

"Indeed." He plunged his feet into the copper bowl, huffing out a satisfied moan at the heat. "And she said nothing else?"

"Only it has been almost a month since William promised to return to her. She's all put out about that. I wish I had a bit of coin to give her. More than she usually asks, that is."

"I think I can help you with that, Orlando. I want to speak with her. See if she'll give me further information regarding Montfalcon's whereabouts. When do you see her next?"

He shrugged. "Few days."

"Excellent."

IN THE SHOE ROOM, Viviane sat with her back to a padded damask column. A loose linen chemise spilled from one shoulder. Lace about her neckline and wrists tickled her skin like a lover's breath. *Rhys's breath.* A red satin shoe with black frogs and an ebony heel she clutched to her heart.

Earlier, Portia had dusted the room with lavender powder, which lulled her. Sleep had eluded all through the morning hours. And now, well past two in the afternoon, she could not begin to start the day. For *he* haunted her thoughts. Her every step. Every time she ran her tongue across her lips she thought to taste him.

Him—the vampire with the warrior's name and the curious scent—Rhys Hawkes.

She touched her mouth and allowed a wicked smile at the thought of Rhys's mouth tasting her. She pressed her thighs together and almost, *almost,* reached a pinnacle. Surely, it would take more than a kiss to bring her to climax. Yet for as agitated as she'd been lately, Viviane was surprised she'd not come from a mere kiss.

What power did the man wield to affix himself in her thoughts—into her very body—like this?

Constantine she never thought about, unless it ended in revulsion.

Rhys, it seemed, could not be near her without touching her, if even through the slightest glide of his knuckles along her skirts, he sought connection.

And he had achieved it. To her detriment. Now she could think of nothing more than seeing him again. Tempting him to touch her, to unleash her from her self-imposed freedoms. To take their kiss beyond.

Did he mark it off as folly? Or did she haunt his thoughts, as well? Did he crave her? Did he wish to feel her teeth against his neck, his mouth, his veins?

"I want more of him," she said on a wistful sigh. "A taste of him."

A taste would not bond her to him as kin to patron. A deeper drink was required for that.

Rolling forward onto her stomach, she teased a red tassel decorating the toe of a cerulean slipper. Each pair of shoes had been lovingly placed on a tilted shelf, the sides of each foldable box down to reveal the contents. It was as if a confectionary shop displayed its wares of satin, lace and ribbon.

Noticing the corner of paper tucked beneath one box, Viviane drew it out. The card was about the size of her hand, and featured a marvelous ink drawing with exquisitely lascivious detail.

"Blanche, you do surprise me."

The drawing depicted a man on a chair, leaning over a woman who sat on the floor. Her dress spilled from shoulders and hips to reveal he teased her nipple with one hand and her quim with the other.

But more interesting in the picture was the chair decorated with arabesques of large male members, and on the woman's shoes were tiny female figures, legs splayed to reveal all.

The erotic art increased Viviane's ache for a sensual touch. She traced a fingernail along the curve of the woman's breast, and tapped the man's delving fingers.

Rhys could touch her like that and she would not stop him.

Even though he disturbs you?

She imagined herself in such a position—with Rhys leaning over her. Sucking in her lip, she slid her hand down her skirts to press between her thighs. Giddy desire stirred. She needed so much more than a kiss.

Portia tiptoed in and leaned a shoulder against the damask wall below an angel-bedecked candelabrum. "Dear, you look so melancholy. It is Monsieur Hawkes."

Viviane hid a sly grin behind the erotic card. "You think to know so much?"

The maid nodded, sure of her assessment. Wilted ruffles frilled about her bosom and mobcap; she'd been steaming Viviane's gown.

Viviane sat up against the padded post and drew her legs into a curl. She displayed the card to Portia. "Were you aware of your former mistress's secret stash?"

"What is that?" Portia bent to examine the card. "Oh my. He's touching her so… And oh." She clutched the card, but Viviane snatched it and possessively pressed it to her chest. "I had no idea. Shall I dispose of it for you?"

"No. It appeals to me. As does Monsieur Hawkes."

Portia's eyelashes fluttered in delight. "He was appealing."

"You think so?"

"Yes, that gray streak in his hair is charming. Makes me wonder if he got it because of some devastating trauma that wounded his heart. And now he bears the scar of it as a reminder."

"You have quite the imagination, Portia."

"Is he a vampire?"

"Apparently." At Portia's wondering gaze she explained. "He seemed out of the ordinary. Not like vampires I've met. Rough-mannered. Dressed poorly."

"Oh, dear, yes, no lace."

"That, and did you see his walk? A bowlegged strut like something right off a pirate's ship. The man was overall..." She searched for the correct summation.

"Wild," Portia murmured with wicked delight.

Viviane hid a smile behind the card. Passion had flared in Rhys's brown eyes as he'd stepped defiantly before her to divert her pace in the salon. When he'd stepped around behind her, she had felt his eyes roving down her back, lingering at the base of her spine. It was as if he had touched her there.

What a divine place to experience touch. And she preferred if it were by a man's tongue while she lay naked before a blazing hearth fire. The tickle of a wet tongue down her spine, tracing into the dimples of Venus that crowned her derriere...

"You're thinking about him," Portia chided teasingly.

"He fascinates me, nothing more." She studied the card

again and wondered if there were more to the collection tucked away.

"Does he desire to give you what Salignac can?"

"What, exactly, is it Constantine *can* give me?"

"Safety. Life."

She liked those things. But freedom was missing from the list.

"You do adore fine things, *ma chérie*. And your coffers are not growing larger. Hell, what coffers?"

She hated that Portia spoke the truth with little reserve. But she did not fault her for it.

All the servants had mutinied following Henri's death. They were owed wages, and Viviane had discovered Henri's caches empty. Upon Portia's suggestion, she'd handed each employee a silver candelabra or two and bid them adieu. But the stable boy, Gabriel, and Portia remained.

Every day new creditors knocked at the door seeking to collect Henri's debts. The furniture in the music room had been carried out yesterday. She had no idea how she would pay Rose Bertin, the dressmaker, yet supposed she could return all of Blanche's gowns.

Viviane studied the shoe and wondered if she could pay off a few leeches with a damask mule or ermine slipper?

"I've pressed the gown with the hummingbirds on the sleeves."

Viviane adored that one.

"Master Rosemont just arrived," the maid added. "He's copying out lessons."

"Excellent. Help me prepare."

IT WAS SATURDAY AFTERNOON and Master Rosemont stood over Viviane, gently guiding and observing as she copied out the word *carriage* on the paper. Henri had seen to arranging for her studies but days after her arrival.

"It's a complicated word," Viviane said as she finished the *e*. "But pretty. Did I make it right?"

"Your penmanship is coming along well, Mademoiselle LaMourette."

Much as she insisted he use her first name, he never did. He was young, and more than a few times Viviane had caught him observing the rise and fall of her bosom as she concentrated over her work. Once she had met his roaming gaze and he blushed so deeply, she decided never to do that again. The man was nervous, but a kind teacher.

"Are there some words you'd like to write today? List a few and I'll write them for you to copy."

Pressing the quill's feathered end to her lips, Viviane perused the many objects in the room, wondering which of them she'd most often need to write about.

"Shoes," she said. "Hmm, and wine."

"Yes, of course." Bemused, Master Rosemont scrawled the words on the page. His strokes elegantly imprinted the ink to paper with an ease that made her marvel. "A few more, and I'll leave them as your homework. How about Portia's name?"

"Oh yes. Portia. And gown. Salon. Book. Park." Her mind wandered to some of the more lascivious pleasures—stroke, tickle, tongue—but she wouldn't do that to him. Would *kiss* be too extreme to mention? Yes, it would. "How about…Hawkes?"

"Very good. Beautiful animals, are they not?"

"I've not seen one close up." Save for the man version. "Have you?"

"Only a dead one. Poor thing. It hung in the taxidermy

shop on the left bank. Gorgeous plumage. I felt sudden anger for the hunter at the sight of it."

The hunter. Like a wolf slayer?

Averting her rising guilt, she studied the paper he turned toward her. "Is that the word?"

"You tell me."

Viviane knew the first word began with an *s*. "Shoe," she said.

"Very good. And the next."

She recited them all, and when the short word beginning with *h* ended the list, she traced her finger beneath the letters. "Hawk." Which wasn't exactly what she'd wanted. "If I put an *s* at the end?"

"It will mean more than one."

"My lady, there's a visitor in the foyer," Portia called as she entered the study. "Lord de Salignac."

"I did not expect him. He knows I do not receive on Saturdays."

"Shall I send him away?"

"No, I will speak to him." There was still half the hour for her lesson, and she did not want to send Master Rosemont home. "I'll send him away quickly," she said. "Write a few more words for me, please. These few will hardly keep me busy the week."

"I agree." With a determined élan, Master Rosemont leaned over the paper.

Flames on a wall sconce flickered as Viviane entered the sitting room.

Constantine wore black, as usual. It was not a color aristocrats embraced, for black was the color of mourning, and of cheap wool they could only afford when they've nothing in their purses. Yet he wore the color as if he'd invented it. The damask coat was shot through with silver threads. In one pose the coat looked black. Yet if he tilted a shoulder or lifted a hand, it shimmered the fabric, turning it a jet silver, and then steel.

"I have told you this is not a day I receive visitors."

"But surely you'll receive me? Is there someone else here?" Constantine peered over her shoulder. "It's a man, isn't it? Viviane, I asked for exclusivity."

"And I asked for proof of your devotion."

"Three kin have left the brood," he stated. Straining his head over her shoulder he glanced toward the study.

"It is not what you would guess it to be."

"Really? So there is a man in the house?"

"Yes, but—"

He flew into a rage so quickly Viviane was swept off balance as he brushed past her. The last thing Master Rosemont needed was a raging vampire interrupting his work. She hurried after him, but he beat her to the study, and held the writing master slammed against the wall when she arrived.

"Let him go!"

"I demand an explanation," Constantine hissed at the reddened teacher. "What are you doing in Mademoiselle LaMourette's home?"

Viviane could but cross her arms and sigh. So the truth would be out.

"He is teaching me to read and write," she confessed. "Now do release him."

"Reading?" Constantine dropped the man, who crumpled to the floor.

"Yes, reading."

The vampire leaned over the table, inspecting her work papers. He jerked a look at her, apologetic yet tinged with a creased anger.

"I believe you owe Master Rosemont an apology."

"Oh, not necessary," the frazzled teacher piped up. "I am fine."

"Forgive me," Constantine said, and Viviane was glad for his humility.

"I think perhaps I should be off." Master Rosemont gathered his leather satchel and shoved the paper across the table. "I completed the list for you, mademoiselle. Perhaps you should send for me next Saturday? I shouldn't wish to intrude."

"No, please, return at the usual time. I promise this embarrassing situation will not be repeated." She delivered Constantine knives with a glance. "Will it?"

"Of course not. Can I ensure your ride home, Master Rosemont?"

"Oh no, no. I'm off." He bowed hastily and made a leg for the front door.

Constantine picked up the list and inspected the words. "Hawk?"

Feeling as though he'd raped her most precious secret, Viviane marched out of the room, hands on her hips.

He followed close on her heels. "So you don't know how to read?"

"What of it?" she spat out.

"I am surprised. I had thought your patron would have ensured a more schooled kin."

"So I am not smart enough for you?" A vicious clarity suddenly focused her, standing off the man who would *own* her if he had his way. "I think you should leave."

"I admit I was in the wrong to approach Master Rosemont so violently. But please, let's put that behind us, Viviane."

Yes, yes, keep the man appeased. "What did you come for?"

He bowed and kissed her cheek, and the other, and

finally a brush of a kiss over her mouth. The man was like marble, only becauseViviane wondered how to ever soften him, find the soul beneath the hard surface.

"Is that smile for me?" he asked.

No, it was not. "But of course. Who else?" She touched her mouth. Rhys lingered there. "Ah, Portia."

The maid brandished a silver tray sporting goblets and a wine bottle. Viviane poured half a goblet and tossed it back while Constantine observed with wonder.

"A bit parched," she offered. She wiped her lips with a finger. "Would you care for some?"

"No, wine tends to sit ill with me. While I was waiting I couldn't help notice your music room is rather spare of furniture. And on the wall." He pointed at the strange bright rectangle of English paper where a painting had once hung. "Are you having trouble, Viviane? Because you know you can ask anything of me."

Pacing away from Constantine to the one remaining settee in the entire house, Viviane decided the truth was not going to harm her, and it would show she trusted him. By all means, she wanted to stay on good terms with him.

"I had no idea Henri was in debt," she offered. "The creditors began appearing with bills three days after his death. All the servants have left, save for Portia and a stable boy, who am I most grateful for."

"If you need money—"

"Not at all. I paid the servants with furniture and silver. The creditors took a few horses and one of two carriages Henri owned. I thought it a fair exchange. I don't wish to make a fuss of it, Constantine. So if we could put the subject aside I would appreciate it."

"I'll not mention it again."

He gripped her wrists and pulled her to him. Viviane

knew he would kiss her, and struggled—only a little. He bruised her mouth with an urgent connection that sparkled in her belly. She had to force herself not to grab at his coat to pull him against her.

It would be so easy to let it happen. To not clasp his fingers in an attempt to stop him from tearing asunder the bows securing her corset. To expose her breasts so he might lick them as she needed them to be touched, tasted and worshipped. But she could not.

Tearing from his embrace, she stepped once before he pulled her back and she tripped on her skirts, falling against him. Constantine's breath whispered down her neck. The prick of his teeth altered her insistent desire as if a penitent's lash to bared flesh.

She managed to slip the side of her hand across his mouth. Skin tore and her blood oozed out. "Don't you dare."

He swept out his tongue and licked the faint crimson trail. Defiance glinted in his dark eyes. "Sweet. As suspected. And pure."

"That is the only taste you will know of me if you do not honor my request to dismiss your kin."

She held her breath, matching his defiant stare. *Pure.* Exactly what he required.

"You are the most exquisite taste, Viviane. To drink of you should murder me sweetly. It is a death I will wait for."

"Constantine, please, tell me what you want from me."

He clasped her hand and his thigh brushed hers. "I would ask you to accept my hand in marriage. To come under my patronage. To have my children."

Hand pressed to her throat, Viviane paced to the table

where the wine decanted. She traced a fingernail along the bottle's thin neck. "Marriage."

"It would make you mine exclusively."

No mention of love.

"But you understand that is impossible, Constantine. I've needs. The hunger forces me to seek others."

"Those men are but donors, vessels to feed your hunger. I don't want to direct you how to go about meeting those needs. But the others, if there are others besides me, I would like you to stop seeing them."

Other male vampires. Lovers? How ridiculous. "You say that as if I've a harem similar to yours."

"Mine is a necessity."

"A patron needs only one or two kin. Henri was an example of that."

"Henri did not lead a tribe. I must set an example by creating progeny."

Poor luck he was having with that.

Constantine was not cruel. Why did she insist on being so cruel to him?

She returned to the settee and sat on the edge of it, offering her hands, which he took and curled before his mouth to kiss. "I will consider it."

"I want an answer now," he insisted. For the first time Viviane felt she'd heard the real Constantine, the powerful lord who got as he wished, and cut down his enemies with one blow. "It is only fair to me."

"You think you can simply *select* me to become yours and I will comply?"

"Viviane, you have been granted such independence—" He stopped abruptly, checking his words.

"It bothers you, my freedom? That does not speak well for my future. As you've said, I have been granted independence. An independence I expect to retain, at all costs."

"That would be a steep price. Viviane, the relationship you had with Henri was unique."

She'd been so young when Henri had taken her under his care. Too young to be pressed into a sexual relationship. And he had never pressed, bless his kind heart.

"Please, let's not speak of him. My heart still aches for his loss."

"Of course." He lifted the talon from around her neck and let it fall from his fingers. "Forgive me. But please consider what the two of us could create."

Quite sure she did not favor being forced into making a decision, Viviane swung her foot and glanced to the floor beside the settee where she spied a box.

"What is in the box?"

Constantine's eyes sparkled. "Curious?"

"Of course. Anything secreted within a red satin box and tied with a bow would make a woman's heart beat."

"But you avoid answering my request."

"Show me what is in the box, and I shall consider your request."

"Ah, so you shall decide our fate by how you judge the value of what I've brought you?"

Of course. If it was of value, and she could use it to pay off one of Henri's debts. "Constantine, you know I will come to you…eventually." It was a sad truth she must soon face. "I need time."

"What if you have not time?"

"I have gone well over six months without drinking from Henri. I am…unique. Older."

"Perhaps it is because you are pure blood."

"If you distract me with whatever you've brought along, perhaps…"

Perhaps she could summon a reason not to answer his question. Ever.

"Very well." He placed the box on her lap. It was flat, narrow, and the red satin box was tied with a froth of black moire ribbon that wavered like oil under the candlelight.

"There is a craftsman in Rouen who designs astonishing pieces of jewelry. I once asked why Marie Antoinette had not summoned him, and he said she had, but he did not enjoy the fuss. Can you imagine?"

"Not everyone lives for the queen's summons, Constantine."

She knew he craved a connection to mortality she would never understand. As well, the fame.

"I saw this piece and immediately decided you must have it. It is as if it were made for you."

Viviane struggled with the knot, but refused to slip the ribbon from the box, as was possible. To delay the surprise was the best moment, and she always took her time when opening the few rare gifts she received.

For his part, Constantine did not rush her. She felt his eyes creep along her face and down to her breasts.

Marriage? He was a fine man. Handsome. Powerful. A tribe leader. All Dark Ones in Paris looked up to him. He could have any female vampire he desired, and she in turn should feel gratitude she'd been chosen by him.

And yet, Viviane had always avoided attachment to men for the very reason immortality meant forever. A woman promises her heart to one man and, centuries later, he may still be in her life. She wasn't ready for that. She'd never fallen desperately or head over heels in love.

And if she should, forever was too long for a commitment to a man whose eyes reflected babies. A baby tucked to her breast was the last thing Viviane envisioned for herself.

Pushing off the box top revealed a wide network of what initially looked like chain mail. Closer inspection found the pewter links were elaborate filigrees, chased and polished to a gleam. Hematite stones were set into the filigree. They shone like polished metal.

Constantine caught her reaching hand. "Careful. The tips of each link are sharpened to fine points."

Viviane lifted the box to eye level to see that indeed, the links were embellished with tiny points, like miniature fangs. "It's absolutely medieval. Like a torture device."

"Do you like it?"

"I believe I do. How delightful, yet dangerous."

"Much like you."

"Thank you, Constantine. It pleases me."

Setting it aside, she dipped her head before his face to accept a kiss. He answered without reluctance. This kiss was hard and demanding, much like—no, she would not think of that other kiss.

The kiss from a man who intrigued.

VIVIANE LINGERED AFTER Constantine had departed.

"You've a letter. Just delivered by a messenger." Portia dropped it on her mistress's lap. "So busy today with the visits and correspondence."

Pressing the crisp paper beneath her nose, Viviane scented the earthy odor and immediately guessed from whom it had come.

"Who is it from?" Portia asked.

"Monsieur Hawkes. Read it, will you?"

Sitting beside her, Portia carefully popped the red wax seal.

The seal of red wax fell away and Viviane caught it.

Interesting crest. The design featured a fleur-de-lis surrounded by pine bows. So provincial. She set it on Portia's lap.

"'My dearest LaMourette,'" Portia began, yet commented, "He addresses you like that? Presumptuous of him."

"I thought you favored him?"

"I do, but the propriety. Please."

"Continue, Portia."

"'My dearest LaMourette. Since we parted last night I have thought of nothing but your warm lips.'" Portia delivered Viviane a gaping O of her mouth.

"Read," Viviane persisted.

"'I know you will take no favor in my listing the many different ways I have thought of our encounter. Nor will it appeal that you have invaded my heart and I've no intention of fighting you from the vanguard.'"

Viviane yawned and patted her mouth dramatically.

"'But I do know how to win your heart, my dark, delicious queen of the night.'" Portia squiggled beside her. "He is so romantic. Oh."

"What?"

"Here is the final line. He writes, 'On my way home I encountered a rat and kicked it most soundly, sending it careening through the night, squeaking to bloody hell.'"

Viviane imagined the rodent flying through the air at the point of Hawkes's toe. How satisfying. How utterly humorous.

"'Good morrow, my sweet LaMourette.'" Portia dropped the letter in her lap. "Why write to you about something so awful?"

Viviane burst out in laughter. She laughed so hard she had to grip her stomach for the corset compressed her ribs. It was most painful, but she was too giddy to care.

"I don't understand," Portia said. "You don't even like rats. You find this funny? What did I miss?" She silently reread the missive. "If he's such an effect on your mood, I believe him dangerous."

"No man is a danger to me."

"To your person. But your heart is something else entirely."

"Nonsense, Portia. Your head is polluted with romanticisms."

"Better romance than dread."

Indeed. Constantine's visit had stirred dread in Viviane's heart. Dread for a dismal future that would see her freedom abolished. Monsieur Hawkes had an awkward, misplaced sense of romance.

Romance?

Rhys Hawkes and Viviane LaMourette? The idea of it tickled Viviane's persistent desire for all things sensual.

CHAPTER NINE

Paris, modern day

RHYS ASKED SIMON TO DROP his things in a guest suite then return immediately to the grand room to go over their plans.

It was good to be home. He owned estates in New York, Daytona Beach and Venice, but Paris was truly home.

Brushing aside the curtain, he admired the sky, dappled with stars. The moon must be on the other side of the house. Two days until it was full. After all the decades had passed, he still took no pleasure trying to sate his vampire or in locking his werewolf away.

Sexually sating the werewolf on the day preceding the full moon and the day following was not a hardship. It was what all werewolves craved during the full moon, sex, or rather, mating. A connection with one's mate they kept for life.

It was sating the vampire that he abhorred.

The difference between Rhys and a normal werewolf was when his werewolf came out, his vampire controlled it. Blood hungry, and armed with deadly talons, there was not a mortal in this world who could stand against him without coming away mortally wounded or dead.

In his first decade following puberty and his initial blooding, he'd lived with the threat of his werewolf coming out at any time during the month. Anger, rage, even a small slight had summoned the wolf. And when a vampire kills, even if in werewolf form, he takes the nightmares of his victims into his soul where they torment for days, even weeks. It was called the *danse macabre*, and he had suffered it over and over until he'd thought surely he would go mad. Moon mad.

Enchanting his vampire had been a necessity he would never regret.

Pacing the imported carpeting stretched before a high-tech titanium fireplace in the grand room, Rhys pushed fingers through his short hair. Tense and jittery, his muscles couldn't relax. It was as if he'd downed a gallon of java, and he hated coffee.

He hadn't taken time to think since learning the urban legend; he'd simply reacted. Now he tried to convince himself this trip to Paris was nothing more than a ruse. And if he were going to tilt at windmills it must be done swiftly, and return him to life before the emotional damage could set in and prod at the heartache he'd thought long and deeply buried.

Because he didn't believe she could still be alive. She had been reduced to *ash*.

The fact this legend resembled a piece of Rhys's life was due to mathematical probability. You doctor a story often enough, it'll eventually match that of someone's recollection.

But how many men had loved a vampiress and then lost her? In the eighteenth century. Paris. A man who was maybe a werewolf or maybe a vampire?

Could she still live?

He supposed a warlock could perform such a spell as to keep a person alive yet frozen, but there couldn't have been a coffin—let alone, one of glass—so long ago that would have been airtight, and would not break over the centuries.

So why had he rushed to Paris?

Couldn't be because hope simmered within him. Some part of him wanted to believe in miracles. He'd walked through the centuries relatively mindful of lacking miracles. There was always a man behind the curtain to erase the wonder.

He'd put her from his memory decades earlier. Hell, a century ago. For decades following her death he'd wallowed in misery and heartbreak. Her sweet kiss lived upon his lips. Those devastating blue eyes, he saw them everywhere. Upon her death, his heart had been shattered beyond repair.

Eventually he'd glued the cracks in his heart—though some pieces could never be replaced—and had finally gotten on with his life sometime after Napoleon's reign. That was when he'd begun to form Hawkes Associates. The work distracted his memory.

Once or twice love had flirted with him, but he'd never again ransomed what little remained of his heart. No, that ghost of her smile would not allow him to consider commitment. Nor the memory of that sweet little curve on the right side of her mouth.

Rhys hadn't looked twice at a female vampire since.

He stared out the living room window. From his estate he could see the Sacré-Coeur basilica, the massive travertine dome lit up as if a beacon to heaven. No heaven for him, he suspected.

Behind him, Simon entered and set up his laptop on the marble-topped writing desk.

"You never did say how you fell in love," his assistant prompted.

During the drive from the airport, he'd been telling

Simon about his first meeting with Viviane at the Salon Noir, and the days that followed.

"For the first time I looked at a woman and did not think about the love I had lost, but the companionship I could gain."

"Companionship?" Simon did not pause typing.

"I wanted to make her my lover. But also I wanted to know her. To know things about her. What did she think of when she was alone? When making love? Did she read the philosophers? Rousseau? Did a violin make her sigh?"

"You thought a lot back then."

"Romance has not changed so much, Simon."

"I know. Now we wonder what she is texting while we wait for the dessert course to arrive. Or why did she dye a pink streak into her blond hair?"

"I thought you liked Stephanie's hair?"

Simon shrugged. "We broke up. It was just as well. She texted everyone but me. I thought you'd decided you were pursuing Viviane to piss off Constantine? Was it for revenge or love?"

"At that moment I wasn't sure. I wasn't paying attention to the mission the Council had sent me on."

"Probably why you're not on the Council today, eh?"

Rhys shoved his hands in his pants pockets. He and the Council had an understanding. Besides, Severo, a lone wolf in Minneapolis, currently represented the werewolves on the Council.

"Arrange to meet the tunnel man this afternoon if possible," Rhys said. "Someplace expensive, so he'll understand I have the means to pay for whatever I wish."

"I don't know about that. I think we'd be wiser to meet on his turf. Probably doesn't frequent the high-class joints, if you get me. Then we could sum him up, get a feel for how he operates."

Rhys nodded. Simon had more experience with the whole cyber world. If he could hook this guy he'd leave it to him.

"Who put her in there?" Simon suddenly asked. "You know, in the coffin?"

Rhys turned a hard gaze on the man.

CHAPTER TEN

Paris, 1785

VIVIANE GATHERED A HEAVY velvet cloak about her shoulders and strode through the kitchen. Hunger called more frequently, of late, which should disturb her, but she set the nagging feeling aside in favor of sustenance.

Before leaving, she eyed a small paring knife lying on the butcher block. Portia used it for the pears she dined on each morning. The pearl handle fit into her palm. She turned the knife, wielding it as if to stab. That would save her from going upstairs to sort about for her fan.

She left out the servants' entrance because it opened aside the back courtyard and walked along the path between the house and the stable.

Just around the stable, a froth of white chrysanthemums plunged out from nowhere to stop her in her tracks.

Viviane stopped a shriek before it shot higher than her throat.

"I knew patience would win me an audience," Rhys said. He turned the corner, his shoulder hugging the building.

Darkness muted his features yet the moon highlighted the gray streak in his hair. It matched the gray wool jacket he wore. Jackboots and no waistcoat this evening. So… pedestrian. However, Viviane decided any fabric more elaborate would distract from the man's unique appeal.

A clever smile curved his mouth. He held out the flowers. Roots twisted from the stems. Dirt had been carelessly shaken off.

"You are trespassing, monsieur."

"Accept the flowers and I will leave."

"I've no desire to accept anything construed as a gift from you." Unless it came with another kiss.

"Then consider them a prize for enduring my purple prose."

About to protest, the mirth Viviane had gained from reading his prose surfaced. She looked aside to hide a small smile. "It was rather lush. You are certainly no gentleman."

He leaned in and his sensual aura cloaked about her. It was a dangerous shadow of male strength and bold defiance. Dangerous to Viviane's desires, which had grown ever-present since meeting the man. "You don't want a gentleman, do you? Unless Constantine is your idea of *gentilhomme*."

She defiantly met his dark eyes and noticed they were gold around the edges, gilded, the only part of him touching embellishment. "You've no idea what I want or do not want. And I have no intention of enlightening you. Now, I am in a hurry so you must leave."

"I will leave if you accept this token of my affection." He turned the flower bouquet between them.

"You promise?"

He nodded. Something in his gaze tickled Viviane at the back of her neck and hummed in her belly. Would he grant her such regard in her candlelit boudoir while leaning over her naked body?

"Very well." She snatched the bouquet from his grasp, and tossed it over her shoulder. A spray of dirt dusted her sleeve, which she shook off with a huff. Hunger called, defeating desire.

"Ouch." Monsieur Hawkes displayed his thumb to reveal a spot of blood. "Must have been thorns on the stems."

"Chrysanthemums don't have—" Yet indeed, he did bleed. How could that have possibly happened?

Viviane held her chin firmly, not about to show him her interest. Or her intense hunger. "Why should I worry for drawing first blood?"

"First? This is the second time you've brought my blood to air, my lady. A man might believe you enjoy the scent of it." He studied his thumb then pointed it toward her. "Hungry?"

Normally only mortal blood roused her hunger. Henri's blood had served to sustain her, but never to ignite desire, though certainly she had swooned when in his arms.

Usually she could go an entire fortnight without slaking her thirst. Why did the blood hunger prod at her so?

"I accepted your gift," she said lightly, yet her fingers clutched the paring knife tightly. "Leave now."

"I don't think so. I've not yet admired your beauty. The shadows make it tricky. Would you let down your hood?"

She looked aside, giving him the hooded side of her face.

"What has changed since the night I stole you away from the rats? You were more open to me then. I thought—"

"You thought incorrectly."

"I was there, LaMourette. You kissed me. You wanted me."

"It was not want." Oh yes, it had been.

"Liar."

Viviane lunged at him, fangs bared and paring knife aimed, but she paused abruptly.

The man displayed his naked wrist, baring the bold blue veins to her. "Go ahead, mademoiselle, slash away. Once you've the taste of Rhys Hawkes on your tongue, I wager you will crave me far more than you do even now."

She relented, tucking the knife behind her back. "I do not crave you."

Crave was too strong a word for the frustrating desire she felt. Though she had seen the vein pulse. She smelled his desire, too. It startled her because it felt familiar, liquid on her skin. Like a gossamer garment she wished to pull over her breasts.

"I would never drink blood from a fellow vampire."

"Why is that?"

"It is a bond I do not desire."

"What of a patron?"

"Are you applying?"

That man's smile bordered on lascivious. "Do you wish me to apply?"

"No."

"Just as well. I've no interest."

She realized her fangs were down but did not will them to rise. It would be viewed as a retreat. "You know we do not drink from one another unless we wish to form an intimate bond."

"The patron and kin bond can be different. It need not be sexual."

Well. That knowledge put him leagues ahead of Constantine. Truly, he was a libertine.

He tutted, glancing skyward where the moon soon promised fullness. "What has happened to you, LaMourette, to put you off your kind?"

"I simply will not risk allowing any male to believe he can patron me, thus owning me."

"I've said I've no interest."

"I trust you little."

"But if you did trust me you'd consider me as, say… lover material?"

Would she? He offended her, and he attracted her. Such a combination did appeal to Viviane's desire for the unique. A man set apart from the myriad who would look upon her as a means to blood and enslave.

Of course, she would take this virile, boisterous man as a lover. But to bond? Never.

"LaMourette—?"

"Possibly," she blurted out. "But your professed infatuation is merely a ploy that has something to do with your investigation into the murders."

"I had no idea, until the other night, you were in any way related to the murdered vampire."

"Henri's wife was murdered, as well."

"Yes, and it baffles me." He leaned against the stable wall, relaxed when she was so tense. "Who would have reason to be rid of Henri Chevalier? Perhaps someone after you?"

The idea had not occurred to her. "Why do you suggest such a thing?"

"Isn't it obvious? You are gorgeous."

"Beauty is no reason for such a heinous crime."

"Many have murdered for lesser raison d'être. The prize of beauty can be a great motivation."

"Does it motivate you?"

"In fact, it does. But not to such heinous acts. What I have in mind is a bit more—" he toed the hem of her gown "—intimate. It would be a pity to spoil such a beautiful evening. And still, I wait for you to make the next move."

He tilted his wrist, teasing. The blood on his finger yet trickled, and it smelled too good to disregard.

The man went beyond preposterous. He bared bold nerve to play with her when she had repeatedly shown him her displeasure. Whether or not she deemed him worthy of her regard would be for her to state, and not him.

Could he not step away and allow her to fulfill her needs? The nerve of him to cause her such trouble!

Time to show him exactly who Viviane LaMourette was.

"You are no gentleman, and so I will not treat you as one." She slashed the paring knife before her, cutting through his palm.

Rhys swore, and shoved her away.

Viviane staggered against the stable wall. Emboldened, she hissed at him, showing her fangs.

Dark eyes flashed betrayal at her. He clasped the wound and growled. Growled!

The air reeked of blood. *Too tempting. Not at all distasteful.*

But that growl. So animal!

Turning, Viviane ran to the house. Once inside, she locked the door and pressed her back to it, arms spread and breaths heaving. Blood covered her fingers.

Beyond the gold embellishment, she had seen something horrible in his eyes. Angry. *Wild.*

Shaking, she clasped her arms across her stomach. Oh, why had she hurt him? He had wanted to give her flowers. The man had been nothing but kind to her.

He'd pushed her to it. He should not have challenged her so.

Portia wandered around the corner with a pile of

laundered linens nestled across her arms. "What is it? *Sacre bleu,* you are bleeding!"

Viviane turned her head. Bloody fingerprints smeared the whitewashed door. She reeled from the gorgeous aroma of it. "It is not my blood."

A knock at the door upset Portia to a chirp. She clasped her throat. "Monsieur Hawkes?"

Viviane nodded.

"Did he hurt you?"

"No, Portia." Viviane drew up straight yet her voice faltered. "I hurt him."

Rich and thick, the blood staining the door invaded her pores. Was this nature's cruel manner of luring her to a new patron? She did not like to be forced to surrender!

Rhys beat on the door.

"Go away!" Portia yelled.

Viviane tugged her maid away from the door and shoved her toward the stairs. "Go to your chambers."

"You cannot allow him in. He's upset you. He may attack you!"

"I am not afraid. Go!"

Portia blinked, affronted, then went off, leaving the linens where she'd dropped them. Viviane suspected she lingered in the hallway.

"I can handle this," she said firmly and heard Portia move away.

Pressing her hand to the door, she felt the tremors as Rhys pounded again.

"Viviane," he intoned teasingly. Not angry, but determined to make her face her cruelties.

The blood scent was too strong. Rich and mixed with meat, wine and bread, and all the things Viviane had sacrificed because she was vampire. She often savored a donor's blood, reeking of mortal pleasures; it was the only way she could enjoy them.

Why did Rhys Hawkes's blood carry such flavors?

She traced a forefinger over the smear on the door. Slick. Red. As if an aperitif spilled from a crystal goblet.

Why had she done something so foolish? He could have easily overpowered her and…well, she wasn't sure what he might have done. Bite her? Take the knife away and cut her? Force himself upon her?

Please, yes.

Grasping her throat, Viviane swallowed. Was that it? Was she playing with him as he played with her? She did not stand down from any threat, unless it was rats.

Might his prowess in bed be so bold and intense?

Yes, she suspected, and secretly hoped it was so.

Viviane flung open the door. Rhys charged the threshold but stopped abruptly, his flat palms pressing the air between them.

Long hair fell forward over his shoulders, loosened from the confining ribbon, and he'd pulled open his frockcoat. Disheveled and dangerously attractive, his earthy scent drowned Viviane's resolve.

"Invite me in," he demanded.

All vampires required permission to cross the threshold of private residences. Viviane reveled in the power it granted her. "Never."

Fitting herself to the wall, she was determined not to broach their distance. To not rush forward and lick the blood from his wound. She would not deny this play intrigued, but she would allow no man the upper hand.

"I accepted your gift," she said coolly. "What more do you want from me?"

Rhys smacked his wounded hand against the invisible

barrier. Blood sparkled in the low light from the candle sitting in a wax puddle on the nearby butcher block.

"You are a vicious one," he said. Brushing the hair from his face put it to disarray. He did not care he presented so wild a demeanor. "No apology is necessary." A roguish grin surfaced. "I do favor a woman who is not afraid to act from her heart. Delicate women are so breakable."

"You break many women?"

He shrugged, and pressed his palms to the door frame. "A few."

A breath caught in Viviane's throat. What must occur to become broken? Kisses, touches, skin upon skin....

Yes, please, break me.

A drop of blood hit the hardwood threshold. She would not look at the crimson spatter.

All the Dark Ones knew what the smell of blood did to a vampire's hunger. He exercised cruelty against her with unfeeling flair. Yet so long as she did not invite him in he was restrained, as if a dog on a leash.

Fangs pricked her lip. Viviane pressed fingers over her mouth.

Rhys revealed a wicked smirk, jeweled with clean white teeth—but no fangs.

"Come, taste me," he said lowly, not quite a whisper, but the tones shivered through her pores, fixing inside her. A lover's entreaty to devour passion and drown in pleasure. "And then I will leave."

She looked aside and tried to scent the acrid cleaning oils Portia used for the wood. Still, his blood invaded all. "Leave now. Before I send for my bravos."

"You've no such thing. Though, I am surprised Lord de Salignac has not assigned a crew to you. If he cares so much for you, should he not protect what is his?"

"I am not his." She lowered her head, twisting farther

from the delicious smell of blood, and clinging to the papered wall. "I belong to no man."

"Do you wish to belong to someone?"

"Never." And she meant it. "Not now. Not ever."

Maybe.

Fingertips stroking the English velvet wall covering, she studied the glint of crimson he offered with a splay of hand and a wiggle of his fingers. Why had it not healed?

"It will be better than a kiss," he alleged. "It is my offering to you, LaMourette. My blood for your pleasure. To slake your hunger. Have you never tasted the provincial blend?"

"I have never…"

Tasted one so different remained in her throat. Making the judgment didn't feel right. Not when his blood scent dizzied her, creeping along her flesh with a lover's touch.

"You are hungry. You were readying to go on the hunt when I surprised you out back. Forgive me. I fear you had no choice but to react the way you did. I deserved this."

Another droplet of blood purled from his palm and dropped through the air. He should have healed by now.

"Think of it not as a means to satisfy a hunger you claim not to have, but instead as a look inside me. You can trust a man after you've drunk from him."

"Trust is possible through sharing blood, but not usual."

"I stand corrected." He reached for her but his fingers bent at the threshold barrier. "And yet I do believe you, LaMourette."

"Believe me?"

"What you show me. One should always believe when a person shows them who they are. You are independent. Strong. Yet you fear."

"Never."

"Yes, you do," he said quietly. Tilting his head aside, he closed his eyes, resigned. "I will not beg. I merely thought to show this side of me to you."

Viviane sucked in her breath. "You confuse me, Monsieur Hawkes."

"I do not mean to. And please, call me Rhys."

"Rhys." Short, simple, the name did not stay on her tongue long enough to make her feel as though she could even know him. "You put me off because there is something about you…"

"Not right?"

"Yes." He nodded, knowing, and she felt as if she'd slashed him again, yet with her words. "And at the same time, I wish to pull you close, because you appeal to some part of me."

"The part that wants to invite me in? To feel me against your body?"

Viviane moved forward, putting herself halfway between the inside of the house and outside. Rhys slid a hand around her waist, but stopped just above her hip. "You're not out far enough."

"This is all I'm willing to offer right now," she said. Touching his chin, she tipped it up to study the thick, dark stubble on his jaw and above his lip. Surprising, since the other night he had been clean-shaven. "Your blood smells of mortal fare. Why are you not like other vampires?"

Smoothing his hand up her corset, his fingers tickled her breasts where they rose above the fabric. Viviane backed away, and his hand stopped at the threshold barrier. Now she knew how far he could move and exactly what his boundaries were.

"We are all different," he said, clasping the front of her skirt and pulling her to him. Their chests hugged. Their mouths lingered but a breath away. The gold rimming his eyes enticed her as if stolen treasure. "Stop seeing all vampires as the same and focus on what stands before you now."

He gripped the top of her stays, and licked the mound of her breast, drawing his tongue slowly to the crease between the two of them. The pointed tip of his tongue embroidered shivers into her resolve.

"So wicked you are, LaMourette. Mmm, you do stir me to such lusty thoughts."

Viviane pulled away, but his fingers hooked in the crossed ribbons of her corset, held her over the threshold.

Sacre bleu, the heat of him at her breast. She raked her fingers through his hair and held him there, controlling him, commanding he please her. She would not cry out in pleasure, she must not give him that, not yet.

The fabric against her thigh began to slink up at his direction. His fingers stroked the satin ribbon that tied her stocking.

Viviane thrust back a shoulder, lifting her breasts high—and Rhys slapped the barrier, his mouth open and hungry for the flesh she had inadvertently moved from his touch.

"Invite me in," he insisted. A tug on the ribbon pulled her stocking loose and the delicate silk slid to the top of her knee.

Viviane drew up her foot, toeing his hard leather jackboot. Hooking her foot behind his knee, she tugged. The man jerked forward, bending and going to his knees outside, one hand sliding down her skirt, the other hand pressed flat to nothing, unable to enter her sanctity.

"Is this what you want, LaMourette?" He peered up

from his position before her, his face level with her waist, his hand moving under her skirts.

Yes, she wanted him on his knees. She wanted him....

Sinking against the door frame, one foot outside and straddling Rhys's knee, the other inside and sliding along the parquet floor, Viviane landed on her derriere.

Never had she desired a man more than now. She knew nothing about him, and all she wanted was everything from him.

"Come inside," she whispered.

And the spell was broken. His hand, released from the barrier, landed on her shoulder and the twosome fell back across the floor.

"Now," he said as he kissed her mouth, her neck and her breasts. "To determine if that invitation was merely to step inside your home, or a more intimate summons."

She pushed his hand down her skirts. "Both. Please."

Fingers stroked her derriere, exploring. Her skirts swished delightfully with movement as he teased down and between her thighs, invading her with such ease it was as if he were entitled.

His breaths came as quickly as hers. A rough kiss landed on the underside of her jaw. His fingers delved into her soft wetness, summoning a heady thrill that she'd not managed for weeks, for her liaisons had been few.

He moaned into her mouth. Viviane clutched the front of his shirt, and drew up her leg to encourage his ministrations. Not once did his mouth leave hers. Nor did his fingers cease their steady rhythm against her most sensitive spot. The man knew exactly how to stroke her, slowly yet steadily, and not too hard nor too lightly. He could not be real, for no man came to a woman her new lover and knew just how to touch her without practice and much exploration.

Rhys's tongue stroked her nipple. Viviane stopped struggling with the surprise of talents. Eyes closed, she surrendered to the insistent longings that had haunted her for weeks. She required this exquisite clutch of passion. And before she knew it, Viviane cried out in ecstasy.

"Animal!" Portia cried, entering the room. She scrambled to the door and grabbed the broom, heading for Rhys. "Get off her!"

Rhys dodged to avoid the swing of Portia's broom. He wasn't so lucky the second time. The broom handle rapped him soundly across the shoulder.

"Beast! Get out, get out!"

With a smart crack, he broke the rough pine handle in two.

Rhys mounted the threshold, and delivered a devil-may-care wink to Viviane. He blew her a kiss. "I've your scent, *chérie*." He dragged his fingers down his tongue. "And now I've the taste of you in my mouth. As promised, I shall take my leave. Keep me in your thoughts this night, LaMourette."

He ducked out as Portia threw the broom head after him.

Shoulders weak with delight, Viviane drew up her knees and sat against the cupboard in a pouf of skirts. Her corset loosened, her breasts jiggled as laughter bubbled up and she released it freely.

"You're laughing?" Portia kicked the door shut. "I thought… But wasn't he—? He was hurting you!"

Tucking her head into her hands she thought her laughter might become tears. So easily he had seduced her to his bidding. How long had she waited for such mastery? When she was staunch and unwilling to allow Constantine such ease with her, she had surrendered to a stranger in a breath.

"Speak to me," Portia said.

"He…he is a most masterful kisser and he certainly does have the skill to please a woman." Breathless, she fluttered her fingers before her flushed face.

"Oh. Oh?" Portia's shocked expression widened her mouth.

"I am thankful you ended the encounter as you did."

Portia lifted her shoulders and dropped them with relief. "Just so. The man is too free with you. But, do you favor him?"

Propping her elbows on her knees Viviane cupped her fingers beneath her chin. "I believe I do."

"But I beat him off with a broom."

"That was most sporting to watch. The man needs impediments if he thinks to simply waltz me into his good graces, yes?"

"Oh indeed." Portia nodded.

CHAPTER ELEVEN

CONSTANTINE WATCHED WITHOUT emotion as the werewolf was goaded to shift into his man-beast form. Bound at wrists, ankles and neck by iron shackles, the strongest beast could not escape. Yet the silver edging on those shackles is what kept this particular beast contained. And here in the damp, deep cellar of his estate, the torture would go unnoticed.

Not torture. A death sentence. Perhaps a little torture. He did enjoy the sound of flesh being rent open. It reminded that no man, or immortal, could stand against him.

Tipping the felt tricorn down over his brows, Constantine leaned against the stone wall, and propped a boot heel to it for support. His men took relish in prodding the werewolf with silver spears taken from the arsenal.

Tracking Henri Chevalier's murderer had been easy enough. He'd waited an appropriate amount of time following the vampires' murders, and then had gone straight to the brothels where William Montfalcon had chosen to hide.

The agonizing howls grew weak and raspy as the candle on the wall guttered. One of Constantine's men approached with bloody spear in hand. He flipped the long sweat-and-blood-riddled hair from his face. "More, my lord?"

Constantine studied the beast's broken body, hanging

now by its neck. The fur had scraped off against the iron neck manacle and blood oozed across its furred chest. The veins bulged and in places where the fur was thin the blood appeared thin runnels of purple.

"Stop for now and let him heal," Constantine decided.

He didn't want to rush things. With Hawkes in town, one never knew if they would require an assassin or a scapegoat.

"I WANT TO KNOW WHERE HE IS staying, where he goes, whom he speaks with," Constantine said, giving instructions to Richard, who had gathered two bravos to track Rhys Hawkes. He tossed the bloodied linen he used to wipe off his hands and neck into the ewer. "The man mustn't take a step without my knowing about it."

"It will be done."

"And send for Grim. He will know what impediments are required to keep Hawkes away."

"I'll have the witch summoned." With a bow, Richard picked up the ewer and left the room.

Constantine stretched out along the new chaise, which had been delivered only this afternoon. He could not abide the blood smell left behind from Sabine on the old furniture. It reminded of his impotence.

Not impotent. *It is the females who simply cannot carry my strong and potent seed.*

Indeed.

Viviane LaMourette could carry his child to term; he knew it. And what a powerful child it could become. Conceived from two bloodborn vampires. Finally, he could begin to strengthen tribal blood.

Constantine rubbed his pulsing temple. While Hawkes

was snooping about he could concentrate on nothing but getting rid of him.

It was preferable not to draw attention to himself with yet another scandalous murder of a Dark One. It would not do for tribe Nava to begin a war against the werewolves. Now, more than ever, discretion must be employed.

Ian Grim, the one witch Constantine trusted not to attack him with his own blood, was just the man to assist. He owed Constantine for a bold rescue from the burning faggots a decade earlier. Grim had been dabbling in devil worship, and had unloosed a malice demon. Villagers never take well to such antics.

Which meant the night was young, and he'd yet to decide whom to bed this evening. His most senior kin was Clarice. She'd been blooded nearly three years now. He suspected she wasn't quite there yet, unable to conceive a child from their union, but until Viviane kneeled before him with desire in her eyes, Constantine could only half-heartedly pursue her. He was no man to beg.

She must come to him. And she would—or he would see she suffered for her obstinacy.

RHYS STALKED THE THREADBARE Aubusson carpeting in William Montfalcon's great room. For as much as he wished the forest floor beneath him and his paws tracking the loamy earth, he could not risk a jaunt at the edge of town tonight. He hadn't yet established a safe storage place for extra clothing. Though every time he sauntered through the Bois de Boulogne his feral heart ached for freedom.

The moon would be full soon. The day preceding and following the full moon, Rhys's dark half growled for release. He had control by a specific means. Only the full moon commanded him completely when he shifted to his man-beast form.

When in werewolf form his vampire mind took over. And the vampire, kept back during the month, was always hungry for blood—and not a mere bite. No, the vampire wanted to bathe in blood, to punish Rhys for enchanting it decades ago and depriving it on a daily basis.

Rhys had only wished to keep his werewolf from harming mortals as the vampire mind pushed the beast to violence, and even murder. The *danse macabre* was a wicked punishment for taking life. He owed a faery a boon for that enchantment.

Had he not sought to control his dark cravings he would have killed hundreds by now, and surely, he too would be dead at the hands of enraged villagers, or from the torturous nightmares of the *danse macabre.*

He must get to his country home before the full moon where he kept an iron cage that would contain his werewolf until morning. Ridiculous he should go to such measures, but necessary.

As for the nights preceding and following the full moon? The werewolf wanted release, but could be controlled. If he were sexually sated—as other werewolves—his werewolf could be satisfied and his vampire mind did not emerge to seek blood.

But who to assist him with that need?

He did not want to ask Orlando for recommendations as to a fitting female. Though he did intend to visit the brothel this day to speak with the woman who claimed to be William's lover.

Only one woman captured his interest. The scent of Viviane's desire, strong and insistent, had melted into him. Clinging to the door frame, she'd wanted his kiss more than she had been willing to admit to herself. And she'd invited him in to more than just her home. Wicked vixen.

Never before had he looked upon a female vampire with interest or desire. Rhys simply hadn't thought it possible. They were too weak and subservient.

How wrong he had been to make assumptions.

The vampiress was divine. Personally strong, a challenge to any man. But her independence was not impudent. She breathed her freedom. It became her quite nicely.

Brewed by a heady sexual allure, she had merely to be in range of his senses to drive him mad with lust. With desire. With love.

Love?

Rhys had loved once. Emeline had been werewolf. She had loved him for his wolf and his vampire. But he'd broken her heart by refusing to get her with child. It was that damned bargain he'd made with the faery. He would not do that to any woman he loved.

Yet Constantine had seen to ending the flicker of hope for a lifelong relationship. Or rather, he had allowed the worst to happen—Emeline's death.

Rhys clenched his fists. *You are not a murderer.*

He wanted to return to Viviane. To look into her azure eyes and read her truths. To continue to believe. Was she so secure? Why did not fear of lacking a patron push her into Constantine's arms? Could Rhys forge an opening into her heart?

He did want her heart. Not some facsimile of a stolen liaison that resulted in sex and stolen trysts. He wanted the woman. All of her.

But must he tell her his truths?

You must if you want her to believe you.

"If she can accept me for what I am, if she can believe me, then I will know she is the one."

"Deep thoughts?"

He startled to find Orlando standing directly before him, open book in hand. In but shirtsleeves and breeches, the pup looked weary, as if he'd been up all night.

"Don't tell me you've been reading?"

"A bit here and there. This one has pictures. It is the Kama..."

"*Kama Sutra?* Hell, boy, maybe I should take care of that one. Unless you are studying? I thought you'd taken up debauchery?"

"It's more difficult than I imagined. Annabelle expects me to, well...you know."

"Please her? Do you not pay her to please you?"

"She doesn't ask me for money now."

Rhys turned his head so Orlando would not see his frown. Nothing good could come of a relationship with a woman who sold her body for sexual favors. And when she stopped charging? Didn't mean she wasn't making her way with others.

"Are we off, then?" he asked, now more eager to meet the woman who would enchant Orlando with her tattered charms.

"Annabelle expects us in an hour."

"WILLIAM SAID HE'D RETURN with money. He said he loved me." The strawberry-cheeked Annabelle, with tiny blue eyes and thick red lips, clasped the hem of Orlando's frockcoat. A love bite, likely from Orlando—or so Rhys guessed—stained her neck violet just below her ear. "He was like an animal, but gentle." She beamed at Orlando.

Rhys read the look exactly for what it was. Manipulation.

"He's never mentioned another home?" he asked. "A retreat in the country, perhaps?"

She shook her head and clutched Orlando's arm. The pup kissed the crown of her head. "Is he in trouble?"

"I don't know. He is missing," Rhys stated plainly. He walked the small room decorated in red fabric and black scarves. It smelled strongly of incense, which he guessed must disguise the taint of sex he picked up, when normal mortals would not. "There's nothing else you wish to tell us about William?"

She tucked her head on Orlando's shoulder. "Like what?"

Like how dare she shill for money in such a manner? Yet how dare *he* judge? Rhys was perfectly aware the women in these establishments often had no choice but to seek this means, and were sometimes even forced to the task. She was so young.

"Nothing, mademoiselle. Thank you for your time."

Rhys made to leave, but as suspected, Orlando did not follow.

"I'll just make sure she is well," Orlando said.

"Of course, I'm going to take a run out to the er…site." Rhys bowed to both and closed the door behind him.

Getting a ride on the back of a wagon headed for Versailles, he reached the kill site fairly soon. Rhys wouldn't shift to wolf shape during the day and so close to mortals.

For all the carriages rushing to and from Paris daily, surely any criminal evidence had been crushed and pummeled to dust. Yet there a distinctive blood scent clung to the earth, impossible to completely remove. It resembled something he knew well. He'd been surrounded by the scent, had lived within its home…

"Oh, William."

He kicked a stone across the carriage ruts and stared back toward the city, which was crowned by jutting chimney tops.

"How could you?"

CHAPTER TWELVE

"THE CHOKER IS AS IF IT WERE made for you," Constantine commented as he moved around to parallel Viviane and leaned in to kiss above her ear. "No bloodshed putting it on, I trust?"

"Actually, we had an incident," she offered.

She did not see Portia amongst the ballroom crush, and suspected she would not until it came time to leave. The maid had been shyly respectful after the broom incident last evening.

"Ah, but she is a blood slave, yes?"

"Portia? No." At the sight of Constantine's raised eyebrows, she added, "And that is how I wish it to remain."

"I am surprised at you, Viviane. Mortals are mere vessels. That you've established a sort of relationship with your maid can be dangerous. The things Henri neglected to teach you."

"She is my friend. And friends are an impossibility to keep when you go after them with intent to bite. Besides, Henri has bitten her. She is marked."

"You require friends who are Dark Ones, *mon amour.* I could introduce you to a few ladies—"

"From your harem? No, thank you, Constantine. I see they attend in numbers tonight. Even masks cannot hide their simpering devotion to you. You are not so eager to prove your interest in me, I see."

"Your words cut me. If you believe I would ask

exclusivity from you, and not give it of myself, then you don't know me as I wish you to. Tonette has gone."

"Yes? Sent to the country to starve?"

"She refused a severance. I had to kill her. She is not missed. As the other kin will not be missed. But I must perform this exorcism, if you will, in measured steps so as not to raise a revolt amongst the ranks."

"I don't care how you go about exorcising your flock, Constantine. I live my life as I've done until you come to me a free and kinless man."

He pressed a hand to the wall over her shoulder. The move caged her with his body. His voice, low and measured, stirred a note of tension. "If you think to tease me with promises to be mine and then to laugh in my face when I have come to you stripped of my blooded kin, I shall retaliate, Viviane."

She leaned forward, which placed her confined breasts but inches from the soft tease of his velvet frockcoat.

"I have promised you nothing. And do not dare to threaten me."

A flick of her fan placed the blade tips under his chin.

Constantine did not flinch. "You are too bold."

"You like me bold."

"I do, indeed. It is what makes me love you." He inhaled her perfume. The heat of his breath prickled at her neck. A swallow set the choker tight against her throat. "I should fall to my knees before you if we were not standing amongst so many others."

As Rhys Hawkes had done upon her threshold? The memory quickened her.

Constantine took her hand and stepped aside to scan the ballroom, and in that moment Viviane's sight fell upon the man standing top of the stairs, scanning the crowd himself.

"Rhys," she said, cautioning her voice to a mere whisper.

"What was that?"

"Just a tickle in my throat."

Her eyes strayed over the blue waistcoat, hugged by brown satin. He cut a fine figure.

"What distracts you? Ah. Monsieur Hawkes. That bastard. He is an eyesore amongst the finery. Does his presence trouble you? But of course, it must, knowing he is so wild, an animal who could strike at any moment."

"An animal? I don't understand."

"Hmm? Oh, of course not. Stay here. I'll see that he is removed."

He made way through the crowd, and it was easy enough to follow his departure for the vampire lord towered over most. He skipped up the stairs, and when Rhys saw him, Viviane thought surely he sneered.

Constantine said something to Rhys. Rhys chuckled. Then they were off, down the entrance hallway.

A wild animal that could strike at any moment? A shiver traced her heart.

Clutching her skirts, Viviane tracked the ballroom perimeter. This was a conversation she did not want to miss.

LORD CONSTANTINE DE SALIGNAC was exactly as Rhys remembered him from the previous decade. Tall, arrogant and possessed of dull black eyes that offered no glint of soul or humanity. The man had a cold heart. Nothing could permeate it. Not even the bonds of family.

"I believe you," Rhys muttered to himself.

All vampires were similar. So mired in the ancient

means of their ancestors, entitled and expectant all should part as they walked through. Cold and soulless—though vampires did possess souls. Rhys shivered to be near such a creature.

Yet he did fear a vampire little. While a match to their species in his human-shaped vampire form, in strength and guile, should he shift to werewolf, the vampire had better run—unless he preferred his head rolling on the ground.

Many times he'd almost shifted while in Constantine's presence. The enchantment that kept back his werewolf was only so effective.

The vampire clad in steel-colored velvet and dripping in silver-threaded lace stalked the hall to the first open door and marched inside, assuming Rhys would follow.

Rhys paused in the hallway, peering into the room. The diminutive salon was done in emerald damask and dark woods. Smaller versions of the grand iron chandeliers from the ballroom hung from sturdy ropes sheathed in emerald velvet. A billiard table fashioned entirely of white marble was topped with red felt.

He scented no others beyond the remnants of whisky, and the hint of sweet wine lingered. Hmm…

Rhys smiled with knowing.

The tribe leader beat a fist on the billiard table. "What in damnation are you doing here, in my home?"

Vampires. Always so melodramatic.

Thank his werewolf's calm mind for lacking dramatics.

Rhys pressed the heels of his palms to the table opposite Constantine. "Enjoying the festivities, drinking champagne and manhandling the wenches."

"There's not a woman in the room who would endure your mangy touch."

"That's an opinion not shared by most women."

"If they knew your nature they would run screaming from you."

"Why so angry, brother?"

Constantine's jaw tightened. He never used that familial word. Probably thought it poison to his tongue.

"Are you not thrilled to see me after so long?" Rhys continued. "Where was it last time? Ah yes, the Conciergerie dungeon. Testing convicts with that devious execution device, the Scottish Maiden. You do back the strangest ventures."

"Lately Monsieur Guillotine has been studying it. I feel certain his modifications will produce a useful method to execution should France ever need it for large volumes."

Rhys clenched his fingers into fists.

"The machine is a marvel," Constantine added. "Slices through flesh and bone so precisely." As did the man's steely gaze. "Now if you will leave."

"I believe the Salon Noir offers an open invitation."

"That is so. Yet it is presumptuous of you to attend. Perhaps I should sic our wolf slayer after you?"

"So the slayer is a vampire?"

"But of course."

"I suspected as much from tribe Nava. What is it you call the alleged wolf who slayed two of your own? Longtooth hunter?"

"The bastard will be dealt with justly."

"But you have not yet found him?"

"I have a suspect."

"In hand?" Rhys eyed his brother, seeking signs of lacking confidence, or concealing a secret. If he knew it was William…

"I am not at liberty to say. What is your concern?"

"I've an interest in the mystery. There is a missing werewolf."

"You run with a pack now?"

"The wolves have always been my friends." Rhys rolled a ball and it clacked the eight ball, landing it in the side pocket. "Unlike the snobbish vampires."

"You label yourself snobbish?"

Affecting nonchalance, Rhys forced a calm tone. "And here I thought you only saw my dark side, brother."

"It is difficult to see beyond your unpolished veneer. You don't belong in Paris and you know it."

"True, this city tries any sane man's countenance. It is a land of falsities and mistruths, all hidden behind the glitter of a porcelain mask and Alençon lace. I hope to leave soon, but not until I learn the truth of the murders."

"And what if one of your werewolf friends murdered the vampires?"

Rhys winced. It was possible William had done the deed. But as a representative for the Council he was to remain impartial. "I want to see justice done. The Council—"

"You're working for the Council now?"

"I've been assigned this mission to prove myself, yes."

"Interesting."

He wagered Constantine thought the idea of Rhys aligning himself with a governing body ludicrous. It was. But time changes a man. He no longer sought to distance himself, but rather gather any who would accept him into his open arms.

"Yes, well, you saw to ensuring I could not form a tribe."

"Was it a tribe or a pack? I'm fuzzy on your original goal." A gesture flashed diamonds on Constantine's fingers. "Must have been a pack for that mangy female you were tupping—"

In an instant, Rhys clamped a vice grip about his brother's throat. He growled, betraying the vampire he was right now.

A master at inciting Rhys's penchant to violence, Constantine's victorious grin widened.

Rhys released him. Flexing his fingers, he fought the werewolf's wish to strike out, to maim and punish. He was not wolf now, he was vampire, a cool, calm creature who could stand against his enemy with utter stillness. Or so coached his werewolf brain.

"I will not tolerate you in this city for one moment longer." Constantine swung an admonishing finger through the air. "Leave."

There were so many reasons Rhys would like to rip out his brother's throat. But he was no murderer. And though Constantine put little worth in family, Rhys would never lose hope. Besides, retreating now would spoil the thrill of seeing Constantine on his knees over the grief of losing his one true love.

If indeed he did love her. His interest must be to win a bloodborn vampiress. On the other hand, Rhys could entirely understand the ease with which a man could fall in love with Viviane LaMourette.

"She is a gorgeous find," Rhys commented. "The one in the red dress you were fawning over. Not very becoming for a man of your stolen rank."

The vampire hissed, revealing fangs. Rhys did not react. Constantine would not bite him. If they'd learned anything about one another over the decades it was their family blood did hold some currency.

Constantine noted Rhys's calm assessment. "The last

thing I desire is your blood curdling at the back of my throat."

"If that it does, literally, curdle," Rhys conjectured.

"She is mine," Constantine said through a fanged warning.

"Apparent from the clutch marks you've bruised onto her wrists."

"I did not— The woman does not realize how desperate she is. She needs a patron."

"Is that the reason? I thought it was love? Rumors say it is so."

"It is. I am."

"Or is it her blood is pure?"

Constantine smirked. "Something you can never obtain, eh, brother?"

Pound the nail in further. So he could never win a vampiress who believed in pure blood and the system of patronage. Nor could he simply attract her through the merit of his mixed breed.

Fool. Abandon this ruse.

No. This was not a wager for love, but for revenge.

Perhaps.

He no longer knew, for sure, what his goal was.

"If you do not see to finding your way from the premises," Constantine said, "I'll have the bravos brought in to throw you out."

"No need," Rhys replied softly.

His brother thrust an angry finger at Rhys. "I am a man of my word."

"Certainly you are. We've engaged in this dance of wills and personal annihilation for decades. If you finally achieve your desire to kill me, who then would you torment?"

"Your death will not come at my hands, brother. I made

a promise to our mother. Beyond that, it is high time our *dance* did come to a finish."

"I agree." Rhys folded his arms across his chest and leaned against the billiard table. "Let's end it here in this city. For once and for all."

The dark lord's eyes twinkled with malice. "May the better man emerge the victor."

Constantine exited with all the fury of the queen's poodle. Rhys chuckled. He crossed his ankles, and pressed his palms against the table behind him.

Was it right he received so much pleasure taunting his brother?

Surely not.

A sniff confirmed what he'd been aware of since entering the room. He had scented her distinct aroma of sweet wine. "You can come out now."

A few seconds passed before the paneling on the far wall cracked in a perfect rectangle, and the secret door opened to reveal Viviane looking like a smuggled princess in red. Her lips matched the deep shade of her dress.

"That color should not be legal on you," he commented as she approached. "Bloodred, eh?"

"You are brothers?"

She had heard it all. Not exactly the way Rhys would have cared to reveal such information, but now it was out, more's the better. But if Viviane had overheard Constantine was his brother, she must have also picked up the other detail about his life.

Hell.

She flipped open her fan and fluttered it curtly. She did not meet his eyes, instead trailing a finger along the slick marble billiard table. "But you don't use the name Salignac."

Rhys slapped his palms to his opposite arms. He wasn't prepared for this conversation.

Her fan stopped fluttering. "Why did you not tell me this immediately?"

"I—"

"No. I cannot speak with you, let alone be in your presence. You have lied to me."

"It was not a lie."

"It was truth hidden." She slapped her fan shut smartly. "Move aside."

He stepped between her and the door, not wanting her to leave without explaining… What? How? Right here in his brother's home? Gods, help him.

Rhys moved to the left, offering her an open path to the door, which she took without uttering another word. The breeze of her scent curled about him in her wake, and he muttered, "Sorry," but she was already too far to hear.

"Damn it!"

Had Constantine won this round? The fact they were brothers should not offend Viviane, unless she truly did have her heart set on being patroned by the tribe leader.

"Have you been completely truthful with me, Viviane?"

CHAPTER THIRTEEN

THE CANDLE GLOW FROM A six-prong silver candelabra flickered madly in Viviane's periphery. She blinked and turned her head slowly. Portia pinned her hair into one of her usual elaborate concoctions, a vision of twists, curls and springy coils.

"One of these days I shall succeed in convincing you to don a wig," Portia said. "Then we've not hours to spend preparing your hair when you deem to so quickly let it down."

Viviane smiled and closed her eyes. "I value your friendship, Portia."

"You deem me a friend?"

"Yes."

The maid's mouth dropped open, then clapped shut. "I just never… Thank you. It means a lot you would say it."

The gentle tug of Portia's fingers through her hair relaxed. Already the hunger pangs tweaked below her rib cage. Or possibly it was the whalebone corset. She wondered sometimes if she might expire from lack of breath, but being immortal wouldn't allow such a dramatic death.

The watered silk gown was the color of rust and shimmered with glints from gold threading shot throughout. It had arrived this morning from the dressmaker, Rose

Bertin, an order Blanche must have placed weeks earlier. Viviane had been dreaming about wearing it all day.

When she was not thinking about Rhys Hawkes.

He and Constantine were brothers. And why such a secret?

She should have asked him last night but she'd been too startled by the information. And he had seemed reluctant to speak of it.

Obviously, the brothers were not on good terms. Constantine's voice had dripped with vitriol when talking with him. Things he'd said, alluding to Rhys being animal, Viviane could not figure.

There was something different about the man she wished to take as a lover. And Viviane was now determined to get to the bottom of it.

Portia toyed with the tiny centers of the roses, hummingbird skulls set with diamonds in the eye sockets. "Where are you off to this evening? The Salon Noir isn't for a few more nights."

Yes, what would be her excuse? For she knew exactly where she intended to go this evening, only she felt she could not come right out and say "to see Rhys Hawkes."

Viviane held the rose piece aside her head while Portia pinned it in place. "For a jaunt in the Tuileries."

"Uh-huh." No belief in that tone.

Her maid flitted around in front of her, her pink-and-brown-striped skirts swishing Viviane's damask sleeve. "You look spectacular. If I were a man I should desire you. Want me to describe your appearance as if I were a magical mirror?"

"I trust your assessment of spectacular. No, no more powder."

"As you wish. You certainly do not require cosmetics

on your beautiful skin, but I worry mortals will wonder why your natural skin is so pale."

"Let them wonder."

Immortality had proven sweet. She would never age. Her skin would remain soft, pale and unblemished. Her body was not too thin, nor was it too plump. She prided herself on her high breasts and narrow waist. And her small feet fit Blanche's shoes perfectly.

"Oops!" Portia snatched for the ribbon she'd knocked off the vanity, but missed it.

Viviane clasped the talon Constantine had given her. "Wolves." She sneered. "Filthy animals. One less werewolf in this world won't bother me at all."

"You wish me to tie the ribbon around your neck?"

The ivory talon felt cool and heavy on her palm. Gauche. "No, leave me."

Left alone in the quiet boudoir, Viviane stroked a finger across her lips. How she craved contact with another body.

What would Constantine think if he learned his brother was engaged in a liaison with her?

THE WOLF DODGED A RIGHT FIST and spat out a boisterous chuckle. He spun around, bending his knee for the kick, but Rhys blocked the high-soaring foot with his elbow. Orlando wobbled off-balance. He jogged around to realign with Rhys in the fisticuffs match they engaged in out in the tiny courtyard behind William's home.

Rhys flipped back his wet hair and bounced on his bare feet, defying Orlando to again approach.

"You are too strong," Orlando declared, huffing, yet smiling. "You've the strength of a wolf, and the cunning of a longtooth."

"You are the only man brave enough to use that slur against me," Rhys said. "Or do I mean foolish?"

Rhys offered a hand and helped the boy to stand. "The match is over."

"But I've not yet won." A bruise spotted the boy's right lower ribs. It would heal within the day.

"We'll pick up where we left off after you've run down the street to procure our meal," Rhys offered. "I'm a bit peckish myself after the run out to the country earlier."

"No clues, eh?"

"Nothing. Though, I could scent the wolf." And should he reveal that scent was so familiar inside the house? Orlando had called William a friend. No sense in speaking his suspicion until he'd solid proof. "There's coin in my purse I left near the bookshelf."

The boy nodded eagerly, grabbed his shirt from the ground, and disappeared inside the house. He shouted he would return with spoils for the victor.

Rhys bent forward, stretching his arms out behind his back.

William's scent had been all over the crime scene. Where could he be hiding? Had he left the country? Rhys hoped for that and then he did not. Justice must be served. And if William was in such a state to have murdered innocents then he may do it again.

Rhys strode inside, kicking the door shut with a heel, and grabbed his shirt from a hook on the wall, but didn't put it on. He wiped the sweat from his face and abdomen.

A daily exercise session appeased his dark side by flexing his muscles and pushing his abilities. Punching the door with a bare fist, Rhys retracted with a wince.

Think of other things. Things that will make you happy.

"LaMourette," he murmured.

Lovely, contrary Viviane. The vampiress with a fierce heart and a desperation that would push her to bold action. He'd succumbed to her allure. Falling to his knees like a besotted, lovesick fop. Even going so far as to offer her his blood.

It would do him no harm. Only the vampiress's bite would enrage his werewolf.

When he was not remembering their intimate embrace on the threshold of her home, Rhys was kicking himself for not keeping her in hand last night so he could explain. But what to explain? So he and Constantine were brothers. Nothing earth-shattering about that. Save the reason why.

"I can't tell her," he muttered, feeling his half-breed blood so painfully. "I must tell her if I wish to win her trust."

On his way to change, a knock on the front door veered him from the bedchamber. He opened the door to pale twilight dazzling off the building windows opposite William's home. Standing amidst that dazzle, Viviane LaMourette.

She gasped at sight of him, and pressed the delicate curves of her black lace fan to rose-red lips. As if she had not expected him to answer? Kohl-lined eyes took him in from head to bare chest.

Rhys offered her a charming smirk and pressed a hand high on the door frame, which tightened his abdomen and flexed his chest muscles.

She turned toward the street, giving him her back. Hair teased into a confection revealed the bare column of her neck. Rhys curled his fingers into his palm to stop from touching her there.

"Perhaps I should return when you are attired more appropriately, Monsieur Hawkes."

"Ah?" He leaned over her shoulder, there, where wine spiced her skin and hair, and took pleasure in pronouncing slowly and deeply, "And here I had thought you were one of those inappropriate sorts."

Lifting her chin, she turned to face him. Twilight played with her azure eyes, dancing devious hell-forged sprites about the iris.

"Won't you invite me in?" she prompted in tones equally as defiant and teasing as his had been.

Perhaps she was not so upset after learning about him and his brother.

"The pleasure is all mine." Rhys stepped back. "Please do enter, mademoiselle."

Her satin skirts swept his legs. Lace at her elbow brushed his bare abdomen. Closing his eyes, he sucked in a breath, savoring the tease of it as if it had been her fingertips.

The vampiress strolled the foyer and into the main room cluttered with furniture, scattered blankets, pillows and books. She eyed a painting on the wall, which featured a pack of eight gray wolves hunting a snowy landscape.

"You are without your maid?" he asked.

She turned and granted him a deviously winning smile. "Apparently I *am* one of those inappropriate sorts."

Her eyes skated from his face, his neck and over his chest and abdomen. A gentleman would have put on the shirt he yet held. Rhys leaned against the wall, shirt hand propped on his hip. "Do you see something you favor, LaMourette?"

She approached with a hip-shifting glide he wanted to contain between his palms while they tangled together in bed. "Perhaps I do."

Boldly, without apology, she traced a forefinger down his chest. Rhys tossed back his head and tightened his jaw to keep from gasping with pleasure. The connection was dangerous. His mind, all wolf now, craved touch, yet his body, vampire, resisted.

"I have thought about you all day," she offered.

Rhys straightened. "Really?"

"And Constantine."

"Ah."

"I had thought to conclude why it should be such a secret you two are brothers. There must be a vicious hatred between the two of you that you choose not to claim the other as family."

"You figured that one."

"What did you do to him?"

"Me? To him?" Rhys's jaw dropped. He slapped his chest. "You think I…?"

She shrugged, pacing before him in a sashay that belied any anger she may feel. "Did he do something to you?"

"We are brothers because we claim the same mother," he said. "But not the same father. I was born a decade after Constantine. We've never been close." Which was putting it very lightly.

Considering his explanation, her eyes traveled the floor along the wall, and back to the painting. She fixed on the pack of wolves.

Now or never, Rhys. You've the opportunity to tell her all. To put your dark secret out there for her to know, and pray she accepts you.

The vampiress twisted abruptly. Curiosity twinkled in her eyes. "You know Constantine wishes to patron me."

"I do."

"Would he be quite angered should I consider a liaison with his brother?"

"You would..." She was stealing the very words from his brain and twisting his tongue tonight. "You are interested in—in me?"

The vixen smirked and fluttered her lashes. "I cannot say I've seen a man in such fine form before."

That bolstered his forgotten vanity.

Her attention strayed downward as her finger glided over his ridged abdomen, marking each rise of muscle. "Aristocrats and men of letters do not put themselves in situations that require strenuous exercise. And while vampires are virile and quite well fashioned, they do not often have so much muscle. Why are you like this?"

He inhaled as her finger trailed along the waist of his breeches, tickling over the dark hair tufting above the brown chamois.

"I am not a man to languish in excess. I find taxing my muscles daily keeps me strong." And his werewolf demanded the vampire maintain his shape. "Viviane, your touch..."

"My touch?" Soft, teasing wonder. A tilt of her head dared him to trace his fingers along her dark lashes. He would not, for he preferred it be his lips when first he touched those dark frills. "Does it disturb you?" Her skirts hugged his legs and the sensual aroma of her skin permeated his senses, dizzying him, loosening his well-reined discretion. And making him forget...what was it? "Do you want me to stop?"

Letting the shirt fall, he pressed his hands flat to the wall behind him. "Touch all you like. You are a woman who is not pleased until she has satisfied her curiosity. Be it blood, or—"

"Flesh. Your body is so hard," she purred, eyes beaming at him. Red lips parted, inviting so many fantasies. "Is it hard all over?"

A flick of her fingers released one of four buttons dotting the left side of his breeches. Would she?

The urge to shove his fingers through her silken hair and pull her in for a hard and brutal kiss flexed Rhys's fingers—yet he did not move. Allowing her the control proved more titillating. Those damned lips; they were the same color as the roses tucked in her hair, but promised less macabre pleasure than did the skulls.

Or would she be so deadly as the skulls nestled within the petals?

Please, kill me sweetly with your mouth.

Viviane cooed, licking her lips. Her eyes dared him to grant her this wicked exploration. It was a dare he silently accepted.

The second button popped free, followed by the third.

She would!

His cock, heavy and hard, landed in her palm with a slap of flesh to flesh.

Exhaling tightly, Rhys's entire musculature tensed. "Hard enough for you?" he managed to ask.

"It is exquisite," she whispered against his mouth. "So… thick. You say I can learn a man by tasting his blood? I disagree. A woman can learn a man by more intimate means."

So much spoken with a flutter of lash. And then… A kiss.

Soft and lush, she claimed his mouth. She tasted sweet, decadent. Forbidden. Apparently she was not at all worried should Constantine learn about them.

Rhys slipped his fingers into the soft hair at the back of her head as she began to trail kisses down his neck and to the center of his chest. He could feel each finger about his staff, tightening, and then, sliding up and down as if taking his measure.

Each kiss tightened yet another muscle he wasn't aware he had, and increased his anticipation tenfold. No rousing sparring session could excite him so thoroughly.

"Bloody deuce," he said on an exhale. "You've quite the grip, LaMourette."

"Mmm…" She pressed a kiss to his neck where his vein pulsed madly. Yet her hand worked its own wicked sorcery, now softly tracing the head of him. "I like to be in control."

"It is something I guessed about you the first night we…ahhh…met."

The ease of her fingers over his thickened head, tugging and squeezing… Hot breath dusted his nipple. Lips drawn over her teeth, she nipped his sensitive flesh.

"Viviane…"

"Come for me." Her eyes held his, their faces a breath apart. "Give me what I want."

A twist of her wrist tugged the sensitive skin of his testicles, which now hugged his body tightly. Rhys could not control the wicked climax that shuddered his bones and weakened his muscles. Head pressed to the wall, he moaned. Madness that he was so close to releasing.

"Show me you are willing to succumb," she cooed. "To allow me to learn you, body—" she lashed his eyelid with her tongue "—and soul."

Her fingers moist with the seed that dribbled from him, slicked him swiftly, drawing him into her power, and claiming him.

He wanted to give her anything she asked. To surrender, to—hell, he couldn't think of any other reason. His brain was fogging. His muscles grew tight. All sensation focused in his groin. He was going to…

Rhys cried out roughly. The force of his climax tightened his abdomen and thighs, and he clenched his fist and beat the wall behind him.

"The deuce, yes," he growled. "Yes, yes and yes."

Viviane purred and licked her fingers, glistening with his ejaculation. Her mouth was red, torrid from him. She smiled wickedly and tapped his hard abdomen beside the evidence of his surrender. "Inappropriate enough for you?"

Rhys cursed softly, yet the heady warmth of elation silenced further response.

She strolled into the foyer and opened the front door. "I had come to also talk about the murders. I feel you are more invested in finding the culprit than Constantine. When next we meet, we'll talk, yes? Unless other things interrupt us." The wicked temptress smiled, revealing the glinting tips of her fangs. "Good eve, Monsieur Hawkes."

And like a ghostly figment the vampiress slipped into the night on a giggle and a sigh.

VIVIANE SWEPT THROUGH THE narrow streets toward home. She could not erase her smile. She'd intended to merely question Rhys about his brother and the investigation and then leave.

She'd never seen a man stand before her with such audacity, baring himself so proudly. She had indulged in sexual liaisons with the finest and most expert lovers. Rhys was shameless, and that had sparked the wanton within her.

Slipping around the stables and entering Henri's home from the servant's entrance, Viviane closed the door and leaned against it. She traced her lips with her fingers, still tasting him on her skin.

"Milady!"

Portia scrambled around the corner, grabbing the door frame to curb her trajectory.

"What is it?"

"Lord de Salignac."

"He was here?"

"*Is* here." She nodded over a shoulder. "I told him you were out, but he insisted upon waiting."

"Bother." Viviane pressed a palm to her sudden rushing heart.

"He's been here most of an hour. In the music room."

Even more bother.

Viviane handed Portia her cape and strode toward the stairway. "Bring me wine," she called back. "And tell him I must freshen up."

Much as she had desired to lie down and dream of her antics with Rhys, she must now erase the taste of him if she was to face Constantine. Why did he insist on calling without prompt?

Portia scrambled about the vanity to place a touch of rouge to her cheeks while Viviane mulled over a glass of wine to settle her vacillating nerves before leaving her chamber to meet Constantine.

WHITE LACE SPILLING FROM HIS sleeves and at his neck, and jet hair curling at his shoulders, Constantine cut a romantic figure, Viviane thought as she approached him. A Romanesque face, square, strong, like a gladiator, and yet refined. He was everything Rhys was not.

We've different fathers.

How interesting. And yet, she wondered if she should bring up the subject now. Constantine was not aware she knew. She'd gotten the impression he was embarrassed by Rhys.

"Lord de Salignac."

Constantine turned abruptly, a frown marring his handsome visage. "My bravo tells me he saw Hawkes leave your home the other night."

So much for niceties.

"I did not allow him entrance." Because they'd embraced upon the threshold. And so much more. Good thing he'd not had her followed just now.

"But he pursues you?"

"I…don't believe so."

She hated lying, but felt it was best in lieu of Constantine's strange anger. He must suspect Rhys a rival for her patronage. Though Rhys had said he was not interested.

Time to steer this conversation on a new course. "Did you notice the hay strewn on the street on your way here?"

"Madame Roux has it laid down in the summer to muffle the noise of horse hooves. Viviane, I must tell you something."

Oh? Well, if he would reveal Rhys as his brother, then she had not to worry about keeping the secret.

"Viviane, I am about to reveal a secret to you. It is a secret I will ask you to take to your grave."

"About Rhys?"

He nodded. Why would their being brothers be such a dire secret? Take it to the grave? She nodded, encouraging Constantine to speak.

He sighed and clamped his arms across his chest. "Rhys Hawkes is half werewolf and half vampire."

Mouth dropping open, Viviane felt as though she shook her head, but she was too startled to gauge her own movements. She sought the love seat across the room, but while her body wavered, she could not make herself move toward it.

"I know. It is quite a shocking revelation."

An actual werewolf? But how could he possibly…? That was not the secret she had thought to hear.

"I believe it best you know since it appears he's been visiting you."

"Only to ask after Henri's murder," she said quickly, not sure from where she'd summoned that.

She had just come from Rhys's embrace. Had been so intimate with him. He was half werewolf?

She flicked her tongue against the back of her teeth. To erase the taste of him? She despised werewolves.

"What does Rhys's—Monsieur Hawkes's—presence matter regarding that? I understand he is investigating the murders."

"You see? Yet he favors the wolves' side, is staying in a wolf's home, even. Because he is one. Or part one."

"How do you have this information?" But she knew. If they were brothers…

"Oh. I just know." So he would not reveal their connection. Too odd. He wished to protect himself but not his brother. "I've known it about him for some time."

"I need to think about this."

"Why is that?" Constantine slipped a finger along her jaw, tilting her head so she could do nothing but look him in the eye. So dark, his eyes. Like Rhys's eyes—because they shared a common parent. Yet when she looked into Rhys's eyes she saw compassion, not the calculated chill she saw now.

Why had Rhys neglected to mention that very large detail? Their familial connection was minimal compared to this.

Where was the wine? She needed a drink. Her fingers fluttered across her breasts. Did she smell of Rhys?

"You are my ally, Viviane. The two of us alone know this secret."

"And Rhys."

"Yes, I would ask you not to name him so intimately. It is Monsieur Hawkes."

"You act as though this information is something we wield against him."

"It is. The truth will see him ostracized."

"But you want that because you believe him your rival."

He clapped his jaw shut abruptly. "You name him my rival?"

This was getting out of hand. She could not continue the conversation and expect not to say something detrimental. "You need to leave. Now."

"If he is my rival, you tread dangerous territory, Viviane," he warned. "No vampire will have a woman tainted by a wolf."

"I am not. But it shouldn't matter." Had she engaged in…? With a wolf?

Viviane fainted.

CHAPTER FOURTEEN

Paris, modern day

THE MERCEDES PULLED DOWN the street toward the meeting destination.

"I don't understand the patronage thing."

On the passenger seat, Rhys looked over the UrbanTrash.com website Simon had brought up on the laptop. "It is an antiquated practice."

"Must be. I thought vamps just did their thing nowadays. I've never seen a female who needed someone to keep her alive. It's not in the lore I've studied."

"Two hundred years ago vampires believed the females weaker, and they were, or at least, they were *designed* to be weak. They were generally kept by patrons, and away from mortal blood sources, which would have strengthened them. Their patron would blood them regularly to ensure survival. But a sort of evolution occurred, and over time the females began to not need the patron. I imagine they might have survived without one even then, if only they had not been afraid to attempt it."

"You think Viviane…?"

"If any female could have survived it would have been Viviane."

"Could you have patroned her?"

"Could I or would I?" The question Rhys had struggled with far too long after he'd last kissed Viviane. "I feared taking her blood would further aggravate the vampire who forces my werewolf to bloody mayhem. As well, a werewolf bitten by a vampire develops a blood hunger."

"Have you ever taken blood from a vampire or allowed a vampire to bite you?"

"No."

"Huh." Simon spied a parking space and swerved into it. "That's strange. I mean, you admit yourself some practices are antiquated. Maybe some of your beliefs are?"

"You've seen my werewolf. You tell me—dare I risk it?"

Simon shifted into Park. "Maybe not."

"A normal wolf would rage and seek blood after being bitten by a vampire. Me? It was unfathomable to me at the time."

"Maybe a vampire bite would tame your rage? You know, a vampiress connecting with your vampire?"

Over the centuries Rhys had toyed with the notion. No matter how many ways he twisted it, he was never satisfied with a solution.

"It's up the street." Simon motioned to the café. "You ready to do this?"

Rhys nodded. Ready, and so not ready.

DANE LEANED AGAINST THE BRIDGE railing across the street from the café. She'd know the marks when she saw them. She'd been hired by tourists wanting her to lead them through the tunnels all the time. That was fine, and a quick way to make money.

It was the fringe crowd who applied requesting specifics that made her cautious and aware not everyone in this world was kind, curious, or out for fun.

She'd lost her life twice in the tunnels thanks to bad judgment.

But how to resist the cash promised for this venture? The guy must be a crazy old millionaire. One last fling before he cacked. She could take him to the deepest depths, which went down seven stories. That should give him a thrill.

But ten thousand a day? Heck, if she could engage the guy for three days, she'd be home free. The bastards who'd been on her back about the loan could be paid, and she wouldn't have to walk with one eye over her shoulder when aboveground.

Slapping at a mosquito that landed on her cheek, she held her palm there as she spied two men walking from the north toward the café. One was tall, wore a business shirt and tie and carried a briefcase. The other ambled, rather than walked, and wore a scruffy leather jacket, his hands tucked in the pockets. Beneath a short, spiky crop of hair his eyes took in the surroundings.

"Bingo," she muttered. "Old man and his accountant, no doubt. I wonder if the codger has had a physical lately. I don't want him to have a heart attack on my watch."

Though he couldn't be that old. His hair was jet-black; he might dye it were it not for the patch of gray streaking one side. His strides were sure, no hunched back or signs of age. Hmm…

Before entering the café, the man gave one last glance up the street. There was something about his movements, preening and focused, that put her on guard. He wasn't like most.

She wasn't like most. Could he possibly be?

"I don't like dealing with Dark Ones," she muttered. But the witches of the Light held no appeal, either.

Humans were easiest to work with. Dark and Light ones had an agenda, or predetermined prejudices that always put her at the scale's bottom. And they always thought they could tell her what to do.

"Money is good. So is food," she reminded herself.

Hefting up her packed duffel, Dane strode across the street. Simon, the guy who'd IM'd her—whom she tagged as the shirt and tie—had assumed she was male. She didn't need to introduce his mistake right away.

Trying to appear as if she was only coming here for refreshment, she forced herself not to look at the two men seated by the front window.

As she waited for her macchiato, she opened her senses to the room. Beyond the coffee beans and the unappetizing lard used in the pastries she could pick up the spice cologne the shirt-and-tie wore.

The other man's scent was feral.

A wolf? It was easy enough to guess at his kind. Rare did she see them in the city. Even in this day and age they usually kept to the country. Explained his sun-browned skin. The wrinkles cresting out from the corners of his eyes? He must be old, indeed. Though werewolves did age less smoothly than say, a vampire, who could look youthful and cold as marble for a millennium.

Would he know what she was? Probably not. And keep it that way.

The clerk shoved her drink across the counter and snapped up her money. "Merci."

Now or never, Dane. Do you want the money?

Hell yes. She was in for the ride, or at least the introductory course.

Dane turned and trod over to the men's table. Setting her cup down, she dragged a nearby chair noisily before the table. She straddled it backward and pushed her duffel between her torso and the chair back, leaning in to sip the hot brew.

"Messieurs," she offered. "I'm Dane Weft."

"YOU'RE SUPPOSED TO BE A GUY," Simon dumbly said around a bite of his croissant.

Rhys delivered his cohort an admonishing nod of his head.

The bedraggled mess of dreads, shabby clothing and a distinct odor—of dirt and lack of soap about her—put him back in his chair. Bold green eyes held him as if defying him to classify her into a neat little slot.

After Simon had mentioned the guide's eccentricities he'd expected quirky. He hadn't expected a female.

He'd traveled three thousand miles on a whim. Now he was thinking to hand over a stack of cash to this scruff of a woman in hopes she could lead him to a chimera?

Simon set down the croissant and offered a hand for her to shake. "I'm Simon Markson."

She looked at his hand, and then tilted her attention to Rhys. "And you are?"

"Rhys Hawkes," he offered quietly.

"The man with the checkbook?"

"Cash."

She couldn't repress a lift of brow. A thick blond dread spilled out from under the dirty hood and plonked her over the eye.

Something about her put up his hackles. That rarely happened. Witches were no longer enemies to his vampire because the Protection spell had been broken years earlier. And vampires, well he had that covered. Yet she was not human.

"What are you looking for?" she asked. "One last fling before you bite the big one?"

"I don't understand."

She shrugged. "You're an old man. Must not have too many years left on you."

Rhys would not dignify her comment by showing

discomfort. He was two and a half centuries old; most werewolves did not live much longer than three centuries. Yet he felt young. Did he look so old to her?

"You want adventure?" she continued. "You're going to have to promise me you won't take your last breath while we're weaving through the depths. I don't need that on my conscience."

"Old is relative," he replied. And she was obnoxious. And her smell was beginning to get under his skin. He could not read her, and until she showed herself to him, there was nothing about her to believe. "I don't intend to die anytime soon. What makes you the expert on the tunnels beyond you claiming to have mapped the majority of them?"

"I've spent the last two decades under the city."

"That would explain the smell," Simon commented. He offered her a wry grimace, but she didn't seem to mind the ribbing. She gained points for that.

"You need a guide? For so much cash, I'm assuming you've a destination or plan in mind. What are you looking for? Lost treasure?"

"The Vampire Snow White," Rhys stated plainly. "You've heard the urban legend?"

She crossed her arms over the huge duffel propped before her. "You're kidding me." Her eyes looked him up and down, seeing more than most. "Yeah, I know the legend. Think about it every once in a while when I'm below. About a decade ago, a local gang of cataphiles used to search for the glass coffin. Never found anything. Why would they?"

"There were others searching for her?"

"Juicy legend like that? Hell, yeah."

Rhys gaped at Simon. Why had no one told him about

this legend sooner? Could Simon not have put two and two together and guessed he might have an interest?

Hell, he shouldn't put the blame on others. Slapping his palms together before him, he pressed his thumbs to his mouth and stared at Weft.

He felt sure her intense green gaze was reading him. There was something *beyond* about her, but he couldn't quite place it. Her smell masked any telling scent he might manage to read from her. Faery?

No, he'd just *know* a faery.

"So you think you'll find the coffin here in the seventh?" she asked. "I can tell you right now, I've been through all the tunnels below us. Nothing down there except a bunch of rats."

I'm afraid of them. Silly, isn't it?

Rhys sucked down his black tea in an awkward swallow. He would not allow himself to grieve or summon emotion for what he knew was lost from him forever. She was dead. No one could have survived for so long and in such a manner. He was merely closing one final door and nailing it securely.

Yet who had nailed the coffin with her inside? Could it have been Constantine? He was the only one Rhys would name Viviane's enemy. And his.

"But if you want to fill my pockets with cash for showing you about below, I'm game." The woman slurped her macchiato, then licked the cup rim as if to get every last drop of flavor.

"Is there any place in the city you've not been?" Simon prompted. "If you've covered the majority, and not found a thing, then perhaps it best we look where you have not?"

"Listen, guys. You two seem nice enough. Human, even. At least one of you."

She shot Rhys a glance. So she knew? But did she know what he was? Good luck with that one.

"And I'm all for entertaining wild dreams of discovering a long-buried glass coffin and opening it to kiss the princess awake. Or whatever plans you have for it. But you do know it's a legend, right? That means it's *not real,*" she whispered to emphasize. "There is no glass coffin. The Vampire Snow White doesn't exist. We'd be tripping about in the dark."

"She may exist," Rhys said.

Pray God, she did not after all this time.

He hadn't seen Constantine in over a century, but was aware he still lived. If he had anything to do with secreting Viviane away…

Simon caught him, warning with a look. They'd agreed not to reveal that Rhys thought this could be real. Only that they were adventurers who wanted to follow the legend for fun.

"Says the werewolf," Dane replied. She held him with a smug grin.

Rhys leaned forward, opening his palm and spreading his fingers over the table. Close to her. An offer of a sort. "You think you know things about me?"

"I picked you out from across the street, wolf. And no, I'm not going to tell you what I am to know such things."

He closed his hand, and sat back. A glance to Simon read his bewildered constitution. The man may have the knowledge, but meeting other paranormals up close? He was always nervous.

"Why would a werewolf be looking for a vampire?" Dane tossed out.

Rhys shook his head negatively. He wasn't about to reveal his truth. If she scented his wolf, but not his vampire, that was her problem. "Just curious, is all. I want to get in, cover the area, and get out. Satisfy the curiosity as quickly as possible. You still interested in such a fruitless venture?"

"Ten thousand, up front?"

"You haven't given us reason to trust you," Simon interrupted. "Where do you live? How can we contact you?"

"I live in the city. You already have my email address."

"She'll come with us and we'll begin tonight," Rhys stated.

She drew her gaze over him again. Beyond the dirt and filth he sensed there might be an attractive woman. But she didn't appeal to his lust in any way, shape, or form.

"You going to put me up and feed me?"

"And bathe you," he added, and stood. He held out a hand. "Have we a deal?"

"I still haven't seen the cash."

He dug in his pocket and pulled out a couple hundred Euros. "I don't carry the bulk with me. Come along with me to my estate, and after you've showered, you'll get the rest."

"So my working with you hinges on my cleanliness?"

He held out the money, waiting for her compliance. "Yes."

Rolling her eyes, she smacked her palm loudly against his. He didn't sense any telling vibrations or get a feel for what she was. Not human, as she'd intimated.

As long as she wasn't demon, he didn't care what she was, so long as she had a work ethic.

CHAPTER FIFTEEN

Paris, 1785

RHYS TRACKED VIVIANE from Rose Bertin's dress shop. She walked with her head held regally, aware of all. He should have told her everything. He must. Now, if he could get her attention.

"Don't give up on me, LaMourette," he whispered. "I won't give up on you."

Viviane's maid had a curiously aloof manner about her. When he saw her stumble into traffic, he picked up his pace.

He made it to Viviane's side as her maid was in danger of stepping before a speeding hackney. Swinging an arm about the maid's waist, Rhys tugged her ample frame against a stone wall. He crushed his body against her skirts and shielded her. The carriage rolled by and Rhys was unable to move quickly. His heel twisted. Icy pain spiked his calf and he felt a bone snap.

"Oh!" The maid struggled, and he released her immediately. "How dare you!"

"You—" Rhys winced, struggling against the sight-blackening pain "—were in danger, my lady."

"I was walking!"

"Thank you," Viviane said to him, then admonished her maid, "You were not watching your step, Portia."

The maid huffed and adjusted the fit of her jacket.

The carriage wheel had nicked his boot heel, twisting his ankle and breaking bone. Shaking his foot behind him, he smiled at the ladies to distract them from the movement.

"You must have been following us," Viviane stated. She didn't meet him in the eye. Odd, but she seemed rather affronted by his presence.

"I was browsing the market," he offered, "and I knew the moment you passed by."

"We weren't anywhere near Les Halles."

"It smelled as though you were close." She had passed by. She knew better than to lie to him.

The woman valued her privacy. He would not refute that.

"Doesn't matter. I wonder if I may have a moment to talk with you, LaMourette?"

"I don't believe I've the time."

Hell, now what? "There is something I need to tell you."

Viviane exchanged glances with her maid, who had no idea how to conceal her wrinkled nose and pursed frown.

"That you forgot to tell me yesterday?"

"Er, yes." The hot, angry vibrations coming off her were tangible. "Perhaps I could escort you home?"

"It is but two houses down the street," she answered curtly.

"Indeed. But then I could be sure your maid is safe. I shouldn't wish her to develop the vapors."

"Nonsense," Portia burst out, yet she did breathe rapidly. And Viviane noticed.

The vampiress threaded an arm through her maid's. "I do not want you in my home."

Rhys shrugged. "I'll wait in the stables until you've assured your maid is comfortable."

"You'll frighten the horses."

"Horses rather take to me." And surely a vampire had hired a witch to bespell her horses, else the beasts would never let her—or any Dark One—get near.

With head lowered, she looked through her lashes. Rhys sought the kindness he knew she possessed. He would not accept refusal.

"You," she said lowly, "are intolerable."

"And you are gorgeous when anger deepens your eyes."

"You are..." She looked aside. What sat upon her tongue she could not voice? He was what? Rude. Aggressive.

Not right.

"Oh, come!" The maid gripped Viviane by the arm. "Walk away. If he is any sort of gentleman he will not follow."

Viviane allowed Portia to lead her away, but a glance over her shoulder lifted Rhys's hopes. He placed a hand over his heart. The vampiress had put him under a spell he wished to never escape. He remained in place long enough to shake off the pain of the injury, before speeding to Viviane's home.

"I TOLD HIM TO WAIT OUTSIDE the servant's door," Portia insisted as Viviane paced before the end of what had once been Henri and Blanche's tester bed. "Why did he not honor your request? He frightens me."

"I've learned some troubling information about Monsieur Hawkes, Portia. I...I'm not sure I can face him. And yet..." She glanced through the open door, down the dark, mirror-lined hallway. He waited below? "...I want to hear it from him."

"Hear what?"

Watching him boldly rescue Portia, to his own detriment—she'd noticed his pain—further set a blaze in Viviane's breast for the powerful and unique man.

"I don't like the way he looks at me," Portia said. "It's as if he looks *into* me."

The piercing stab of caution should have decided her against allowing Rhys in tonight. Instead, it hummed in her chest, warning, and yet needing to know more about the man who tread two worlds.

"What's that noise?" Portia dashed to the doorway, and let out a chirp.

Rhys Hawkes marched down the hallway, his boots rapping the marble floor as soundly as Viviane's heart beat her ribs.

"Leave us." She pushed Portia into the hallway.

The maid slammed herself against the wall and crept past the dark-eyed vampire—who was also a werewolf—and scrambled off.

As Rhys neared her bedchamber, Viviane slammed the door in his face.

THE WOMAN HAD AN IRRITATING habit of contrariness. Rhys pounded the wood once. "Viviane." He contained his desire to shout. He was not here to admonish or accuse. "We need to talk."

"I can hear you quite well where you stand."

"Please, Viviane, let me inside. I can't do it this way."

"Do what? Make a confession? Tell me what should have come from your mouth, but instead, I had to hear it from your brother?"

From his brother…? Hell. Constantine must have revealed all. Though why he would—

The only reason Constantine would tell Viviane would

be to gain her confidence, perhaps hoping to scare her away from him. It is how their duels ensued over the decades; he should expect nothing less.

"I'm sorry."

He could sense the rapid heartbeats not a dash away from him. Her scent carried through the wood barrier and tickled his nose.

The latch clicked, but the door did not open. Soft footpads walked away on the other side. Rhys clutched the door handle. It opened inward freely.

Viviane stood at the end of the grand bed layered in silks and lace, hands clutched to her breast. The soft round glow of a candle flame behind her radiated a halo about her head. Pink skirts dashed through with silver threading shimmered like twilight upon snow. Her flesh, paler than the fabric, absorbed the reflective flame. Pearls on fire.

Her expression held no anger, and Rhys was glad for it. Yet it did neither invite him to step forward into her embrace.

"An apology is due," he said, straightening. Hands behind his back, he paced before her. "Constantine told you?"

"Your father was a werewolf," she hissed accusingly.

"Yes." She stepped away as he approached, fleeing as if he would harm her. "I won't touch you, Viviane. You're frightened, I know—"

"I fear nothing," she proudly insisted with a lift of her chin. Yet still she stepped backward, and when she reached the threshold to a small room, she put up a hand. "Stay back!"

He saw the room was lined with racks of shoes. A veritable haven for a woman of fashion, he guessed. Honoring her fear, Rhys stopped in the doorway.

"I am half wolf, half vampire," he offered.

At once the confession humiliated, and yet part of him pined to claim his mixed blood and be damned to any who would sneer at him.

"Why did I have to learn that from Constantine?" Her back against a pillar, she was now trapped, but he would not think to make her feel so. "Why was your big secret that you were brothers? Did you not think you being wolf was more important?"

"Only half," he replied.

"What of your parents? If Constantine is bloodborn, and you are of two natures—"

"My mother was vampire. My father, werewolf. We've different fathers, but the same mother."

He'd never known his father. Was he dead or alive? Searching for his son? Did he even know he had a son? Questions asked so many times they'd become nonsensical to him now.

"Why didn't you tell me?"

"I—it's not something I reveal unless I must."

"You are ashamed?"

Yes, and no. "Viviane, you named me not right the moment we met. Do you think I would invite further disdain with my dark truth?"

"Then you have lied to me."

"Only—" Not revealed all. A pathetic excuse he would not attempt. Rhys leaned a shoulder against the door frame. "Forgive me. It is ingrained in me to protect myself against what others will think of me."

"You struck me as a man who cared little for what others thought."

"Indeed. Yet what *you* think of me means more than I can explain."

She considered what he'd said. The hurt in her eyes

was too bright, impossible to disregard. *Please let her accept me.*

"Viviane, I love you, I would not harm you."

Her eyes glittered with flames. "Love me?"

Shoulders dropping, Rhys read her disdain. "Yes."

"You find love easily, wolf."

"Ah?" Rhys met her gaze, fitful, but not quite angry. "I offend you."

"I do not take offense easily. It is that you are new to me," she said coolly. "Rhys, make me believe you."

She turned his own philosophy on him?

"Very well. I am vampire now." He splayed his arms. "Yet my mind is werewolf."

Azure eyes scrutinized him from head to boots, and decided upon a shrug and a head shake. "I don't understand. You think like a wolf?"

"Yes, and when I am werewolf, my vampire mind holds court. It is confusing, and I don't even understand it completely. Only that I must control my vampire mind at all costs."

"I should think your vampire more civilized."

That one cut him to the bone.

"On the contrary, I can never shift to my werewolf because when in wolf form my vampire rules. Do you know what we vampires want most, Viviane?"

"Blood," she replied boldly.

"Exactly. And when my werewolf is told by my vampire mind it wants blood, it kills. It goes after any mortal, male or female, to get it. It bites the pretty neck and sucks out the blood, and then reaches a taloned paw inside and rips out muscle and ribs to get to the thick, beating heart."

She sank against the pillar, slipping down to sit in a swish of skirts.

"And so I never shift," he said quietly, and squatted to

remain on her level. "It is difficult to resist when the moon is full. And mostly, I cannot resist. I take myself far away from people whenever I possibly can."

Tears glittered in her eyes. "You murder?"

He shook his head. "I have not for decades."

"But you have."

"Before I had my vampire enchanted, yes."

Again, she carefully considered the information. Fear did not contort her brow, and even her confusion was beginning to shed. The woman gained control with knowledge. He took pride that he could give that control to her.

"Have you ever shifted when the moon is not full?"

"I do not, though there are times when my anger forces it on me. I feel my bones begin to shift, but with determination I can prevent it. Constantine always puts up my werewolf's hackles."

"Henri was killed on the night of a full moon."

Now Rhys twisted and sat against the door frame and caught his forehead in his palms. "Your accusation is inappropriate."

"It wasn't an accusation. I'm sorry, Rhys. You've startled me with your admission."

"But you knew I was a half-breed. My brother told you."

"Yes, but I've little time to sort out how that makes me feel. And only now must I face the information because you insisted upon barging in—"

"My manner may be crude but I had to tell you, Viviane. I could not let this go one moment longer."

"One moment too late," she said snidely.

Rhys felt her words slice through his heart. "Yes, I suspect my brother could not wait to reveal my truth to get you on his side."

"I stand on no man's side."

"Of course not. You've listened with a very open mind. I commend you for that. If you should decide to hate me, I can only be grateful that you first learned the facts before settling upon such a decision."

"I'm not sure what I believe yet. It must be difficult for you. Have you been alone so long then?"

"Are you worried my colliding natures have scared off lovers?" Rhys glided his eyes down from her cinched breasts to where he imagined the apex of her thighs was hidden beneath so many layers of frivolous fabric. Idiot, to court such thoughts at this moment. And yet… "I meant what I said about continuing the pursuit, LaMourette. Love me or hate me, I still want you."

"Because you've some twisted desire to wage war against your brother. Love? You are not interested in me but for the triumph winning can grant you."

The woman was no fool, and yet he admired her direct manner.

"Constantine will stand good to his word about having you thrown out," she said. "You should leave Paris. It cannot be safe for a man such as you."

"So you're to be rid of me when we've only come together?"

"We are not together."

"Says the woman who has handled intimate parts of me." He leaned forward onto a palm, pleased she did not flinch away from him. "We would make a marvelous pair, LaMourette. Have you already promised yourself to him?"

"Never," she snapped.

"But isn't it a need for female vampires to have a patron? Do you not suffer without one? On the other hand, I thought it only was created vampires who required patronage."

Regaining her composure, she said, "I don't know. I will not be forced to a decision."

Rhys wanted to take her in his arms, and feel her acceptance in a return embrace. That she had not scored her deadly fan blades across his face proved a small victory after the truths he'd just given her. She would accept him. She must.

"We bloodborn females do require a patron," she said. "But I will not sacrifice my freedom to be blooded anew."

"No, I should suspect not. Do you wish me to protect you?"

"How can you?"

"I could talk to Constantine. Make him understand you have no desire—"

"You know nothing of my desires."

"I beg to differ."

Now she stood and he did, too. He reached for her as she slipped from the room, but did not dare touch.

"No man knows how to please me," she insisted quietly yet with a sharp tone. Her anger deepened her color. Rhys wanted to press her against his bare flesh to divine the heat from her.

"You are marvelous when angered, LaMourette. Won't you allow me to steal another kiss, or perhaps this time let me please you until you moan."

"And yet…" She stepped forward. "It isn't often my curiosity is pricked by vulgarities."

"I know you are a woman who indulges in all manner of pleasure."

"I should like to engage in many forms of pleasure with you, Monsieur Hawkes, but I am put off by your staunch need to compete with your brother. And this new information."

"You've never been kissed by a wolf."

Her thick lashes dusted the air as she tilted a look over his body. "Apparently, I have."

"Only in mind, lover." He dared to swing around before her, trapping her against the side of the high tester bed, a hand to either side of her skirts. The lush perfume of her grew bold, heady, like grapes on the vine. "Would you accept a kiss from me right now?"

"Are you vampire or werewolf?"

"Vampire. But wolf in mind."

Her tongue traced her lower lip. Rhys wanted to feel the firm tip of it licking his skin, gliding low to taste his hardness, the heavy weight of his need. If he did not kiss her right now—

"You smell wild and..."

"And?" he prompted.

Her parted lips, so red, screamed for him to bruise them.

"Rhys, I..."

He crushed her mouth. Devoured it. Stormed her gasps and pressed his tongue to hers.

If she wanted vulgarities, he could give them to her. Grasping her skirts, he found the curve of her derriere and squeezed it, pressing her mons against his erection. She did not wear the restrictive wooden panniers, which normally kept a woman caged and far from his touch. He felt her heat beneath the damask and silk. He felt the hum of her desire, the shudder of her uncertainty.

"I adore you, Viviane."

"Adoration is boring."

So she would challenge him?

"True. So is infatuation. Passion is exquisite. Desire—"

"Commonplace."

She pushed him away from her, and though he stood defiantly waiting for her to pull him back, she did not.

"You disturb me, Rhys."

"You like being disturbed."

Her eyes lit like stars. Indeed, she desired the unknown, the fantasy, the mystery of what he was.

Pacing immediately before him, she teased at a loose curl of dark hair. "Can you change shapes?"

"I will not. It is a darkness I will not unleash on anyone."

"You've been thinking wolf since we've met?"

Another nod. "Yes. But now I've revealed my dark side, you must know my truth completely."

"And that is?"

"I want to make love to you because I desire you, but also…because I am compelled. I need to be sated to keep back the wolf tomorrow night before the full moon."

"And you wish me to comply?"

"I want you, Viviane."

"Because you must have a woman."

"No, not any woman. Only you."

"But you have come to me before the one night you need me. How should I take that?"

"You are right. This is wrong." He turned finding his reflection in the vanity mirror—and not hers. So odd.

"Leave," she said quietly.

"No."

"Now," she insisted. "Please, Rhys, if you care for me at all you must leave."

He sensed her turning onto the bed, sniffing at tears. He could not look. He should look, for it was only he who had given her such a mood. Sadness. But not fear, no. She did fear little. Save rats.

"I want you, Viviane," he said softly.

"I know you do."

"Will we ever…?"

"I'm not sure. Good eve, Rhys."

He nodded, and walked out. Walking away from the only woman he cared for, the one woman he had thought may care for him.

Had he destroyed his chances to win her heart by revealing his truths?

"I BELIEVE YOU'VE COME TO THE end of your usefulness," Constantine said. "There is another who may provide me the scapegoat I require."

"You'll set me free?" William pleaded.

"Nonsense, you murdered two vampires."

"At your request! I wasn't in my head. I was forced! It was that witch!"

Constantine ripped off his leather glove, wet with wolf blood, and tossed it in the fire. He strode toward the stairs, snarling at his men as he passed, "Kill him."

Three spears pierced the werewolf in heart, groin and throat. The wolf's head jerked up in agony. Its yellow eyes flashed open and met Constantine's dark, steady gaze.

The beast's head dropped and death came with a brilliant explosion of blood from its every vein.

Constantine stepped back and wiped the blood from his face. He did not dash out his tongue. The enemy's blood held no favor.

The Council must not learn of his duplicity, which meant Rhys Hawkes must be silenced. And if anyone could command a werewolf, it was Ian Grim.

HE IS HALF WEREWOLF.

The man she desired was not the man she thought him

to be. And yet, Viviane was not frightened. She was only slightly offended he'd not told her. What had been Monsieur Hawkes when she had kissed him and touched him so intimately at his home? Vampire or werewolf? Should it matter?

It did matter. As Constantine had intimated, for a vampire to be intimate with a wolf would forever mark her against her own kind.

A man who was not what she thought him to be. She'd known that first night they'd spoken that he was not right.

"I wonder what it would be like to be kissed by a wolf?"

You already know.

Indeed. Rhys could be the very man she needed in her life. He desired her. And he was not interested in her because of her bloodborn status. He simply wanted to be her lover.

Why refuse him?

Viviane's heart quested for noise, commotion, excitement. The thrill of being pursued. The intensity of pursuit.

"Portia!"

The maid appeared immediately, as if she had been lingering outside the bedchamber door.

"I wish to write a letter," she said. "Or rather, a short missive. Gather the pen and ink and some paper. I'll need help to spell the words."

"Of course, *ma chérie*."

CHAPTER SIXTEEN

FROM A DISTANCE, RHYS COULD not discern if the rider were male, female, or fanged. She sat on the gelding like a bandit.

His anticipation lifted.

He'd received the note this morning just before the sun rose on the horizon. Delivered by Portia. It was an invitation to meet Viviane in the Bois de Boulogne at midnight for a jaunt.

She was aware what he needed tonight. Surely, she had not forgotten. His idea of a midnight jaunt involved shedding their clothes and breathing in her skin. Pray, let hers be the same.

The horse, a fine mount, slowed as it approached, stepping in a high trot as if trained to march. Sitting sidesaddle, her deep crimson skirts swept the barrel of the horse. One small foot secured in the stirrup was all that kept her from sliding off. Stars sat in her eyes, which narrowed as she drew rein. High, pale cheekbones soaked up the moonlight.

That same moonlight teased Rhys's werewolf. It wanted release, to mate and be sated. But he must sate it in vampire form to keep his werewolf from raging.

"Mademoiselle, the forest is empty of human souls," he confirmed.

She nodded approvingly. "As I'd hoped."

"You've had time to consider all I've revealed to you?"

"I have." She walked the horse beyond him, around and in a circle that took her off the path beaten to dirt by carriage wheels.

Rhys stood patiently, taking in her essence. Traces of desire wafted from her skin, intense and sweet. His vampire scented her blood.

The moire ribbon at her neck was a new purchase for he could hear the rub of the raised weft against her skin. The leather gloves gripping the reins must be an old and favored pair for they hugged her flesh as if a second skin and smelled of beeswax polish.

"I won't ask what you concluded," he said.

"Isn't it obvious?"

"It is. I want you, Viviane."

"You need me," she boldly challenged, staring down at him. She favored the position of authority. It tickled him to grant it to her.

"Yes," he confirmed. "I need you."

"Show me what you are, wolf," she challenged. "And that I can trust you."

"Right now?" His wolf shape was neutral; neither his vampire nor werewolf mind really controlled it. He was most like an animal in that form, yet still retained the human knowledge of a mortal.

"Yes. The forest is a fine place to reveal one's truths," she prompted.

"And then what?"

Viviane hitched a heel to the horse's flank. It took off at a canter, and she called back, "If you can catch me, you can have me!"

A flirting challenge? His werewolf demanded the satisfaction of capturing her and pushing her to the ground, shoving up her skirts and claiming her roughly.

The vampire he was right now decided the werewolf rather wise.

But the four-legged wolf he could become wanted to run, to lope through the grasses and dash after the wind.

Twisting his foot, Rhys pushed off the ball and into a run. The heavy frockcoat slowed him, making it difficult to pump his arms. He veered toward the forest lining the path.

VIVIANE HEELED MORDAUNT and left Rhys in a wake of upended turf. While her brain was still trying to order out this new information about Rhys, her heart rushed ahead, urging her to abandon caution.

She had sent the letter, knowing he would not refuse her. Yet she had been unsure she would attend this midnight appointment until only half a turn of the clock earlier.

Vampires did not engage with werewolves.

Yet Viviane favored the idea of tossing tradition aside and gambling with risk.

The first time she glanced back, she almost lost balance. Riding sidesaddle was difficult, especially at breakneck speed. She'd not worn breeches under her skirts as she usually did when she went for a ride, yet she'd changed into a riding corset, which was cut high so as not to dig into her gut as the horse jostled.

Rhys followed closely.

She felt her breasts flush and held back a giggle at this spontaneous adventure. The second time she glanced back, the wind loosened the hair pinned at the top of her head. She tucked a long swath over her ear and searched the hazy darkness. Rhys dodged toward the thick forest, disappearing.

Did he know of a shortcut? There could be unmarked paths lovers used for liaisons, or by killers to hide their deeds. Last month two bodies had been found in this park.

She heeled Mordaunt and the horse snorted in response. Darkness and the loamy grass impeded the gelding's footing and kept it from a full-out run.

A wolf dashed out from the woods, parallel to them and kept pace. Mordaunt may be aware of it, but would not balk for the witch's spell.

Rhys? It had to be. How marvelous. He'd shifted to show her his animal form.

She wanted to look at the wolf, to watch it race across the long grasses, but more she needed to pay attention. A low hanging branch swept the crown of her head. The next time she looked, the wolf was gone.

Mordaunt's front legs stiffened as the horse dug in its hooves to a stop. It reared. Viviane slid from the hot withers, crying out.

She hit the ground, hip first and rolled to her stomach. Slapping the ground, she moaned. Mordaunt reared once, and stomped the ground too close to her head. A large gray wolf growled, frightening the horse off the path to wander the edge of a field.

The wolf loped toward her. Its fur was thick and healthy. Gold eyes tracked the area. It circled, its nose dipping to sniff at her, yet it kept ten paces away at all times.

Viviane pushed to sit, and shook her head to loosen the leaves from her tousled hair. Though she had no proof this was Rhys, she was not afraid.

"So you have won," she declared proudly. "I am pleased for your victory." She drew her fingers across her breasts, wet from the dewy grass. Licking them, she drawled, "It is more than a mere race you have won."

The animal stalked before her. It gave no indication it understood, but neither did it growl. Its eyes matched the elegant rim of gold she had noticed on Rhys's irises.

"How am I to speak to a wolf?"

The wolf yipped once, and released a whining, shrill tone, which reminded Viviane of the submissive dogs the king kept at Versailles for the hunt.

Mordaunt bristled its withers and trotted off, clearly offended by the beast, yet not willing to get too far from his mistress.

Apprehension doubled her heartbeats. The man favored her, but would such admiration manifest while in wolf form?

Maybe this was not Rhys. There were wolves in abundance at the periphery of Paris, though rarely were they sighted in the park. She reasoned now perhaps that was because they entered the park after all humans had left.

Did it sense she was not human? Or did one human-shaped being appear as tasty—or threatening—as the next?

She had killed one wolf; she could kill another.

Exhaling, she shook her head. No, she would not again kill a wolf. Not now, knowing Rhys was half wolf.

"Show yourself," she demanded. "Or I shall mount and ride off, and never speak to you again. Rhys?"

The wolf pranced about her, jumping to land its fore-paws, and dashing about in a circle. Playful in its motions. Or perhaps teasing the prey before the attack?

"You're frightening me," she admitted. Did the wolf understand? "Do not tease me, please."

Skipping out before her, the wolf growled and yipped, yet the vocalizations were abruptly cut off. The beast flipped to its back, its legs kicking out at odd angles, as if an invisible force had pressed it down and pinned it with a hand to the stomach.

Viviane leaned forward, fingers curling into the wet grass. No longer could she sense her heartbeats. Perhaps her heart had stopped to witness such a sight. To know what was happening, and to also know it could not happen unless he trusted her.

She heard the crack of bone, the leathery tear as flesh and fur stretched and elongated. Whiny snarls amplified, and she wondered would the whole city not hear. Quickly the whines grew low and tortured. The wolf, gyrating in the darkness, kicked up leaves and pawed the grass.

The voice of a man emerged as the legs lengthened and she watched the broad, bold, back stretch. The spine curved as muscles banded beneath mortal flesh.

Not at all horrified, Viviane clutched her chest. There, her heart raced. Her wondrous sigh underlined the creature's agonizing moans.

Never had she witnessed a Dark One change. Not even after she'd killed the wolf, for it had changed to a man while she had not been aware. Fascinating. And so personal.

When he was completely man, Rhys knelt before her, one hand on the ground, and squatting on his hind legs. Naked. Long hair tousled about his shoulders. The gray streak gleamed in the moonlight, as did the sweat on his muscles. Muscles she wanted to touch, to press her palms to and draw in his sensual heat.

Gold animal eyes held her. They had yet to change.

He stretched back his head, twisting it as if to draw out a kink in his neck. Easing back his shoulders, he worked them up, one, then the other. Standing, he worked through his entire body, stretching and tensing the muscles until he shook one foot loosely and then the other.

"Shifting shape is always difficult," he finally remarked.

Viviane released her held breath. Laughter felt wrong so she aborted it with an effusive smile. Yet inside she giddily celebrated what she had just witnessed and was relieved she'd the courage to invite him tonight.

"One disadvantage of the change is clothing does not come along during the process." Rhys flexed a biceps and inhaled deeply, which lifted his broad chest. "But I'll wager a naked man does not offend your experienced disposition, eh, LaMourette?"

"Not at all."

Viviane drew her eyes over his tight stomach, row after row of hard muscle emphasized his strength, his wild virility. Moonlight glistened silver on his sweat-beaded flesh, plating him as if a statue. Gluttony was not one of his vices.

Nor was humility. As her eyes traveled lower, she fixed upon the gorgeous weapon at the apex of his thighs, so boldly erect. Defiant. Ready.

"You keep staring at my private bits, I'll begin to wonder if that's all you're interested in, *chérie*."

"I wouldn't call them bits." Pushing to stand, Viviane approached. "They've changed," she said of his eyes. "I like them gold."

"Then you favor my wolf. Ahh…"

She clutched his erection. So thick and hard, her fingers did not completely span the width. It was a prize she would take in reward for the race—win or not.

"It is a most spectacular thing." She stroked it, keeping a firm grasp. The skin was smooth, silken, the thick head of it hot and wet with dew.

He moved in and nuzzled his cheek aside hers. A throaty sigh signaled his pleasure.

"You said your werewolf needs to be sated?"

"Yes, if I am not sexually fulfilled by midnight on the night preceding the full moon the werewolf takes over."

"And your vampire?"

"Will take over the werewolf's mind. It will not be so playful as I was in simple wolf form."

Viviane paused her astute ministrations. She stroked his cheek, bristled with beard stubble. A smudge of dirt cut a line across his skin. "You don't like your werewolf," she stated.

"It's not a matter of liking. It's a matter of not wishing to murder anyone."

"Nothing can be done to stop it once you have shifted?"

"I keep an iron cage at home for the full moon."

"You poor man. Do all werewolves endure the same struggle?"

"Only me. Measures have been taken. I was enchanted by a faery decades ago. But that only keeps my werewolf away until the full moon."

"A faery? And what did you give her in return?"

"Can we not discuss this right now? I am standing naked before you, LaMourette."

"Yes, and displaying quite a healthy regard for me." They both looked down to her hand clasped about his hard staff. "Shall I take this as a metaphor for your truths? All bold and out there?"

"You may." He nuzzled aside her cheek. "You know my darkest secret now, Viviane."

"Well, then—" she kissed his dirt-smeared shoulder "—we had best see to taming the werewolf."

"What did you have in—"

Viviane fell to her knees and kissed his erection.

"The woman is a libertine," he said on a strained tone.

Her fangs tingled, wanting to taste, to pierce him, but she relinquished that desire for the fascination of exploring the delicate boundary that kept him wanting and submissive at her touch.

A lash of her tongue along his hard length drew out a moan from her lover. His staff bobbed, pleading for her to take him into her mouth. And so she did because the control this position offered her was insurmountable. Drawing her hands about his thighs and up his buttocks, she held him there, a prisoner that she would make suffer as she pleased.

Salty and verdant, the taste of him belied his simple exterior, but spoke of his intricate nature. She could not take him too far, but she read his moans as evidence she served him well.

"Viviane, you will kill me."

"You don't like what I'm doing?"

His deep groan scurried over her flesh and prickled her every pore to a wanting receptor.

"If you continue, ah…*le petit morte*."

"Come, wolf," she cooed. "Do as I request. Surrender to me."

"The deuce, Viviane!"

And he relented. His body shuddered. Twice now she had mastered him. The triumph emboldened her. She could trust this man, no matter his wicked darkness.

Viviane stood and tugged at him, and led him toward the trees.

Her heel stepped on a branch, upsetting her balance. Rhys caught her by the elbows and brought her down in a thicket of long grass. He tore at the bodice seam high on her shoulder where it was sown to the corset. It came free easily. Portia wasn't the most exacting seamstress. Viviane would thank her later.

He ripped the bodice from her gown. "What's this? It is half what it should be."

"My riding corset."

"I like it."

He bit the ribbon securing the corset through wide grommets. Releasing the tight ribbon unloosened her voluptuous breasts. Rhys's tongue grazed her nipple and Viviane arched her back to receive his hot lashes. A hot lick about her rigid flesh giddied. He suckled, drawing all sensation to the exquisite center of her.

Her entire body reacted, tensing, relaxing, toes curling and chest rising. Her being tingled, wanting all he could give to her and then flinching with sweet reluctance, until she moaned and set back her shoulders, opening herself to receive whatever his tongue, his fingers, his skin could offer.

He struggled at her skirts, but lifting her by the hips, he managed to locate the ribbon in the back, and tugged it loose with a rip and a tear. His hips rocked, his penis nudged at her thigh.

"You are a wicked woman."

"What? For taking advantage of a naked man? I hardly feel any challenge was presented."

He smiled against her mouth and kissed her deeply, roughly. She clung to his shoulders, tearing her nails into his moist skin. She would not draw blood—not yet.

Moving hard kisses over her neck, Rhys caressed her breasts, pinching the nipples, massaging her flesh, and again finding the hard peaks with his mouth. His mouth may be at her breasts, yet she felt his touch at the apex of her mons, deeply, teasing at her.

His erection thumped her stomach. Hard again so quickly?

"That was excellent," he whispered, "but a far cry from utter satiation. We've much to do with *la lune* watching over us tonight. Are you willing?"

"Oh yes."

He dragged the skirts from her thighs and the smooth intrusion of his fingers into her sex filled the night with a dazzle of stars Viviane could only touch in her dreams.

"So wet," he growled. "Ripe for me. Viviane, I must…"

"Yes, now. All of you. Inside me." She nudged his hip, beckoning. "I must feel you, all of you."

He entered her slowly, aware of his width and that she winced with the introduction of it. As he eased inside, Viviane spread out her arms and gripped at the wet grass. Filling her. Mastering her. Putting himself in peril.

"I must warn you," she gasped as he thrusted. "Sex brings up the desire for blood in me."

"Do not bite me, Viviane. Just…do not. Please?"

She stretched her mouth wide, wanting to sink her fangs into the hot flesh. Taking blood would increase the pleasure tenfold. A deep drink would bond her to him.

She did not want that.

He does not want that. The realization stung.

And then she released, crying out into the night for the sweetest, most wicked coupling she had ever experienced.

Yet it was only that—a coupling. Not the connection she now realized she really needed. A connection with a man like no other, the only man who saw into her heart and respected it.

CHAPTER SEVENTEEN

RHYS HOVERED OVER VIVIANE'S moon-dappled body, watching as the climax tensed her stomach muscles. Her back arched to lift her gorgeous breasts, and her slender legs were wrapped about his hips. Sharing the pulse of their connection brought him to another orgasm. Clasping her around the shoulders, he clutched her to him.

The werewolf growled lowly; it was sated.

His vampire was not complaining, either.

Stretched out upon the folded bit of her gown and the forest floor, Viviane grinned, a pleased cat. Twisting her arms above her head, she sighed.

"Viviane, you have given me a gift."

"Climax?"

"Acceptance."

"Easy enough."

"Really?"

"Yes, but you did imply sex was necessary to keep back your werewolf tonight. And I must confess to a certain curiosity."

"I see."

"Do you? Because I'm not sure I understand. I have made love with a werewolf."

"Half."

"Yes, and it bothers me little when it should." She bracketed his face with her hands. "I want you, Rhys Hawkes. I want your vampire. I want your werewolf. I want your ineffable complexity and your simple ugliness. But most of all, I want the beauty of you."

"And so you have me." He tapped the fang jutting over her lip, careful not to cut himself. "Pretty."

"You speak the truth?"

He shrugged. "Mine are bigger when I'm the werewolf."

She traced his mouth. "But mine will bring you ecstasy."

"More than what I've just experienced?"

"Close." She slid her tongue along the gleaming fang. "You want to try it?"

"Your bite devastates. For once bitten I'm sure a man can dream of nothing but you endlessly after."

"Don't say that. I don't wish to harm. I do it to survive. Do you not?"

"Yes, but as vampire it is my werewolf who controls my mind. It doesn't need blood, so I oftentimes have to remind myself to bite someone for sustenance."

"That is incredible. To have to *remember* to drink blood? I cannot imagine." She leaned back, her breasts high and pale in the moonlight. "So you won't take my bite?"

Rhys stroked softly over her nipple. "You know if a vampire bites a werewolf that wolf then develops an unnatural hunger for blood."

"But if your wolf has already a blood hunger…"

"I don't know what can happen, Viviane." His kissed her aside the mouth, careful not to touch her fang, and then kissed her eyelid. "I do not refuse you. I refuse the unknown. Can you accept that?"

The tip of her fang receded into her mouth. Disappointed, surely.

"We've only begun," he offered. "We've time to learn one another."

"Yes. And I trust you, Rhys. Thank you for trusting that I would understand."

He leaned on an elbow and skimmed a hand over her other breast. Her body was hot and sticky, still panting from their incredible exertions. "You mean that?"

"I actually do. I trust you more than any man."

"What of Salignac?"

"What of him?"

He tucked his head against her neck and nuzzled her skin. "I feel I've done you a disservice. Constantine can patron you. I shouldn't wish to spoil your prospects."

"On the contrary, you've opened my eyes. Had you not come along I might have been cowed into entering a relationship with a vile and boring vampire whose only interest in me is for progeny."

"I suspect he does love you."

"Why do you speak your brother's defense? Have you changed your mind about me so quickly? Do you regret our making love, Rhys?"

"Not for one moment." He rolled to his back and closed his eyes. "And yet, I cannot give you what he can."

This is what he'd wanted. Win the girl and shame the brother. But victory did not feel right. Not if Viviane were merely surrendering to a need. She'd been curious about him. And he had asked her for this.

She could have no idea tonight had brought his victory.

She drew his hand over her breast and positioned it flat upon her ribs. Her heart beat boldly against his palm. "Do you feel that?" she whispered as softly as moonlight on skin. "That is you. You have gotten inside me, and I don't understand how it happened, only that it has."

He smirked. "Were you not there when I put myself inside you just moments ago, lover?"

She chuckled. "I'm being serious. We should not be here, lying happily in one another's arms. We are enemies."

"Is that how you see me? Vampires and werewolves are not enemies."

"They do not particularly care for one another."

"I am vampire in form more than I am wolf."

"Yes, but your mind is more wolf than vampire."

"So you have been paying attention. You know me now, Viviane, ugliness and all."

She stroked his hair. "Your wolf is gorgeous. This is your wolf, yes?" She dug her fingers in where the gray streaked his black hair.

"I believe so."

Nuzzling her face against his hair, she breathed him in. It humbled him that she accepted him fur, fangs and all.

This was the easy part though. If they were ever to bond, the werewolf would insist upon mating.

"I am sorry for naming you not right. You are more man than I have ever known. Your differences dazzle my heart." She traced his beard with a fingertip.

"I like the sound of that. You must understand when I've tried to take vampire lovers in the past, they eventually learn my secret. Well, I tell it. It is not something I can hide and expect to have an honest relationship. And that makes them flee. Always."

"I don't want to flee your arms, Rhys. Your brother suspects I admire you. I am sure that is why he told me your secret. He wishes you out of the city."

"And you in his arms."

She looked aside. “Can we do this?”

“I would never put you in a position of risk. If you do not believe we can manage a secret affair say so.”

“And you would release me?”

“Reluctantly.” He nuzzled into her hair. Drown in her forever, and he would not ask for air. “But yes.”

“No, I want us.”

She sat, her bare back to him, and combed fingers through her hair. A broken green leaf fluttered from the moonswept strands. Rhys stroked the soft skin down her spine, gooseflesh rising in his wake.

“What of your lacking patron? What if— Could I become your patron?”

She turned about and bracketed his face with her cool palms. Sadness clouded her eyes. “You will not take my bite. Why even ask?”

So true. He did not know what her bite would do to his already lunatic werewolf. But oh, he felt sure his vampire would love to lick Viviane’s blood and devour her whole.

It was the devouring part that sickened him.

He traced her gaze as she sought his in the darkness. He couldn’t see depth or light in her irises, but he sensed her nervous enthusiasm.

“Viviane, I will secrete you into my heart and keep you safe, I promise. I will let no harm come to you as long as I am able.”

“So many secrets. I don’t like it.”

“But you are my best secret. The secret that makes me strong.”

“That’s silly. You are strong all by yourself. You dare to walk before the tribe Nava when you know they look down upon you.”

"Only the one man despises my treading his halls."

"Your brother. Oh, Rhys, let's not talk of dark things. Make love to me again."

RHYS WOKE TO THE STEADY BEAT of Viviane's heart against his chest. If a vampire drank the blood of another vampire, they could synchronize heartbeats, always know where the other was, merely by pulse alone.

He wanted that, but not the risk that accompanied sharing blood.

She lay sprawled upon him, her head heavy at his throat and one leg bent across his hip. They'd made love again and again. Both had surely climaxed half a dozen times before surrendering to a blissful sleep.

Now, with the sky lightening he felt the day—

"Viviane." He nudged her shoulder urgently. "Viviane, wake up. We've been here all night."

She stirred, wrapping her arm across his shoulder, and nuzzled in again. "Tired yet."

"The sun is rising," he hissed.

She shot upright, looking about. It was yet dark, probably five in the morning, Rhys guessed. Dawn was not far off.

He shoved the gown into her arms and scanned the field for Mordaunt. A glint of orange peaked on the horizon. Rhys had never feared the sunrise. "Where's the damn horse?"

"He must have wandered home. The witch's spell gives Mordaunt a homing instinct."

"We must find cover for you. Some place dark until I can find you more clothing and a means of travel."

Rhys lifted her in a swaddle of her gown; the stitches torn from the bodice would require a maid's hand to be worn again. Leaves spilled onto the ground and a branch dropped onto his foot.

"What about you?" she asked, her eyes straying to the orange line across the field. "You've misplaced your clothes."

"My werewolf makes me immune to the burning effects the sun has on my vampire flesh. All, save my eyes." He scanned their periphery. Across the field stood a small stone building. Rhys raced toward it. "Keep your head under the dress."

A mausoleum sat nestled beneath mature oak trees. Setting Viviane on the ground in the shadows, he inspected the lock. It was new, and a thick iron chain held the door securely.

Charging the door, Rhys rammed his shoulder against the solid stone. He slammed again and again, but eventually the lock snapped and sent him stumbling inside the small enclosure. Must and dirt choked him. A fine beam of gray light spilled across the entryway. Windows in a mausoleum?

Viviane entered, sniffing the dingy room. "There are dead bodies in here?"

"Just bones. Their souls were claimed long ago by the soul bringer. You'll be safe until I can return with protective clothing. Come sit over in this corner."

He helped her sit on the dress and pull up the skirts to wrap about her shoulders. Her tousled hair scattered about her face and shoulder. Bits of grass and earth impressed her pale skin. A ravaged angel, he wanted to devour her, draw her into his soul and keep her safe there. Hugging her, he clung to what had become more valuable than breath to him.

"I'll go quickly. I'll find my clothes and Mordaunt."

She gripped his hand. "What if there are rats?"

"None in here, LaMourette. It is dusty and there is no food to attract rodents. I promise you will be safe from them. Now I must be quick. My wolf has prowled the city on a few occasions. If I don't find the horse, can I get another from your stable?"

"Of course. Tell Portia I insist. You must have something to tell her so she will know to trust you."

"Something only she knows about you?"

"Yes, but what?"

He waited.

"Monsieur Rosemont," she blurted out. "Every Saturday afternoon. Tell Portia, and she will know I've taken you into my confidence."

"Every Saturday afternoon. Viviane?"

"He's my teacher. I am...learning to read."

"Ah? Good for you." He kissed her on the cheek. "You'll be safe, *chérie*."

PORTIA HAD A BATH WAITING for her mistress in the tepidarium, and fussed over her as Rhys stood by the door observing the frenzy of concern. She needed to be fussed over, to get clean and put the horror of nearly burning behind her.

Settling into the bath, she looked over her shoulder and beamed a smile at him. "You'll stay?"

After Portia left, Viviane tugged Rhys into the bath with her and after they'd cleaned away the dirt and remnants of forest, she spent the day entwined within her lover's arms. Kissing his mouth. Stroking his muscles and learning his tender spots, the places where the slightest breath made him flinch and moan with pleasure.

He carried her to the bed and laid her beneath the confection of silk curtains, tassels and fringe. Stretching back his arms to yawn he noticed the table beside the bed and picked up the card Viviane kept tucked there to admire as she drifted to sleep.

He jumped onto the bed, landing on his back beside her and studied the card. "LaMourette, is this the type of reading material you prefer?"

"It is." She snuggled aside his body, firm and muscled and so warm from their shared lovemaking. "I found it tucked in Blanche's things. It deserves to be seen, not hidden."

"You want me to do this to you?" He tossed the card over a shoulder and didn't wait for an answer, turning her to her side and hugging her from behind.

His fingers clasped her nipple and squeezed it hard, while he slid his other hand between her legs to play at her wetness, mimicking the card. Viviane gasped boldly.

His slow, attentive moves to her swollen clit hummed throughout her body. She slid a palm back and down his thigh, holding him against her. His cock nuzzled her spine. His moans matched hers and her breath increased.

Gasping, she clutched at the air, wanting, standing at the edge…

Released, she fell freely into bliss, crying out loudly. Her body shivered and bucked, answering his command.

The sound of her lover's long and satisfied moan was more valuable than any precious stone. He stretched out on the bed. Candlelight played across his flesh.

"I love you, LaMourette." He leaned in and kissed her breast. "I do." Bright brown eyes twinkled at her.

Viviane had never known love, save for in the blood crossing her tongue. When she drank from a donor, she could taste the vivid spice of love flowing through a mortal's blood. Most often she tasted love in mothers of small children, but not always, contempt was a strong flavor, as well.

So while she had not felt it herself, she knew love's essence, and would recognize it the moment it assaulted her heart. Surely.

In truth, she may be in love. With the idea of love, with the heady rush of claiming a new lover. With Rhys's truth, and yes, his wolf. She tasted love, liquid and sweet at the back of her throat and in her veins. But she would not speak it. She could not.

For eventually, she must go to Constantine.

"That makes me happy," she answered. It was all she could give him. "Your werewolf did not show at all during our lovemaking last night," she said, changing the subject.

Rhys lazily rolled off the bed and padded over to the vanity. Candlelight played across his muscles, powerful thighs for running, sleek yet broad back.

"Indeed. You are a powerful witch, LaMourette. I've never found a mortal woman who could do the same."

He palmed the vanity and stretched, easing each shoulder forward then back. He sat on the padded chair and splayed out his legs, unmindful of his nudity, or perhaps proud of it. So much to be proud of, and already jutting up stiff and ready.

"No woman?" she entreated.

"Well, I've not tried to make love all night with a mortal woman. Because what if the sex should not sate me? I would shift and then…"

He looked aside, his reflection in the mirror peaceful. Yet behind his lowered lashes Viviane sensed he shuddered at the horrors of which he was capable. And she had kept back those horrors?

A tingle of pride scurried through her veins. She was a woman of great strength, and this proved it. She had tamed his werewolf. No longer was she the wolf slayer. Now she preferred to be wolf enchantress.

His reflection grinned at her.

His *reflection*. What marvel.

"I must leave the city this afternoon," Rhys said. "Tonight the moon is full."

"I will miss you."

"Will you? That pleases me."

"Is that the only thing I offer to please you?"

His cock bobbed, and he smiled wickedly. "Apparently not."

Viviane lazily stretched her hands along the sheets between her legs to lean forward. Sex-tousled hair spilled over half her face. "What of your wolf? I've heard werewolves mate while in their beastly form."

"It is the only way we bond with one another."

"Does your beast wish to mate with me? Could I mate with it? Are you…?"

"Beastly?"

She shrugged, unsure how to put into delicate terms what she could only imagine as a wild and raging animal.

"The werewolf is able to mate with its own kind, as well as mortal females. While most werewolves would never choose a vampire, I promise that is not one of my problems. I would love to mate with you, Viviane. But I cannot."

"Because your werewolf has the vicious vampire mind?"

He nodded. "I've never mated in werewolf form. Much as I wish for it, the vampire has more wicked needs that must be kept contained."

"That makes me very sad. I wish I could tame your

werewolf. Or rather," she considered the arrangement of the man's dual nature, "your vampire."

He smiled, looking aside. "I adore you, LaMourette. I dare say if there was a woman on this earth who would dare stand before my werewolf, it would be you."

"Challenge accepted." She tongued her lip, inviting him back to her arms.

"What is this?" Rhys clasped something from the vanity. "Is this—" he dangled the talon on the blue velvet ribbon, then clutched it and brought it to his nose "—what I think it is?"

Viviane could feel the punishing waves of his sudden anger, and wondered if such an abrupt change in emotion would bring on his werewolf.

"Constantine gave it to me," she blurted. Lunging, she gripped the iron bedpost, but dared not step down to approach him.

A breathy cry broke from him. Shaking his head effusively, he dropped the talon on the vanity, and stood so quickly and violently the chair toppled.

"It is hers!" He looked for answers from her. "I can smell her on it."

"Hers? But who?"

"I loved her," he cried. "He killed her!"

The macabre artifact's truth made itself plain. Constantine had claimed the prize from a kill—that Rhys had loved.

"Oh, *sacre bleu*."

Rhys stuffed his legs into his breeches. He grabbed his shirt and frockcoat, stepping hastily into his boots.

"No, Rhys! I did not know. Constantine told me it was a trophy—"

The man spun on her, his fingers clutched in a claw

as if to choke her. His face screwed into a tormented cry, but no sound came from him.

"Your lover," Viviane said, so softly, yet feeling those two words cut into her heart as if a blade. "The one…he murdered."

"You wore it?" he pleaded.

She nodded and turned away. Her fingers trembled as she clutched the bed linens, wanted to pull them up to hide from him.

"I must be away from here." He stomped toward the door.

"Rhys, I did not know." But he did not hear her for he was already halfway down the hall.

Cracking glass and then the clatter of shards hitting the floor indicated he'd punched the mirror-lined wall.

Viviane clutched the bedpost and pressed her forehead to the iron. "Have I lost him?"

CHAPTER EIGHTEEN

RHYS RAN THROUGH PARIS as if it were a blurred nightmare haunting his sleep. He made the city gates and leaped over them. Once a league out of Paris, the muddy roads began to hamper his footsteps and he shifted to wolf form.

The shift was quick, but complicated. With the midnight hour so near, his body wanted to shift to werewolf form, yet, fighting the inner vampire, he clung to his were mind and commanded the shift to four-legged wolf.

From here on, he raced the moon.

Loping across the lands, the wolf panted, its tongue lolling. Rhys pushed harder, faster. He was too near the city. And her...Emeline.

He wanted to hurt something—anything—to claim revenge in her name.

He veered west, tracking the edge of a forest.

Damn, Constantine!

He would shame the tribe leader by revealing he was related to a half-breed. He would take his brother's blood. All of it. He would destroy what his brother needed most—Viviane.

Wodges of grassy dirt kicked up behind his paws. Dodging into the forest, he slowed as the wolf navigated the close-spaced birch and pine trees.

Rhys fought to redirect his wolf onto the road where he could make distance, but the wolf had self-preservation in mind. Pine sap and rotting undergrowth called to his wolf. Here was home. Here was safety.

The scent of human blood made him snap his muzzle and come to a heaving pause. The wolf lifted its nose and sniffed.

Must avenge Emeline. Must...take blood.

No, his wolf did not care for human blood. *Do not listen to the vampire! Fight the moonlight. Do not...succumb.*

The wolf let out a howl, which was abruptly bit off with a shrieking whine. It rolled on the forest floor, fighting the burning snap of bones and stretch of muscle.

Too late. The werewolf was upon him. The vampire wanted blood.

God help the nearest mortal who wandered onto his path.

VIVIANE STALKED THE DARKNESS. Her skirts made no noise. Her shoes were soled with thick leather, a necessity for silence.

The midnight moon sat full and bright above the Notre Dame cathedral like a halo proclaiming its divinity.

Viviane wondered how Rhys saw the moon right now. Did he view it with human eyes or through animal eyes? And what did the werewolf look like? She had not ever seen a werewolf completely shifted, only in the animal wolf shape, which she obviously had little difficulty taming, or killing—once wounded, of course. She wasn't sure if she could take on a fully shifted werewolf.

Had Constantine taken the talon from the wolf or the werewolf? Had she still been alive?

A shudder rippled up her neck as she listened for mortal heartbeats.

That she had worn his lover's talon! She hated Constantine for that. She hated the vampire lord for his fascination with her wolf kill.

Might his knowing she was sleeping with his brother turn him away from her? She suspected it would ignite a bloody war between the twosome and she would not care to guess at the outcome.

Constantine must not learn of their liaison. Hell, she wasn't sure how to label it. Merely fascination? Curiosity? Or something deeper, something that touched her heart.

It is love, you know it as you know nothing else. You have tasted love from the veins of others. Know it now as it pulses your heart.

Shaking her head adamantly, she picked up the slow thud of life. Behind her and moving at a shuffle. The odor of vile, unwashed flesh overwhelmed her senses.

Viviane slipped out from the alley and quickened her pace. She was not so hungry that she would stoop to feed on a disgusting human.

Would Rhys's werewolf be compelled to drink blood this night? He'd been repulsed by his dark side. What horrors would his werewolf commit at the direction of his bloodthirsty vampire?

"Oh!" A fop in pink damask and powdered wig exclaimed as he stumbled right into Viviane's arms. The intriguing scent of opium smoke coated him. "Sorry. Not so sure where I am right now," he slurred. "Was on my way home."

"This way," Viviane said, and directed him into the darkness behind a cart of loose hay.

She clutched the threadbare damask, her fingernails cutting into the pink fabric. Not unhandsome, even the skewed wig could not hide his glittering eyes. Viviane had been in opium houses before, and didn't mind the small high she got from drinking an addict's blood.

"This can't be right," he muttered against her breast. "You are too beautiful."

His hands groped for hold against the cart and her hip. Hot breath upon her bosom gave her no thrill. It made her sad for her absent lover. A lover she had betrayed by wearing the talon.

With a resolute sigh, she pushed up the man's head with the heel of her palm. "It will be right, you'll see."

Tilting his head put him off balance, and Viviane clung to his body as his legs gave out. Sinking her fangs into his neck she sucked the blood. It was warm and not undesirable. But that was all.

She stopped drinking before he could be granted the orgasmic swoon her bite promised. One last lick of the blood curling across his throat and she whispered, "You stumbled against a cart and cut yourself. Safe journey home, my tattered prince."

Standing, she turned right into Constantine de Salignac's arms.

"YOU WOULD NOT NEED TO succumb to such lowly tactics as drinking from any drunk fop you encounter if you would simply accept my patronship, Viviane."

She backed against the hay cart. Constantine moved in, his legs crushing her skirts. She could feel his desire for her. *Wolf slayer.* It disgusted her.

Tugging out the black lace fan from her sleeve—Constantine grabbed it, preventing her from unfurling the weapon. "You really wish to show me your disapproval?"

"I tire of your pursuits, Lord de Salignac. Leave me be."

"I thought so." Fisting the fan, he squeezed, crushing the delicate wood pieces. "My bravos tell me he was in your home again. How can you do this to me, Viviane?"

"You know nothing. Not of my heart."

"So he is in your heart now? That damned half-breed! You consort with an animal!"

"He is your brother!"

"Indeed." Constantine sniffed and smirked. "Henri was a fool to give you so long a leash."

She tried to push by him, but he would not relent, keeping her caged against the cart, and with the fop lolling at her ankles muttering nonsyllables.

Constantine leaned in, drawing his nose along her jaw. Sniffing, scenting. If he thought to bite her—

He reared, his eyes black coals in the darkness. "I smell him on you."

"It surprises me you would recognize his scent. You deem to keep your brother at such a distance."

The slap to her cheek was unexpected. Viviane sneered and this time managed to wrestle her fan free. But she did not slash it across Constantine's face, only held it before her, defying him to make that move again.

The vampire lord held back his shoulders, his chin up, and looked upon her. "He taints you, Viviane."

"You've no idea," she purred. A flick of the fan stopped his move to touch her. "You do not care to patron me, you simply want me to birth bloodborn vampires to strengthen your tribe."

Constantine slapped a palm across his heart. "But I do love you. Genuinely. And you do need a patron."

"Perhaps. But he must be as Henri, kind, loving and willing to grant me rein."

"Ridiculous! Why can you not see the honor in supporting our tribe?"

"It is your tribe, not mine. And I will not submit to you."

"You!" He fisted the air, then released the tight, brutal grip. "You are lying through your fangs, Viviane. You were devastated to learn he is a half-breed," Constantine surmised. "And where is he now? Ah, I am foolish to forget. He is out howling at the moon like the animal he is."

He pressed her shoulders to the cart and Viviane retaliated by drawing the fan blades across his forearm. It cut fabric, and in the next moment, the vampire broke it in half, and flung it over his shoulder.

"You bastard," she said. "Why do you hate your brother?"

"Is it not enough he is a half-breed? An abomination! Viviane, don't do this to me. Do not stray from the one man who wishes to care for you, to see you patroned."

"Take your hands from me, Constantine. I will not be forced to anything."

"But I've dismissed two more kin. If I am releasing my lifeblood for no reason—"

"They are your lifeblood? I thought it the kin who relied on the patron, not the other way around. Are you addicted to them as the man who lies at our feet is addicted to opium?"

He growled, exposing his fangs in a manner any vampire would take as a threat.

Viviane did not back down. "Show me you can embrace your brother and I will not find it so difficult to consider you as a patron."

"We have been at each other's throats for decades. A man cannot change overnight."

Viviane stepped away from him. She walked swiftly.

Her home was down the street. "Do not come to me, Lord de Salignac. If I deem you worthy, I will come to you."

"He does not love you," he hissed. "This is a game against me!"

She reached the front door of Henri's estate as Constantine grabbed her arm.

"Unhand me! You're hurting me."

She shoved open the door and clattered inside, but was unable to keep Constantine from following.

"You will be mine."

"Even after I have tainted myself with your brother?"

"You admit to it, then? What insidious notions live in your small brain, woman? No vampire will have you, let alone patron you, if he knows you've been touched by the mange."

"He is not contagious!"

She hurried away, matching her footsteps to her heartbeats. A frantic pace, both. It had only begun. For the vampire lord would not release her so easily. Today he had thrown down a gauntlet.

Heartbeats pounding, her breaths came too quickly. Desperate sobs were merely gasps.

Portia spun into the room, a wondering look on her face. *"Cherie?"*

Viviane wanted her to stay, but would not show Constantine her worry. "I am busy as you can see."

The maid bowed and backed from the room.

Hands on hips, she paced. "Don't think to assault me in my home, Salignac."

"Assault you?"

"You'll never have my blood, nor do I wish yours."

"We are two of a kind. The children we could have—"

Viviane chuckled.

"You are yet a viable mate for me," he insisted.

"Do not put it that way. It is as if I am a commodity."

Constantine lunged for her, pinning her shoulders against the wall. He stretched his mouth to show her his fangs. A power play she would be wise to submit to. Instead she lifted a knee and managed to just brush his thigh. Her skirts were too cumbersome to do any damage.

"I will expose you, Viviane. Surrender to me or risk the entire vampire nation learning of your digression."

"Why would you have me after you've said no other vampire will?"

Constantine thrust Viviane to the floor and swept out of the room. The maid scrambled from his path and he gnashed his fangs at her. And then, he grabbed her, and sank his fangs into her throat.

"No!" Viviane crawled into the doorway and, skirts impeding her swift rise, struggled to stand. "Unhand her!"

He tore his teeth from the maid's throat, ripping flesh and quickly dropping her to avoid the spurt of blood.

"What have you done?" Viviane lunged to Portia's side. Her fingers slipped through hot blood. "This cannot be stopped. She will die!"

She stood and beat her fists against his chest. Grinning, Constantine licked the maid's blood from his lips.

"Get out of my house! You will never have me. Rhys was right about you."

He gripped her wrists and crushed the fine bones within his grip. She twisted her head down and screamed.

He shoved her away, to land near the maid's bleeding body, and stormed from the house. "You will submit to me, or you will never have a patron."

"I will not!"

"Then I will tell all. All the vampires who walk the

streets of Paris will know Viviane LaMourette has lain with a hideous half-breed."

"No!"

"Word will travel quickly. There is not a vampire in this world who will patron you."

"No, Constantine, please."

"Submit to me. If you do not wish to save yourself, save your lover."

He marched out, leaving Viviane sprawled in the growing pool of Portia's blood.

CHAPTER NINETEEN

Paris, modern day

POOLE, THE BUTLER IN RHYS'S Paris home, pushed a food cart laden for a crowd into the great room that also served as a dining room.

"How do you think Dane knew you are a wolf? At least half," Simon asked as he tapped away on the laptop at the dining table. He paused to select a plate with red potatoes in rosemary sauce and half a boned game hen.

Rhys sat across the table from Simon. "She's something else herself."

"But what? Faery? Demon?"

"Not something I've been around. Ever."

"Seriously? Hell, you've worked with all sorts at Hawkes Associates."

"She puts up my hackles. Could be a familiar."

"Ah, a cat shifter."

"You know I'm not a fan of cats."

Simon had given his cat to a neighbor after taking the job as Rhys's assistant. It wasn't so much the cat hair as the lingering feline scent that stirred up his werewolf.

"She could be dangerous," Simon said. "Can we trust her?"

"I have a feeling cash will keep her in line."

Simon nodded. "Do you remember where William

Montfalcon lived in the eighteenth century? I'd like to plot out a city map and mark our progress."

"You think we should go underground near his former residence?" Rhys considered it for the first time. Yes, why not? They must explore all possibilities. And yet. "I believe William was dead well before I thought Viviane dead."

"So the question I've avoided asking..." Simon began cautiously.

Rhys nodded, knowing. "Who put her in the coffin?"

"I understand you thought her dead, so didn't even consider it back then. But now, have you thought about it?"

On a heavy sigh, Rhys said, "Constantine de Salignac."

"Your brother?"

"You know our history."

Simon whistled.

"I lost track of him at the beginning of the twentieth century." Rhys paced the floor, sure he'd mark a path in the rug before the day was dark. "Who is the Council representative here in Paris?"

"I believe the vampire rep is Vincent Lepore."

"Contact him," Rhys directed. "He should know where I can find Constantine."

"Will do."

"That smells so freakin' good."

Both men glanced at the vision that sauntered in from the hallway. A huge black-and-blue-striped beach towel wrapped about her body. The long dreads gleamed with water droplets. Her skin glowed after a good scrubbing.

"Wonders do not cease," Simon commented. "There was a real girl beneath all that grime."

Dane flipped him the bird.

"Or not." Simon focused back on the laptop, while managing to fork in food with his free hand.

"Help yourself," Rhys offered.

Dane gobbled a carrot stick in crunchy bites. "Where are my clothes? They're not in my room."

"Hopefully burned by now."

"And what the hell am I supposed to do now?" The woman grabbed a plate of potatoes and chicken. "Tromp beneath the city naked? If you guys have some weird sort of ménage planned, I am so not interested."

"I've ordered new clothes for you," Rhys offered, "and proper skulking equipment for Simon and me. I expect the entirety to arrive within the hour. There's a robe in your closet you may use until then."

The woman nodded and seated herself. "This place is pretty spiffy. Mercedes in the garage. Gold fixtures and silk sheets. How rich are you?"

"Filthy," Simon said.

"Filthy is my kind of rich." Dane dug in, smashing the small red potatoes and pouring butter over them. "You get me some pants with big pockets to hold all my loot?"

"No, I ordered you a purse," Rhys assured her.

The look she gave him stirred up a rare grin. She was one woman who wouldn't be caught dead dangling a strappy little purse at her side. He had never taken to those kinds of women. Simple and unassuming was more his sort. Nothing at all like *her*.

"I'm kidding." He poured a goblet of wine and offered the bottle to Simon.

"So," Simon asked as he filled a goblet, "how did you know Rhys is a wolf?"

"He's got the wolf walk," Dane said. "Loose and loping. Predatory and sure. He didn't miss a thing of his surroundings when walking toward the café. But he's different than most wolves."

Rhys inspected the food displayed on the cart. "Maybe I'm not a wolf after all."

She raised her brows. "I'm never wrong. But you could be a half-breed."

"And what, exactly," Simon said quickly to defer the thread from dangerous territory, "are you, then?"

"That's for me to know and you to get screwed."

"I don't think she's trustworthy," Simon offered to Rhys.

"Children, quit fighting."

"But she's an idiot to accept your generosity without then divulging the smallest requested detail."

"She was smart enough to mark me as wolf."

"Lucky guess," Simon said. "And only half-right."

"I knew it," Dane said, with a slash of her fork, which dripped butter across the table. "Now to figure your other half."

"And how long do you think she'll lead us on a goose chase knowing every day puts another ten Gs in her pocket?"

"I can answer that." Dane tapped her fingers methodically on the glass. "I figure I need at least three days and then I'll be able to pay off my debts. A week will set me up for a year."

"Find the coffin—" Rhys pushed his plate aside "—and I'll set you up for life."

"Seriously? Why?"

"Because I can."

"Huh." She swiped a finger through the butter on the plate. "Now I wish it wasn't a legend. Wouldn't mind never having to worry about money again. Will any coffin count?"

"No."

Rhys sensed her disappointment.

While the food looked appetizing, he reluctantly selected the potatoes and meat. He had no hunger, but knew he would need the energy to see him through whatever the days would present.

"So who's the evil vampire in the legend?" Dane asked.

Rhys turned a stare on the woman. "His name is Constantine de Salignac." The evil vampire, indeed. "You heard of him?"

"Sounds not unfamiliar."

"Because you are a familiar?" Simon prompted.

Dane lifted her chin and shoved a forkful of food in her mouth.

"If you know anything about Salignac," Rhys said, "you must tell me."

"I don't, offhand. But I promise you if something comes to mind, I will tell you right away. Deal?"

Rhys nodded, but Simon interrupted with a triumphant, "Yes!" He looked to Rhys. "That was quick. I just emailed Lepore. Told him you wanted to meet him. He's available tomorrow."

"Set up the meet," Rhys said.

One step closer to resurrecting a relationship with a brother he had hoped to never see again.

CHAPTER TWENTY

Paris, 1785

VIVIANE PAID A MAN WEARING ragged wool breeches and a filthy shirt to take Portia's body away on a tumbrel to Les Innocents, the city graveyard. She had no coin, but the silver candelabra from the tepidarium had made the man's eyes light up and he quickly agreed to accept it as payment.

She'd bound Portia's body in the skirts torn from a few of Blanche's gowns. Fine damask, she suspected, would be stolen from her body before it was buried.

"Wait." She scanned about for something of value, and spied a dented pewter pitcher on the cupboard. "Take this," she said, and gave the pitcher to the man, "and promise me you will not unwrap the body."

The man looked over the pitiful piece.

"The candelabra alone will feed your family for a month," she said before he could argue. "Please, respect the dead."

He nodded, and tucked the pitcher under an arm.

A BEAM OF SUNLIGHT MARKED across his ankle. It wasn't warm. It wasn't cold. Rhys stared at it for a while, gauging his slow, relaxed breaths, noting his surroundings in the moist scent of hay, rotting wood, and something fresh… Clean.

"Water," Rhys croaked.

He scrambled across the hay strewn over the hard dirt floor and lifted a tin cup to his mouth. Never had something so simple tasted so good. It washed away the taste of blood.

As the cool water wet his throat, he remembered. His vampire had gotten what it wanted.

Dropping the cup, he gripped the iron bars before him. He knelt, naked, inside a ten-foot-square iron cage, set at the back of an empty barn. Sun beamed through a space in the rotting wood roof. Birds chirped overhead, sifting down straw from a nest.

Rhys pressed his forehead to the bars. He sensed a presence standing off in the shadows near the open barn doors. And he knew what had occurred within the hours of dark and dawn.

"Thank you," Rhys said. And then, "Forgive me."

"Do not ask that of me." Claude Mourreigh stepped forward.

The werewolf was the Marsauceux pack's alpha principal. The pack inhabited the valley east of Dreux. They were a secretive and much maligned pack. Since the Gévaudan attacks midcentury, Claude had been adamant with rules and safety procedures. It had not been one of their own glorified as *La Bête,* but a wise wolf kept his nose to the trail and did not reveal itself to the enemy—man, toting firearms loaded with silver bullets.

Rhys hadn't realized he'd gotten so far from Paris.

No, he would not ask forgiveness from this man who had seen it all, and had suffered far worse for his breed than Rhys could ever imagine. The scar cutting from cheek to cheek and across Claude's nose was ever a reminder of man's fearful stupidity about the unknown.

"What were you up to last night?" Claude asked in his

hoarse, tired voice. He was three centuries old, surely. Werewolves did not live much longer than that. "You are much smarter, Hawkes."

"I left Paris too late. I had not time to find an isolated place for the shift. I didn't realize I was so close to home. Did I… Is the human…?"

"He took talons to the shoulder and across his back, but is not dead. Yet. But he saw you, and a few pack members. You know what that means."

"It would have been better had I killed him." Still kneeling before the bars, Rhys hung his head.

Better for the pack, for then no mortal could claim to have seen a mad wolf that walked on its hind legs and was larger than a man. He and *la lune* engaged in a bitter duel each month. She would ever control him; no enchantment could defeat her silent strength.

Claude turned and stalked away, his well-worn jack-boots flapping against the backs of his knees. When he returned, he stuffed folded clothing through the bars, which landed beside Rhys.

"Dress, and we'll talk. I am not pleased with your actions, Rhys Hawkes. Things have changed between us."

The pack leader strode out of the barn, leaving Rhys nodding in agreement. Werewolves respected him for his darker side, but Claude was well aware the vampire ruled Rhys's werewolf. Claude had been the one to suggest Rhys seek help from Faery to contain his violence.

They had known each other decades, and Rhys had kept his promise to Claude he would harm no one by putting himself away during the full moon. It was a promise he had made to himself, as well.

Now as Rhys gathered the clothing, he saw the blood on his fingers and dashed across his chest. He picked up the tin cup, and with the few droplets of remaining water, tried to clean his transgressions from his skin.

AFTER DRESSING, RHYS FOUND Claude standing before a half-buried boulder that rose from the earth no higher than his knees. Set upon the boulder, a cross had been carved from granite; its highest arm was crumbled and covered in lichen. A single grave marker for so many comrades murdered during the Gévaudan frenzy. The fear of wolves had spread across the country; no wolf—whether natural or a werewolf—had been safe.

Rhys stepped beside Claude and bowed his head. He whispered blessings and crossed himself in deference. Yes, he believed in a god.

"The pack is doing well?" he asked.

"Two births last month," Claude said. "Both healthy baby boys. I am proud of them."

Whether or not the pups were Claude's progeny mattered little; the principal claimed a certain foster parentage to all those born within the pack. It made a tighter group. But it was not always a sexual situation. Each wolf mated for life, and did not have affairs within the pack.

It was the difference between the werewolves and vampires. Rhys suspected vampires would tup whoever was standing before them, be they wife, lover, friend or stranger. Well, he knew it for truth.

Fortunately, when vampire—as now—he followed his heart, which was werewolf.

"I envy your family," he said.

"You will have family someday, Hawkes. You already do."

"Salignac is not family." The words felt bitter on his tongue.

"But he is your brother. Honor that connection."

"I do." He stubbed his toe against the boulder. "I do not always honor it. I will. I must try."

The pack had been Rhys's first look at real family after his mother had died, leaving him to fend on his own at the age of seventeen. Loving, caring, protective in all matters, pack wolves respected one another. It had been his first taste of romantic love as well, for Claude had introduced him to Emeline. She had not been chosen to mate by a pack member because she'd been lame with a gimp right leg after being caught in a trap. Rhys had cared little she limped.

She had stolen his heart, and Claude had approved of their bond. Rhys had not allowed her to be present during the full moon, but he'd always felt his werewolf would never harm her. Emeline had pined for the connection they might share during the full moon; it was when the female werewolf went into heat and needed sex.

Rhys still did not think it cruel to have denied her.

Would his werewolf harm the vampire he now loved? For to think on it, as werewolf, his vampire mind reigned. Surely the vampire should take well to another?

It wasn't so simple as that. It would never be simple.

"I…have fallen in love."

"With a mortal?" Claude's tone was too hopeful. Leave the packs alone, it suggested, find a common mortal and hope she can accept you. You, who are not right, and never will be.

It was the first time Rhys had sensed disdain from Claude.

"She is vampire," he said quickly.

Claude whistled lowly.

"My brother also loves her."

Without looking, Rhys knew Claude shook his head.

The old werewolf was a man of few words. His actions always spoke loudest.

"You are no longer welcome to visit the Marsauceux pack, Hawkes."

Rhys's heart clenched at the announcement, much as it was deserved. "I understand."

He had brought the pack out in werewolf form last night. They'd sensed him, and Claude had known if Rhys were not captured, he would kill.

"What of Orlando?" Claude asked. "Where is the boy now?"

Rhys had taught Orlando to get away from all humans during the full moon, though as a full-blood werewolf, Orlando had not the worry he would attack someone for blood. Werewolves sought to mate during the full moon, and if they came across a mortal female, well, then…

"He is safe, I'm sure."

"You have no idea where he is," Claude hissed.

"He's been doing well in Paris. Enjoying the city's extravagances."

"Tupping whores, no doubt. Send him home. I no longer trust the boy in your care. The pack will welcome him."

Rhys nodded. "I will send Orlando to you immediately."

It would be as if sending away his only child. But for the danger his neglect may cause Orlando, Rhys knew it was the only option.

"Thank you for your lenience, principal. I will not set foot on pack territory again."

And he walked away, knowing the werewolf tracked him until he could no longer see him. It was the hardest walk Rhys had ever to make. To walk away from his mentor in shame. To walk away from trust because he had destroyed that fine strand of acceptance.

To give up the one piece of family he had.

Swallowing, he beat a fist against his heart, but it did not stop the tears that watered his eyes.

He had never felt more alone.

"SHE ARRIVED BEFORE SUNRISE. Refused to leave," Orlando said as he took Rhys's coat and shook off the rain.

He'd stopped by his country home after leaving Dreux to check that it was still locked up tight, and spent that evening alone, away from mortals and gorgeous vampiresses who would tempt his werewolf.

There he'd pulled on some boots and a serviceable coat. He tired of wearing the satins and silk stockings required to attend the Salon Noir. He simply wanted to be himself. Focus must return to investigating the crime.

But she was inextricably woven into every breath and movement Rhys made, or intended to make. "Viviane?"

"She is in William's bedchamber. How are you, Rhys?"

"Well enough."

He could not meet the boy's eyes. So many good times he and Orlando had shared. They lived simply, working the land for their food and chopping wood for warmth. Play, entertainment, love, it was all fashioned from the heart. "I did not make it to safety on the night of the full moon."

"Oh." Horror in the boy's utterance.

How many times had Orlando been the one to lock up Rhys as the clouds moved away to reveal the moon? Rhys would see to it he would never bear that burden again.

"The Marsauceux pack prevented me from committing murder. My vampire wanted blood." Rhys exhaled. "Claude wants you to return to the pack."

"I won't." Orlando fisted his hands and thrust back his

shoulders in sudden defense. "I am not a pack wolf. I'm like you, Rhys. We make our own way. Just like you've always said."

"Orlando, I regret ever giving you the idea a wolf alone was a boon. The pack provides family."

"You are my family. You are—" He swung about and punched the closest thing, which was the bookshelves. Books tumbled to the floor. "You are like my father."

"And you, my son." Swallowing, Rhys clamped a palm on the boy's shoulder. Neither looked up. Orlando huffed, fighting a yowl or perhaps sobs. "Claude does not trust me as your guardian. I do not trust myself. I should have never left you alone in the city."

"But I can take care of myself. You know that! I roamed the woods edging the city and my werewolf was content beneath the full moon. It is you who must be away. You were doing what you must…."

"Boy." Rhys pulled him in for a hug. "Please, do this for me. Just while I'm in Paris?"

"But if I go to the pack—"

If he joined the pack he would have family, might be mated with a female and would have a good life. They both knew it was for the best, but not necessarily the better.

Orlando nodded and looked away. "Another day, then. I am to see Annabelle today. I won't leave her waiting as William had done."

"You didn't promise her riches?"

"No." A sly smile cracked the boy's solemn expression. "Only a tumble."

AN ANGEL SLEPT, HER HEAD nestled upon the pillow. Pale skin, dark hair, pursed rosebud lips. A study in dark and light. Much like himself. Yet Viviane's soul did not struggle against itself. She could walk the world knowing exactly who she was, what she wanted, what she must do to survive.

And what she must do was succumb. A cruel notion to Viviane. To Rhys, as well. What if he could find a patron who would agree to blood her, yet stand back and allow her and Rhys to have a relationship?

Fool. No vampire would do such a thing, not when the prize of a bloodborn vampiress was offered.

Rhys stroked her cheek and she stirred.

"I could not stay away," she murmured. "It's been two days. You were able to get to safety?"

He mumbled a positive tone, and leaned in to bury his face in her hair. What was safety? Nothing tangible, that was sure, more a feeling.

She slid her hand into the placket of her skirt, pulled something out and placed it on Rhys's palm. Clasping her fingers over his, she held there for a moment. "I had no idea what it meant, or who it belonged to until you told me."

At first sight of the talon, Rhys sucked in a hissing breath. He clasped his fist about the precious memento and pressed it to his mouth.

Emeline's pleas to allow her to approach his werewolf during the full moon screeched at him now. Would things have gone differently if he'd trusted himself?

No.

"I am sorry," she said. "I removed the ribbon. It is not a thing to decorate, and should not be considered jewelry, but instead a piece of your heart. Keep it close, and remember the good times."

He nodded. "It is hideous, but it is as if you've returned her to my heart. Thank you."

"Do not grant me favor. I took it willingly and with macabre fascination."

"It is no longer in Constantine's hands. That is all that matters."

He kissed her brow. Inhaled her innocent beauty. Indulged in her seductive allure. "Thank you. Simply…thank you."

"You, Rhys Hawkes—" she leaned in, her lips brushing his ear "—are all that I want."

He needed that acceptance.

CHAPTER TWENTY-ONE

"THIS IS A WARM, comfortable home," Viviane commented as she strode past the table where Rhys sat finishing the last of his meal.

He offered a chunk of bread but she shook her head. The man ate as if famished. She couldn't understand how his vampire allowed it. Surely, it must make him sick.

He followed her, baguette in hand, as she took the steps to look over the small library. A few books lay on the floor, which she picked up and replaced on the shelf. "So many books. You said this is a werewolf's home?"

They'd come to terms after she'd given him the talon. She could never erase her guilt—she had worn the talon taken from his lover—but they understood one another.

Viviane knew she could never replace Emeline. She didn't want to. But should she tell him about the wolf she had slain? It felt like betrayal not mentioning it, but she wasn't confident he'd accept another brutal truth so soon after the other one.

"William was peaceful and contemplative," he said. "I'm sure he read them all. I fear he is not missing, but rather dead."

"Why so?"

"I spoke to a woman who knew him intimately."

"A lover?"

"A prostitute, actually. She has been waiting for his return. William gave her no indication he would not return. Has Constantine said anything to you about his investigation?"

"Only that he would find the wolf responsible and punish him justly. You don't think—?"

"William's disappearance is too curious not to at least wonder if there is a connection. I…went to the site where it happened."

Viviane pressed her fingers to her mouth. To imagine the horrors Henri and Blanche must have experienced.

And you fret, wolf slayer?

Oh, she wanted to confess to Rhys but could not.

"It was cleaned up, but I scented William distinctly."

"So he was the one?"

"I suspect so, but until we find him in hiding, there can be no justice."

"Constantine sent his men out searching. Perhaps you and your brother—"

"Should work together? I don't believe that will go over at all."

"I suppose not." Viviane ran her fingers along the books. A dizzy wave fell over her.

Rhys wrapped his arms around her waist from behind. He smelled like the burgundy sauce that had seasoned the roasted fowl and it distracted her from morbid thoughts.

"Are you all right here? We can leave?"

"No, I need…distraction. To think about something else."

She felt safe with Rhys. As if she could tell him anything. So why did she not?

A kiss tickled along her neck. She would not walk away from this gift. The gift of love. Yet she was duly aware she had not spoken her love to him. She could not speak it out loud, for that would make it too difficult when she must betray him.

Viviane slid her fingers over the book spines, and spied a brilliant red one. "This one is pretty."

She tugged out the narrow volume. Red moire covered the end boards and glossy gold embossing styled the title. "So…." She hadn't seen the word before, and sounding it out was a challenge.

Rhys traced beneath the next letter with a fingernail. "That's the *n*. How does it sound?"

She made the letter's sound, and added it to the first letters. He spoke the next letters to her, patiently waiting for her to put them all together, and finally she declared, "Sonnets!"

"Yes, very good. Shall we read a few? It may distract your thoughts."

"That would be splendid."

He twirled her about. The worn gray velvet chaise longue was wide enough for both of them. Her back to his chest, and one of his arms about her waist, Viviane paged through the book until she arrived at a short verse with many small words. She recognized one of them. "Love!"

"You know all the important words, I see. Now, do you want to give this one a try? A few sentences?"

"You won't mock me?"

"Darling, lover mine." He kissed her head. "Why would I do that?"

She remembered the cold reception knowledge of her lacking skills had gotten from Constantine. The two men could not be more opposite. Pity Constantine had not learned compassion and kindness from his brother.

Nestling against her lover's body to study the page, she sounded out the word following *love*. Rhys only suggested help when she paused overlong. He did not rush or chide her for mistakes, gently encouraging she retry the sounds together.

"'Love alters not with his brief hours and weeks,'" she reread, gaining each word after much practice. And then the next line, "'But bears it out even to the edge of doom.'"

"Excellent," he encouraged. "Shakespeare wrote some gorgeous verse. You're coming along well with your studies, Viviane. Soon you will be reading through the entire wall behind us. Want to try another line?"

In fact, she read two more lines, and was rewarded with a kiss. Master Rosemont never did that.

"You will spoil me if I am rewarded with a kiss for every sentence I get correct."

"You deserve to be spoiled."

"Mmm, you taste like rosemary." She kissed him again, gliding her tongue along his lower lip. "I haven't been able to eat for two centuries. Sometimes the smell of food maddens me. I want to taste, but know it'll make me sick. You give me that splendid taste. But how can you eat?"

"My werewolf must be fed."

"Your vampire does not get sick?"

"No, but it retaliates against the wolf during the full moon."

Spreading her fingers over his chest, she tugged the drawstring around his neck loose. The soft hairs beneath tickled as she explored. Finding his nipple made him tense when she touched the hard little bead.

"Seems you've decided the lesson is finished," he remarked.

"Oh no, more, please. Will you read to me?"

"Only if you promise your hand will not stray lower and distract my concentration."

"I'll try my best." She glided her fingers over his abdomen.

"Wicked vampiress. Pity there are no pictures, eh?" He paged through the book and began to read.

Viviane closed her eyes to the melody. Rhys's voice entered her mind on soft intonations, and touched her soul with a resonating timbre. And in the deep, abiding recitation, his words glided along her flesh as if a lover's tender kisses. She'd never been read to before. It was as much an aphrodisiac as foreplay.

When finished, Rhys paused, sighing, as if to take in what he'd read. Viviane did the same, nestling her head against the hard muscle strapping his shoulder. "More," she whispered. "Please?"

She spread her fingers across his stomach, riding the tips of hair under his breeches. He moaned as a fingernail grazed his erection. "One more, and then..." she prompted.

"Very well, one more. And then."

This sonnet spoke of a lover searching for his heart and finding it in the most unlikely of places. In a woman he had never thought to consider. Viviane smiled to think they were much the same. What love she would not have known had she not given this man the slightest of considerations? For his pursuing her without relenting she must be thankful. She trusted him completely. So much so, she could lie next to him and expose her greatest secret, and have him but embrace her and encourage her to master her reading.

When the last word was read, she whispered, "I am yours."

"Are you? Can you be mine?"

She didn't reply. Rhys clasped the hand she'd held across his stomach and kissed it. It was a bitter truth that must be abided. They both knew she must go to Constantine for patronage.

"Tell me how the faery enchanted you," she said. "I've always wanted to meet a faery, but is not their ichor addictive to vampires?"

"Very. I did not take her ichor. But she gave me a great gift. Claude Mourreigh, a pack leader, is the one who suggested I seek help from Faery to tame my vampire. He had said the faery would come to me if I called...."

Rhys had never seen a faery, though he believed in them. They were supposed to take quite well to a werewolf. Rhys's werewolf, though, was always controlled by his vampire, so he doubted a faery would enjoy the vicious company.

Cressida was the name Claude had given him, but he had been told not to use it until invited to do so.

Rhys fell to his knees deep in the forest surrounding his home, west of Versailles. Spreading out his arms, yet keeping his head down, he opened himself to what may come. He called out blessings to the forest, the trees, the earth, and all things natural, over and over.

The leaves rustled. Not far off a ground snake slithered across the crisp autumn leaves. A cricket chirped. A crow squawked, midflight.

A shimmer of cold air touched him as if frost. Rhys gritted his teeth at the icy sensation. Something glittered in the air before him. And amidst that glamorous atmosphere, she materialized.

Small, thin and pale, yet so beautiful. Streams of white hair spilled over her shoulders and past her hips, wavering like the sea. She wore a gossamer sheath that exposed her legs and arms. Rarely had Rhys seen a woman wearing so little.

"I am Rhys Hawkes," he said, still kneeling.

"I know who you are. I missed your birth, Rhys Hawkes."

"I'm...sorry?"

"Too late for you now. We prefer half-breeds when they are newly born." She walked to him, yet her feet did not crunch the leaves. Perhaps she floated above the ground; he didn't want to look too closely. "You have had a time of it. Your dual natures have no intention of embracing."

"My vampire is vicious," he explained. "It needs to be shackled. I...don't wish to harm innocents."

"What of those who are not innocent?" She bent before him, bringing her bright violet eyes close to his face. "What of murderers and cutpurses, and lechers most foul?"

"I am no man to judge," Rhys answered. "I do not wish to take life. Ever."

The faery stood abruptly. "Honorable. But dull." She sighed, obviously disappointed in him. "So, what shall it be?"

"Claude Mourreigh tells me you might enchant my vampire in a manner it no longer controls my werewolf."

"That is a tall order, Rhys Hawkes. You think I can control the moon? You are quite ridiculous." Pouting, she gave him her shoulder, arms crossed.

"Forgive me. It is what I was told. What...what can you do for me? Please."

"I may be able to shackle your vampire throughout the month. Keep it buried within you. But anger and violence are too powerful to harness."

"I would avoid getting angry."

She smirked. "You would be a man alone if you could master that. And do not expect me to challenge the moon. Surely your werewolf requires release once in a while."

"Yes, during the full moon. But only then. I will do anything you ask, give you anything—"

"Of course you will." The faery shook her shoulders and wings unfurled behind her, stretching out to touch the canvas of branches and glistening like oil on water. "You will owe me a boon for enchanting your vampire, Rhys Hawkes. Do you agree?"

"Yes," he hastened to answer, and then wondered what exactly the boon would be. And in the next moment, he did not care. The prospect of finally controlling his vampire was too great. "What need I do?"

"Stand. And do not move."

It happened swiftly. The forest floor seemed to rise and smack Rhys in the face.

In actuality, the faery lifted a great glamour and forced it into Rhys. His body took in the ancient faery magick and sorted it through his veins and muscles and clung to it as a starving man to a cleaned bone. It became Rhys. It tendriled about his vampire. It slid along his werewolf.

Rhys landed on the forest floor, stomach first, arms slamming the ground, his cheek smacking cold earth.

When he woke the sky had darkened. Wind brushed leaves over his arms.

Rhys rolled to his back and examined his hands. He was alive, though he felt as if he'd been plowed over by a team of horses.

Had the enchantment worked?

"Of course it did." The faery appeared right before his face.

Rhys scrambled to stand. The faery hovered, beating her gossamer wings slowly.

"Now my boon," she instructed.

"Anything."

"You will give to me your firstborn, Rhys Hawkes."

Rhys gaped. That was quite a boon. And yet, why not? He had no designs on family. What was a child to him? "Very well."

"I will return for the boon when it exists," the faery said. "You have earned the right to name me Cressida."

"Thank you, Cressida. How will I know—"

She fluttered away, through the treetops, seeming to grow smaller until she was the size of an insect.

"How will I know when the boon exists?" Rhys finished. "She will return? When the child is born?"

It confused him, but semantics mattered little.

Now, he would walk through the month and see if his vampire riled his werewolf to murder. If he could make it to the full moon, then the faery had served him well.

"That's incredible," Viviane whispered. "But she asked very much of you."

"It was easy enough to make the bargain when I gained so much. Of course, I was young then. Children were not something I would have considered."

"Do you want a child now?"

"No," he said. "And yes. But I try not to think about it, because I know the power of Faery is great."

He shifted on the chaise and the book slid across Viviane's lap.

She caught the book and a small folded paper fell out of it. She handed it to Rhys. "What do you make of this?"

Rhys studied the paper. "The handwriting is small and erratic. It's difficult to decipher. It appears a check of sorts for services rendered. Exact services are not stated. Nor are the parties involved listed."

"How much?"

"Hmm? Oh, about a thousand livres."

"Is that very much?"

"About two of your fancy gowns. Enough to feed a man for a year."

Rhys stroked his thumb over the embossed letterhead. An intertwined *C* and *S* formed the monogram. He sat up abruptly.

"What is it?"

"Huh? Oh…" He winced. "Just a bit of an ache in my belly. I tend to eat for my werewolf, but forget my vampire body cannot endure a feast. Why don't you let me walk you home, then I'll go for a run?"

In spite of his outwardly calm demeanor, Rhys's anger brewed inwardly. He knew the initials on the paper could only be from one person.

CHAPTER TWENTY-TWO

RHYS GROWLED AT THE FOOTMAN holding post in the Hôtel de Salignac lobby. The man, a mortal enthralled by receiving a regular bite, wisely stepped back.

As he marched down the grand marble hallway toward the ballroom, Rhys's honed senses did not pick up a particular scent. There were plenty of odors, most of them female and hungry.

Ahead, the rumble of male conversation grew louder, more aggressive. Rhys rushed down the steps and into the ballroom.

Two tribe vampires prowled before Constantine. They were dressed in breeches, shirts and jackboots, riding attire or fighting ready.

Rhys lifted his chest, bulking up his frame and bringing all attention to him. The vampires sought command from their leader. Constantine stepped between them, making a small gesture they remain back.

A mirthless smile curved his brother's mouth. "The cat comes to the mouse," Salignac announced. "Or is that the dog to its master?"

"You are not my master," Rhys stated. "Are you so enamored of your patronship over so many you automatically include all as your underlings? Do your tribe members bow to you, as well?"

"Not at all. We respect one another. My men are of their own minds. Why are you in my home?"

"I thought a brotherly chat in order."

"As a matter of fact, I was coming for you."

"Is that so?"

Constantine looked aside. One tribe member dropped a length of chain and on the end of it dangled an iron shackle. Or was that silver?

Rhys felt his hackles rise. "What is this? Doesn't look like a simple escort from the city."

"You did it to yourself, brother."

The feral instinct to shift tingled in his shoulders, but Rhys fought against it. He would not give Constantine the satisfaction.

"You deny you murdered Henri Chevalier and his wife?"

"What?" Constantine shifted uncomfortably. "You mock me."

"I don't know why I didn't guess it immediately. The one person standing between you and the prospect of a bloodborn child. It was you who hired William to murder her patron. I found the bill!"

Constantine chuckled, small and self-important.

"So you could have Viviane for yourself." Rhys made the connection like that.

He wanted to swing the chain about his brother's neck and choke him, but that was not the way to kill a vampire. Nor to serve justice as a representative of the Council.

"Brilliant lies to cover your bloody truths," Constantine said slyly. He approached Rhys, not cowering, and perhaps anticipating Rhys would not swing out at him. Their rivalries had always been private.

"Do not think my men will believe your stories. We are united in Nava. I care for them. They see justice done to any who should act against us."

Rhys would not allow Constantine to work this in his favor. "Henri Chevalier was not a Nava member."

"He was a friend."

"Is that how you treat your friends? Wait. Yes, I believe it is so. For if you treat your very brother so poorly, surely friends receive the same lacking regard. Henri's death was a means for you to gain the bloodborn female you crave."

"You filthy dog."

Rhys mirrored the vampire's circling moves, keeping an eye to his next attack. "That epitaph is tired."

"Lice-ridden mongrel."

"Much better."

"You stole her from me! You put your filthy hands to her!"

A triumphant smile curled Rhys's mouth. But the triumph lasted mere moments. This revenge was bittersweet. While he enjoyed serving the coup de grâce to his nemesis, he no longer wanted to involve Viviane.

"She is mine!" Constantine swung at him with his fist.

Gripping the man while he was midswing, Rhys brought up his knee to crush into Constantine's face. The vampire, released, stumbled and landed on the ballroom floor. He spat dark blood onto a white section of the harlequin tiles.

The tribe moved in.

"Stay back," Constantine growled at his underlings. "This is between me and the abomination."

Rhys pounced and landed before his brother. "She belongs to no one."

Rhys pounded the vampire's face with a fist. He did not fear injury, for he knew when attacked so directly the vampire couldn't summon its fangs, a protective means that kept its weapons from being broken. "Most especially not to the vampire lord who thinks to place her within a silver cage and keep her for himself."

"Would that I had such a cage. The silver would keep you out!"

Constantine shucked off his frockcoat. The two circled one another. The acrid scent of aggression flooding from the tribe stung Rhys's nostrils.

Constantine charged. Rhys blocked the first punch, then took a boot to his gut. He did not relent. As a child, he had watched his older brother spar with other boys, cheering him on, hoping some day Constantine would teach him his scrapping skills. The day of his puberty arrived too soon, and Rhys came into his werewolf and vampire in one remarkably horrific night.

His brother did spar with him after that, but it was not to teach but to accuse and pummel.

Constantine had taught Rhys real hate. Yet always, he'd attempted to win his brother's approval by luring unsuspecting mortals in for his brother to bite. But Rhys's vampire had been wild in those early days and his werewolf could not be contained.

Constantine had been disgusted by his brother's mad blood hunger. He'd once found Rhys naked and hiding in the shed the morning following his werewolf's rampage. Rhys still remembered the hot spit hitting his face—his brother's assessment of his worth.

He'd grown stronger and more skilled over the years; finally, he and Constantine would have their match.

Constantine's men did not move to stop the fisticuffs.

"She will die without me," Constantine said, huffing from exertion as a mortal would. "Do you think to steal her away only to watch that happen? Or perhaps that is your finest revenge? I understand now. Seduce her toward a slow death. Well played, Hawkes."

Rhys took another fist to the face. His blood tasted foul. "Viviane has asked you to leave her be. Why will you not respect her wishes?"

"Because she is being tupped by a bloody wolf!"

Rhys swung wide, his palm stiff. The heel of it connected with Constantine's shoulder and sent the vampire flying backward.

"Love knows no prejudice," Rhys said. Rolling back his shoulder, he prepared for the next blow.

"Love?" The vampire, sprawled before his tribe members, studied his bloody skull with a fingertip. "You are incapable of loving a vampire as she deserves. Most especially Viviane. She is one of a kind."

"Yes, the ultimate broodmare for your tribe. Did you ask Viviane if that is her desire?"

"Females have no say!"

"You are incapable of knowing her heart," Rhys said. "Your idea of love hurts her."

"You have poisoned her mind. How dare she? To take up with a wolf?"

To mate with a wolf, Rhys thought proudly.

"Stay away from her," Rhys said. He spat bloody spittle onto the marble floor. "She's mine."

"You have ordered her death," Constantine countered. "Slowly. Cruelly. Do you know what happens when a female is denied her patron?"

"Viviane has survived for months without taking from her former patron. As you've said, she is unique. Because she is bloodborn she needn't take from a patron so frequently."

"She cannot survive forever. She needs vampire blood running in her veins. She's lived over two centuries. Can you imagine waking one evening to a woman aged two hundred years? It happens swiftly. She will rapidly age and change to dust. Can you do that, Hawkes? Hold the dust of your lover in your hand and be thankful for your selfish decision to make her yours?"

"You know not."

"I do! I have let many of my own die recently. She demanded it of me! Promised me her heart if I would devote mine to her. Wicked vampiress. And look how she thanks me?"

"What did William do for you?" Rhys insisted. He must get his brother's confession.

Constantine stood. "You know."

"He killed Viviane's patron. But he would not have done so. Ever. I know William. He was a gentle man. What did you do to Montfalcon to make him commit murder?"

Constantine spat blood, and dragged his tongue along the bottoms of his fangs. "It is helpful to have a witch in one's pocket."

"A witch?"

"Do you know what our children could be?" Constantine continued. "A son would be the most powerful vampire Paris has seen. He would be the key to strengthening Nava's fading bloodline. I must have Viviane."

"As a commodity," Rhys barked. "Could you patron her knowing she would never love you?"

"With the blood comes a certain attachment. The swoon. Eventually she will not know what it was like to be without me. I have kept your secret too long, brother. Now you force my hand."

"My secret?"

The vampire lord whistled. From across the ballroom

half a dozen more vampires marched forth, wielding chains. The clink of iron threatened.

"You are the only man I know of in Paris who is possessed of an unnatural lust—a werewolf who seeks blood. Seems to me you are the only suspect."

"That is madness! You've confessed—"

"To nothing, save the heartbreak in knowing my brother is guilty of a heinous crime."

Much as Rhys wanted to stand and fight, he did not want the justice Constantine would mete out should his minions manage to wrangle him.

Lifting a foot, he heeled Constantine in the chest, shoving him backward, into the klatch of oncoming vampires.

Rhys clenched his fists. Turning and running away felt wrong. It was not like him to *not* stand and face whatever challenge sneered at him.

Yet his werewolf wanted free. To slash out at injustice. To prove Constantine's mad accusation by revealing his wicked darkness.

"You run, brother!" Constantine called from the ballroom. "I will not relent. You've gone too far. You will be punished!"

Rhys slapped the wall nearest him and swore. He had no doubt Constantine would accuse him and find success for he had the entire tribe behind him and Rhys had no one.

Racing toward the exit, he struggled with his new cowardice.

But it was not a fear of facing his brother that pushed him down the cobbled street and toward Viviane's home. It was the call to keep her safe. For now Constantine had played his hand, he would not cease until he owned the one thing he desired most.

RHYS DID NOT RETURN to William's home, so Viviane had returned to Henri's estate and waited. He did not appear the following day, and she began to worry. He'd walked from her arms after a blissful afternoon of making love and reading poetry to one another. She did not suspect she had said anything to keep him away.

Which meant he was either investigating the murders, or something was really wrong. Had he decided against an affair with her? He'd been relentless in her pursuit, and now…nothing.

A half-moon scythed the sky and drowsed through a window above the butcher table. Out of sorts, she passed through the silver-shadowed kitchen, fists clenched at her thighs. When her skirts snagged on a chair leg, she kept walking. The chair clattered onto the tiles in her wake.

Here the moonlight glimmered on the crystal chandelier still on the floor. The currier would pick it up tomorrow in payment of Henri's bill for the stable supplies. The vultures had picked this home clean.

Viviane stopped before the constellation of crystal droplets, guttered candles and arabesquing iron. A tear dropped onto her cheek. Feeling her entire body begin to quake, she struggled to maintain composure.

Never let them see your weakness.

Never had she shed tears for anything. Anyone. Now she cried for herself. She had begun to love Rhys. Where was he? The moon was not full; he did not need to be away from her.

Shoving the heavy iron chandelier, she managed to push it against the wall. Crystals shattered and beeswax candles snapped in half and clattered across the floor. The tinkle of crystal skittering on the tiles mimicked the furious anger racing along her spine and neck.

Grasping the heavy iron bar that circled the chandelier,

Viviane sank to her knees and pressed her forehead to it. Her skirt spread out behind her and she tore open the top laces on her constricting bodice.

Viviane slapped a hand across the broken crystals.

Her heart had abandoned itself to a promise of happiness in Rhys Hawkes's arms. And tonight, without a word to her, he had taken her heart and crushed it beneath his heel.

"I must go out. Erase Rhys's brutal betrayal from my thoughts."

With blood.

CHAPTER TWENTY-THREE

RHYS ALMOST WALKED PAST the thin girl in tattered dress and no shoes, but her bird chirps were too sweet to ignore. She held a tiny carved shape in her frail hand. The long beak of it immediately told the species, and his heart pulsed.

She asked but six sous, a pittance that would likely buy her a loaf of bread. Rhys pressed a gold louis d'or into her palm and told her to spend it at the bread shop on rue Dauphine, one of Orlando's favorite haunts. He knew the proprietress would give the girl correct change and not steal from her.

Striding the bridge, which crossed at the end of the Tuileries, Rhys shoved a hand in the deep pocket sewn inside his frockcoat and felt the wooden bird. Smooth and small, so delicate. Like Viviane's trust.

He strode by the hawkers and merchants edging the bridge and landed the soft grass fronting the octagon pool at the end of the royal gardens. The day had been overcast and now night had fallen, an eerie fog hung level with the second-floor windows. Rain sprinkled his face. The weather had cleared the park of the finer crowd who did not care to get their clothing wet or muddied.

Happiness carried him through the heady perfume of roses and greenery and toward the rue Saint-Honoré. Despite the weather, the street was abustle with carriages headed toward the Palais Royal for a night of gambling, drink and debauchery. He had never felt the desire to drink himself to oblivion. In Viviane's arms he'd found a sweet surrender beyond bliss.

He'd not been able to face her after speaking with his brother. He'd needed time—and needed to shrug off the change that had begun to shift him to werewolf. He'd sent word to the Council today that his efforts had uncovered a suspect but that he needed confirmation.

He'd then gone to the brothel and given Annabelle more than enough gold to see her put up in an apartment on the left bank, with the prospect of doing seamstress work for the landlord. It goaded at him that Orlando cared for one of such little means. And though Orlando must leave the city, he could at least allow that he would know Annabelle would be well in his absence.

A scream cracked through the cluttered streets like a pistol shot. Rhys followed the carriages and people through twilight's glitter of street lamps toward the noise. They gathered about someone.

Stretched at an awkward angle, her head back and one leg wrenched under, the young woman's arm bled, the flesh shredded at her shoulder. Held by an elder woman, her close-spaced eyes were wide, her screams frantic and laced with bloody spittle.

In the middle of the cobbled street, sprawled across the muddy gutter, lay a wolf, blood oozing from its midsection.

A wolf in the city? The sight clenched at Rhys's gut. It was larger than the average natural wolf. It had attacked the woman; Rhys knew to glance at the wounds. But the beast had not done fatal damage—it hadn't time.

The wolf's killer, poised over it, her hand still on the knife blade, did not see Rhys approach. She panted, her arms strong, muscles flexing and fingers firm about the knife handle. Jaw gritted tight, she finished dragging the blade from sternum to gut.

Brave to approach a wolf attacking another. Yet so vicious, animalistic, as she remained over the kill, breathing in its death scent.

"It attacked without provocation," someone muttered from the crowd circling the hideous scene. "She is so strong."

"It was ravenous."

As he approached, arms spread in placation, Rhys bent cautiously to allow the killer to see him. He heard a whisper from the crowd, "Wolf slayer."

The killer turned to him, her blue eyes vibrant. Blood smeared her lips.

"Viviane?"

Recognition softened her tense jaw. She released the knife and it clattered onto the cobblestones.

Rhys moved quickly to pull her from the wolf's body. She did not fold herself into his embrace, nor did he do anything more than hold her back when her body wanted to remain crouched over the kill.

"Mon Dieu." He recognized the fur, a unique ginger fur, the belly streaked with white. Such knowledge cut him through the sternum with an intangible blade.

He pushed Viviane aside.

Aware she stumbled and landed her palms on the street, Rhys muttered a negligent apology. His focus remained on the wolf's body, not long dead.

"There is nothing to see here!" he shouted to the crowd. Anger crackled his words. Heartbreak delivered them with a tight cut. "The beast is dead."

It pained him to name it a beast. But better to clear the crowd quickly. He wasn't sure how much time he had.

"See to the woman," he directed someone standing before him. "I'll remove the wolf."

Legs shuffled and people were drawn out of their marvel to action.

He lifted the wolf's cumbersome body. Blood spilled from its gut over his chest and arms, soaking hot against his skin. Rhys tightened his jaw to keep his composure and hold down his rising bile. His hackles stiffened and his innate senses wanted to howl at the moon for this tragedy, but he bit off the urge.

Viviane held his gaze, the knife somehow again clutched in her hand. Her gaping mouth said nothing. There was nothing to say. She'd protected innocent mortals. Yet she had also committed a heinous crime.

Rhys nudged his way between two people. "Stand back! It may be rabid!" He gritted his teeth to speak the foul accusation. "Do you wish to be exposed?" That cleared his path.

He ran, Viviane in tow, down the street and dodged into the first narrow alleyway. He wanted to run from this cruel city and into the country. No time. And he would never get past the guards at the city wall with a dead wolf in his arms.

"Rhys, where are you taking it?"

"To safety."

He heard Viviane flick her blade out at someone and say, "Do not follow! The beast is foaming at the mouth!"

He reached the Chevalier stables, and Rhys slipped inside and gently laid the wolf where straw had loosened from a neat stack. Blood pooled onto the dirt floor.

Viviane closed the door and stalked before the corpse. "I will not have that thing in here. It would have killed the woman!"

"You ensured that would not happen," he hissed.

She reared from his vitriolic response. He had no patience for reassuring kindnesses now.

"Why would he have done something like that? He would not," Rhys said firmly. "He must…not be well."

"What are you talking about? It is but a beast. I don't know how it got through the gates—oh, *sacre bleu.*"

The shift began. Fur stretched and receded into flesh. When a werewolf died, or was murdered in its wolf form, it always, eventually reverted to were shape. Rhys had recognized the fur and was thankful he'd gotten to him when he had.

He would be more thankful had this hideous crime never occurred.

Viviane slapped her palms over her mouth. Her muffled scream disturbed Mordaunt, who snorted and heeled the floor. The horses hadn't so much as moved during the wolf's shift.

Rhys put a hand over the man's blood-soaked ginger hair and stroked it from his closed eyelids. His gut was split open, the intestines spilling out. The smell viciously assaulted his nose and he choked back a howl.

Viviane gasped. "It is the boy."

"Orlando Thomas. His parents died when he was twelve. I've looked after him since. I considered myself a father to him. He never disputed that."

"But— Why would he attack? Werewolves, they do not—"

"I cannot know. Orlando would never harm anyone."

Forcing himself to look over the young man's body, Rhys winced at the sight of his genitals. The flesh was dotted with pustules, forming an angry rash. A symptom he had never before seen, but had heard of.

"Syphilis. He must have contracted it from a brothel

whore." And he'd only just come from seeing Annabelle. He hadn't noticed her ill. "Damn, I should have kept a closer eye on him. Claude will never forgive me."

"Sickness made him do this?" Viviane approached, but did not lean down. "I am so sorry. I... *Sacre bleu,* I've killed your friend. Yet another wolf..."

Yet another? Rhys closed his eyes. God help him.

Her skirt swished Rhys's shoulder as she turned away. Quick to react, he caught her at the open door and pinned her against the frame. "You did not know."

"Please, do not think this is retaliation against the hurt you have caused me. I reacted," her words warbled. "He would have torn off her arm. Or worse! His wolf was so big, standing on its hind legs. He was a monster!"

"In retaliation?"

"You do not love me. You just left me!"

Must they do this now? "I was busy today, with Constantine," he said lowly. "We will discuss this when the time is appropriate."

"Yes. Yes. Please, I cannot look at him. Take him away. Get him away from my home."

He pressed her hard against the door frame, keeping her from escape. "You do not get to control this situation. He was my friend."

Tears stained her cheeks. "I'm sorry."

"I know you are." Rhys touched her cheek, his fingers shaking. So difficult not to slap her, to deliver her punishment. *Wolf slayer.* "Give me time with him. Yes? Send the maid out with sheets, blankets, something."

"Portia is—" She nodded, and he released her. "I'll be out with them right away."

HOURS PASSED AND RHYS did not come inside. Viviane paced the vast music room floor, now empty of furniture, including the harpsichord. She wondered all sorts of scenarios. Had he wrapped the young man's body in the blanket and taken it away to be burned or buried?

Or was he still out there, mourning a lost friend?

She had murdered his friend!

There had been times Viviane had walked right past a battling domestic couple or once witnessed a horse biting an old man. She tendered no concern for mortals and their pain. Yet the victim had been so young. Blond ringlets springing at each ear. Pretty in her blue gown. She may have been a fine lady's maid. *Like Portia.*

Rarely did a wolf enter the city and attack a human, even in the winter when food was scarce.

Rhys suspected the boy had syphilis, which she did know could drive a man to insanity. In proof, the hospital Bicêtre overflowed with the sick and insane. How awful to have watched the wolf change to human form and then to see the injury cleaving open his abdomen. A cut she had delivered with macabre zest.

A vicious reaction she could have stopped, for that first stab had killed the beast, cut into the heart and ceased its struggles. But Viviane had continued to pull the knife through fur and cartilage to the soft, giving belly.

Some darkness in her had arisen. The same had emerged when she'd first journeyed to Paris. She'd wanted to cut out the untouchable wickedness within her. To release it. To punish it for her descent into an abyss she feared never escaping. And to strike out for Portia's death.

If she had accepted Constantine's offer that first evening after Henri's death none of this would have happened.

But self-preservation was firmly embedded within her psyche.

As she paced the floor, the hungry pining in her gut told her nothing could be as she wished. She needed a patron.

A consistent supply of blood so she would not wither from the weak mortal blood, which made her *believe* she were living.

Why were the females so weak? Male vampires who had been created required a few draughts from their creator to survive, and then they went on to patron their own kin.

She clasped her throat, feeling a genuine need for sustaining blood, which she had not got to answer before encountering the attacking wolf. But was it normal hunger, or a more life-preserving desire? She did not know.

"I am not weak. I refuse to be!"

Drawing aside the window sash, Viviane gasped at sight of Rhys, standing knee-deep in a large hole in the center of the courtyard. A body wrapped in a wool blanket lay at the edge of the hole.

Viviane leaned out the window. "You cannot bury him there!"

Dirt landed the mound at the head of the grave. Sweat and mud smeared Rhys's face.

"Bring him to Les Innocents!"

"He is my friend. He deserves more respect than tossing him into an abysmal mass graveyard."

True, the cemetery was overflowing with centuries of bodies tossed unceremoniously upon one another, most during mass death such as plague. She'd had Portia taken there. Cruel of her.

"Then take him to the country. It is his real home."

"I cannot get him out of the city without inspection and too many questions." Rhys jammed the shovel into the dirt. "Here he lies."

"No! I do not want him buried here." Her conditioned disgust was difficult not to acknowledge. "He is a wolf."

"What is wrong with a wolf?" Wrist resting on the

shovel handle, he tilted a condemning glare on her. "You suddenly hate us all, wolf slayer?"

Viviane gaped. "Do not name me that awful title."

"But it is yours to own. You killed the wolf outside of Paris in the spring?"

"It was self-defense."

Rhys smirked, shaking his head in disbelief.

"Please, don't be ridiculous. I know the boy meant the world to you, Rhys, I do."

He climbed from the grave and stalked to the window. His jackboots were muddy, his bare chest smeared with sweat and dirt. "I wish you were not like the other vampires," he said.

"What does that mean?"

"You claim to care for me because you think I am safe. A vampire, yet not." He looked at the ground. "Emeline accepted me when everyone else would not."

"I accept you!"

"Yet why do you only see my wolf? Why does not my vampire threaten you?"

"Because you are a wolf in mind and heart. I accept that, Rhys."

"And it is my wolf you should fear."

"No, I—" She shook her head, but could not find words to protest.

"Wolf slayer," he recited acidly.

Viviane's heart cracked open. She should have told him before this. She'd wanted to. Now she understood how he had been unable to present his complete truth to her. "The wolf killed the driver," she whispered. "It was rabid."

"It—he—was not rabid," Rhys pronounced fiercely. "And his name was Pierre Rebeaux. He was upset over the recent death of his wife and stillborn child."

She did not like knowing the name or the wolf's

circumstances. It made him real. A thinking, feeling being.

Two werewolves she had killed now. What monster had she become?

Truly, she had won the right to wear the wolf's talon. Perhaps if she wore it still, Rhys would stay away from her. She would infect his life with her darkness.

"And you think I will take your heinous act as retaliation? You know me so little, Viviane. I love you. I would not harm you."

"So many secrets revealed lately," she said, her mind aspin with so many different perspectives. "I know you love me, but…"

"Constantine wants you to believe I would use you. Well, it did not start out that way. The first time I saw you in the ballroom, I fell in love. Your eyes, so deep and blue, they spoke for you before you could open your mouth. I had to have you. I spoke with you not long after, and became more determined to have you. Later, Orlando mentioned he'd heard Lord de Salignac was in love—with you."

"You learned that *after* you saw me?"

"Yes, after we'd spoken in the hall. The relationship between my brother and I has been a constant battle over who is better, who can win the most, who has all the gold, so to speak."

He propped an elbow on the shovel.

"We have, through the decades, beaten one another down, taken from the other, tricked and stolen if it would see the other in misery. A wicked sort of game I'm sure you believe vulgar. It is, but it is all I know, to go to heads against Constantine over the years."

"What has this to do with me?"

"The moment I learned he was in love, I decided I

would take that love away from him. It would be my next turn at revenge, for the last time I saw Constantine he had stood over my murdered lover."

Viviane turned away and clasped her hand to her breast.

"It mattered not to me who the woman was, what she looked like, or that she was a vampire," Rhys continued. "I simply wanted to hurt Salignac. And what better way than by aiming directly for a man's heart?"

Viviane pressed a palm to the windowsill.

"And yet I had already fallen in love with you. What to do? Revenge or love? I knew revenge would be much sweeter for your beauty rivals all. What a tremendous prize for Constantine to lose."

"Say no more," she insisted.

"It began as revenge, but I think my heart abandoned vengeance even before my mind understood the futility of such a ruse."

"I don't want to listen to this. I've heard quite enough."

Rhys slammed the windowsill with a dirty fist. "You promised to listen until I was finished."

"I promised nothing. I never promise a thing to any man! And you are finished. We are finished."

"There is a we, Viviane." He grabbed her wrist and would not relent. "You cannot deny it, nor can I. I had thought I could simply seduce the girl and she would not look twice at Salignac. Yet revenge lost its sweetness. Viviane, please, I have fallen in love with you. I am in love with you. Please hear my truths. I have never wished to harm you. That is why I am confessing. I want you to know what brought you to me, and now I know you better, understand I cannot continue to deceive."

Claiming the frockcoat from the ground, he drew out the small wood carving from the pocket. Grasping

Viviane's hand, he placed it on her palm and folded her fingers over it.

"No jewel would do you justice. But this—this is your heart, Viviane. Wild, steady, ever beating. I love you."

She opened her fingers. A tiny wooden hummingbird wobbled in her grasp.

A woman should be devastated when the man she has realized she wants more than life itself has confessed to betraying her.

While Viviane's heart thumped with the words Rhys had unleashed upon her, she remained surprisingly rational.

She stroked the smooth bird's body. *Always, she must beat her wings quickly, to stay one step ahead.* He knew her heart well. Better, perhaps, than she did.

"Leave me to finish," he said softly, his attention on the open grave. "Close the window."

"We must talk."

"Not tonight. I must away…from here," he said. "I need to breathe. And I must go to the Marsauceux pack to tell them about Orlando."

Bowing her head and nodding, Viviane stepped back and shut the window.

She had lost him.

CLAUDE MOURREIGH STOMPED the loamy earth beneath a willow tree. "You are positive it was the vampires?"

Antoine nodded. "She stabbed Orlando before all. They cheered her! The bloody mortals were cheering a vicious longtooth for slaying one of our own. And then Hawkes arrived."

"What did he do to her?"

"He scooped up Orlando and the vampiress followed

him as they ran off to her home. He buried Orlando in her courtyard!"

Claude stopped his erratic pacing. "That is most offensive. You can bring me to her home?"

Antoine nodded.

"If the vampires think to take justice upon themselves for the murder of their own, then we, too, will show them we will act swiftly should any deem to murder our own. Let's go."

CHAPTER TWENTY-FOUR

RHYS TAMPED THE DIRT over the makeshift grave. His arms ached from digging. His heart had been shredded and buried alongside Orlando's torn body.

The summer night had turned cold and threatened rain. He shivered and stumbled backward to sit on the stone bench hugged by frothy night jasmine.

"Forgive me, Claude," he muttered. "Pray the entire pack can forgive me."

Yet he did not expect forgiveness. It was not owed him.

He had been Orlando's guardian. Instead of allowing him to gallivant about the city seeking pleasures in all the wrong places, Rhys should have accompanied him to the inns. Rhys could have pointed out those women he'd felt were safe.

Rhys had failed the one person he'd ever felt was his family.

The loss strangled his breath. He heaved, seeking air and fighting sobs.

Tilting his head, he let out a long and mourning howl. He cared not that he sat in the center of Paris and the neighborhood would surely think a real wolf was again stalking the streets. A few dogs joined his miserable tone with yips and howls.

Rhys pulled his palms down his face. His vampire

prodded at him; it wanted blood in the form of revenge. He swallowed to keep back another howl.

An odd thought occurred. If Orlando had been sleeping with Annabelle, and she had also slept with William Montfalcon—could Montfalcon have developed the same affliction and gone mad, thus killing the vampires?

No, Rhys knew differently. He'd been bought by Constantine. But what if Montfalcon had required some nudging to do the heinous deed? Would Constantine go so far to ensure his wicked plan succeeded? How could he know the whore would cause the werewolf to rage? There were yet questions he wanted to press upon his brother, but would it matter?

William was dead. The vampires were dead. And Orlando was dead—at the hands of the wolf slayer.

Anger twitched his muscles. Rhys felt the uncomfortable shift in his bones. The werewolf wanted revenge for what had been done to his companion. It mattered not the vampire had been sated a few days earlier with the blood of an unsuspecting mortal. Together, werewolf and vampire would be avenged.

"No." Rhys winced and clutched the bench, straining against the powerful darkness, struggling for release, for vengeance. "Can't..."

With the stroke of a blade the vampiress had destroyed his family.

Rhys's arm jutted out and his skin crawled as the flesh prickled. Fur grew beneath his sodden breeches. He kicked off his boots, anticipating and cursing the imminent shift.

This could not happen here. In the city. So close to her. The woman he loved despite her mindless cruelties.

She had been protecting an innocent.

Orlando had been innocent.

A throaty howl curdled in Rhys's throat. His ankle bones popped and the marrow liquefied. He tore at his muddy breeches. Fingernails grew into adamant talons. His chest expanded and fur pelted his skin.

As his werewolf mind struggled to hold to one last vestige of sanity, the vampire within scented the betrayer's blood.

VIVIANE CLUTCHED HER NIGHT robe close to her body and scurried through the dark hallway toward the music room. She could not sleep knowing Rhys was outside. Even if he had left, knowing a dead werewolf was buried in the courtyard disturbed.

The estate felt wrong as she moved through its cool confines on a ghostly stride. No longer did it welcome her as Henri had by sweeping her into his arms and offering her his redeeming blood. The walls and quiet air pressed against her skin and made her wish to be away, far, far away.

With Rhys.

Could he forgive her the horrible crime she had committed tonight?

"I would not expect it—"

She pushed open the music room door—at the same time the window across the room shattered. A massive shape leaped inside and scrambled over the glass pieces on the floor.

The werewolf stood on its hind legs and stretched out its arms, talons cutting the air. A rangy howl clutched at Viviane's heart. Never had she seen a shifted werewolf. Her legs wobbled.

Rhys had not forgiven her.

The beast sighted her and snarled, revealing long, sharp fangs.

She screamed. Scrambling away, her low-heeled shoes slipped on the marble floor. Stumbling, she slapped the wall and managed to stay upright.

Behind her, the werewolf careened out of the music room. Claws and padded paws slapped the floor. Heavy, grunting breaths punctuated its loping advance upon her.

The tepidarium door was open. It was not an escape, Viviane realized at the worst moment. As the wolf's talon tore through her robe, she scrambled across the tiles and tripped, hitting the floor with a bone-jarring shock.

The wolf leaped over her, landing at the pool's edge. It growled and snarled.

Viviane backed away, her voluminous silk robe impeding and slipping from her shoulder. Rhys had said his vampire mind ruled while in werewolf form. The vampire should not be so angry over Orlando's death as the werewolf, but she could not reason that right now.

She did know one truth. The vampire wanted blood. And it would not take a sip, but rather influence the werewolf to take her head from her body to get at the blood.

Talons clutched her ankle. Blood scented the wine-drenched air. Viviane's body dragged across the tile floor. She dug in her fingernails, clutching the slick tiles, but they bent. Kicking backward, she managed a heel to the werewolf's maw.

She had kicked her lover!

Did some part of Rhys know who she was? Please, let him see her. To believe her as he'd once said. He must believe she would never mean him harm.

Turning, she darted away and reached the wall where she fit herself into the corner.

The wolf growled and slapped a paw onto the water's surface. Cold white droplets spattered her face.

"Rhys, it's me!"

Another howl felt as if the blades of her fan were fixing into her spine, one by one, burrowing deep.

Viviane eyed the doorway. The wolf crept toward her, blocking a straight retreat to freedom. Its gold eyes raged. Talons cut through tile. If she ran left she'd be caught in the corner. To the right, the vanity with fresh linens. She could shove it at him, and hope for a moment's distraction—

The wolf lunged.

Her foot slipped in a puddle and she toppled, landing in the pool of cold water. Her head went under. Flailing her arms and kicking at the pool's bottom, she struggled to surface. Her feet slipped and she swallowed the horrible mix of water, stale milk and wine.

Something sharp cut into her gut. Blood bubbled on the surface. A taloned paw dipped in and scooped her around the waist. Viviane's body went flying and she landed against the wall, her jaw clacking and arms flinging out as if boneless. Sinking to the floor, she sputtered out the offensive water.

The wolf landed before her, crouched like a man. Its wet nose touched her shoulder. Fur tickled along her jaw. Its head was exactly as the wolves in the wild, with long snout, vicious teeth and ears pricked high. Only at its neck did it form into man shape, though broader, more muscled and furred.

But he was no man right now. The paws and talons, the shape of his legs, formed for fast running, were all wolf.

A scream hummed in her breast. Some part of her denied fear. She pushed against the beast's muscular neck with ineffectual fists.

The werewolf roared, exposing its thick, long teeth. Made for tearing meat, not piercing a vein for a polite drink.

"I..." Viviane gasped, unsure words could still the beast.

It sniffed at her. One paw landed upon her thigh, the talons cutting through her sodden robe and into flesh and opening up streams of blood. Growls, low and warning, continued.

"I love you, Rhys." Oh, that she'd not the courage to admit her heart until she thought to lose that precious life. "I'm sorry."

The wolf slammed her shoulders against the wall. The tongue lashed under her jaw. The *vampire* tasted her blood. Could her blood—somehow—tame this beast? She had to try.

"Take what you must from me," she warbled. "Anything. All of me. I am yours."

The werewolf reared onto its hind legs. The size of it was surely two or three heads taller than Rhys normally stood, the shoulders twice as broad. It was a creature to fear. Not a man to love.

And yet, its gold eyes glistened with Rhys's truths. He believed her when he looked at her now. And she believed him. He was a man who wanted a different reality. A man tortured by a darkness that would never loosen its grip on his gentle soul.

Turning and leaping across the pool, the werewolf took off, leaving Viviane against the wall, her heart racing, and tears pouring down her cheeks.

WHEN FINALLY SHE MANAGED to stand, Viviane tore away the tattered remnants of her night robe. It was soaked, as was she. The tiles beneath her feet were cracked from the werewolf's weight. She wrapped a linen about her torso.

Hair dripping down her back and tears still spilling, she took trembling steps down the hallway. Realizing her entire body shook as her fingers fluttered over the walls, she sought calm, but could not find it.

Her lover had stolen her bravery. She did not fault him.

Stunning what she now feared most, she also loved.

Ahead, three slashes cut through the wall. The music-room doorway was torn apart, the wood frame hanging. She did not go in. The glass would cut her feet, and while she wanted to feel the pain, she did not want to track blood through the house.

She paused at the stairs. Dawn must be so close. She should secrete herself away in her bedchamber and draw the bed curtains. Yet she walked to the servant's door and opened it to a whisper of cool air.

He sat outside on the bench before the grave. He'd shifted to man form, and had tugged on his breeches, though they were split down one side to reveal thigh. A tattered shirt hung on his shoulders, yet covered little.

Clutching the linen about her chest, Viviane padded out, barefoot, across the loosened dirt courtyard. He sensed her, lifting his head, but didn't turn to acknowledge her.

"It's almost dawn," he said.

She touched his shoulder, but he flinched, nudging her away. Viviane sat beside him on the bench and he moved aside so they would not touch.

"Did I…" He sighed heavily, and sucked in a breath. "Did I hurt you?"

"No," she said quickly. Her thigh hurt, but it had already healed. "Though you had every right."

He turned to face her, his expression stabbing her as no talon could. "Do not say that."

"It is true. I killed Orlando."

"Be quiet, LaMourette." He beat the bench with a fist. "The vampire, *my vampire,* wanted blood."

"And yet when your werewolf scented my blood, it did not harm me. Rhys, your werewolf would not—"

"You know not what I may or may not do to you! What I am capable of. Do not think to understand me. This is wrong."

"What is wrong?"

"Us!" He stood and grabbed the shovel stuck into the dirt, and thrust it toward the stables. It hit the wood with a clatter. "Do not accept what little I can offer you. Hold yourself to higher standards." He thrust an arm out, pointing. "Go to him. Go to Constantine if you want to live."

Viviane swung about to reproach his ridiculous suggestion, but Rhys gnashed his teeth at her and swiped the smear of blood from his cheek. He thrust his bloodied fingers toward her.

"Do you see? This is what the vampire wants from you. He wants it all. To drink you dry, to crack your bones and suck out your marrow."

"Don't say that."

"It is true! I will never rise above the darkness clinging to my soul."

"That is an excuse. You can be as good or as evil as you desire. The werewolf in you demands you choose well. You are not a monster, Rhys."

He grabbed her by the shoulders and shook her. "Don't you see me?"

Viviane calmly said, "Yes. And I believe you." She placed her palm over his heart. So frantic, the pulse racing.

"Do not believe this," he spat and shoved away her hand. "Go to him! I demand it of you."

With that, he tugged from her and marched out of the courtyard, picking up to a run by the time he rounded the stable.

Falling to sit on the bench, Viviane could not find tears now. She did believe him. His real truth. And she would not deny her love.

He thought himself a monster. She knew better.

But he was not wrong when he claimed Constantine could give her a better life. Did she want the safety of a patron or the danger of true love?

RHYS WANDERED THE STREETS, a soused man who had not consumed spirits. His clothing tattered from the shift, he kept to the early-morning shadows. Ahead, the cobbles were dusted with fine white powder. A rotund pastry chef walked out and around the corner, a load of empty flour sacks in his arms.

Rhys's vampire stirred. *You still have not fed me. You denied me the vampiress's blood.*

Rhys turned the corner. He hated doing this.

You need this. Me, your vampire. Do not deny me!

And why not? He'd already made a mess of things by chasing Viviane, scaring the hell from her, and then demanding she go to Constantine.

His grand design to get revenge upon his brother had turned itself on its head, and now he had become the recipient of the vengeance. Served him right for dallying with the ruthless plan in the first place.

Viviane must hate him now.

The more the better. It would make it easier for her to go to Constantine.

"What's that, then?" The chef turned to look over the sorry man, clutching at his breeches to hold them up. "I don't have any scraps this morning. Be gone with you!"

Rhys lunged, his fangs sinking into the dry, dusted skin of the tumescent neck.

CHAPTER TWENTY-FIVE

Paris, modern day

THE WORLD BENEATH THE SURFACE of Paris toyed with Rhys's sensory perception.

Though in vampire form now, he could follow Dane's feline scent with his eyes closed. His werewolf instincts weren't sure whether to follow her or swat her about, which proved it a good thing he wasn't in that form right now.

The petite, dreadlocked spelunker led the way, her headlamp glancing off the hard limestone walls. Chalk, paint and charcoal marks designated meaningful info to those who had made them. Dane would occasionally tap a red circle or arrow as if confirming her mark on this underworld.

Dane moved slowly Rhys suspected to allow him and Simon to adjust to the uneven terrain and darkness. The darkness did not bother him.

"We're going down, messieurs," Dane informed them in the no-nonsense tone she had adopted and which he appreciated.

He'd been right to take a chance on her. She knew what she was doing.

Rhys waited while Dane directed Simon to step carefully along the edges of the circular, vertical tunnel.

"You'll have to drop the last six feet," she instructed.

Simon yelped. His feet gave from the last foothold.

His body thudded against stone. Dane turned to offer Rhys help.

"I'll bring up the rear," he said.

"You don't trust me?"

"I do, but a gentleman never allows a lady to go last."

"Now you think I'm a lady?"

"You're no gentleman."

She took it with an accepting nod and dropped out of sight into a lower tunnel. Rhys followed, finding he was growing less keen on the tunnel's tight confines, and knowing worse was to come.

If a person were confined here for any amount of time surely they would struggle with sanity. And worse, what if their confinement were inside a coffin?

He could not bear to think it, for his stomach convulsed as if the vampire was hungry. It had been weeks since he'd taken blood. So he grasped his werewolf mind, sane, calm and wise. For now.

"I am so sorry, Viviane. I pray you are not alive."

TWO HOURS INTO THEIR TREK, the threesome squatted in a three-foot-high tunnel that Dane had—remarkably—not yet explored.

"I've been thinking," she said, directing her headlight beam onto the dirt floor in respect for the men's eyes. "This coffin was supposedly buried in the eighteenth century?"

"1785, if it was done immediately," Rhys replied.

That statement put him to a sudden panic. He couldn't get past the possibility that this could be a farce, or perhaps it was that he *did not* want to go beyond that, to actually ruminate on the "evil vampire" from the tale.

Had the vampire lord kept her prisoner for a time?

Before burying her alive? Truly, had it been his brother? Why had he not killed the bastard long ago?

"It's all right." Despite Simon's nervousness the assistant knew when to offer Rhys reassurance. "We'll find her."

"You really believe this, don't you?" Dane asked him.

"No. Yes. I don't know," Rhys said, feeling sweat sheen his forehead for the first time. "I have to follow this through to put my heart at peace."

"I understand. But we're losing battery power, guys, and should be heading back up." Dane dug in her backpack and drew out a fresh piece of red chalk and turned to make her mark on the wall, along with compass and longitude directions. "You cool with calling it a day? Or rather, night. It's almost four in the morning."

"We should organize a bigger search party." Rhys spoke his worries out loud. "We'll never manage this alone. There are miles of tunnels to cover. We need another half a dozen men."

"And we need to spread out," Dane agreed.

Rhys sighed. The air was heavy and he was exhausted. In spite of the meal he'd eaten earlier, he knew what he needed was warm human blood.

He glanced to Simon, whose eyelids blinked with exhaustion.

"Fine. We retreat and regroup."

CHAPTER TWENTY-SIX

Paris, 1785

VIVIANE SAT BEFORE THE VANITY looking over the various pots of rouge and face powder. Kohl for her eyes. Carmine for her lips. Portia normally made up her face because Viviane could not see herself in a mirror to know how she looked.

Now she had not the heart to fuss over her appearance. For she only faced Constantine this night. Not as though she were going to meet a lover, a man she cared for. A man who would ask her to share his life.

A man who had unleashed his darkness upon her—and yet had not harmed her—because he could not. He would not, no matter of what he believed his vampire capable.

Outside her bedchamber window, torchlight flamed and invited late-night revelers to view the carnival on the Seine. Magicians and contortionists entertained well past midnight, entreating one and all to satisfy their macabre curiosity.

A tear dribbled down Viviane's cheek. The mansion was so quiet now. Her peace had been ripped asunder by Constantine's cruel act.

And now she was preparing to sacrifice herself to him. Because Rhys would not have her.

"He is trying to save me."

A sacrifice she knew must wrench at his heart as

wretchedly as it did hers. He believed his werewolf would harm her. She did not believe that. She had looked into his eyes and had read his soul. So bold, yet gentle.

She slapped the back of her hand across the vanity. Glass pots, brushes and a ewer of stale water clattered across the floor. The crash muffled her despairing wail.

She cried for the loss of her lover's pride and she cried for the girl in the blue dress. She cried for Orlando, whom she should have gotten to know better. But she could not cry for herself.

"I will go to that bastard, but I will not have his child. He will have to force me—"

And she knew he would. If she were to give Constantine a male heir that would mean a new beginning for him, and his tribe. A beginning that did not involve his brother, Rhys.

SQUATTING BESIDE A SOOTED gargoyle, a hand curled about the stone wing, Rhys observed the city from atop the Louvre. The revelers had passed, their path snaking them north along the Seine to the Place de Grève for their macabre festivities.

The air was so still he could hear voices murmuring in houses. The shifting of horses in their stables. The slithering rhythm of a knife across the whetstone.

The single candle flame in her bedchamber flickered out.

Rhys's heart thumped. He anticipated the seconds it would take for her to arrive on the town house's street level. The kitchen candle extinguished. She would leave out the servant's door, as was usual.

Going to *him,* the leader of tribe Nava. To claim her future and ensure her survival. Rhys did not fault her that need. He wished it was he who could meet that need.

You told her to go to him.

It had been the life-giving option. Viviane would thrive under Constantine's care. He could give her anything she desired.

Save love, whispered Rhys's heart.

Opening his hand, he inspected the single black hair he'd twisted round his forefinger. Now he carefully threaded the precious strand through the threads torn loose on his sleeve. A part of her.

"Don't do it, Viviane," he murmured, fingers curling about the gargoyle's neck. "I love you. Maybe I can patron you." It would require he take her bite and further enrage his werewolf—but if it meant Viviane's life? "You could be my mate."

And he knew she could not, because his werewolf would rip the vampiress's head from her neck the moment he saw her. So much for saving her life.

And yet he had not harmed her this morning. His werewolf had looked into her eyes, and even goaded by the vampire, but had not the desire to harm her. She had bestilled him.

A moment was all he'd required.

Had he sacrificed his only hope for love?

VIVIANE REFUSED RICHARD'S suggestion to show her to Constantine's study. She preferred to walk the long, winding path to Hell alone.

It had come to this.

The dark halls creaked under her wary steps. This elaborate palace housed a murderer. Surely, Constantine had killed many mortals in his lifetime. Dark Ones, as well. As tribe leader, a fierce mien was expected.

Only Portia's death mattered to Viviane. The maid

had harmed none. She had been a constant and faithful companion.

She did not want to bow before Constantine.

She could think of nothing but standing in Rhys's arms, because right now those arms, even if they ended in talons, were more giving than any others.

However, the truth could not be disregarded.

She would not sulk about her fate for one moment longer. With head held high, and heart shaky but determined, Viviane LaMourette would begin a new chapter.

One she must learn to tolerate.

Ahead she sensed the heartbeats from more than one being. Constantine's dark allure drew her forward. Lavender and blood spiced the air. The walls were mirrored, yet not a single shadow darkened the silvered glass as she neared the oil lamp.

Drawing her gaze along the seam in the wall, she decided the small knot on the wood chair rail must be the release. A push triggered the latch, and the door swung outward, gushing out a drowning roil of candlelight and the heavy scent of incense. Harpsichord notes tripped out too gaily, warning Viviane that she must remain on guard.

She inhaled resolutely and pressed a palm to her stomach.

Ruby velvet hugged the walls. Black, tooled leather decorated the chaises and ottomans about the expansive room. The carpet looked animal fur. Viviane would not be surprised were it wolf. The crystal chandelier hung low, so one had to walk around it to navigate the room's perimeter.

Everywhere lounged females in all states of undress. Vampires—once mortal—blooded by Constantine. His harem. Their eyes were glassy, their movements lethargic.

One lunged forward, but was caught by the arm of a companion.

Constantine lay sprawled, his shoulders against a tumble of elaborate velvet and satin pillows. His leather breeches were unfastened at the waist to reveal dark hairs tufting out. He wore nothing else. Candle flames worshipped him, flickering smartly across his bare abdomen, not so muscular as Rhys, but neither soft. He was a vision.

Silver flashed as he flicked his fingers to silently command the slender woman draped across his lap to move. She crawled off, leering at Viviane and revealing she was not so neat when taking blood for the crimson drool at the corner of her mouth.

Uncivilized, Viviane thought. The room housed a harem of hobbled animals, kept reined by their master.

I cannot do this. I do not want to be kept like them. Do they not see they are nothing more than chattel?

"Mademoiselle LaMourette," Constantine said on a lazy drawl. His fingers played with the vampiress's garnet hair. "Did I request your presence this evening?"

She met his dark eyes. No compassion, not a hint of her reflection there. It was not a stare she could endure overlong. Most especially, not for centuries. "I wish to speak to you in private. Send your minions off to their cages."

One woman snarled. The poor things. They would never know the freedom Viviane had known all her life. Could she master a rescue mission right here and now? Release them to their own designs?

No. They would never survive.

"Whatever you wish to say to me can be said before my kin." Constantine lay back, his fingers finding the loose curls of a blonde woman who lay on her stomach, her backside completely revealed amidst the sheer fabrics draped across the divan. "Soon enough they will become your sisters."

Viviane gritted her teeth to keep from screaming. "No."

The harpsichord abruptly stopped.

Constantine tilted his head. "What was that?"

She could not do this, could not kneel, or bow or whatever it was he required of her.

"I am not comfortable with this arrangement. Will you please grant me your audience in private? Just a few moments?"

"Not tonight, LaMourette. I've suffered your rebuffs to a certain degree of humiliation. I will no longer bow to your requests. Tell me this—you are untainted by the half-breed's blood?"

She nodded. She would never harm Rhys by biting him, and thus giving his werewolf a greater hunger for blood than it already possessed.

"Then I will consider you."

Her neck muscles tightened. He would *consider* her? How dare he!

Viviane kept her lips pressed together. Standing here was humiliating enough without the women leering at her.

"I had thought you'd intended to come before me on your knees?"

She had promised nothing of the sort. But it was apparent he would milk this to his advantage. He would bring her to her lowest to show all he could control her.

In a fluid movement, Constantine stood. He turned Viviane toward the chandelier, which was so bright it made it difficult to see. In reaction, she stepped closer to him.

I cannot do this. I will not. Even if I must die alone and starving.

Constantine's touch raised gooseflesh across her skin. Fingers glided to her neck and stopped at her pulse. Normally such a touch would quicken Viviane, draw up her desire. Now it curdled dread throughout her being.

Run. Get away from him.

"Will you or will you not accept me as your patron?"

"She will not!"

Rhys barged into the room and tugged Viviane from Constantine's grasp.

CHAPTER TWENTY-SEVEN

VIVIANE MELTED INTO HIS embrace, yet Rhys sensed her muscles were tense, unsure.

"How did you get in here?" Constantine demanded.

Hordes of glassy-eyed kin congregated behind the vampire lord, curious and unembarrassed by their exposed flesh, yet ridiculously shivering at the sight of him.

To validate their fears, Rhys snarled at them. Surely, their master must have told them about his half-breed brother.

A half-breed who currently waged an inner war against his dark side. It wanted out. It wanted to put taloned paws about Constantine's neck. He could feel the shift tighten his shoulders and pectorals.

"I walked in," Rhys said through a tight jaw. "Your porter was taking a nap. Happens when you've mortals working the night hours." He clasped Viviane's hand. "I won't allow you to succumb to his bullying. Come with me now. You don't need to do this."

"She will die without my patronage."

Rhys snarled. "She can find another patron who is not so power hungry. One who is willing to love her and treat her with respect."

Gratitude flashed in Viviane's eyes. Yes, he knew exactly what she desired. And though he could not give it to her, he would walk the world to find someone who could.

"Not you." Constantine narrowed his eyes. "Never an atrocity such as you."

The accusation would never cease to hurt. Rhys twisted his neck and tightened his jaw. His fingertips tingled, signaling the werewolf's growing rage.

"Would that I could give Viviane the lifeblood she requires."

"You're fighting it right now," his brother said coolly. "You are a beast!"

Viviane buried her face aside his neck and into his hair. "You've the same blood in your veins," she said to Constantine. "I wonder should your kin not fear you?"

The women suddenly looked at their master anew.

"She lies!" Constantine shouted and beat his chest. "I am bloodborn!"

That insistent declaration Rhys had heard over and over when they were younger. *I am better than you. I am not half-breed. I am bloodborn. Only I am right.*

He had agreed with Constantine then. Now, something inside of him shook its head and raged at the entitlement. Rhys would make his own way.

"Will you come with me?" he whispered to Viviane.

She nodded, and he lifted her into his arms.

Constantine growled.

"She's mine," Rhys announced, his voice growing rough with the emerging werewolf. He twisted his neck, fighting the beast. "If you try to take her from me, or harm her in any way, I will kill you."

Rhys loped out from the Hôtel de Salignac and into the night, Viviane draped in his arms.

For some reason the shift did not abate. The werewolf was coming upon him. Now.

"I love you," he said as he took the narrow alleyway to her home. "I can't stop this. I'm shifting. I pray some day you will forgive me the darkness my soul will not relent."

"I already have. I love you, Rhys. Always."

It was the first time he'd heard her say it. But it was too late.

He dashed into the stables and set her down awkwardly. Bones snapping and muscles stretching, Rhys yowled as his beast demanded release.

And the vampire in him sneered at Viviane.

BOLD YELLOW EYES BEAMED at Viviane. The werewolf rose on hind legs, looming over her. She stumbled when Rhys had released her. He'd been fighting the shift all the way from Constantine's palace. She'd felt his muscles bulge and his voice strain. He'd picked up speed and seams had torn on his sleeves.

The werewolf turned, inspecting the open stable door. With a slash of its paw, it slammed the door shut.

Viviane shuffled backward, her skirts impeding successful escape. Her spine hit the sharp corner of a wood supporting post.

The horses did not stir to have the beast stalking but feet away from them. It was as if they were silenced by the power of Rhys's man-beast form, respectful even.

They'd done this once before, werewolf against vampire. She could survive it again. This time fear did not rise. He'd rescued her, taken her away from a horrible fate. He had won her freedom.

Now she must help him see that truth, to know the honor he possessed, and to claim it.

Lunging forward, Rhys went on all fours, his wide, powerful paws slapping the straw-littered dirt floor. The wolf's body was large, elongated and did not walk as a real wolf for the insinuation of man.

"You want blood, yes?" Viviane defied bravely.

The long maw opened, stretching back black flesh to reveal moon-white fangs. Should those teeth graze her skin, they would open it to bleed.

"You want to bite another vampire?" she challenged. "I know you. You use this big, scary werewolf to frighten others, but you are not, and never will be, the man the werewolf is. You are the vampire."

Its nose brushed her cheek, none too gently. Talons dug into the dirt beside her thighs. A snort hushed hot breath over her lips.

"Yes, the vampire who is so angry he has not control all the time, he forces Rhys to heinous acts. How dare you. You know, should he be caught, it would be your death, as well."

Viviane grasped the werewolf's head, one hand behind an ear, the other along its jaw. The hard fangs cut her palm as it wrestled with her grip, but she would not relent.

"Hear me, wolf! You don't want what the vampire pushes you to do. You do not want to harm me."

She struggled to maintain hold but realized the wolf could shuck her off with ease, so some part of it had to be hearing her beyond the raging vampire who pressed it for blood.

"You love me, Rhys. Your werewolf does. You want to mate with me."

The gold eyes blinked. A snort hushed breath across her cheek. And Viviane gasped. There, on the shimmering surface of his eyes, she saw her reflection. A blurry, moving image of dark hair and blue eyes. And love.

Is that how she appeared? And only in her lover's eyes. Fitting.

"Fight the vampire," she whispered, for she had fallen

into his gaze. Into the mirror of her own desperation, her desires and needs. "For us, Rhys."

The werewolf tugged from her grasp and thrust back its head to howl. The sound reverberated through Viviane's bones, imprinting the perilous cry of one enslaved by a darker half. She dug her fingers into the soft fur behind his ears, wanting to never let go. To believe in his goodness.

The werewolf wanted freedom. The vampire wanted what it needed to survive.

Rhys's neck snapped oddly to the left. The wolf yelped. Viviane sensed he would shift again, and did not try to scramble away, though he stood right over her. Nothing her lover did could scare her.

Fur brushed her face and legs. Grinding growls were abruptly cut off. Whimpers segued with the wrenching noise of snapping bone. A human hand slapped the air and landed on her stomach. Wolf ears changed, the fur receding and the smooth pink ear shell tucking against human skull.

Rhys flipped back his hair, revealing human face, muscles tense and jaw biting as the final changes returned his body to vampire and his mind to werewolf.

He collapsed on her, his head hitting her lap. Viviane embraced his shuddering shoulders. He sobbed softly against her stomach. A man broken by his own inner demons.

"I love you," was all she could say.

AWARE SHE STROKED HIS HAIR and drew it across his bare shoulders, Rhys lay still, wallowing in the calming touch. Viviane had spoken to his werewolf mind while the vampire had dominated it. Somehow, he had heard her, and had stopped his werewolf from attacking her for the blood the vampire craved.

He was weak now. It had been but a day since he'd drunk blood, yet the vampire was never satisfied. He would not—must not—harm Viviane. And in his core, he knew his werewolf would always protect her from his dark side.

That relieved and horrified him. Ever after, she would need protection from his vampire.

Had he done the right thing by taking her away from his brother?

Emotionally it had been right. But physically? Perhaps there were some evils Viviane must endure to survive.

No, you will not relent to Constantine. She is yours. You will make it work.

Her head tilted against the wall, her eyes were closed, yet a soft smile sat on her lips. The tiny curve that had initially captured him now teased him to touch it. "Thank you for trusting me."

"I will never give up on you, Rhys. On us. Take me inside," she said, eyes still closed. "Make love to me."

He carried Viviane through the quiet shadows. Dawn would soon crush the night and he wanted to tuck her away in her bedchamber before that happened.

He laid her on the bed and on the vanity found a tinderbox. Striking the flint sharply, he lit the tinder and a warm glow suffused the room. The draperies were drawn, no sunlight would enter this sanctuary.

Viviane shrugged off her cape. Her hair was tangled. Together, they looked like gypsies come in from the storm.

"My werewolf heard you, even shackled by the vampire," he offered.

"I know. I wasn't afraid of you. Either of you." She gestured he come to her.

"You dared me to mate with you."

He climbed onto the bed and tugged the ties loose about her neck. "I am ready for your werewolf. I want to know all of you, Rhys."

"Would that my werewolf was ready for you."

"I wonder if you did bite me, or vice versa, if it may appease your vampire?"

"It would further enrage my werewolf."

"What if it tamed your vampire?"

He leaned over the bed, putting his palms to each side of her hips. Despite her distraught appearance she smelled luscious. "I will not risk harming you, Viviane. Please accept that."

"I can. I love you, Rhys. And no matter what my fate holds, which is likely a swift and painful death without a patron, I wish to spend that time with you. If you will have me."

"If?" He crawled over her and kissed her mouth. So soft and giving. Tender curls slipped beneath his stroking fingers. The heat of her seeped into his body, melting him upon her limbs. "Not if," he whispered. "Only yes and yes, a thousand times over. I will have you, LaMourette."

He searched her azure gaze. He would find her heart there. Her truth. Her desire. His sanctity.

A kiss pushed away the world from around them. Limestone walls crumbled in silence and gray night sky wilted. The half-moon dazzled over all.

He did want to bite her, to draw her life into his body. He sensed his vampire was weak, but that merely placed him on a strength level to the common mortal. He could wait until later to feed on a random mortal.

And yet, what harm could drinking her blood do? Only

her bite would aggravate his werewolf. To bite her would simply feed the vampire's hunger. Dare he? They both wanted him to try.

Rhys slipped his hands under her gown and tore the cotton shift down the middle to expose her breasts, her stomach, her mons. Unwilling to do this slowly, to dance with foreplay and ensure she was ready for him, he slid his fingers inside her, seeking her moist heat. She moaned at his entrance, and ground herself against him, indicating what she wanted, what she needed.

Kissing her stomach, he licked to her breasts. There he worshipped her nipples, biting and sucking so hard he brought blood to the surface in a delicious bruise. All the while, he stroked her and she rocked upon his hand in reply to his motions.

"You belong to me."

"Yes. Yours."

"I will not own you," he murmured, "but I will serve you. Please you."

"Yes."

"Love you. Adore you."

"Yes, Rhys, yes!"

She came, her thighs squeezing his hand as her head thrust into the lace counterpane and her hips bucked. He wanted to claim her but more so he wanted to experience her pleasure. To give her what she needed, and bask in the stolen bliss.

And yes, his werewolf mind wanted to allow the vampire to taste her blood.

The vampiress pushed him onto the bed, and crawled over him. She ground her wetness against his erection. Sharp fingernails clutched his arms as she rubbed her breasts over his chest.

He clutched her derriere and squeezed, loving the

rock of her hips as she worked her mons against his hard cock.

"Take it all," she managed. "Oh, Rhys..."

She slipped her fingers along his tattered breeches. The torn fabric fell away. Her fingers circled him, stroking, following the rhythm of her tongue.

"The deuce, Viviane, you will be the end of me."

"It will be a sweet death, I promise. Yes, faster. Like that."

Viviane shoved Rhys into the pillows and climbed upon his naked body. His erection bobbed against her mons. She palmed his shoulders and leaned in for a kiss.

And in the pale light he saw the glint as her fangs descended.

"Now I'm going to claim you. Let no other woman touch your body or desire your kiss. You are mine, always."

VIVIANE SLID ONTO HER lover's hardness. It filled her, thickly, snugly, finding its place while marking its claim. She rode him to a swift climax, thrusting back her head when her fangs descended. The agony of denying herself the blood only increased the intensity of orgasm. She felt it would never end, and the exquisite pleasure of it would kill her.

Falling onto the bed, and stretching her arms above her head, she cooed, "That was too good."

Rhys rolled to his side, fitting his body against hers, his cock, still hard and thick, snugged against her hip.

She hugged him, silently knowing she would die alongside her lover. And she was prepared to do so every moment until they were exactly as blissful as this one.

The only thing that could be more pleasurable prodded. "Let me taste you," she whispered. "Please."

Rhys nodded. "I want that. But you must not bite me. Your saliva must not enter my bloodstream."

"Then how?" She sat as he slid off the bed and sorted over the serving tray left near the bed.

Tinging a fingernail against the goblet released a gorgeous chime. Rhys handed it to her, then searched the floor of her boudoir. It was a mess. Earlier, she'd pushed all the things from the vanity onto it. Displaying the small scissors Portia had used to trim Viviane's hair, he slashed it across his wrist.

Blood scent blossomed in the room, whetting Viviane's hunger more than she could imagine. She'd been sated sexually. Now she would be fed true sustenance by her lover.

She leaned forward, offering the goblet, and he held his wrist over it to dribble the sweet crimson elixir into the shallow glass.

She licked her lips in anticipation, and almost got lost in the hunger, when Rhys tipped up her chin and fixed her gaze with his. "I want to patron you, lover."

Neither knew if it was possible. But she sensed his hope rose as high as her own.

When he snatched back his hand and pressed it to his mouth to seal the wound, Viviane brought the goblet to her lips. Reverent, she closed her eyes and tilted it back.

The rich elixir assaulted her senses. Headier than a bouquet of rare roses, like an entire forest, the scent entered her brain on a heavy, cloying note. Is this what the world tasted like? Steeped in the earth and air and the very flavor of humanity? It was bright and soft, liquid and fresh. Like sunlight in her veins.

Viviane smiled over the rim of the goblet at her lover. He had given her life.

CHAPTER TWENTY-EIGHT

RHYS HAD PURCHASED SIX clutches of six roses each for a grand gift to his lover. He'd left her to sleep through the dawn, while he satisfied the werewolf's craving for real food. His previous attempt at giving her flowers had failed, so he intended to strew the petals up the stairs and into her boudoir.

She had taken his blood last night. Sweet wonder, he'd reveled to watch her swallow every last drop. If only he could do the same. It would bond them as vampires, yet, well, he would not consider the detrimental effects it could have.

Burying his face in the soft white petals, he inhaled the scent.

Before he could knock on the servant's door, he noted it hung open. Someone rushed out from the stables toward him.

"They've taken her!"

"What?" Rhys grabbed the stable hand by the wrists.

The boy—must be Gabriel that Viviane had mentioned—was frantic. Tears streamed down his eyes. He bled at the shoulder, which made Rhys wonder if he had tried to protect himself—but from what?

"The men!" the shaking teen pealed in sobbing huffs. "They broke down the door and pronounced my mistress the wolf slayer, then grabbed her and took off! I…I think one of them looked like a wolf?" He shoved a hand through his tangled hair. "I could not have seen right. He must have worn a helmet made from a wolf's head."

Werewolves had been here? Rhys dropped the roses.

"I tried to beat them off with the scythe."

"Hell." Someone from the pack must have witnessed Orlando's death. "When were they here? How long ago?"

"Not long. They pulled a tumbrel behind two horses. She didn't scream. But she did slash and bite at them. I couldn't protect her! What will they do to her?"

"Nothing good. Stay here, and nail up the door. Then you go home. It is Mademoiselle LaMourette they want. They won't come after you, but you'd best stay away, boy."

"But the horses?"

"I'll see to them."

"You must save her, monsieur!"

"I will." Rhys raced out the courtyard behind Henri's estate. "I will get her back!"

Rhys ran without slowing and leaped the gates near the porte de Auteuil, which he knew would be unguarded this time of night, for key guards were posted west at the road to Versailles.

Midair he shifted, shedding his were form and clothing, and landed the ground on four paws. Charging along the beaten trail, the wolf kept his nose to the ground.

He scented the pack before he scented Viviane. But her scent was also strong. Wine and...no fear, but defiant aggression. She had no idea the danger she was in.

THE CART WAS MANNED by one horse and driver. Two werewolves in wolf form loped before the horse.

Wrists and ankles aching, Viviane struggled against the heavy iron shackles binding her to the tumbrel. Her guard, a swarthy were named Antoine with long, dirty hair hanging in his eyes held a whip, the handle carved to a point, on her.

He taunted with a sneer of brown teeth. Viviane worried one bump in the dirt road would topple him forward, stake aimed toward her heart.

Whatever they did to her, she deserved it. She may have saved a mortal's life, but the paranormal nations did not value the life of a mortal before their own. Any punishment she received from the wolves would be just.

Yet while she maintained a fierce indifference, she wanted to fall to her knees and beg freedom. Rhys had made her see the world anew. She did not want their relationship to end because of her stupidity.

A shrill yip from behind the tumbrel alerted all the wolves. Viviane's guard searched the star-spangled night and let out a howl.

A lone wolf sped beyond the cart to race against the wolves in the lead. The cart slowed to a rough stop. The driver tossed the reins to her guard. "Hold the horses, Antoine, and keep an eye on her."

Viviane twisted at the waist but could not see over her shoulder. Wolves growled and yipped.

"What have you done to him?" Antoine growled at her. "He's fighting his own kind!"

That meant the new wolf was Rhys.

Viviane bared her fangs at the man. He responded by revealing his, which were thicker and designed for tearing meat. He didn't have an inner vampire she could appeal to, either. Suddenly, she felt helpless.

The wolves snarled and growled, snapping at one another. She wanted to see what Rhys was doing, if he were winning.

The guard slammed the whip against her throat, pinning

her shoulders against the rough wood slats. "No lone wolf would fight a pack leader. What does he want?"

"Don't know," she managed to say against the hard whip handle.

"You've done something to him."

"No."

"You've bitten him, made him blood hungry!"

"No, he did not...."

Her guard shoved the whip harder against her throat. Unable to prevent showing her fangs, she knew he took it as a sign of aggression.

The angry snarls ceased, and now Viviane recognized male voices as they shifted from wolf to were form. She saw one man stalking the darkness, his bare skin gray for the night was black, clouds covering the three-quarters moon.

"You dare to stop the pack from seeking justice?" called one man she could not see.

Viviane closed her eyes and listened fiercely.

RHYS SHIFTED TO WERE FORM. Three pack wolves also shifted. Growling lowly, and yipping, fur changed to flesh, and bones realigned and lengthened, leaving them naked and sweating from the vicious squabble they'd briefly engaged.

They stood at the edge of the less traveled road. Forest surrounded on both sides, the foliage so thick even a wolf could see in no further than the first line of pine trees.

The Marsauceux pack members stepped into a row, flanking Claude, their principal.

Rhys had promised Claude he would not return to the pack's territory. They weren't close to Marsauceux territory, the pack had been poking about Paris—

likely looking for Orlando—but he would not argue semantics now.

"You go back on your word, Hawkes," Claude announced.

"I had no choice."

"Why so? For her? The longtooth bitch murdered Orlando!"

Rhys twisted a look over his shoulder. Antoine held a whip across Viviane's neck. The pointed end wasn't going to cause lethal damage, yet he was thankful it was not poised before her heart.

"You have been in Paris too long," Claude said. "The bitch would not have killed Orlando if you—the two of you—had been home."

"I am conducting an investigation. You knew Orlando was coming along with me before I left for Paris. Viviane was protecting a mortal girl from Orlando's attack. He'd syphilis and was mad."

"She is a wolf slayer!"

Indeed. The truth of her prodded at his very soul, yet he saw beyond the foul crimes and into her heart.

"Orlando would have required putting down no matter."

"Putting down? Do you hear yourself, man?" Claude stalked before him. His dusty shoulders were as broad as Rhys's and the scar digging into his abdomen and across his face claimed him the elder and more experienced of the two. "You sound like a mortal. A pompous mortal hunter. What's come of you?"

"I am civilized. As are we all."

The pack leader sneered. Who was Rhys to claim such a thing when he warred within his own skin to master his uncivilized counterpart?

"This calamity tonight." Rhys gestured at the tumbrel.

"What madness has infected your mind, Claude? This is not how you handle injustice against the pack. Not without a fair hearing and proof of the crime."

"Do not presume to tell me the order of things. Antoine saw her kill the boy. What further proof do you require?"

"She did not purposefully attack Orlando."

"No, not an attack, but still vicious murder. Perhaps if you had watched over Orlando as promised he would still be alive."

Indeed. Rhys felt the man's words cut open his heart and bleed it into his entrails. It was his fault Orlando lay buried in Viviane's courtyard right now.

One by one, Rhys met the surrounding pack members' eyes. They sneered and stretched back their shoulders making themselves broader, fiercer, a show of superiority. They were in the right; he was not.

"Forgive me, principal Mourreigh. I assume all the blame for Orlando's death."

The old wolf cast a glance over his pack, seething, wanting to avenge their own—as was their right. When he looked at Rhys, Claude's jaw tightened. "I say you should be the one to cut the vampire's throat and spill her blood in remembrance of Orlando."

Rhys took a step but cautioned his anger. Within, the vampire stirred. What foul darkness he possessed that part of him could pine for blood? Thankfully, it was easiest to maintain a grasp on his wolf mind when in the company of fellow wolves that he admired.

"I've a suspicion about you, Rhys Hawkes," Claude said. "I think you've just confirmed it."

"What, that I've a civilized bone and don't wish to watch a slaughter?"

"That you've developed a dangerous folly for the

vampiress. Have you been tupping her? Worse, have you taken her blood?"

Back in the tumbrel, Viviane's chains clanked and she shouted, "Never!"

Rhys winced. Was she trying to protect him? It wasn't necessary.

His brother had been right; he would never belong to the vampire race or the werewolf breed. He was a man who stood alone.

Spreading out his arms to expose his chest and torso put him in a vulnerable position before the pack members. Rhys lifted his chin and announced, "I love Viviane LaMourette."

"Love makes men do stupid things," Claude hissed. "You should have stayed away. You promised."

"Doesn't matter what has been done or what has not. I love her, and I accept whatever punishment the pack wishes to enforce upon me. Will you release her if I surrender myself?"

Claude shook his head, as if to confirm Rhys was acting the fool. The old wolf stomped the loamy earth. "Release the bitch."

The leader eyed him. "You surrender nothing, Hawkes. I have already marked you from this world. But I will take justice for the vampiress's crime."

CONSTANTINE CLIMBED DOWN the curving, narrow wood steps into the dark cellar beneath Ian Grim's house in the Marais. This section of the city had been built over marsh. Stench of rot and dampness overwhelmed.

As the stairs twisted and the walls changed from stacked brick to hard-packed clay earth, he assumed he was at a level to the tunnels that traversed beneath the city.

The tunnels were rumored to snake and twist for hundreds of leagues, some plunging five stories into the ground.

Close enough to touch Hell?

"Salignac," Grim acknowledged without looking up from the table before him.

The witch was Scottish. Salignac hated his provincial brogue. Even more he hated that the man never deigned to present him with due respect. As one of the Light, the witch knew he wielded a powerful weapon over Constantine. Thanks to the great Protection spell, all witches' blood was poisonous to vampires.

Constantine strode beneath a ceiling hung with desiccated, dried herbs and a dead rabbit dangled in the mix. The smell of decayed flesh put him off, and he mined for the handkerchief tucked up his frockcoat sleeve.

"What brings you to the earth's bowels?" Grim asked, still focused on the vials before him. He tilted the contents of one into the other. Both liquids were clear, but when combined, transformed to a murky blue.

"You ignored my summons."

"Busy."

Quelling his ire, Constantine fisted his fingers. "I need silver bullets. Silver blades. Silver in liquid form to institute into food. Something."

"Werewolf problem?"

Constantine smirked. *Problem* made it sound so small. He stroked a thumb along his jaw, which still ached, despite the crack Rhys had pummeled into the bone having healed hours ago.

"It is Rhys Hawkes. Again."

"Well, it *is* his turn."

"I didn't ask for a tally on our encounters."

"Encounters." Grim chuffed. "That's a way of putting it. What has he done now?"

"He's stolen her from me."

"Her? Ah, yes, the one you've lost your heart to. The bloodborn vampiress?"

"It is no longer love. It never was."

"Merely need, eh?"

"She's chosen a slow death over a secure life with me."

Now Grim set the vials in a brass rack and twisted his blond head to give Constantine his full attention. He pushed up the spectacles perched at the end of his nose and sniffed. "That's a cruel blow to your ego, I'll wager. But how can she survive without a patron?"

Constantine swallowed. How could she choose death? His brother was not so powerful, so appealing to women. Was he?

What, about him, repulsed her so?

"How soon can you have the silver prepared?"

"Hmm, a couple days. You'll have to provide me with ingots. I've not the coin to invest in silver."

"I will, I'll send Richard with some later—"

"I cannot guarantee a werewolf eradicator will work against your brother since he is only half wolf. And isn't he enchanted?"

"Superstitious blather. He is a living being, as I am, and can be killed. You just have to provide the correct means."

The witch toyed with a pearl-handled anthame placed beside a bloody rabbit's ear. "I thought you had vowed not to kill your brother."

The witch had the obnoxious manner of always being right.

Pacing beneath the gruesome ceiling, Constantine's mind opened wider and revisited the blissful memory of he and Viviane, during sweeter times. She'd been so pleased with the choker. A deadly gift that could thrill none but his perfect mate.

If she were not to choose life, perhaps he would give her exactly as she desired.

"No," he said. And then, more decidedly, "No. I don't want my brother dead. If he is dead, he will not feel the anguish of my revenge. One that will require your assistance, Grim."

"I am at your service, my lord. What do you require?"

"I must see to the details first. If it is even possible. There is a glass-smith on the Rive Gauche. Yes, that is how it will be. I shall exact the perfect revenge and bring the dog to his knees."

CHAPTER TWENTY-NINE

THE PACK SHIFTED TO WEREWOLF shape and stalked toward him. Rhys shifted in preparation. His werewolf roused and snarled, snapping his toothy maw, but it maintained deference. His vampire mind sensed it was in no position to fight, so did not prod him to lash out.

Behind him chains clinked as Antoine released Viviane. Claude would ensure honor was maintained. The pack wanted his blood now.

So long as someone's blood flows, his vampire mind hissed with macabre glee.

There was one brand of pack justice. First strike took Rhys across the forehead, the talon cutting through flesh and skull bone. He did not cry out. In werewolf form he could not speak—nor would he howl.

Talons went at all angles to his body, tearing fur, muscle and bone. The vampire in him roiled in vicious delight as blood coated fur spattered the air.

It seemed the torture went on forever, but finally, when Rhys could barely stand, the pack shifted. In were form they stood, their bodies bloodied. Two jumped onto the cart and hastened it away, while two had shifted to wolf form and loped along behind the cart.

The pack leader said not a word to him. A scornful look spoke volumes.

Rhys collapsed, landing in a thick nest of leaves beneath an oak tree. His vision red, the world smelled of blood, pain and agony. He hated his vampire, who writhed in near sexual climax at the joy of it all.

At this moment he could curse his mother her indiscretions, but then his wolf mind grasped hold of the vampire and shook it. He shifted, crying out as the painful cuts tortured anew his human flesh. He would heal in were form but not as quickly as if he'd remained in werewolf shape.

Exhausted, completely shifted to vampire form, yet in his werewolf mind, he could barely lift his head to scan the sky. Dawn crept upon the horizon.

"Viv..." he gasped out. He prayed she had gotten to cover before the sun rose.

"Rhys!"

She landed at his side and stretched an arm across his chest. Rhys groaned as the contact abraded the cuts and tore at the open wounds. Yet her presence worked a balm to his bare and shivering soul. "You should not..."

"Oh, my love, they could have killed you."

"Never. Claude does not condone murder. I am...no longer welcomed by the pack."

"*Sacre bleu,* you're covered with wounds. Does it hurt terribly? No, that was a foolish question." She touched his neck and looked at her finger. Would the vampiress lick off the blood?

"I'll heal." He clasped her hand.

"Rhys, you shouldn't have done that. I killed the boy."

"I love you more than my werewolf family, Viviane. I would sacrifice my life to save yours again and again."

"Don't say that. I want you alive, in my arms."

Her mouth brushed his cheek. Pain flickered into the background. Blood wet his skin, and she could dash out her tongue and taste it, but she did not. Instead she tendered gentle kisses over his face. He felt his muscles band tightly and a few rib bones snapped into place.

"You need clothes," she said, as if just noticing his nudity.

"More important, you need protection. We'll never make it to Paris before the sun rises. But we might make it to my home."

"You live close? But you can't walk."

"Give me a few moments, and more kisses, and I'll have healed enough to hobble. Tear your skirts, love. Make some protection."

She ripped her skirts and fashioned a hood to pull over her head and face. Rhys arched his back, and popped one last vertebra into place. A satisfied groan masked the yip of pain. A flash of orange light hit his eye.

He lifted Viviane into his arms. "Pull the fabric over your face. Quickly!"

He dashed deep into the forest, tracking the scent and indications his home was near. But when he arrived on the west side edging his property, Rhys stopped and pressed his shoulder to an oak tree. His breaths exhaled across Viviane's hooded head. The pain returned, but it was not because of torn muscles.

"What is it?" Viviane peeked out from under the hood and gasped. "That is your home?"

Rhys swallowed back a howl. "It was."

Flames engulfed the small country cottage Rhys had lived in for three decades. He had built it himself, cutting the wood and taking care in fashioning the joins to create an airtight fit in the walls. Fieldstones that he'd plastered about the fireplace tumbled to the ground. Fire sparks danced hundreds of feet in the air. A few pine trees had ignited close by.

The pack had shown their disapproval over his actions.

No longer could Rhys claim an alliance with either side of his nature. The vampires hated him on principle. The werewolves, he had betrayed.

Even Faery would haunt him relentlessly, yet never embrace him.

Wrapping his arms about Viviane he squeezed away the need to shout his anger to the world. Because he could not be angry for the choices he had made. He would make the same choice again if he knew in advance the results would be so devastating.

"You can live with me," she whispered against his ear. "We'll return to my home in Venice. You will like it there."

"We will take care of one another," he agreed.

He turned and stomped into the forest, where sunlight filtered through the tree canopy, and laid Viviane on a bed of leaves. Not nearly as soft or fragrant as the roses she deserved. "I'll gather pine bows to make you a shelter. Stay put."

THEY EMBRACED BENEATH THE shelter all day. Rhys snoozed. Viviane sensed he needed the rest for his body to completely heal. She drowsed, but was aware, not far off, of the fire that tore apart her lover's home.

By late evening, the couple broached the gates of Paris. Viviane stood a-tatter, a gray wolf at her side. Viviane was able to slip through behind a large tumbrel packed with cabbage heads nestled in hay, Rhys loping ahead of her and using the shadows as cover.

By the time she reached Henri's home, her feet ached, for she'd not been wearing shoes when the wolves had kidnapped her, and her back felt as though she'd carried a load of stones for leagues.

Rhys was tired as well, for as soon as they reached

her property, he scampered to the back courtyard and lay down, panting, his tongue lolling out his mouth.

"I'll bring out some water."

Rhys whined and tucked his nose under a paw. He lay before Orlando's grave. So much he had lost.

"Because of me."

She turned and stepped on a scatter of roses. So many of them, wilted and strewn by a breeze. She bent and collected a few white petals and pressed them into her palm. If only he had arrived with these earlier, before the wolves had taken her.

Sniffing away tears, she found a bucket, and filled it from the well inside the tepidarium.

AFTER SHIFTING, RHYS WRAPPED up in the wool blanket folded neatly and left outside the back door. Viviane had brought his wolf water, and left him alone, which he appreciated. The waxing moon shimmered the water remaining in the bucket.

He glanced to the grave. "Forgive me, Orlando. And blessings for your rest."

He tried the door handle, finding it open. Navigating the dark town house on bare feet, his fingers tracing the walls, he felt the gouges his werewolf had left behind when chasing Viviane. It was a part of him he could never change. She would have to accept that if she truly loved him. Pray, she could.

He ascended the stairs and sought the small glow of light lacing a guest chamber door, and walked in. Viviane sat in a copper tub lined in white linen.

"Come to me," she pleaded on a whisper.

He dropped the blanket and settled into the tub. There wasn't much water and it was tepid. She soaped his hair and picked out leaf fragments and sticks. The talon wounds had all healed.

Viviane eased a cloth gently over his skin. Could she touch the wound that had bruised his heart? He didn't want her to. It should remain a reminder of his faithful companion, Orlando, and of what Rhys had sacrificed for his own happiness.

Two scars he wore on his heart now. Orlando and Emeline.

Meeting her silent eyes, he was not sure he could endure taking another scar, yet he would fight vampires and werewolves and any other who attempted to part the two of them.

He nestled his cheek against her breasts and closed his eyes. "Mine," he whispered. "You are mine."

She kissed the crown of his head and traced lazy circles across his back. No longer did he care his physical home had burned to the ground. In Viviane's arms he found home. A man required nothing more than love and acceptance to survive.

"I love you."

"You are loved," she replied.

He melted against her breast and dared to sleep.

RHYS WANTED TO START putting affairs together for William Montfalcon. He would tidy up his home and find the title and ensure Claude Mourreigh received it all.

Viviane had come along because leaving her behind was unthinkable. The two could not move more than arm's reach from one another without feeling alone.

They closed the front door and Rhys did not have to seek a candle. The moon was high in the sky, but a day until it was full.

He stroked the hood from Viviane's head and it caught

on the lacquered stick piercing the chignon. Midnight hair spilled over her shoulders.

"Mmm, I've undone you, LaMourette."

"Not completely, lover." Drawing her fingers over her neck, she lazily moved across her breasts, then tugged the thin blue ribbon, which barely closed the gray bodice over the black corset beneath.

Rhys bent to bite the ribbons free from the tight bow. They didn't make it upstairs to the bedchamber. This evening they christened the chaise longue with their sexual antics. And the Aubusson rug stretched between two chairs in the sitting room. And the wall of books where Rhys's fingers slipped into the space left by the missing volume of sonnets as he plunged himself inside his lover's hot body.

Well after midnight, they had made it to the stairs.

His shoulders and arms stretched across a stair riser, Rhys dropped his head to rest against the next step.

"I don't want to leave you for a night," he decided of his departure tomorrow evening.

"We sated your wolf tonight. Why can we not do it tomorrow?"

"The full moon is the one night I must give my werewolf rein. Or rather, my vampire."

"Twice now your werewolf has not harmed me."

"Which baffles the hell out of me."

"Perhaps your werewolf was confused?"

"Please, Viviane, let's take this slowly."

"Very well. I am willing to do that because I love you *and* your werewolf who is ruled by a bloodthirsty vampire. I've been thinking about what you said, the boon you owe Faery. I would sacrifice our child for you."

He touched her mouth, seeking with his silence.

She nodded. "I have seen your vampire's rage, and

know it is a good thing it is not allowed release more than a day or two a month. Besides, I could have more children. To be honest, I am not sure I'd make such a good mother."

"You would be a fierce mother, Viviane. You've a protective instinct about you. And I would marvel to stand over you with our child cradled in your arms."

"Our second child," she corrected.

That she accepted his bizarre bargain warmed Rhys's soul. He did not deserve Viviane, but he would challenge no man to take her from him.

"What shall I do with myself when you are gone? I'll miss you desperately."

"Whatever you do, be sure you don't go out on your own. Promise me, Viviane."

"I promise. But I don't believe Lord Salignac is going to do anything to me. He's more bluster than bite."

She knew the enemy so little. Constantine had allowed Emeline to die. He made it clear he would kill or torture Rhys if given opportunity.

"You need to understand Constantine is never the one who wields the killing blow, but rather the one who orchestrates heinous deeds. Viviane, I did not want to tell you, but…"

"He sent William Montfalcon after Henri," she guessed.

Rhys nodded. "I figured it out after seeing the bill and confronted him about it."

"As a Council representative what will you do to him?"

"I must report him to win my position with the Council." He hugged her tightly. "They would kill him. I don't know if I can do that to my brother."

"He killed your lover."

"I want to tell you how it happened, so you will understand why it is not so easy for me to condemn my brother. Constantine did not kill Emeline." Rhys exhaled heavily. "He allowed her to die."

"But you said—"

"I know. At times it feels as though he was the one to draw the silver blade across her throat, but in reality, he merely stood back and let it happen when I could not get to her fast enough."

She drew up his hand and pressed her lips to the palm. Her breath tickled. "Tell me?"

And so the last of his secrets would be out.

"We had come to heads, Constantine and I. A few decades ago I had the grand idea to start a tribe of half-breeds. I located a few here in Paris. Same as me, half wolf, half vampire. Naturally, Constantine was appalled and he attacked.

"We were battling one another at the edge of a forest west of the city. We faced Constantine and three vampires. I don't believe in shifting to werewolf form to gain the advantage, and he was my brother, you understand. Emeline was strong and fancied herself a warrior. I didn't like that."

"Were the others in your tribe like you? Enchanted to tame their wolves."

"No. Far as I know, I'm the only one with the particular problem where my mind is not as my body. Anyway, I was standing off two vampires, and I noticed Constantine standing inside the forest before two hunters."

"Vampire hunters? The Order of the Stake?"

"Hunters of all sorts, possibly the Order of the Stake, though I had thought they only pursued vampires. We had noticed them, my men and I, in the city earlier that evening. I knew they had been stalking us, but had not thought they had followed us out of the city. I saw they held a woman and knew it was Emeline."

Rhys bowed his head, catching it in his palm. Viviane hugged him, holding him closely. He felt her heart pound against his chest, her pulse thud against his neck.

"I saw Constantine step back, lifting his arms as if in retreat. And the hunters took off with Emeline. I knew he had no investment in keeping her alive, yet I could not believe he would just let them take her.

"Enraged, I shifted. I took the heads off the two vampires and leaped to pin my brother on the ground. I howled and raised my paw to slash at him, but stopped before doing so. He was my brother. Even goaded by my vampire mind, my werewolf would not harm him. Isn't that incredible?"

"Not for you, Rhys. You are kind before cruel."

"Not if I do not know you." She slipped her fingers along his hairline, dashing back the strands from his face.

"I raced into the forest and found the hunters over Emeline's body. One had drawn out the silver blade from her heart. I took off his head in one swipe. The other hunter I let run a ways before taking him apart with talons. I slaughtered them.

"By the time I returned to Emeline she was dead. Constantine was nowhere to be seen. I should have followed him to Paris and killed him."

"No," Viviane cooed. "You would not have."

"He didn't kill her," Rhys murmured, "but he didn't stop it from happening. And so I cannot kill him, but if ever the chance to stop his death were presented me, I would not stop it. And do you know..." He grimaced, fighting tears. "I had no idea she was pregnant, but it was apparent when looking over her body."

"I am so sorry."

"When I saw the talon on your vanity... Constantine must have returned to her body while I pursued the hunters and claimed the talon. What kind of monster is he?"

"Not a man who will ever find peace, surely."

Rhys didn't say more; he did not need to.

"You did not continue with the tribe following that?"

"No. I became a recluse for years, then decided Emeline would have wanted me to live, and so I kept to the country and the packs that accepted me. It is also when Orlando came to me. He gave me hope. I wanted to forget the pain from my past and move forward. As now. You are my future, yes?"

"Oh, yes."

"Then I'm going to secure the bravo we discussed a few days ago."

Loose hair tumbled down her back as she sat. "He won't come inside, will he?"

"No, I'll have him posted outside. But, Viviane, one day. Twenty-four short hours. You can catch up on reading sonnets."

"I hold a sonnet in my heart for you."

She turned into his arms and laid her head upon his shoulder. Rhys traced her mouth and slid his fingers down her neck. "When I return let's leave the city."

"Yes."

"So simple as that?"

"Of course! During your absence I'll spend the day packing Henri's estate. "

"How many trunks will I need to provide?"

"Two. Or perhaps, three. I'll send them on to Venice. It is a magical city."

"To magic," he said. But she'd already filled him with more magic than he thought possible.

CHAPTER THIRTY

IT WAS NIGHTFALL BEFORE they dragged their sex-wearied bodies from the bed and Viviane tugged a chemise over her shoulders. Rhys dressed in breeches and his leather greatcoat and gathered his tricorn.

She trailed him about the house, her fingers laced within his, as he checked the doors and windows.

He repeated what he'd explained more than once already. "Be sure to have the bravo escort you when you go to Henri's to pack, Viviane."

"I will be quite well, lover."

He stopped at the front door, and drew Viviane's lithe body against his. The chemise was so thin her nipples darkened the fabric. He pressed a palm over one to enjoy the hard play of it against his flesh.

"I know you are capable, and not like the weak mortal women. But you understand my concerns?"

"I do, and I don't know what to say to keep you from worry."

"Nothing will calm my worry until I return to hold you in my arms again. I love you, Viviane."

She kissed him, a sweet, blissful lingering of their mouths that filled him with regret.

"I am yours," she said into his mouth. And turned her head to nestle against his neck.

TO THINK, HE HAD GOTTEN RID of half his kin for her, Constantine fumed. Prove your alliance to me, she had said. And so he had. Only to have her slap him across the jaw with a humiliating repudiation.

"A half-breed."

He wanted to shout, to yell, to tear things apart and beat upon them until they were bloody. Instead he would exact perfect revenge against the two of them.

Lord de Salignac prowled the brothel's close confines. He visited when all options to finding a stray blood source were unavailable. Incense and sex salted the air. Fabric smooth and silken brushed his hands and legs. Tonight he did not want a street beggar or a foul-smelling orphan who lurked beneath the bridges strapping the Seine. He needed a very specific beauty.

The madam Celeste Demorreau, a young thing who had inherited the position from her mother, hooked her arm along his, and walked him about the receiving room where dozens of potentials lounged and preened at one another. Some kissed lazily in hopes of attracting his eye with the subversive display.

Looking over the top of his round, violet-lensed spectacles, Constantine scanned the room. He favored an encounter with the twosome embracing at the wall.

"My lord?" the madam prompted.

Constantine focused. "She must have dark hair," he said in a low voice that kept their conversation private from the women. "Slender, and…an ample bosom."

"There is a new girl. She's rather shy, but I think she will fit your requirements. This way."

Leading him through the halls draped in alternating white and black velvet fabric, the madam stopped before a threadbare tapestry and cast it aside to reveal a woman seated before a vanity. Her reflection pursed small red lips. A narrow face with wide, bold eyes, a curious sadness gave her a solemn grace. She looked similar to Viviane. Not as beautiful, but she would do.

"Have her sent to my home."

"But that is not usual—"

"Your mother has not told you of our arrangements?"

She nodded. "Forgive me, my lord. Yes, I am aware. Tomorrow evening?"

"Excellent."

RHYS HAD SENT WORD to the Council that the werewolf who had murdered the vampires was dead. He hesitated mentioning Salignac's involvement; if it should later be learned, Rhys's integrity would be questioned.

Which was why he thanked the Council for their consideration, but explained he could not accept a position at this time. They need not know he was in love and wanted to spend every moment by his lover's side. Nor need they know he could not betray the brother he hated.

It had not been a difficult decision. Perhaps later he would develop renewed interest to serve, but for now, love ruled.

The German landau coach was exactly what Rhys needed. Actually, it was what Viviane needed. He stroked a palm along the highly varnished black exterior. Inside the seats adjusted on hinges to fold down for sleeping. And the windows had sturdy wood shades that blocked all light from entering.

They could travel during the day, allowing Viviane to sleep completely protected from the sun. And it was well sprung, necessary for the journey to Venice, which Rhys guessed would be well over a fortnight.

After indicating he'd purchase the coach, he was thankful he kept most of his money in gold with a *notaire* in Paris. It hadn't been destroyed by the fire at his home.

What he needed was a place where he could keep his valuables for centuries. An institution he knew would always exist, no matter where Rhys's travels took him, and a *notaire* who would keep his secret.

"Some sort of bank for the Dark Ones," he muttered. "I like the idea."

Today had been successful, for he'd secured this smart coach for his lover, and now his future looked bright. He had the full moon to meet tonight, and then he could step into the future, with Viviane at his side.

"MADEMOISELLE."

The bravo who Rhys had hired spoke so little, the hairs at the back of Viviane's neck stiffened at the sound of his warning voice.

She'd pushed the key into the lock on William's front door, and turned to find the bravo gesturing she move inside, quickly.

"What is it?" she asked.

"I heard a commotion around back. Go inside and lock the door. I'll come around to the back and knock once for entrance. Yes?"

She nodded agreement, and slipped inside. The key tumbled down her green satin skirt and clinked onto the stone floor. Too nervous, she left it where it lay. Pacing twice before the door, she suddenly remembered to turn the bolt.

Stepping back, she peered out the window into the street. No shadows moved. Here, where the buildings towered four stories, and hugged one another so closely, very little moonlight was permitted through.

She forced herself away from the window. Her fingers brushed the writing desk where the wooden hummingbird sat upon the volume of sonnets. Rhys's melodic recitation comforted her as she remembered the afternoon spent entwined on the chaise lounge.

She clutched the bird, fitting her fingers about its smooth body. To have selected this specific gift, he knew her heart.

"Rhys," she whispered. "Hurry home to my heart."

A crash at the back of the house sounded like wood breaking and something heavy hitting the ground. Viviane clung to the stair rail. Her senses honed on a disturbing scent. Blood.

And another presence she could not sort out.

Before she could think to flee out the front door, Constantine de Salignac marched into the room. Adorned in silver and black, his mirthless smile stabbed at her. Blood spilled from his mouth, which he wiped away with a handkerchief.

"Viviane, *chérie*." Salignac spread his arms wide in invitation.

She backed away. The sonnet book dug into the arch of her slippered foot.

Another man stepped alongside the sneering vampire lord.

"You've met Ian Grim before, I'm sure?"

The witch was an ally to vampires. Dressed in emerald velvet, his blond hair a frazzled mess, the man looked insane. But the true insanity was in the wrist he displayed to her. It bled.

Witch's blood was poison to a vampire. One drop of it upon her skin would sizzle through to her insides and eat away at her organs and heart and finally reduce her to ash. A slow but sure death.

"What do you want?" she firmly asked, glad for her lacking fear. "You dare to intrude in Monsieur Hawkes's home?"

"I see the mongrel nowhere in sight. Does he not give a care for his lover's safety?"

"I should be safe in my own home."

"Ah? You two are sharing the place now? I know for a fact Hawkes squats in this home. It belonged to William Montfalcon."

Grim stepped forward, brandishing his wrist as a weapon Viviane could not put herself far enough away from. Her hips swiped the writing desk, setting her off balance.

But it was Constantine who approached and spread his fingers over her hair and down her cheek. The touch chilled her blood. He had watched, waited for his moment when Rhys was not around to protect her.

She struck out, slicing him on the cheek with a fingernail. "What did you do to the bravo?"

"The oaf bowed before me and begged me to bite him." Constantine wiped the blood from his skin then licked his finger. "The big ones always do fall the quickest. You did not place false hope in the lackwit actually protecting you?"

She had. She had underestimated Constantine.

"What do you want?"

"Revenge. It is a family game, to put it appropriately. Rhys has had his win, now I shall take mine."

Viviane tightened her grip about the hummingbird. All she had right now to bolster her courage. A glance confirmed Grim's blood dripped on the floor, not a step from her skirts. She drew back her toe.

"Rhys changed his mind," she said. "He no longer wishes revenge against you."

"My brother is backing down? Doubtful. That mongrel is vicious with his cuts."

"He has never killed someone close to you."

"Does he have you believe I killed Emeline?"

"No." Viviane looked aside. "He told me what really happened. But you did not protect her."

"He blames me for not protecting his own? Isn't that a fine excuse."

"Leave us to live peacefully, I beg of you."

"You beg to me now?" Constantine splayed beringed fingers across his chest. "That is rich. After all I have sacrificed for your pleasure, and you have mocked me for those sacrifices, *now* you would beg my mercy?"

"You have sacrificed nothing."

"I have killed half a dozen of my kin for you!"

"I did not ask you to kill them, merely to be rid of them."

"Does that not imply death?"

"You are heartless."

"You are a bitch, Viviane LaMourette. You think you can survive with the half-breed as your patron?"

"Honestly? No. But I prefer dying in Rhys's arms to living in yours."

Constantine moved swiftly. He wrangled her arm around behind her back and twisted so she could not struggle free. And with her head forced forward, she could smell the filth in the witch's clothing.

"Begin the spell, Grim," the vampire lord commanded.

"What are you doing?" She struggled, but he held her with ease, pressing his clawed hand about her neck and wrenching her arm higher across her back.

Grim chanted in Latin, a language Viviane recognized from the intonations only. A spell? The devil take Constantine and all his bloody kin!

"If you wish your revenge on Rhys then kill me," she cried.

No, please. She did not want to die.

Pulled upright by a yank of her hair, Viviane felt Grim's words enter her mind. The bellicose tones shimmered and ignited. The rhythm of his incantation seduced.

Viviane blinked. Her shoulders relaxed.

"You think my revenge is against my brother?" Constantine's teeth dragged down her neck, not cutting, but warning. "You betrayed me by taking my love, twisting it, and tossing it at me. Wicked bitch. You will spend the rest of your days unable to move, yet your mind will be alive and vital. Think of me, Viviane. Think of me when the rats scurry over your body and you try to remember what your lover's touch felt like. And know because you betrayed me, you will have unending horror."

The witch's chanting grew to a shout.

Viviane's body stiffened. Her hands cringed into claws. The hummingbird's beak dug into her palm. She tried to fight the movement, but it was as though her muscles were being commanded by Grim's voice. Constantine's hold slipped away, yet she sensed him at her back, supporting, holding her.

Viviane opened her mouth to scream.

Did she scream? Had she opened her mouth? She couldn't feel her lips.

And as she stretched her jaw and pleaded with the witch to cease, she knew she was not moving at all. Her body was frozen. Held motionless by a spell that enchanted her to a drowsy, mirthless smile.

"It is complete."

In her peripheral view, Constantine's hand spread open to receive. "The choker," the vampire said.

He spoke of the iron-maiden choker. Had he been to Henri's home? She'd left the thing behind for the sellers to include with the house.

Why could she not move? And how long would this miserable spell last? To keep her immobile yet conscious?

"Bind that wound on your wrist," Constantine directed the witch. Then he clutched the roses on the side of Viviane's head and tugged them off. "I will need this."

Grim must have brought along bindings, for but moments passed before he confirmed the task complete. "Shall I hold her for you?"

Shuffled into the witch's hold, Viviane could feel his hands grip about her shoulders. His stench reviled.

Constantine's pitiful smile stabbed. "Frightened?"

"Yes," she screamed silently. "Make this stop. Rhys!"

"You should be."

He lifted the choker before her. She saw the small black stones and the sharp points. If he intended to put it on her, it was backwards.

"You should not have accepted my gift if you intended to deny my love. I have only ever been kind to you, Viviane," he said. "You would have been safer with me, your own breed. But you are tainted now. You've the half-breed's blood in your veins."

Thank the gods she had taken Rhys's blood. Viviane could feel it within her now. Hot, strong. Life sustaining?

"I can smell him on you. It is more filthy and wretched than Grim's odor, I assure you."

Something warm spattered her cheek. Tears.

The cold choker clutched her throat. Constantine tied the ribbon behind her neck. The points pierced her flesh, burning. Agony slid a delirious scream through her mind. Yet she could but experience and not react.

He touched a bloody finger to his mouth, but did not

taste it. "Tainted," he pronounced, and wiped the finger on her bodice. "Help me lift her."

Her body was handled roughly as Grim gripped her shoulders and Constantine groped about her skirts to get her stiff legs in hand. "Set her on the chaise, will you?"

Grim asked, "What of the—?"

"This first."

Viviane's world tilted, her vision scaling along the shelves of books and the ceiling. Her skirts shuffled up her legs. Metal buttons clacked as Constantine released his breeches.

"You are a voyeur?" he asked the witch. "Give me a moment. I want to send my wicked lover to hell with part of me inside her."

Viviane's bile curdled. She wanted to lash at the monster, to win her freedom.

He entered her. She could feel nothing. But the horror overwhelmed as he pumped quickly, gruffly, and gave an abbreviated cry of pleasure.

"Remember me, Viviane, as I drip down your thigh and you are unable to wipe it away."

He stood and refastened his breeches. "Help me now, Grim."

Through the house and out the back door they carried her. Were they setting her on the ground? She could not move her eyes, and could see only directly before her. The sky glittered with full, gorgeous moonlight.

Rhys. *My love.* At this moment he must be loping freely across the countryside beneath the pale full moon.

Constantine kissed her on the mouth. She could not feel the touch. His face blocked out the moonlight.

She wanted to see the moon. To connect with her lover.

I am yours. Her last words to him.

"Grim, hand me the crown."

Her tormentor held a hideous thing before her. A ring of skulls. Small skulls similar to the rose hairpiece she often wore.

"Rat skulls," he said, his eyes glinting. "I crown you Queen of the Rats."

The moon flashed. Something moved over the top of her. It was glass, set in a narrow frame, for she could see the leading that connected it as if a box to the sections on the side.

What horror is this? They'd put her inside something. And now it was lifted from the ground and she could feel her body floating.

"You had your chance," Constantine said. "And now I condemn you to eternity."

A scream exploded behind her eyes.

CHAPTER THIRTY-ONE

Paris, modern day

DANE TOLD RHYS SHE'D START making calls to gather a team when they returned to his estate. But as soon as she sat on the bed in the guest room, she fell into a deep sleep and dreamed of soft, cushy beds layered with satin sheets, and with men like Rhys Hawkes tucked between them. She woke later, smiling, thinking that was the best dream ever.

In her peripheral view, she noticed Rhys sat on the chair near the window, his heels on the windowsill. His profile revealed closed eyes to the high-noon sunlight.

"I thought I locked the door," she said groggily.

"You did not," he replied. "You going to sleep all day?"

She'd like to. "Sorry. Guess the lure of a real bed got the better of me."

Rest would come soon enough. She'd already pocketed ten grand.

"What are you?" Dane boldly asked.

He tilted a smile at her. The sunlight admired his face, slipping along the lines fanned out at the corners of his eyes and in the crags wrinkling his forehead as he lifted his brows. "Half vamp, half wolf. What are you?"

"Familiar," she offered plainly.

"I suspected."

"Aversion to cats?"

"Their fur, not their demeanors," he offered.

"How can you soak up the rays if you're half vamp?"

"My werewolf protects me. How can you sit in the same room as a wolf if you are a cat shifter?"

"I'm not afraid of wolves. Nowadays, they're plain stupid. But vampires are smart."

"I would argue that summation, but to each his, or her, own."

She had insulted him, but she wasn't sure how.

"How did it happen?" she asked. "I mean, if the legend is true. Where were you that some vampire was able to kidnap your lover?"

"It was the full moon. I'd left the city to put myself away from her. I had hired the biggest, strongest bravo I could find to protect her. I only wanted to keep her safe."

Hell of a lot of good that had done.

"I thought the only problem a werewolf had during the full moon was wanting to mate. Why would you need to be away from her?"

Dane couldn't imagine what he must be struggling with right now. If it were true—which it wasn't—he must feel tremendous guilt.

"Because of my mixed blood my vampire mind controls my werewolf. Makes it bloodthirsty. It's never good. I should have taken her along with me. I could have chained myself. I should have…"

Dane felt Rhys's anxiety burst through to the top of the scale. At that moment the butler knocked and brought in breakfast.

"You want some?" she asked, hoping to alleviate his tension.

"No, I will leave you. I am eager to return underground. An hour?"

"Less than that. I'll round up a team. Thanks, Monsieur Hawkes."

He nodded. "I'll have the next ten thousand waiting for you before we leave."

RHYS FOUND IT DIFFICULT TO do nothing, waiting for Dane to gather a larger team of spelunkers, but it had been centuries. Much as it pained him to admit it, a few more hours was not going to matter.

Viviane had taken his blood the day before the fire. But he had not taken hers. Rhys now believed, with two centuries of knowledge under his belt, if she would have bitten him, cursed his wolf with the blood hunger, his vampire mind may have been appeased.

Or rather, he wanted to believe.

"Master Hawkes." Poole stepped into the living room. "A Monsieur Lepore is here to see you."

"Show him in."

Rhys fisted a hand in his opposite palm, anticipation growing. One step closer to locating Constantine.

Vincent Lepore was a tall, slender vampire with gray hair and a nose that curved west. He'd served on the Council for a century, though, and Rhys knew from hearsay, his word was impeccable.

"Hawkes." Lepore offered a hand and the two shook. "Your assistant tells me you are looking for your brother?"

"Yes, and I assume since you've come directly to me, you've information on his location?"

"Actually—" Lepore scratched the back of his neck "—I've discussed this matter with a few Council members."

It had become a matter? That didn't sound promising.

"We've determined it unwise to reveal Salignac's location to you."

"You protect a criminal?"

"What crime has Constantine committed?" Lepore asked, and for good reason for he could not be aware of Rhys's suspicions.

"I cannot say. I want to speak to my brother. Can you not, at the very least, give me a phone number?"

"Don't think he uses technology. He's very private, Rhys."

"And yet you seem to know much more about him than I, his own brother."

"The Council is aware of the bad blood between the two of you. You know we keep tabs."

Yes, and yet another reason he'd been fine with his decision not to pursue a seat on the Council. Big brother, he was not.

"Constantine may have buried my lover alive, beneath Paris, two centuries ago," Rhys blurted out. "Had her bespelled by the witch Grim."

"The warlock is on the Council's watch list."

Rhys chuckled. The Council had a tendency to watch more often than get involved.

"He lives in France," Lepore offered. "That is all I will say. I can attempt to contact him on your behalf if that will serve?"

"Do so," Rhys said. "Tell him I need answers regarding Viviane LaMourette."

"CHANGE OF PLANS, BOYS." Dane entered the living room a few minutes after Lepore had left and plopped onto the sofa next to Simon, who protected his laptop from her elbow.

"You weren't able to gather a team?" Rhys wondered.

"Got the team. But today all efforts are focused in the Bois de Boulogne. Two of our own have gone missing."

"*Our* own?" Simon intoned skeptically.

"Fellow cataphiles."

"They are of no concern to our mission," Rhys stated, still angered that the Council deemed it wise to protect his brother from him.

Dane jumped from the sofa and met him in the center of the room. "Look, wolf, if I spend the day helping my cohorts search for their friends, then they'll reciprocate. And it's not as if one more day is going to matter on your quest, is it?"

Rhys's heart clenched. Chimeras should not have such power over a man. "Twenty-four hours, then. You return to this mission promptly at eleven tomorrow morning."

"I will. I'm going to take off."

"She won't come back," Simon commented as Rhys strode the floor. "That was a ruse. She got ten grand. She's going to run."

"She'll be back. And you'll be sure of it. Grab your gear. We're going to join the search party."

CHAPTER THIRTY-TWO

Paris, 1785

NORMALLY RHYS WOULD RUN to Paris as a wolf, and shift in the forest edging the city. Today, he returned by carriage, feeling rather tall and high as the driver's box placed him.

As he gained the rue Saint-Honoré, carriages and horses stood at a standstill. An ashy scent overwhelmed. Gray flakes floated in the air.

Hackles stiffening, Rhys pressed the horses, but to no end. He was trapped, unable to navigate forward.

Leaping from the driver's seat, he squeezed between horse flesh and carriage wheels.

Heart racing and fists pumping to increase his speed, he did not see the world as he passed through the streets, turning and dodging to avoid carriages and people. Turning right, he shouldered an old man but did not call regrets.

As he neared Montfalcon's neighborhood he could smell the lingering sulfurous miasma of what must have been a raging fire.

Try as he might, he could not find Viviane's scent. But he could smell none of the people he passed, so that gave him hope.

He rounded the corner to havoc. A portion of the neighborhood had been charred to a skeleton of wood and stone framework. Smoke wafted from the simmering wreckage.

Three houses had burned to black crenellated stumps. And the center house was where Rhys had left his vampire lover to await his return.

Legs going loose and wobbly as he approached, he reached out, but did not grasp a reassuring hand or land his lover's slender waist.

One man picked through the ash.

"Get out!" He stomped through the charred remains. It was warm yet for steam rose amongst the wisps of ash.

A man bent over the remains straightened and tugged smartly at his cloth-buttoned coat. A smear of ash dashed his white jabot. "And you are?"

"This is my home," Rhys gasped. Well, it had been for the short time. He had no home at all now. Two burned in so little time… "Do you scavenge in the ruins of my life?"

"Forgive me, monsieur. I am Philip LeMarck, the city inspector. You are just arriving?"

"Yes, I've been away…but a day." His voice broke. Rhys clasped his throat.

The city inspector. So he was not poking about, looking for something to steal. At once Rhys wanted to fall against him for support, and yet he would not allow any to see his shock.

He rallied strength with a deep inhale. "When did it happen?"

"Burned through the night. Only got the flames extinguished early this morning. Bit of rain fell a few hours ago, which helped."

Feeling his bile rise, Rhys stumbled forward. He landed his hands on the inspector's forearms. The man braced him.

"My lover," he gasped. "Viviane LaMourette. She was

here. Though…she was to be at her home packing." Hope momentarily sparked.

The inspector's face bowed and he shook his head. "This way."

Frozen in the middle of the destruction, the wind stirred thick gray ash flakes before Rhys. A storm to match that within his heart.

"Monsieur?" The inspector stood before the study, which had been directly below the bedchamber. "Perhaps you should sit a moment before we do this? I'll call for the water carrier, and you'll have a drink. Better yet, some hard ale."

"Do? Do what?" Innately, Rhys knew where the man wanted him to go. Tread forth into hell. Open his eyes to a truth he could not bear. "What is over there?"

"Are you sure you're ready—"

"Just tell me!"

"We found two bodies."

Rhys dropped to his knees. Sulfur tangled at the back of his throat. Tears spilled down his cheeks. Had his hands ever shaken so horribly?

"One body appears male," the inspector said. "Found him outside the back door."

The bravo. Had he tried to get inside to rescue Viviane from the flames? How could she have been trapped inside? It wasn't as if he'd locked her up tight. Had the flames eaten at her gown, the smoke smothering her cries?

No. *Please don't let her have suffered.*

Lifted from his knees by the inspector, Rhys shoved him roughly. "Show me, then."

"I walked through quickly when I arrived this morning, monsieur. I'm waiting for the surgeon to arrive to help me, er…recover the bodies. Over here where the top floor dropped down and the bed…"

A charred bedpost jutted out as if it were a stalagmite in a dark cave. Here the ash swirled like summer snow. Flakes landed on Rhys's shoulders and hair. His hands trembled. A reedy moan escaped and he again landed on his knees before the charred hand visible amidst scattered lumber.

The inspector squatted and gently pushed aside a heap of ash, revealing the bottom of a jawbone and the reticulated spine bones. Black and charred and—Rhys looked away, closing his eyes, but that did not stop the tears.

His heart pounded. Dead!

He felt his muscles grow slack. The world wobbled.

Mercy. He had not been here to save her.

He heard a snick and turned to see what the inspector had tugged from the body. But a few strands of black moire ribbon were intact. Coated with a black smudge, tiny skulls tumbled away and dropped.

Rhys plunged his hand into the ash and grasped a skull no larger than his fingertip. *Red roses clutching skulls.* The first time he'd seen her wearing that piece her azure eyes had sparkled.

He clutched it to his chest and reeled forward, rocking. He was aware the inspector rose, patted him on the shoulder, then left him alone with his agony.

His heart spilled out in wretched cries. And when they turned to howls, he pressed his face to his knees to stifle the strange sounds that might see him revealed for the creature he was.

CHAPTER THIRTY-THREE

Paris, modern day

SIMON KEPT PACE WITH DANE and didn't grumble as they descended to the third level beneath the park west of the city to track the missing cataphile, Marcus Leonard. They were on the trail now. If Marcus had come this way, and gotten lost because his equipment had failed, they would find him.

Rhys had joined the search with a separate crew, which surprised Dane. Simon explained the man did have a tendency to draw into himself when troubled. Being with strangers was probably less stressful for him right now.

"I'm impressed you didn't take the money," Simon commented.

They strode, side by side, rubber boots occasionally slipping on the slick stones. This tunnel was ten feet high and about as wide. Ahead, lights from two on the rescue team flashed across the walls.

"Wasn't mine to take," Dane said. "Look, I know you don't trust me, and that's your prerogative. But if you knew the big bads I owed money to, you'd know I'm in this for the big payoff."

"Human or other?"

"Other."

"Vampires?"

"Something like that. It's tribe Anakim. You know about them?"

"I know vampires form tribes, but that one is not familiar to me."

"They are night walkers. Can't access the daylight unless they can restore their bloodline."

"How do they do that?"

"By getting their hands on a nephilim."

"Isn't that a—"

"Yep."

Simon whistled.

Dane had said enough. "You really think we'll find the coffin?"

"Honestly?" Simon paused to lean against the curved wall and swiped sweat from his brow. Dane was impressed he'd tracked in this far. He was no athlete, to gauge from his spare frame. "No. But, as you have discovered, it's worth the search."

"My brand-new purse is doing the happy dance. But are you getting a bonus for this adventure?"

"I'd do anything for Rhys. The man has integrity dripping from his pores. He would walk the world for me if I needed him to. I hate to imagine what this will do to him if we find out it's true."

A shout ahead set the lead lights bobbling. Dane gripped Simon's hand. "They must have found something. Come on!"

As they raced through the tunnel, a terrified scream joined the melee.

Dane's hackles lifted. A foul scent alerted her she wasn't going to like what was around the corner. If she were in cat form right now her back would be arched and her tail high.

One of the lead team members pushed past her, hand

over his mouth. He didn't make it far before she heard him retching.

"Oh, Christ." Simon wrenched his forearm over his nose. "What is it?"

She pressed a palm to his shoulder as a sign to stay put. Two others stood glued to the wall, eyeing her, shaking their heads miserably.

"I'll take a look," she offered, and turned the curve where the rock ceiling suddenly dipped.

On the dirt floor lay a body crawling with beetles. The stench of death was so strong Dane had to swallow her bile. "Marcus?"

One of the leaders nodded and rushed past her to join the others.

Moving her head to direct the headlamp away from the body, Dane surveyed the area. The wall behind the body was splattered with a dark glistening substance. Blood.

"Something attacked him?" she muttered.

"Attack?" Simon called. He kept out of keen vision of the body. "What do you see?"

"Marcus's body," she relayed to him. Her nose could not adjust to the odor and she spat to get the foul taste from her mouth. "The wall and the floor are spattered with his blood. It's like an animal attacked him. Or someone went after him with a weapon."

Simon gagged.

Dane leaned over the body. The insects were not en masse, so the body could not have been dead long. Dane was no forensics expert, but she figured it should take at least a few days for massive insect invasion. Peering over his neck revealed claw marks. Not deep or wide. She wouldn't say wolf or any particular creature. Could simply be fingernails. In fact, when holding her fingers near the wounds without touching, they were a good match.

Another shout alerted her to a turn in the tunnel ahead.

"Stay there!" she called to Simon. "I'll go check it out."

Around the corner she found Roger, a burly German whom she'd dated once—until she'd met his six real cats; she did not do fetishes. He beamed his headlamp upon a scatter of thick limestone pavers. They'd been toppled from what looked to have been a half wall. Here and there a centuries-old skull pocked the wall.

"Another body?" she asked cautiously.

"I've heard the legend," Roger said in wonder, "but dismissed it."

His statement giddied her belly. Dane scampered over to view what Roger's headlamp illuminated within the torn limestone wall.

"A glass coffin." Broken, or rather shattered.

From the inside? Or had Marcus found it and broken the glass to get to what had been inside?

RHYS, WHO STOOD TOPSIDE after assisting a guide who'd twisted his ankle, spied Vincent Lepore standing on the street corner, another man at his side. At sight of the tall, dark-haired man, Rhys rushed across the street, fists bared.

Lepore stepped before the man, grabbing Rhys's wrists to keep him from an attack. "He's come to talk! Honor that, Hawkes."

Growling, and shoving into Lepore's body as if he could move through him to get to the man standing behind him, Rhys gave a surrendering growl and disengaged. He fisted the air and yowled out his frustrations.

"You bastard!"

Constantine stepped forward. The vampire had not

changed in appearance save his shoulders sagged and he appeared submissive, beaten down. His dark eyes did not fix to Rhys for more than a nanosecond at a time as he swept the area back and forth to Rhys.

"How could you do this?"

"It took you a long time to miss her, brother."

The statement prodded his werewolf, and Rhys lunged, shoving Lepore aside to slam Constantine's shoulders to the brick wall behind him. Talons grew out of his fingers and into his brother's flesh.

"Still so quick to anger." Constantine gritted his jaws, and met his glare. "I was jealous of you."

Pulled from behind, Rhys snarled as Lepore detached him, his talons dragging bloody gouges in Constantine's shoulders. "You said you wanted to speak to him. It will do no good to kill him now."

"I will do my heart a world of good to slaughter this vile creature."

"Before the world? Mortals walk across the street and drive by in their cars. Be smart, Hawkes."

Rhys huffed and stepped back of his own accord. He flicked a wrist, drawing his talons back in. Blood dripped from his fingertips. "You could never step back and allow me to have happiness, could you?"

"You stole her from me!"

"Gentlemen." Lepore stood between them, his arms out to grab the next one who made a move. "What's been done is done."

"She could be dead," Rhys argued.

"You thought her dead centuries ago," Lepore reasoned.

"What if she is alive?"

Constantine smirked.

"I will kill you!" This time Lepore delivered a gut

punch to Rhys as he charged, which caused him to bend over. The vampire had a mean right lunge. "Why do you protect him?" he muttered, slowing rising straight. "The Council should not take sides."

"The Council has only just become aware of a situation that may or may not be deemed a crime. Have you found a coffin?" Lepore insisted.

"No. But he's alluded to it. You did it, didn't you? Tell him of your crime!"

Constantine wrapped his arms across his chest and eyed the sidewalk. "If I cannot have her, then no man shall."

Rhys felt the tingle of his rising werewolf goad at his neck and spine. It would be so easy to shift, take his brother's head off, and Lepore's, too. He was not a man to murder, but sometimes even the staunchest must surrender to pure anger.

His brother had taken Viviane from him.

The jangle of his cell phone momentarily diverted his rage. Normally, he would ignore it, but Simon and Dane were still below ground. "Don't move," he said to the two men.

He answered and Simon's excited breathing startled him. "Take a breath, man. I can't understand you."

Simon huffed through his short, rapid sentences and the staticky connection, but Rhys heard a few key things. Murdered. Coffin. Escaped.

"A coffin? I'll be right there," Rhys said.

"I'll meet you topside to guide you."

"Not necessary. If there's blood, I'll scent you right to the location."

He shoved the phone in a pocket and stepped up to his brother. Without touching him, he stood face-to-face, seething. "They found the coffin."

"Is she alive?"

Lepore said, "Make a deal, gentlemen. If she is alive, you walk away with the girl, Hawkes, and leave your brother with the guilt over what he has done."

He didn't like that idea, but the growing excitement that there might possibly be a girl to find made him nod. "And if she is dead?"

"I will leave you two to fight it out."

"Deal." Rhys smacked a handshake with Lepore, then turned to walk off.

Just off the curb, he twisted and rushed back to his brother. A right swing caught Constantine's jaw and he felt the bones crack and saw the broken fang fly through the air.

Constantine dropped unconscious.

"Keep an eye on him," Rhys said to Lepore.

RHYS TRACKED UNDERGROUND through miles of tunnels, agility moving him swiftly. He located the rescue team in less than twenty minutes. Strong blood scent tickled his vampire's hunger. He had not fed in weeks. Over the centuries his blood hunger had grown lesser and his werewolf mind had but to appease the vampire once a month. A wise man would have done so before descending, but it was too late to worry now.

More than one team member had been sick, and he avoided the evidence as he raced around the corner and ran smack into Simon.

"You've found her?"

Simon gripped Rhys's forearm. Sweat drooled down his face and he trembled. It wasn't hot down here. The man must be in shock.

"No, but there's a coffin."

"Of glass?" His heart already sat in his throat. After

all these years, Constantine still had not changed. The arrogance of him!

Simon nodded effusively. "Glass. It's real."

Feeling the tingle of change at the tips of his fingers, Rhys shook his hands, fighting the vampire's menacing hunger. Inhaling, he maintained composure and clamped his arms across his chest. "Show me."

Simon pointed. "There's a body around the corner. I put my head around but didn't want to add to the stench with my own sickness. Dane's with it right now."

Rhys left the man and swung around the corner. He'd seen many a dead body. This one was a fresh kill. The blood had coagulated, but it was still bright red.

Fortunately, the stench consisted of more than blood, for the foul scents of death and trauma rose. He felt his vampire cringe, backing from it like a mongrel from rotting meat.

Something glinted in the eye….

Rhys leaned in and plucked out a small object from the eyeball. It was no longer than an inch, like a straight pin, yet fashioned from—

Heartbeats scurrying, Rhys gasped. This was— It looked as if it had been carved from wood, and had been broken off from the larger piece.

A strange elation eddied through his system. It could really be her!

He took in the surroundings. Blood everywhere. Ancient skulls were tucked in the walls and strewn on the cave floor. It looked a slaughter, not a simple killing. Whatever had done this…

He could think what had done this, and it hurt his heart to imagine it.

All these years, Constantine must have reveled in

the notion that he had achieved the greatest and most devastating triumph between the brothers.

"Rhys?" Dane swung around the corner. She seemed comfortable with the body and smell, and he gave her credit for that. "This way. I suspect Marcus found it and broke the glass."

Dropping the small wood piece into his breast pocket, he followed her down a passage. Her lamp lit the narrow tunnel. Spiderwebs glittered with blood droplets.

A small cove was blocked off with limestone blocks. Looking at the fallen blocks and glass shards wrenched his soul out through his pores.

Emitting an agonized cry at sight of the broken glass coffin, Rhys caught a palm against the limestone wall. He leaned forward, knowing he would not find anyone inside, for it was obvious whatever had been inside had escaped.

Breathing deeply through his nose, he separated the blood and sickness from the humid air. His vampire picked out the metallic taint of mortal man's blood glimmering on the glass shards.

Rhys rolled his shoulders back, stretching his muscles to stay relaxed, in control.

No other scent lifted beyond the blood. He slapped a palm to his forehead and clenched his jaws. What had she smelled like? It had been so long. Curse him, but he had forgotten what she had smelled like.

Concentrate. Give yourself to her memory.

Soft, silken hair veiling his face after they'd made love. The warmth of her skin steeped in the luscious aroma. It had been...like summer fields and rich, sweet grapes.

"Wine," he gasped, recognizing the smell. "Yes, it is her!"

Clamping his hands to his shoulders, he moaned at the horror of it, unable to celebrate the fact she may still be alive. He had done this to her! He had abandoned her after the fire, fully believing she had perished in it.

He had seen the burned body. Who had been the one wearing the hairpiece with the tiny skulls? Constantine was a foul bastard.

"Ouch! What the hell?" He spun to search the dim light where Dane stood. Rubbing her arm, she bent to inspect something on the floor.

He didn't care what it was. His world had changed. His soul had been wounded. Hell, it had been torn out and slashed to ribbons. No matter the remnants of violence surrounding, he could not get beyond his futile abandonment of the woman he had loved.

Still loved.

"It's some kind of necklace or medieval choker thing. Black stones on it. Lots of dried blood. It's sharp."

Swinging around, Rhys gripped the metal choker Dane dangled. It pierced his palm. Traces of what had once been ribbon fluttered from each end. As he touched it, the blood coating the filigreed iron permeated his skin, and her scent flooded him.

"Viviane."

He had never tasted her blood. What a fool he had been. Things could have been different for them. He could have patroned her. Hell, she could have survived without a patron. The centuries had taught him that.

"Here's something else," Dane said. "Nah, it's a bunch of rat skulls. Probably died ages ago."

Clutching the choker to his chest, pressing the sharp points through his shirt and flesh, Rhys fell to his knees and howled. "Viviane!"

CRESSIDA RUBBED HER BARE ARMS against the chill of the tunnel. All this strange talk was unfamiliar. Was she still in the mortal land of Paris?

The fresh blood scent sickened her. But more so, it angered. Grim's spell and the enchantment had bound her to the vampiress the moment the warlock had spoken the Latin words. She had been ripped from Faery.

Constantine de Salignac had stolen so many years from her. She and the vampiress were bonded in a means that had initially pleased Cressida—until the years had started to pass.

She stomped the ground fiercely, centering all her rage and vitriol into the ground. The stone rumbled with her fury, shaking and loosing pebbles from the ceiling.

Yet finally, she would have her boon.

CHAPTER THIRTY-FOUR

RHYS HELD OFF TEARS until they'd reached the estate. He had brusquely told Simon and Dane to give him peace, and had insulated himself behind locked doors in his room.

He wept now. Not loud, but a silent mourning of constant salty pain sliding down his cheeks.

Opening his palm he dropped the choker onto the table. Blood puddled on the wood laminate. His palm was pocked with crimson holes as if he'd slammed it upon a bed of nails.

As the wounds closed and pushed out drops of blood, he felt the greater wound expand and bleed profusely. His heart had fissured the moment Simon had called about the find. At first sight of the broken and blood-stained coffin, his heart had broken into pieces and fallen into his gut.

The choker had been tied around her neck backwards, so the metal points pierced flesh. The dried blood was proof of that.

He rubbed his knuckles. They still ached from the blow he'd delivered Constantine. He'd once considered his brother may have started the fire, but he'd never approached him about it. As the French Revolution had begun, Constantine had been ousted as tribe leader. Creedence Saint-Pierre assumed control.

All those decades—centuries—of exile and confinement in the coffin. She had suffered so much!

He'd promised Lepore he would walk away from his

brother if he found Viviane alive. And he would. But he had not found her yet.

He bowed his head. Legend told the spell had kept the vampiress conscious but frozen. Feeling, as well?

He remembered the wood piece and dug it from his pocket. It was the beak from the hummingbird.

"Forgive me, Viviane. I should have known. I should not have walked away from this city without viable proof of your death."

Yet he'd thought her ashes proof enough.

Moaning, Rhys dropped his head. While he knew no time must be lost in tracking the vampiress, he could not rally himself from the deep misery that racked his muscles and reduced him to a whimpering soul.

AN HOUR LATER, SIMON opened Rhys's door and peered inside. Dane followed and the two cautiously entered. The gentle vampire-werewolf sat by the window, hands flat on his thighs.

"Sorry to intrude," Simon started. "But Dane and I have determined there may be a time issue here. Hmm, how do I put this?"

Dane jumped in. "If she's topside, we'll want to find her before morning, and before someone else does. Like the media," she added. She spied the choker on the table. The blood scent was vile. "There's already a story on the news about the body found in the tunnel. They're spinning it as one friend who attacked another, and now he's hiding out. No references to an attack from something *other*."

"Which is good," Simon said. "Until the bodies start piling up."

"Bodies?" Rhys asked quietly.

"I hate to be so blunt," Dane said, "but she ripped out Marcus's throat. Obviously, she needs blood. And you know she'll be drawn to it. And what will her mental state be? She hasn't seen the world for centuries. "

Rhys swiped his hands over his face and sighed. "Enough."

Simon crossed his arms, defiant in his stance, but he didn't say anything. Dane's job was done. She could take the money and leave. But she didn't want to leave now.

Rhys looked to her. "I'll have Simon open a bank account for you today. Switzerland, of course. You're free to go."

"I'll stay and help, if you'll have me. I'm not as keen topside, but another set of eyes in the search can't hurt."

"I don't think I can afford you anymore."

She grinned, pleased he could find humor. "We're good, Hawkes."

"Very well, then I would like you to help us. I want a team sent out through the Boulogne park. She may have surfaced there. Another team should start in the eighth *arrondissement.* Perhaps I should put teams in other surrounding neighborhoods."

"I'll track the media," Simon said. "If word of any strange attack gets out, I'll find it. It shouldn't be difficult to find a vampiress who must be wearing a dress from the eighteenth century."

"The fabric would have decayed," Dane decided. "There were fibers and threads on the glass. She could be half naked."

Rhys slapped his arms across his chest. "I need to go out now. I can't sit around wondering. Tune the walkie-talkies to the same channel, and Dane keep me updated as you disperse the teams, yes?"

"I'll have them out within the hour."

He strode through the room, lifting his leather

jacket and checking it for the walkie. "Simon, keep me posted."

Dane followed his swift pace to the elevator bay. "You should eat, perhaps rest before going out."

"No time. And I have rested. She's out there, alone, likely manic. She needs me."

"Do you think you can catch her scent?"

He nodded. "I caught traces of it. If she's topside, I may be able to track her."

The elevator pinged, but Dane grabbed Rhys's arm. "This isn't your fault."

He pressed the heel of his palm to the doorway, and let the doors close. "I buried her, Dane. I believed her dead."

"So you see? Not your fault!"

"I found her in the ashes of William Montfalcon's home. When I touched her bones they disintegrated to ash. A human would not have completely ashed like that. The skull and the femur and hip bones would have remained mostly intact. I had every reason to believe it was her. Do you know, I sat there all day, carefully plucking her ash from the building remains and placing it upon my frock-coat. Then I bundled it up and took it to a mausoleum in the Boulogne. I spent the next three days in there, crying and asking her forgiveness."

"But it wasn't her."

"He planned this so well!"

"The evil vampire from the legend?"

"That bastard Constantine." He chuckled. "Yes, the evil vampire from the legend. He must have found a vampiress who looked like her. Or made one. Poor thing. She could not have known what her new patron's evil plans were.

But do you think he bespelled Viviane and buried her that same day? Or did he keep her awhile?"

"Don't think about it. Just concentrate on finding her."

CHAPTER THIRTY-FIVE

STEVE MONROE BOUNCED on his sneakers toward home, a backpack slung over his left shoulder. He'd been in Paris six months thanks to an exchange-student program. His major was cryptozoology. So long as he kept his nose to the books and didn't flash his Dracula T-shirt or his chupacabra obsession he was cool. And, okay, historical studies was what was listed on his syllabus.

It was late and the sun had set an hour ago. His stomach growled. "Hope Jack remembers it's his night to buy pizza."

He heard a noise at the end of the alleyway edging his building.

He hated *the end.* It was dark. Not that he feared the unknown. Hell, he wanted to *find* the unknown. But the neighbor's cats always pissed on the garbage bin and left half-eaten rats and mice strewn at the end.

Someone was crying and sniffling. A woman?

Sneakers squidging the wet tarmac, Steve set aside his distaste for the smell and peered around the narrow metal bin. A woman sat huddled there. Dark, disheveled hair spilled over shoulders and chest. With minimal illumination from a distant streetlight he saw her face, arms and legs were dirty. Was that blood on her face?

"Lady?" His voice warbled when he was nervous. Dude, he could handle an encounter with a ghost or shapeshifter, but a pretty woman? "Lady, are you okay?

"Uh, do you speak English? I am an American," he explained stupidly and then realized he'd better speak to her in French.

Wide blue eyes set in a dirt-and-blood-smeared face peered up at him. He glanced over and saw a man's body. His legs were hidden behind the garbage bin.

His neighbor? He'd never met the neighbors who lived below him, but he'd heard the brutish husband yelling to his wife on occasion.

"Oh, hell. Did he hurt you? Lady? Are you— Come here, let me get you out of there. Is he—is he dead?"

No. Duh. What woman could do something like kill a guy?

"You knocked him out?"

She nodded and reached out a hand, which he clasped to pull her up. When she stood before him, Steve slapped his palms to his chest and took a step back.

"Oh, hell, you are naked. Did that bastard…?"

He didn't want to think the dastardly stuff that could have happened to this chick. Her body was dirty, and her hair hung over bare breasts. She wasn't wearing any pants and he could see everything. Yet there was some wispy thread stuff hanging from her arms and waist.

"Okay, let's get you out of here. You beat him off? Good for you. Dirty bastard deserved whatever you gave him." He glanced down the alleyway. "Did he throw your clothes somewhere? In the trash? Clothes." He patted his shirt and pants.

She must not understand French, either. Or else he was conjugating the wrong words.

She nodded and patted her arms as he did. A dash of her tongue tested what looked like a bloody split lip.

Tugging off his T-shirt, Steve held it out with both hands. "Put this on." He shook it, but she merely stared at it. “Come on, it’s one of my faves. *The Wolfman*—1941, directed by George Waggner. It’s long so it’ll cover your, uh…”

Her tongue swept out to lick the corner of her mouth. He hastily tugged it over her head but she didn’t stick her arms through the sleeves. He wanted to help her, but, man, she was *so* naked.

And had probably been attacked or raped by the asshole lying on the ground. She must be traumatized. And the police would want to do whatever they did, so he shouldn’t touch her too much.

Don’t leave your prints on her, man. He wasn’t that stupid.

God, she was beautiful, in a bruised-and-battered kind of way.

“Your arms,” he directed. “Stick them in the…push them up and out. Right. Good.”

She clutched the shirt against her chest. A weary innocence danced in her bright eyes. She had cut her hand and he saw something on her palm.

“Looks like…a little bird?”

She nodded and clutched it to her chin.

“Nice. Uh… My apartment is up those stairs. I could call the cops for you. You need the police. You want to come up with me? I won’t hurt you. Promise. Well, you can sit on the step if you don’t trust me.”

Her smile stopped him cold. Definitely blood at her mouth. Whatever she’d done to the bastard on the ground—kicked, punched, clawed—he deserved worse.

“Um…” Her weird smile made him feel cornered by a cat and he the rat. “I think I have some sweatpants that’ll fit you, too. I can get those for you while we wait for the cops. You don’t have to come in if you’re scared. I’ll hand them to you out in the hallway.”

When he walked she followed him up the stairs, her eyes scanning everywhere. As if she'd never seen this alley. Could she have been attacked and left here?

The outer door led into a hallway and six apartments. Steve slammed a shoulder against the door. "It always sticks," he explained.

Her eyes flickered along his neck. "Hungry." She spoke French.

"Hu—you're hungry? Okay. Uh." Steve scratched his neck. "Did you just—" She had not just gazed longingly at his neck. He had watched too many horror flicks. "I've got some day-old pizza you can nosh on while we wait for the cops."

"Cops?"

He had to stop mixing his English with French. "The police. *Authorités?*"

A door down the hall swung inside. Madame Nesbitt's cat meowed and poked out its scraggly black head in tandem with its owner. The old woman stepped out, always on the alert for intruders. She kept track of everyone's coming and going.

"She could work for the CIA," Steve muttered sotto voce as he led the tattered woman toward his door. Aware he was half dressed—and more embarrassed for that than the naked chick—he slapped a palm across his chest. "Hey, Madame Nesbitt."

"Hungry." The woman approached Madame Nesbitt.

"Who is this, Monsieur Monroe? And why is she wearing but a shirt?"

"She's my friend. She's hungry." He smiled sheepishly. He'd never had a girl in his apartment before. How to explain that one?

Madame Nesbitt cried out. Steve froze at the old woman's utterance. A scream was abruptly cut off. Her body went stiff.

The cat yowled.

The chick from the alley was—was she biting Madame Nesbitt?

"No, this isn't right. You said you were hungry, but, dude— Are you a zombie?"

Madame Nesbitt slumped in the doorway. The chick wiped her lips of blood and smiled proudly at Steve, revealing fangs.

"Oh hell. Not a zombie. "

Aware he was stepping backward as she took steps toward him, Steve calculated how fast he could run, stick the key in his door and slam it in her face before she might latch onto his neck.

He'd studied paranormal creatures. It was more fascination than scholarly. He'd watched every version of *Dracula;* including the one with Gerard Butler, which had been a total chick flick—

Focus, Steve!

"Don't get too close, lady. Keep the shirt. It's yours. Did you—hell, did you *bite* the guy in the alley?"

She nodded. Another smile. Only it wasn't a sweet smile, it was wicked. Wickedly sexy. Because now those bright blue eyes twinkled as if she'd been revived by blood.

"Are you a…vampire?" It sounded ridiculous. He'd seen people biting others and drinking their blood—*in the movies.*

"I am. Vampire." She tapped the door. "You…know about me?"

"I…I think I do." And how odd was it to converse with one if she was for real? This was a moment he'd dreamed about. She did look a bit like Vampirella. But seriously?

"You are for…for real? You bite people? Did you kill Madame Nesbitt?"

"Kill? No. *Jamais.* Just in a swoon," the woman offered.

"A swoon. Right. Like a sort of unconscious compliance introduced by you taking blood from her. Oh, hell, what am I saying? Don't come any closer. I…I don't think I taste good."

"I have no fight with you. And I am sated for now."

"Sated. That's good. Maybe. Uh, wh-who do you have a fight with? If you don't mind me asking."

"Salignac," she said firmly. "And Ian Grim."

"Okay. Two guys. But not me, right?"

"No, not you." She knocked on his door. "Inside?"

Steve stumbled through the door and before he could slam it shut the vampire walked in.

"I thought I had to invite you in."

"You did. Down in the street."

Hell, he *had* invited her inside. *Idiot!*

"Okay, lady, wait. Stop right there." She took directions. A dribble of blood stained the Wolfman's cheek.

A vampire? It was all a joke, right? One of his classmates was going to get it on Monday. Probably it was Sydney. She was always making fun of him for his paranormal interests. And she was in the drama club so she would have access to makeup and props.

"Whew. That's got to be it."

Flicking on a light verified the woman was naked. And filthy from tangled, bloody hair to dirty toes. It was as if she'd crawled from a grave. And, dude, she did not smell fresh.

"Sydney really worked some magic on you."

"Magic." The woman hissed. "Grim will die."

"Okay, lady, here's the deal. This is a great act. But on

the slightest chance it isn't, and you took a bump to the head when that bastard beat on you, I'm going to call the cops. I'm not sure anymore who the victim is and who needs to be put behind bars. But we gotta have a rule."

"Rule?"

"Yes, a condition you must follow while you are in my home. Just in case, you know, you really are a vampire."

She nodded, understanding.

"All right, so the rule is..."

She leaned in, waiting.

"No biting Steve."

"No bite Steve," she repeated. A drool of blood trickled down her chin.

Steve's stomach lurched.

"Right. No biting Steve. Steve is nice. Steve—" he pointed to himself "—is the guy who's helping you, right?"

"Steve help Viviane. Steve good."

"Yeah, but not *good* like in *good to eat,* but *good* like in helping. Your name's Viviane? That's pretty."

The bloody smile ruined any dreams about making out with a sexy Vampirella.

"I need a shirt. And you need pants."

"Pants?"

"Yes, sweatpants, or something. You stay put. I'll be right back."

He dashed through the living room and closed his bedroom door. Frantically he pawed through the stack of dirty clothes mounding in the corner. But he didn't care about stupid clothes.

"A vampire? Right, Steve, you need to call the mental ward for yourself. You may fancy yourself a cryptozoologist, but you're not stupid. Any mythological monster can easily be explained through historical epidemiology and research. Vampirism developed during the plague times. They weren't vampires, but everyone thought the chewing dead were going to come after them and suck their blood. Vampires do not exist!"

He dug deeper into the clothes pile and pulled a black turtleneck over his head. The last time he'd washed it he'd dried it too long. He'd never get the hang of the French washer and dryer. Now it hugged his skinny ribs and his hard nipples popped up like beads. Embarrassing, but necessary protection.

Eyeing the bedroom furniture he cursed the lack of bedposts, or even a bed, for he had but the mattress on the floor. Nothing that could be used as a wooden stake.

The lightbulb flickered on over his head. "I have garlic in the kitchen."

Working through the garlic myth in his brain he conjured historical research that it had once been used as a mosquito repellent. Mosquitoes sucked blood, and thus, people once thought it would work against vampires.

"Stupid."

But still.

Swinging out of the bedroom, Steve noticed Viviane wandered his messy living room, examining the television, running her hand over the open laptop. She tripped on the pizza box from two days ago, and landed on the couch, hands first, flashing Steve her pale, dirt-smeared backside. He'd forgotten about the pants.

She turned and sat, grimacing and tugging down the shirt, which went to her thighs.

"Sorry." Steve gathered the pizza box and shoved a stack of *Warcraft* discs aside with his sneaker. "Late night studying. Exchange student. I'm from Iowa. So, you live in Paris long?"

She nodded. "This is Paris?"

"Yep. Always has been. Your accent is different from the locals though. Where did you come from?"

"Paris." She tilted her head, as if watching something flicker close to her cheek. "It is different."

Looking over the counter and lifting books and food-crusted plates and a dirty pair of boxer shorts, Steve roamed for the cell phone. He clasped the garlic clove, which crumbled to dust on his palm. And when had he ever made a home-cooked meal for himself?

Swiping the garlic dust over his forearms, in case it did ward off vampires, Steve swung a hip around the side of the counter. "So. Viviane."

Viviane the vampire? Steve, you are screwed.

"So, I'm looking for the phone. Then I can call the cops for you. Send you on your way. Oh, hey, don't touch that." He jumped around the counter and carefully removed the USB drive from her fingers. She displayed the small bird happily. "That's a bird. But what kind?"

"Hummingbird. He gave it to me."

"He?"

"You smell." She winced, then yawned. "I'm hungry. Need—"

The door buzzed and Steve shot upright. "Don't freak," he said urgently.

Wide blue eyes merely stared at him. Steve had a thing for blue-eyed girls with dark hair. They were so otherworldly.

Otherworldly? No kidding.

Was she wondering what his blood tasted like? He clutched the turtleneck. How to keep a hungry vampire satisfied without losing a pint?

"I think that's Jack. My friend. We study together. I'm going to see who is at the door," he said slowly and a little too loud, as if she were deaf.

As usual Jack never waited for an invite. The door opened and Steve's three-hundred-pound friend charged through, dropping a fresh box of chocolate croissants on the counter and heading for his favorite easy chair with the duct-taped arms.

A curious, half-naked woman met Jack in the living room.

"Dude!" Jack's astonishment lit his round face like a Christmas tree. "Where did you find her?"

"Behind the trash bin. Uh, Jack, I don't think you should get too close to her."

"Why? She's wearing nothing but a shirt. Dude! Your favorite shirt!"

"Hungry."

"Oh no—" Lunging to rescue his friend, Steve tripped over a stack of textbooks.

A half-gnawed croissant went flying. Jack's hefty bulk slammed against the wall, knocking the Bela Lugosi figurine from an overhead shelf. Viviane fixed her teeth to his meaty neck.

Landing on the living-room floor, Steve groaned a weak protest. "Viviane!"

"Not Steve!" she sputtered, drooling out Jack's blood. With a happy grin, the vampire again latched onto Jack.

Steve muttered, "Mercy."

Jack gurgled a strangely satisfied cry, like a happy, sexual kind of noise.

Then his friend collapsed on the floor.

Scrambling upright, Steve splayed out his arms. "What did you do that for?"

Viviane wiped blood from her lips and shrugged. "Hungry."

"But, but he's my friend."

"No bite Steve."

"You really are a vampire, aren't you, lady."

VIVIANE THE VAMPIRE SAT in the tub. Steve had drained the dirty water once and now poured warm water over her hair, helping her soap it with the shampoo he got at the discount drugstore down the street. It was weird, but Steve felt like she needed to be taken care of. Despite the fact she was a bloodsucking vampire, she had been through something awful, and needed a kind touch.

Jack was still out cold in the living room. He wasn't dead. Steve had checked for a pulse to be sure.

"So, Viviane." He poured clean water over her hair to rinse out the shampoo. "Where did you come from?"

"Below."

"Below? You mean—" he swallowed "—from the grave?"

"No, not Les Innocents. Below this city."

"Oh. Oh? You mean like the catacombs?" Paris was a virtual web of underground tunnels. Steve had once partied in them at an all-night rave. "Seriously? You live underground?"

"Not living." She shook her head. "Forced. Grim."

Yeah, that would be grim. Another pour of water rinsed the suds from her shoulders.

"Someone forced you underground? Uh…how long have you been down there?" To judge from the dirt on her it had been a while.

"Can't decide. Lost track of time. No day or night. All darkness. Too long. Now the city is different."

"How so?"

"No horses! The buildings are the same but not. People in strange clothing. I…feel the same. Only hungry."

"Well, you can't have been below for long. What do

you last remember? I mean, was it winter? Summer? It's summer now."

"Summer. Very pretty. Flowers were blooming in the Tuileries."

"Yes, I sometimes have lunch in the royal gardens. " He handed her the soap, but it slipped through her fingers.

"Marie Antoinette had given birth to her third child," she said with a sigh.

"Marie Antoin—" Steve chuffed. "That was in the eighteenth century."

Viviane fluttered her blue gaze. "Yes."

"No way. That would make you like two hundred some years old."

"What time is it now?"

"Time? You mean the date? It's the twenty-first century, lady. Oh, wait." He stood. A glance out the doorway saw Jack was moving. "Oh, man, you guys got me good."

He marched out to the living room and gave Jack a hand up. "Dude, that was classic. Where did you find her? She's such a looker. I really believed she bit you."

"Bit me?" Jack slapped a palm over his neck. Blood colored his fingers. "What the hell?"

"You can stop the act. I know I'm being punk'd. That fake blood is amazing. What is it? Corn syrup and red food coloring? But what did you add to make it smell so real?"

"Dude, I am not punking you. And that bitch bit me? Why didn't you warn me? She's like a vampire or something."

It was rare Jack didn't opt for a joke right away.

Steve rushed to the bathroom. Viviane stood outside the tub, dripping onto the ripped Metallica floor mat.

Over his shoulder, Jack whispered in admiration, "Dude, she is so naked. I don't care that she bit me."

"Grab a towel," Steve said, and when Jack stood stupidly unmoving, he shoved his friend aside and grabbed the biggest towel he had, which was frayed all around the edges. He held it before her. "Wrap this around you. Seriously? The eighteenth century? Like with the big wigs and the goofy tights on the men?"

"Steve." Sad blue eyes entreated. They were like two pieces of sky, but rained on. "You tell me true? Twenty-first century?"

"Yeah, it's been, like…two hundred and thirty years since Marie Antoinette was queen. France doesn't even have kings and queens anymore. Have you been underground all that time?"

"I was bespelled by Ian Grim," Viviane said. "And Constantine, he…" She swept a hand before her loins, indicating something Steve had suspected of the guy in the alley. "I will kill Grim! And I will find Constantine and rip out his heart."

Jack exchanged raised brows with Steve.

"Yeah, cool. And go you with the dramatics, and all." Steve put up a placating hand. "But listen, you gotta be careful, Viviane. This is a new world. People don't take kindly to vampires running around biting them. It's gonna get you locked up. Or something worse."

"So the world has not changed."

Steve led Viviane into his bedroom, and between he and Jack scrounged up sweatpants and a clean Jekyll and Hyde T-shirt.

"People don't believe in vampires, Viviane," Steve said, as he stepped back to look over his handiwork. She looked pitiful, but she did work the shirt. 36C, he guessed, and then chided himself for the lascivious thought.

"It is the same, then," she offered sadly.

"Yes, but if you go around biting people, you will be arrested and put in jail."

"No." Viviane shoved past both men and rushed out into the living room. "No more confinement! I want freedom!"

"SHE'S GOING TO ESCAPE!" Steve shoved Jack ahead of him and grabbed his jacket. "Come on, man, we've got to go after her."

"I don't know, dude." Jack studied his neck with a fingertip. "I think we should let the bloodsucker go. Since when did you develop a death wish?"

"Jack, are you dead?"

"No."

"Right." Steve slapped the bite marks on the side of Jack's neck, and his friend yelped. "She could have killed you, but she didn't."

"But she's, like, insane. Living underground for centuries. And now she's risen to stalk those who have betrayed her. You heard her. She's going to kill someone sooner or later. And I don't want it to be me. I think I'll sit this one out."

"Fine." Steve opened the door and started hurrying down the iron stairs.

The guy was no longer behind the Dumpster.

"He must have got up and wandered off." At least Viviane wasn't killing. Yet.

Where would a vampire who was familiar with the city two centuries previously go? The Louvre? The Seine? Notre Dame?

The closest landmark was the Arc du Triomphe up the street. No, that was after her time.

"Viviane!"

A black Mercedes squealed to a halt across the street. The door opened and a man charged out from it.

Turning and tripping on the curb, Steve lunged forward in an awkward sprawl. He was tugged upright and slammed against a brick wall.

"Where is she?" the man demanded.

Big and muscled, a gray chunk dashed through his short black hair. He reminded Steve of thugs on television shows. Thugs who twisted necks and broke bones.

His dark eyes tracked Steve's face and down the front of his shirt. "You called her name."

"V-Viviane?"

"Yes, you have seen her?"

"Dude, I don't think we're talking about the same lady here. There are lots of chicks in this town called Viviane. It's a spat with me and my old lady, you know." Why was he protecting her? "C-could you let go of me?"

The man relaxed his grip and Steve's feet hit the ground.

"It is the same Viviane," he said. His French was a little different than most of the accents Steve had heard. Similar to Viviane's French. "You must tell me where she is. Now!"

"Chill, dude. In case you weren't paying attention, I was calling to her because I *don't* know where she is. And the longer I'm delayed…"

"Yes? What will happen? She will be lost? She will what?"

"Dude."

"My name is Rhys Hawkes. Did she say that name to you?"

"No, but she wasn't exactly coherent all the time. Listen, I don't think you know what sort of chick this Viviane is.

If you did—" Slammed against the brick again, Steve bit the edge of his tongue. "That hurt!"

Rhys slapped his hand aside Steve's face and roughly shoved it to the right. He examined his neck. So maybe the guy did have a clue. Why else the interest in his neck? Unless—

Steve kicked and scrambled against his attacker, who held firm. "Not another one! We have a strict no-bite-Steve rule."

"Your name is Steve?" The man leaned in so close Steve winced and wondered if that were aftershave or some kind of vampire pheromone that would put him under a spell and make him beg for the bite. "Steve, how long have you known about Viviane? Did you find her?"

"She sort of found me. She's a vampire and you are, too!"

The man grinned, but Steve did not see fangs. Only smug satisfaction. "I won't bite you. Promise."

Despite his dangling status, Steve exhaled in relief.

"But I will tear your head from your neck if you do not become forthcoming this instant."

"I don't know anything! I don't know where she is. I brought her to my place, and she took a bath because she was all bloody and naked—"

"She had no clothes?"

"No, but don't worry, dude, I didn't touch her. She's, like, dangerous. She bit my best friend."

"Did she kill him? Is she…mad?"

"She's definitely some kind of angry. Oh, you mean insane. Maybe. I think she's been out of the loop for quite a while, if you ask me. But I held a conversation with her. I think the blood makes her sane. Anyway, I was going to keep tabs on her but she walked out. She needs help, man. That's all I know."

Rhys dropped Steve.

He knew he was going to regret getting too friendly with the muscle-bound thug, but he couldn't help himself. This was a cryptozoologist's dream come true. He had to take advantage of it.

"So," he asked casually, but tugged up the neck of his turtleneck, "how do you know this chick?"

Rhys turned and scanned the street. "She's my lover," he said over his shoulder. "*Was* my lover. I believed that she was murdered over two hundred years ago. I was wrong."

"Sooo, you're going to take over looking for her now? Awesome. Glad to leave you to the task. I'll just be going—"

Steve hadn't seen the man move, yet he held him by the collar now, his toes barely touching the ground.

"I need you," Rhys said. "You are the only person she's had contact with since coming aboveground. You may have some influence with her."

"Oh, I doubt it."

"I was following her scent, but it's grown weak. You said you washed her?"

Steve nodded. "I used grape shampoo. You could sniff that out, right? Store where I got the stuff is behind us."

The man sniffed Steve's head. "I can smell it on you. Sweet and artificial. You are positive this is the scent she wears?"

"Yep."

"Why do you smell the same?"

Steve gulped down a swallow. "Dude, I didn't touch her."

"You'll come with me." Shoved roughly, Steve crossed the street to where the Mercedes was parked. Not much of a chance to break free unless he wanted broken bones. But seriously? Get in a car with a vampire?

"We have to hurry. The moon will be full and high in less than two hours."

CHAPTER THIRTY-SIX

AS HE TRACKED THE SIDEWALK edging the Seine, Rhys was hyperaware that the clock ticked faster than his tracking efforts. The moon was nearly at its apex.

He could not sense her at all. He should be able to scent her by the disgusting sweet fragrance that filled the backseat. It was all over the kid, which would make finding Viviane impossible unless he split away from Steve.

He couldn't imagine what she must be like now. Steve had said he'd discovered her naked, with strips of decaying fabric hanging from her limbs.

And according to the boy she'd taken blood. That had to mean something. But it also meant she was a menace. Add in her unfamiliarity with the times and the city, and— No time to waste.

Quickening his footsteps along the boulevard du Seine, Rhys gestured to Steve, who walked the opposite side of the bridge with Simon pacing him in the car, to keep his eyes peeled. The boy was being helpful because Rhys had intimated he'd wrench his neck from the spinal column and leave him in an alleyway.

He would not, but it was a good scare and it had put a healthy fear in the kid who wore a turtleneck sweater like armor.

Ahead the bridge that crossed before Notre Dame hummed with night traffic. An ambulance peeled by, its siren silent, yet the lights flashed red at the periphery of Rhys's ever-scanning gaze.

Steve rushed across the bridge and met Rhys as he gained the parvis before the cathedral. "Dude, it's almost midnight."

"Soon."

"Yeah? Well, your driver said you have to be out of town before then. Otherwise you, like…rampage."

"I do nothing of the sort. I merely…"

Shift to man-beast form. Scare the shit out of common mortals. And his werewolf answered to his vampire's hunger for blood. And yes, he did rampage.

His estate sat east of the city, the safe room already prepared for tonight. "I need but twenty minutes to broach the city's walls."

Ready to grip the boy's shirt and admonish, Rhys paused. "Listen."

The doors before the cathedral opened and a slim man staggered outside. No one paid him mind; there were perhaps a dozen tourists still lingering though the church had closed for services hours earlier.

"What?" Steve took a step but Rhys stopped him with a palm to his chest. "Do you see her? Smell her? She's inside. That man is bleeding from his neck."

The squeal of tires pulled up left of where Rhys stood and parked on the parvis. Simon stepped out and waved to him.

Struck by a breeze curling about his head, Rhys turned to spy a vision striding across the street. Clad in white, and tall and slender, her white hair flowed out from her head as if blown by the sudden wind.

He couldn't remember her name but recognized her species—faery.

There, approaching with the confidence of a preying

lioness, the faery held out her arms as if he should rush forward and kiss her.

Recognition thumped his gut, teasing his dual nature. The werewolf growled. His vampire wanted to tear out her throat. He had not seen her for centuries.

Steve shoved him, and Rhys growled. His hackles stretched and the werewolf pined for release.

He glanced to the west facade of Notre Dame. Guarded by gargoyles, saints and centuries of ancient ritual—including pagan—the cathedral was no place for a vampire. Yet Viviane, as he, was not baptized. Holy objects would serve her no harm, so she could safely seek shelter within.

"I'm going after her," he said to Steve. "Tell Simon to keep one foot on the accelerator."

The faery paralleled his path toward the cathedral, emitting a spring breeze around him. "Why now?" he asked.

"You've found her, haven't you? Your tragic lover."

"Cressida." He remembered her name. "Now is not a good time."

"Now is the time I have waited for over two centuries. Rather, I've been imprisoned along with your wicked vampire bitch. I've only just been freed."

"I don't understand."

"You don't need to. You must hurry if you wish to beat *la lune*."

Rhys felt her gaze tickle his neck and move across his mouth. He dashed out his tongue but only tasted air.

He slipped into the cool darkness and turned to inspect the narthex. The faery appeared beside him. It was as if he'd stepped through time. If only that were true and it was the eve before he had lost Viviane. He would not have left her. "Never."

The faery touched one long, graceful finger to his lower lip. A scurry of sensation moved across his mouth and fizzled deep into his being.

"Are you going to rescue your mad lover, then?"

"Cressida!"

"I do hope you will."

"Why? Why are you here?"

"You'll discover soon enough. But the moon calls to you. Best snatch her quickly."

"I intend to." He slapped a palm over his aching heart. "Where could she be?"

"Outside."

"What? Why didn't you say something?"

The faery shoved open the door. A woman, long black hair flowing in her wake, ran toward Steve, who stood at the car. Simon and Steve grabbed her.

Rhys lunged into the Mercedes's backseat. The woman struggling with Simon screamed. Her fingernails slashed Simon's face. One of her bare heels clocked Rhys aside the jaw.

He clamped a hand about her ankle, but didn't want to push her beyond what precipice of fear she balanced—he released her right away.

"Can you secure her?" Simon said.

"Don't hold her," Rhys instructed. "Let her go." He moved aside to allow Simon to slink out of the backseat beside him. "You okay?"

Simon touched the blood on his jaw. "I'll be fine. Who's the blonde chick?"

"Faery."

"What the— She coming with us?"

"No. Give the kid some cash and let's get out of here."

Simon closed the backseat door behind Rhys. He would

handle Steve, and the faery would follow one way or another, Rhys felt sure.

Right now, he struggled with elation and caution.

It was her.

"Viviane."

She blindly kicked at him, and with her hands beat against the car door, apparently unaware how to use the handle to open it. The kid had clothed her in baggy gray sweatpants and a T-shirt that boasted a monstrous face demarcated by a normal face. Jekyll and Hyde? What kind of sick joke was that on him?

She smelled like the boy, a pitiful replacement for the Italian wine she'd once bathed in.

He wanted to pull her against him and crush her into his body. To know her once again. To somehow apologize with an embrace, because where to even begin with words? But how dare he when he had been the one who could have prevented her cruel imprisonment?

God, he wanted to touch her. He wanted to shout. He wanted to punch someone—*Constantine*. He wanted…

…what he did not deserve.

"It's me, Viviane," he said softly. She stopped kicking, and impressed her shoulders against the door. Simon drove swiftly, and the car swerved once in a while. "Rhys Hawkes."

No longer did he wear his hair past his shoulders, but instead military short. It was still black as coal, with the gray patch over his left temple. A few wrinkles had settled around his eyes and mouth, but he was the same. Would she recognize him? Could she?

She looked as if she had just stepped from the eighteenth century. And been attacked by a mad mob.

"Regarde moi."

He reached forward, hand held up and fingers loose, but waited for her to make the next move.

Her eyes flashed from his face to the front seat, to the back window where the night lights of Paris flickered in a dizzy rush. Did she recognize him?

"Hungry," she said quietly.

Yes, surely she must be starved for blood. She'd fed three times according to Steve. He could give her his blood. If she bit him, yes, he would develop a vicious hunger that would strangle his werewolf, but he owed her for the two centuries he had stolen from her.

"Rhys?"

His name, gasped from her lips, touched his chest and beamed into his heart. Rhys nodded, unable to speak for he feared he'd begin to blather and frighten her.

"Rhys Hawkes?" She opened her hand, and on her palm sat a small object. The wooden hummingbird, of which the beak still rested in Rhys's breast pocket. "My Rhys?"

"Yes, your Rhys." The words spilled like tears from his mouth. "I'm sorry, Viviane. I thought you were dead."

"Not dead!"

She put up a palm before her face. Tucking her knees to her chest, she was so tiny on the huge leather seat. So frail. Indeed, her arms were thinner than usual, and her face gaunt. She really did need blood.

"How much longer, Simon?"

"Ten minutes. I just crossed the *peripherique*."

"Viviane, it's the night of the full moon. I…I know you may not understand, and this is cruel, having only just found you, but…I must lock myself away. My werewolf. I can feel it straining for release right now."

"Your vampire," she whispered. "It is cruel."

He bowed his head. "You remember."

How to touch her heart? A bruised and tormented heart that beat a pace to match no creature's life. Mad surely, and perhaps wicked with grief, vengeance and spite.

The Mercedes spun on loose gravel. They took the curving drive to Rhys's estate. Rhys directed Simon not to turn on the garage light, and when they stopped he scooped up Viviane. So frail in his grasp. So insignificant.

She could become whole again. They could have a good life.

Would she still feel that way? Could she remember him?

"Sorry," he said as he strode the dark hallway toward the entertainment room. It was closest to the safe room. "I know you must hate me. I have no right to beg forgiveness. Simon, prepare the room!"

His assistant had already rushed ahead.

"I will take care of you," he said, and kicked the door inside. "I beg your forgiveness."

"Not dead." Her plea was a battle cry against him abandoning her. Rhys's heart dropped. He deserved her disdain.

Only the flashing LED bulbs from a multitude of electronic devices lighted the room. A small red-and-green glow sheened across two large theater chairs.

He set Viviane on a chair, and she slid back on the slick leather. He knelt there, feeling the tingle in his fingertips and fighting the change.

Grasping his wrist, she worked the wooden hummingbird into his hand. It killed him she had kept this. She must have clutched it before the spell had been put on her. Had she been aware it was in her hand all through the centuries? Did she love him for that or hate him?

A small blessing was that she did not appear insane.

"Rhys!"

Simon waited at the door.

Rhys leaned in and kissed Viviane on the forehead. Her soft skin begged him to remain, to embrace her, to earn forgiveness. But his arms tingled now. His werewolf was coming.

"I'll see you in the morning," he said, and stroked her cheek. "Do not harm Simon. But you can use him to slake your hunger. And whatever you do, you must not leave. You are safe here."

"Safe?"

"I promise." He choked down a hard swallow. Much as he had promised then, she had not been safe in the eighteenth century.

CHAPTER THIRTY-SEVEN

THE MORTAL MAN SLIPPED from Viviane's embrace. She wiped blood from her mouth. She had dreamed about blood for centuries, though she'd lost her grasp on time. Good thing that, or she would truly be lunatic now. She was not. She was completely sound.

Mostly, a little voice inside her head whispered.

The man groaned and stretched out along the carpeted floor, a satisfied smile on his face. The men today—had it been over two centuries?—wore their clothing to conform to their bodies. The soft white shirt hugged his thin torso and the trousers were nicely tailored. He wore a small diamond earring in the left ear only.

No lace. No frockcoats. Not a single horse and carriage out on the streets. The moving machine they had put her into to get her here baffled. Yet she'd found Notre Dame. It had looked the same, had been a refuge.

Now here she sat in a dark room with chairs in a row and a large white wall on one end. How had she gotten in here? Had this man put her here? It was difficult to recall things that had happened before she'd taken his blood. Only bits and pieces, like Notre Dame and the noisy machines.

The man beside her moaned and tucked his hands under his chin. He tasted rich. She would keep him until he died.

An animal howl echoed through the building, clattering

the walls. Viviane searched in the darkness and found the door, threw it open and dashed into the bare hallway.

Again the howl skittered up her spine. It sounded wild, feral. Familiar. Viviane hated wolves. Yes?

Oh, yes, wolf slayer.

So long she had been trapped underground. Frozen, yet ever knowing. Seeing all. Which hadn't been much. Though occasionally rats would swarm over the glass coffin.

She cried out in disgust and wrapped her arms about herself. So many of them, crawling, stirring, swarming over her. Their long horrid tails flicking across the glass. And she, so fearful the glass would crack and they would spill over her like a hideous flood.

She crouched, eyeing the floor. They crawled along the walls, silent, until they were not silent. Their chattering squeaks still rang loudly in memory.

Again the howl rippled through the atmosphere. The wolf summoned the rats, hordes of them, surely. Unwilling to remain and discover the source of the sound, Viviane dashed down the hallway.

"Must get out of here. Need to be safe. I am free!"

And yet, what would she do? Where would she go? The world had changed. She was not dead!

"I will survive." Yes, she was strong. "I always survive." She would take the man with the rich blood with her.

Pushing open a door, she entered an open port that housed two of the noisy machines. They had wheels but no horses. Both were shiny black, like the sheen on Constantine's eyes.

"I will kill him," Viviane ground through clenched teeth.

She touched the slick surface of one machine, yet at

that moment the howl again tapped against her brain. "Rhys?"

The name came to her, unattached to memory or image, yet it weighed so heavily in her mind that she turned to the door and stepped back inside the hall.

He'd sat in the back of one of the machines next to her. Pleading her forgiveness. So big and strong. Not familiar. But—yes, something about him.

"Rhys Hawkes," she said on a gasp. Images of her running her fingers through his hair, gasping as his kisses traveled her skin…

"My lover, you are here? Where are you?"

Following the insistent howl, Viviane tracked past the open door where the mortal lay enthralled from her bite, and onward down a long passage that turned sharply right. There were no lights, but she saw well. Ahead, a small green light blinked beside a door handle.

The howl came from behind the door. Viviane slapped her palms to the cold metal door. "Rhys!"

She remembered now. She had thought of nothing but Rhys Hawkes the moment Salignac and Grim had abandoned her in the dark depths beneath Paris. Her fingers had frozen about the hummingbird she still grasped, yet she had thought to feel the warmth of her lover's skin imbued within the polished wood. He had been there with her.

Why was he not here for her now?

He put you in the machine.

Had he? Her thoughts were scattered. *Not dead.* Why did he abandon me? *So alone. The rats…*

She pounded the door, but howls answered.

One thing she did know; her lover only howled during the full moon. There were no windows in the hall. She did not know if it was night or day, but she guessed the moon must be high and full. Which meant Rhys must be werewolf.

A form she had once run from. A form she had defiantly stood up to. A form she recalled had been ruled by his vampire.

Viviane had contemplated Rhys's double nature for ages while underground. Could it have been centuries before her mind had finally gone blank and her eyes void?

She had decided one truth. One pertinent detail they both had overlooked. It was…

She clutched her gut. "Hungry."

The mortal donor lay close. She could feel his heartbeats. Many times she had felt a heartbeat near. In the darkness. Others had come close but had never found her. She wanted blood. She needed blood. Blood would—

"He needs my blood!" She beat the door. "I can tame your vampire! Let me in!"

Down the hall, the mortal stumbled out from the room. Viviane dashed to him. "Rhys is trapped. You must help me."

Drunk from the swoon, the mortal eyed her cautiously as she grabbed his hand and dragged him down the hall.

"He's in there for his own safety," he said. "And to protect you."

"Get him out! I can save him."

"Save him?" He laughed. "He just saved *you,* lady."

"My name is Viviane." She sauntered toward him and ran her fingers down the front of his shirt. Warm, so warm. *Never get warm again.* The mortal's eyes tracked hers, sobering him instantly. "Rhys is my lover."

The man nodded. "I know about you two. You remember him? You're not…mad? Insane?"

She tilted her head. The scent of his blood hypnotized.

"Would you not be insane after being buried alive two centuries?"

"Yes. But you seem pretty rational right now."

"The blood makes me clear."

And it would make Rhys clear, too.

"You will open this door right now."

Lunging, she bit into his vein again. Hot, thick blood oozed over her teeth and tongue. He did not struggle but instead embraced her as she forced her persuasion into his thoughts.

Open the door. "Now."

"Yes." He leaned aside and tapped on the number pad near the door. "But this only opens the outer door. He's locked in a cage inside."

"You'll open the cage."

"I—" She gripped his chin and squeezed. "I will," he hastily agreed. "Anything you ask of me. But as soon as I do that, I'm closing this outer door. I will not let him loose to torment innocents. You'll be trapped inside."

"Trapped with my lover?" Viviane stood aside. "Open the door for me."

The square cage stretched to the ceiling, twice as high as a man. Around the top tiny blue lights cast an eerie glow over the creature who now stood at the center of the cage, seething, its fangs revealed, its talons bared and prepared to strike.

Not a creature. "My lover." A man who had taken her away from the despicable Constantine de Salignac.

A man who had not rescued her when Salignac had enacted his greatest revenge.

"Rhys?"

The wolf huffed, and slapped a paw about one thin bar.

It was him, her lover. The gray fur declared it so. She was not afraid.

"Why? Why did you not save me?"

The werewolf twisted its head and reared back, howling long and loud so that the sound cloaked Viviane like a sodden garment she could not shuck. It charged the bars, slashing out with an arm. It meant harm.

"Your werewolf does not scare me." She lifted her head, drawing a breath through her nose for courage. "You couldn't be there," she said, remembering now it had been a night like tonight when the moon had reigned. "I wish you had been. I thought of you. Always." She lifted her head proudly and beat her breast. "Not dead!"

The bars rattled, but no matter how much the wolf beat against them, they did not budge. Strong metal. Must be magical, she decided. But the cage door had been unlocked. The werewolf was unaware. She sought the door, eyeing the far side, and found it.

Dare she?

So many years she had thought about this. Decades, surely. And then the rats would make her scream. Silently. Achingly. She had only desired Rhys's warm embrace. To know safety. To remember love.

"Do you love me?" she asked, walking toward the cage door. "I love you, Rhys. I think."

She glanced aside, opening her palm. A wooden hummingbird? Who had given her this?

Viviane shook her head. Her thoughts jumbled so easily. "Blood," she whispered.

Yes, the blood.

Gripping the cage door, she swung it wide. The werewolf leaped out and slammed her body to the floor. Her skull hit the floor hard, and she winced, blinking at the bright flashes interspersed with blackness.

The beast roared, exposing its long maw of glistening teeth. Teeth that could take off her arm or head with one bite. Fearless, Viviane clasped his head, determination forcing her actions before she lost focus.

"I love you, Rhys Hawkes, and I will tame you this night. I know what you need."

Chasing the painful and unanswerable desire she had lived in for two centuries, Viviane lunged. Her fangs descended, and she bit into the werewolf's leathery neck where the fur receded to bare skin. The wolf bucked, but she held tight, wrapping her legs about its waist and clinging. Hot blood gushed into her mouth and over her lips, streaming down her chin and neck.

It was difficult to hold fast, but she shoved her hands into the fur on its scalp and licked at the heavy, throbbing vein. So sweet, virile and hot, his blood. The werewolf's blood.

It was all that she needed. Knowledge fit into that empty slot in her mind. She knew. She remembered. She was Viviane LaMourette, strong, free. Rhys Hawkes's lover.

Yet right now her lover, while in werewolf shape, had the mind of a vampire. A vampire who had been enchanted to shackle its vicious desire for blood. A vampire who needed to know a new master, a new patron, a new lover who would blood bond with him.

That master would be her.

With a ferocious twist of his shoulders, Rhys shucked her off him. Viviane landed on the floor, sprawled, crying out at the pain of landing on her hip. The wolf charged her.

She bit into her wrist, opening the flesh raggedly, and the blood spurt. It hit the wolf's maw, staining its teeth crimson.

"Take it," she gasped. "Taste me for the first time, lover. Know I am yours, and you are mine."

Dizzied by the gush of blood from her vein, Viviane's lashes fluttered. She closed her eyes to the tug at her wrist as the werewolf lapped in her life's blood.

RHYS CAME TO, SPRAWLED facedown in a sticky puddle of blood. It did not offend. It smelled sweet. Like wine on a summer afternoon.

He studied his hands, covered with blood, and looked down at his naked body. He had survived the full moon once again. Yet he lay outside the titanium cage.

"Viviane."

Slapping a hand in the blood, he twisted at the waist to spy her frail body lying next to him, her hair strewn across the floor and curling into the crimson puddle. Her wrist was caked with dried blood where his werewolf had fed, spurred by his vampire to take every last drop—yet he had not.

He must not have taken it all.

"Viviane?" He tugged her into his arms and shook her. So pale, her skin. Her mouth lolled open. "No, you cannot be dead. Please." Tears dropped onto her blood-stained lips. Rhys cried out.

Just then the lock clicked. The outer door moved inward a few inches. No one entered. It was merely the timed mechanism setting him free.

Never free. Not if you have killed her. Again.

He slapped two fingers aside her throat, searching for a pulse, but he could not find one. Too much hair in the way. He scrambled to move it aside when suddenly her body jerked and she sucked in a breath.

Azure eyes blinked open and fixed to his. The tiny crease at the right side of her mouth appeared.

"Rhys, my love," she managed to say in the smallest voice. "I've saved you."

Had she? Hell, the notion of it made him chuckle.

Had their sharing blood indeed tamed his vampire and released him from the darkness? Had she traveled through time, frozen in a glass coffin, to finally set him free?

Only time would tell—and the next full moon.

He wanted to tell her how sorry he was. To explain why he had thought her dead. He wanted to erase the centuries and do it all over again.

Right now, all he needed was to hold Viviane. To kiss her.

Deep in Viviane's kiss he found the man he once was. The man who had walked through the Enlightenment in dark clothing and with his head held down stepped aside. The proud half-breed who had pursued Viviane without relent stepped up and breathed in.

Her breath moved into him, warming him and reigniting his spirit. And he noticed their heartbeats, pressed chest to chest, pulsed in synch. He had consumed her blood, as she had his. Only time would determine their fates.

"Lover," she whispered against his mouth. For the first time since he'd found her, her eyes were bright, so clear. She moved his hand down to her belly. "Can you feel it?"

The odd question redirected his focus and when Rhys pressed his fingers gently to her smooth stomach, he thought he felt another rhythm. Rapid and small. But how was that possible?

"A child?" he asked.

"I've been aware the entire time I was in the coffin." She slid her bloodied hand along his cheek. "The first will not be ours."

"No, but it must—"

And she kissed him silent, so that his protests rang in

his heart and regret surfaced, and he knew then why the faery had appeared outside of the cathedral.

"The future promises to be quite challenging," he said, then bowed to kiss her again.

They spoke no more, instead answering the centuries-long hunger for one another as Rhys stripped the clothes from Viviane, and found his place inside her. A place where he belonged. Home.

CHAPTER THIRTY-EIGHT

Nine months later...

MOONLIGHT SHONE THROUGH the nursery windows. A twinkle of stardust seemed to beam over the twin cribs nestled against the wall. Rhys helped Viviane stow away the diaper-changing supplies, quietly closing the cupboard doors so as not to wake the newborns.

Two of them born two days ago, one but moments after the other. A surprise. Rhys had sent Poole out to buy another crib before the midwife had left.

Viviane nudged a shoulder against his chest and turned to nuzzle against his neck. His beard was thick for the moon was soon full. But he needn't fear a raging werewolf. Since Viviane had lured his werewolf to take her blood, he had continued—as vampire—to drink from her once a fortnight. And he allowed her to take from him. It bonded them so deeply he had never thought it possible to love someone more.

And it seemed to keep Viviane sane. She had to take blood every day from a donor, because if she missed a day, Rhys noticed her mind wandered.

She would ever struggle with insanity, but he would not allow it to win.

Simon had actually been doing research into post-traumatic stress disorder and anything he could find regarding madness and possible cures. He had been Rhys's rock since he'd gotten Viviane back. And to pick up the work Simon could not manage, he'd hired Steve Monroe to assist at the Paris office of Hawkes Associates.

Viviane kissed him, and he indulged in the moment, holding her in the moonlight, the babes sleeping peacefully nearby. Her dark hair veiled his neck and tickled his skin, stirring him as her touch always did. Life could not be more perfect.

How odd that they had journeyed through the centuries, each at their own pace, and while once she was the one two centuries older than he, now they were both the same age. Time had literally frozen her, and the gestating babes, until the moment of her release from hell.

Grasping his hand, she led him to the cribs and the two looked over the tiny beings. Viviane stroked the thick sprigs of hair on the first infant. "Red," she whispered. "And so much of it."

"I've been told my father had red hair," he said quietly.

"Yes? That explains it, then." She pressed a kiss to her fingertips and placed it to the baby's nose. "Trystan, who makes me laugh to look at him."

She delivered a kiss to the next infant's nose. "Vaillant, my dark prince." The babe's hair was black as Rhys and Viviane's hair, and he was not such a tubby bundle as his brother and had yet to cry. "They are blessings, yes?"

He hugged her from behind, resting his chin on her shoulder. "Truly, we are blessed. Have I told you today that I love you?"

"This afternoon when I rose, and then an hour later after I'd fed, and just ten minutes ago. Don't ever stop, lover. I need to hear it always."

"I love you, Viviane. Ever after."

Viviane suddenly stiffened, and Rhys momentarily

wondered when was the last time she'd drunk blood. It had been a few hours earlier when they'd stolen a moment in the shower while the babies had been snoozing.

"What is it?"

She turned toward the open nursery doorway where a brilliant shimmer danced upon the opposite wall in the hallway.

Rhys's heart dropped. Viviane slipped from his embrace. *Not now.* Not ever, he pleaded fruitlessly.

His lover kissed his lips, and lifted his hand to clasp against her mouth. Bright azure eyes spoke things they had not spoken since the eighteenth century. A promise had been made.

"I cannot stay in here," she said. "This is for you to do."

"Viviane, I—"

She kissed him silent. "I love you, Rhys. Now you must pay the boon."

And she slipped noiselessly across the room to the door that adjoined the master bedroom, closing it with a click of the lock behind her.

Only then did the faery enter the room. With a dazzle, the faery's wings swept the door frame and the top of the vanity and dressers as she approached.

"So soon?" Rhys asked. And then he had the brief thought that perhaps sooner was better.

It can never be better. This was the most horrible thing.

And yet, two had been born. Almost as if... No, he would not think it.

"Two?" Cressida said as she approached the cribs.

Rhys wanted to wrest her away and fling her out the patio doors. If he could harm the faery he would—and then he would not. He was a man of his word. Hell, he'd not been able to bring himself to seek out Constantine. Much as his brother deserved to die for his crime, he was not the heartless man to enforce that punishment. And besides, he now spent every moment with Viviane. He would not taint the time they shared with foul acts against his brother.

"I have waited a very long time," Cressida announced.

"You have."

"Which one shall it be?"

He joined her before the cribs and looked over the sleeping infants, blissfully unaware that both their lives would now be irrevocably altered.

His chest tightened and his throat squeezed. How could a father be expected to make such a choice?

"You must do it," he said, and turned his back to the cribs. "Quickly, please."

Eyes closed, he listened intently and sensed the faery leaning over one crib and studying the child.

"So bright, his hair," she commented.

Rhys winced. Trystan now slept on his back, a bit of his plump belly showing beneath the soft shirt he wore. His thumb was always securely in his mouth, a habit he'd assumed but moments following birth.

"This one is rather thin. He barely breathes as he sleeps."

And Vaillant, Viviane's dark prince. The quiet one who never cried, and would not suckle from his mother no matter how Viviane tried. But she cooed to him and rocked him, with bottle in hand, and seemed to spend more time with the babe, perhaps because he was so different.

Would they both be half-breeds? Or would his vampire

blood and Viviane's make them full vampire? Impossible to know until puberty.

Viviane was brave to grant him this situation without raging or protesting. He knew she loved them both, as did he. How dare he cast away one of his own children?

"Cressida, there must be some other manner in which we can—"

Rhys turned. The faery no longer stood in the room.

He rushed to the cribs. Trystan lay untouched.

Vaillant's crib was empty. A glitter of faery dust stained the sheets.

"No." Rhys grabbed up the sheets and pressed them to his face—soft, powdery, baby scent—then flung them down, and quickly grabbed up Trystan.

He pressed the babe's warm head to his cheek. Tears wet the thick crop of red hair. Falling to his knees before the cribs, Rhys rocked back and forth, struggling to hold in a raging howl.

EPILOGUE

Fourteen years later in Faery...

VAILLANT HAD ACHIEVED puberty last eve. Cressida had seen the wild look in the young half-breed's eyes, and had expected them to go completely gold as he then shifted to werewolf for the first time. He must shift. His mother had been vampire, his father a half-breed. Vaillant's blood was mixed to a delicious brew. Faery rejoiced in those of mixed blood.

He did not shift.

Instead he'd claimed intense hunger, and she suspected it was his vampire half that needed mortal blood. She'd had a mortal brought to Faery.

He did not drink blood.

But still he insisted hunger.

Frustrating. She had chosen the half-breed child as her boon in repayment for enchanting Rhys Hawkes's vampire so long ago. Half-breeds were valued to mate with the sidhe. Their mixed blood combined with faery ichor produced powerful hybrid offspring.

"What have you determined?" Cressida asked the seer, who had just come from Vaillant's quarters. The sylph in red silks floated beneath a canopy of intoxicating honeysuckle. "Is he ill?"

"No, he is a perfectly well, bloodborn vampire." The seer cringed at Cressida's sharp inhale.

"What?" Cressida drew the seer to her with a crook of her finger. "You lie to me. I have no need for a bloodborn vampire. They are common and unusable."

The seer shrugged, then shifted to small size and fluttered off into the bright white sky.

Seething, Cressida spread out her wings, which swept the honeysuckle, and scythed off the fragrant blossoms in a golden storm. She keened long, high and loud, and it shook all of Faery. The entire Unseelie court shuddered to recognize the faery's anger.

She had chosen incorrectly.

And yet, how was it possible Vaillant was bloodborn?

* * * * *

Watch for Vaillant's story,
FOREVER VAMPIRE,
in May 2011.

Award-winning author

SARAH McCARTY

delivers the first three titles of the steamy Hell's Eight series.

January

February

March

"Definitely spicy…[and] a great love story, too."
—*RT Book Reviews* Top Pick on *Tucker's Claim*

Available for the first time in mass-market paperback!

HQN™

We *are* romance™

www.HQNBooks.com

PHSMT2011

Try these Healthy and Delicious Spring Rolls!

INGREDIENTS

2 packages rice-paper spring roll wrappers (20 wrappers)

1 cup grated carrot

¼ cup bean sprouts

1 cucumber, julienned

1 red bell pepper, without stem and seeds, julienned

4 green onions finely chopped—use only the green part

DIRECTIONS

1. Soak one rice-paper wrapper in a large bowl of hot water until softened.
2. Place a pinch each of carrots, sprouts, cucumber, bell pepper and green onion on the wrapper toward the bottom third of the rice paper.
3. Fold ends in and roll tightly to enclose filling.
4. Repeat with remaining wrappers. Chill before serving.